MEGAN WOOD

The Naidisbo

NORTHWEST
TERRITORIES
ARTS.®

Registered Trade-mark owned by the Government of the Northwest Territories

Megan Wood is pleased to publish The Naidisbo with the help of the NWT Arts Council.

First edition

ISBN: 978-1-9991781-0-9

Cover art by Ana Chabrand Design House
Editing by Sigrid Macdonald
Illustration by Seth Tomlinson Cartography

This book was professionally typeset on Reedsy.
Find out more at reedsy.com

to Josh

Contents

Acknowledgement

Thank you to the NWT Arts Council for sponsoring this piece of work.

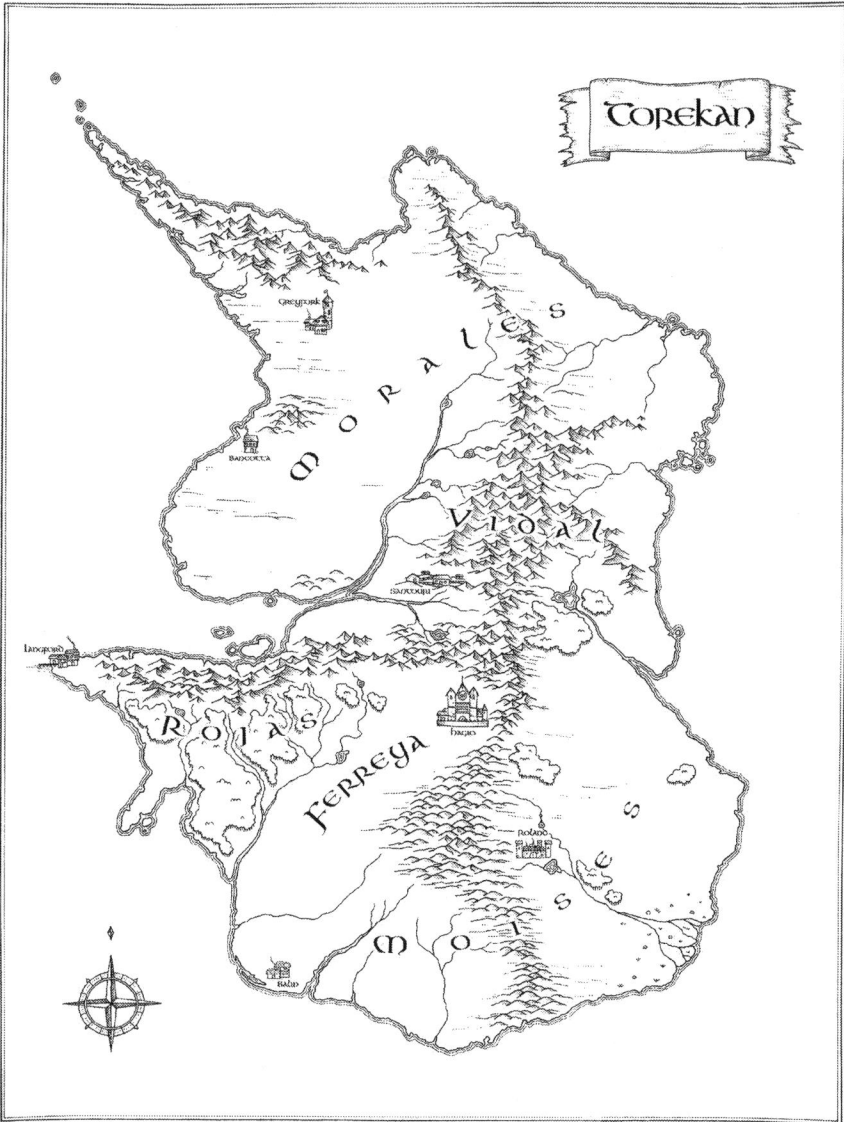

Prologue

She breathed deeply into her hands, grimacing at the lingering scent of mint. It was still better than the smell of burning flesh. The man's body, limp and charred, hung on display in the courtyard. His screams had faded long ago, and yet people still stood shoulder to shoulder, waiting for the Apaiza to announce the man's crimes against the Order of Alvar.

"Do you see this man who hangs before you?" The speaker swept his arm toward the charred body with a look of disgust as he shouted to the crowd around the platform. His white robe swept behind him as he paced in front of the body. "Alvar has shown us that the way to retribution is through truth, peace, and utmost respect for our elders, and yet this man chose to lie to his people! This man brought Urki wood on to the streets of Hagio and thought it would be missed, but we see everything!"

Weak cheering came from those in the religious quarter of the crowd as the Apaiza paused in his declaration. "This man was executed to protect you, our people, from the evil that naturalists call magic. This man died as commanded by our Aita, our great leader. Do not let his actions sway you; do not let his mistakes lead you to evil! We are weakened by their lies, and we let the naturalists win!"

The woman turned away as the cheers grew louder, keeping her head down and pushing through the crowd. She breathed easier with each step, increasing the distance between herself and the beginning of the celebrations. Today marked the 150th year since the Order of Alvar took control of the continent, banning the naturalists, the people who drew power from the land and the roots.

* * *

"Anika!" Margaret yelled as Anika hurried to join her, the mint and sugar poultice in hand and ready to apply. A young soldier sat quivering beneath Margaret as she examined the open gash on his arm. "Idiot! What soldier manages to stab himself while training? Alvar help you if you enter actual combat."

The soldier looked away, squeezing his eyes tightly as Margaret took the poultice from Anika and applied it liberally to the wound. Anika stepped into his line of sight and smiled when he looked at her; he was a good-looking young man, despite the green tinge. She suspected he was more distressed by Margaret than his wound.

"She isn't nearly as ferocious as she seems," Anika said in a half-whisper, knowing full well Margaret could hear. He didn't answer her, but he did smile sheepishly as he took a shuddering breath. Margaret didn't scold them, so Anika knew the distraction was appreciated. She closed her eyes and, for just a moment, let herself listen to his body. She let the slowing inhalation and exhalation wash over her like waves, the steady beating of his heart singing in her head like faraway drums. Pushing away the sounds, she passed Margaret more bandages. Satisfied he would be fine, she returned to the infirmary, Margaret's unrelenting insults still ringing behind her.

Being a nurse in the church was a job that others considered dull, but in the city of Hagio, it tended to be anything but. The current Aita of South Torekan, Reynard, seemed set on keeping the capital of each district prepared for any potential threat. Hagio, capital of the territory Ferreya, was the largest and most well defended of all capitals, so Anika never had a lack of work.

She spent most days in the infirmary, tending to soldiers wounded while training as they adjusted to their newfound abilities as provided by Reynard. Upon being accepted as a soldier they were branded by Reynard himself, their physical strength and capacity to withstand injury growing beyond the normal traits of men. She also provided cures for everyday ailments to the visiting Komandantes, Doctors, or Liders who feasted with the Aitas as their soldiers trained. When the Aitas met or hosted company, it was always in Hagio's church.

Things in the church, or Reynard's place of power as she preferred to think of it, were routine and settled with the typical comings and goings of a place of worship. However, since the celebrations of the 150th anniversary of the Order of Alvar being in control had begun, things had become busier. The North Aita of Torekan, Edyta, had arrived three days ago with her own army, and the increase in training caused more work for Anika and Margaret.

Not only did the new soldiers add to the workload in the infirmary, but it also meant she was required to help in her 'downtime' by serving at the nightly feasts. It wasn't that serving itself was horrible but having to change from her comfortable nursing clothes to the ill-fitting uniform was irritating. Worse than the black skirt and button-down top was standing for hours against a wall in silence as members of the order gossiped about politics, money, and rebels.

She allowed herself to daydream during the long suppers. The distraction provided relief from the boredom, and she didn't have to hear each person's heart rate or the hitch in their breath when they disagreed with Reynard but chose to keep quiet.

Dreading the supper for that evening, but knowing she'd be late if she didn't leave, she called to Margaret, "I'm going up to change." Margaret grunted something inaudible in response as Anika closed the door behind her, eyes squinting against the abrasive sunlight in the cloudless sky. She took a deep breath, steeling herself for the evening as she walked toward the church. She stopped to admire a bed of roses in the courtyard. The yellows and pinks stood brightly against the harmless trees. As she reached a hand out to cup one of the roses, a fox slinked out of the bushes and crouched in front of her, snarling as it looked her over. Anika bit back the curse at her lips as the fox, eyes eerily human-like, continued to hold her in its hostile gaze, sparks springing from its tail as she turned away.

The foxes were one of the worst parts of the church. They crept among the grounds, hiding and spying. While the church maintained that they were simply fire foxes, everyone knew they were Reynard's eyes and ears. Rumour was that a soldier had once been caught sleeping on sentry by a fox; the soldier had disappeared shortly after, but the fox remained.

Walking into the barren servant quarters, she made her way down the hall. As always, the lights were kept low, and the doors shut. It was quiet, the silence poisoned only by the sound of water dripping somewhere in the distance. Most of the servants were preoccupied this time of day, just as she soon would be. Her door creaked as she opened it. Their quarters were always in need of repair, but it was on the lowest list of priorities for the church.

Her room was small, a single bed against the far wall with a tiny armoire and chest that contained her personal belongings. In the other corner was her little table and chair. Even though it lay coated in dust from lack of use, she appreciated it just the same as some servants didn't even have that.

She opened the armoire and took out her serving uniform. It was drab. The black skirt and shirt were large, more grey than black, and obvious hand-me-downs. Despite their drabness, she was grateful for them. While she wasn't sickly thin, she was shapely and well enough developed that she tried not to bring attention to herself. Most people thought that working in a church would be enough of a deterrent from unwanted advances; the order, however, may have been saintly in the past, but things certainly were different since they began ruling as a theocracy 150 years ago.

It wasn't unusual for servants to have more than one job. She often juggled being a server, nurse, and maid if necessary. The servants did what they had to do to get ahead when working in the church. Anika had seen servants flirt with members of the order for as little as a glass of good wine. Usually, they didn't bother flirting with the common soldiers, but the Liders and Komandantes were known to provide presents or money for the girls they enjoyed. Liders and Komandantes were mid-ranking soldiers who led small fractions of the Aitas' army. Most servants had the sense to stay away from the second in command, the Doctors, who were known to be cruel and angry. Doctors played the part of enforcer for the Aitas, and as such, they did what they wanted, and there were never questions asked.

Closing the top button of her shirt, she pulled her black hair out of the ponytail and brushed it, letting it fall around her shoulders. Fully dressed and ready to withstand an hour or two of serving, she entered the kitchen, waving hello to the other servants. They were so busy filling platters with fish and decadent sweets that most weren't able to stop and talk. Relieved, she went to her usual place at the entrance to the dining hall and waited.

The gathering of the north and south was, as always, a boisterously entertaining event. Officials mingled, army Liders and Komandantes wore their finest military clothing, and, while there were few women who were part of the order, the companions of the officials were dressed for a royal function. She sighed in relief as she scanned the room. Neither the Aitas nor their Doctors had arrived yet, so she wasn't as late as she'd thought.

John, a young serving boy, thrust a serving platter with champagne flutes into her hands as he walked by. Steeling herself, she moved into the crowd, ready to flutter at the outside of conversations, available enough to provide drinks but far enough away that she hoped they'd not speak with her. She was small enough that she could slide between groups without causing much disturbance. Officials reached out, exchanging empty flutes for full ones as she adjusted her grip to the changing weight of the tray. She tried not to listen, but it was impossible not to overhear. She knew that later the others would gossip about it anyway.

"Did you hear about the rebels in the south?" a slender woman in red said to her well-decorated companion. Anika paused for his response.

"Ha!" he chuckled. "I suppose they feel they have to do something on the 150th, but we extinguished the problem easily."

The woman smiled, painted lips pursed as she nodded, seemingly oblivious to the officer's hand now running up and down her arm. Anika moved on to another group. This was a usual topic of conversation, and she knew always to take whatever she heard with a grain of salt. Rumour was that the rebels did more damage than the order allowed people to believe — otherwise, it wouldn't be discussed at all — and she was inclined to agree with the assumption. While she tried to remain indifferent to gossip, it was difficult not to hope for change. Things were so stifling in the church. Sometimes she fell asleep feeling like the walls were falling in around her. She didn't dare to dream of change, even if part of her hoped for it. Sometimes, the other servants would discuss news from outside, but to Anika, that was like asking for trouble; if they were overheard, they would be punished. She reminded herself that the order had been in control for 150 years, and the likelihood of anything changing was slim.

She ducked back into the kitchen, and John passed her a newly filled tray. It would be a long evening, probably longer than usual, given the occasion. Lila, one of the other girls, mouthed 'drinks' as she passed by. Anika raised one finger; she never stayed for too long; the other servants didn't have to get up and deal with Margaret in the morning.

* * *

"Did you hear the news?" Lila passed her the wine, her eyes twinkling with the newly heard gossip. Lila was one of the servants who hadn't yet learned the value of silence, but Anika would be lying if she said part of her didn't want to know what she'd share.

With a smirk to Anika, she turned toward John, who was leaning forward in his chair and listening intently. "There are rumours that the rebels are making headway. I overheard the Doctor himself say that the rebels have been gathering forces to march on Hagio."

"Pft," one of the other girls interjected from across the room. "The order is smarter than that. If anything, they make these things up so they can tell us about how powerful they were when they neutralized the threat."

Anika sat her wine down, yawning, and already regretting that she stayed for more than one drink. She was halfway out of her chair when the girl said, "I overheard that they think there's a Naidisbo alive."

"What?" Anika snapped at the girl. The attention of the three of them shifted to her, each looking puzzled by her sudden outburst.

The girl continued, watching Anika warily. "I was serving the Aitas their supper tonight, and Reynard and Edyta said they want all three powers to sit as one in the order. Then they can be the most powerful rulers in the world. Reynard seemed to think they could find a Naidisbo."

Lila shook her head. "The Naidisbo all died in the last uprising. The order even killed the ones who tried to escape to the continent — Edyta sunk their ships herself."

John, always trying to win more affection from Lila, nodded eagerly. "You must have misheard. You need to catch real truths, not half stories when you're serving."

Trying to hide her shaking, Anika said goodnight, shutting the door behind her and taking a moment to lean against it quietly, letting her thoughts and their ongoing mumbling behind the door roll off her before heading to her room.

Sleep normally came to her easily, but that night she slept fitfully, tossing, turning, dreaming of sinking ships. She did nothing as the water pooled at her feet and the people around her drowned. Even though she could feel their life painfully leaving, she felt frozen, unable or unwilling to aid them as their lungs became overwhelmed in the ocean water.

In the morning, she felt as if she hadn't slept at all, and apparently, she looked like it too. Ignoring the look from Margaret she sat and pulled a stalk of garlic toward her, her eyes fluttered closed for just a moment before Margaret started.

"I suppose you partied last night with the others?" She was pulling herbs off the top shelf, the ladder precariously balanced on one leg as she stretched for something just out of reach. Anika bit back the instinct to offer her help; she was just as short and didn't feel overly generous toward Margaret at the moment.

"No, thank you very much. I went to bed at a very reasonable time. I just didn't sleep well." The piece of garlic popped free of its husk, the heavy smell filling the air.

Margaret scoffed, an eyebrow raised as she left Anika alone, going to attend to their first patient of the day. Rolling her eyes at Margaret's brown bun disappearing over the door, Anika went back to work on her poultice. She spent a lot of her time making remedies under Margaret's guidance. It helped her to learn traditional medicine, and she had an excuse to do something other than dress soldiers' wounds all day.

"Hello?" The door behind her creaked as it opened. A young man poked his head in tentatively. "Is anyone here?"

Anika wiped her hands on her skirt as she stood to greet the young man. The robes of an Apaiza in training were beige and horribly unflattering on most, and this young man was no exception. His only saving grace was his ebony skin and enough height that he was able to pull focus away from the terrible uniform.

"Can I help you?" She gestured to a chair, and he sat obediently.

"My apologies for interrupting. I seem to have burned myself." He pulled his sleeve up, wincing as he revealed the reddened and bubbling skin along the inside of his left forearm. "I was trying to put out the fire before bed, and I slipped."

"My Aita, did you ever!" She fell to her knees as she pushed his sleeve up farther, wrapping a ribbon around his arm to keep it from falling. Her hand hovered over it, and she felt the heat rising from the wound. She didn't need her power to feel the intensity. She let herself quickly dive into his injury, just long enough to see if his body had already started fighting the infection. Knowing it had, she smiled as she got to her feet, letting him know she could aid his healing with a simple cold wrap, ointment, and regular bandage changes. He stayed silent, smiling, and nodding as he watched her flit around the room, collecting ingredients for the ointment.

"You're smiling an awful lot for someone with such a bad burn," she said, rubbing the ointment over his skin gently.

"You're easy to smile at." He flashed her a grin, quickly replaced by a grimace as she pushed a little harder. He shook his head and looked away from his burn, fixing his gaze on her as he smiled again.

"Are you flirting?" Her chair scraped across the ground as she moved closer, pulling the bandage taut as she secured it to the burn.

"What would give you that idea?" He laughed, but she noticed his eyes didn't leave her face.

"Well, you are. But I feel that I should probably let you know that Apaizas don't flirt. The Apaiza are married to their cause. Women — or men — are not something that should even interest you."

"I'm not an Apaiza yet. I haven't vowed to give up women."

"You are brazen." She pushed back her chair, wiping her hands on her smock as she gestured to the door. "I don't think your Apaiza trainers would like to hear that."

He ignored her. "I'm Michael." He held out his uninjured arm to her. She held his hand loosely as she questioned her judgment. "Anika."

1

Thinning Blood

"Let us sit together as one nation, bound by our achievements and our continued growth. Let us remember that we will continue to work together to ensure safety, that no naturalists will corrupt our people and that we will protect them with the elements which we wield. I ask that you raise a glass to our people, our nation, and ladies and gentlemen, to us."

Cheers erupted as Reynard raised his glass, the red wine he always drank swirling ominously as he smiled to the crowd. His toast — as it usually was — was meant as both a reminder of his power and a threat to the naturalists. Head bowed, he looked almost humble as he lay a hand over his heart, the red and black robe swaying softly at his arm as the cheers finally subsided.

"Thank you for your energy. Let's eat!"

Anika rolled her eyes behind closed lids and stepped forward. She leaned, as she had been taught, between every second person, gesturing to the mashed potatoes on her tray. Most of the men would serve themselves, but women were always a gamble.

The one she stood beside now looked at her and smiled. "Oh, just a tiny bit, please!"

Anika nodded and scooped a small amount on her plate, the smell of the woman's perfume becoming overpowering as she stepped away.

"These servants always give me way too much," she said to the man beside

1

her. "I swear they want me to burst out of my dress." Anika held back another eye roll as she leaned around the man's shoulders to offer him the tray.

"I can't imagine anyone would dream of doing such a thing to a beautiful woman." The man turned away from her to look at Anika, smiling and winking as he did. Anika held back a smirk as she recognized Michael, the training Apaiza. She nodded respectfully after he'd taken his potatoes and moved on, glancing back at him as she leaned between the next two. He was strangely friendly and didn't fit in with the other solemn priests in the order. And she noticed that he hadn't heeded her warning about the flirting as his hand drifted to gently squeeze his neighbours.

The man next to Michael was well decorated and deep in conversation with one of the southern Komandantes seated beside him. Forced to interrupt and offer them the dish, Anika murmured her apologies and moved the platter between them. Hardly breaking stride, he turned to her and pulled a scoop of potatoes to his plate, but he paused as he went to put the spoon back. Sneering, he set the spoon down, shifting to face her in his chair. He let his hand wander, falling to firmly grasp her ass and squeeze as he turned back to his companion. Anika moved on to the next person, ignoring the creeping feeling of sickness in her stomach. Her neck was burning and her heart beating faster as she forced her hand balancing the tray to remain steady.

As she circled the table, she noticed that there were now two pairs of eyes following her, although they were both trying to hide it. Michael and the other man's eyes drifted to her, each drinking her in as she moved. She struggled not to let her face redden as she finished her round. Finally, at the end of the table, she took a deep breath of relief. Defying her instincts and walking slowly, she made it to the kitchen and thrust the tray at John, excusing herself before he could pass her another.

She let herself walk fast, half-jogging to the bathroom where she shut the door and locked it behind her. Her heart was racing. She started to slow it down, but she still felt unsettled as she studied her reflection in the mirror. She shook her head, trying to rationalize her racing thoughts. *You're being ridiculous.* She ran the water in the sink, grounding herself in the coolness on her hands. *Pull yourself together.* She put her frigid hands against the base of her neck, feeling better as the shiver ran down her back. *Chances are you're overreacting. They' re drinking. They aren't focused on you.*

She took a deep breath as she examined herself in the mirror, straightened her hair, and braced herself to go back to work. She was right; nothing else interesting happened during the rest of the meal. The men and women drank and joked, conversation seemed light and at ease. But she remained conscientious of the man that had grabbed her, and she noted how many bottles were emptying at his seat. He seemed to have his attention captured by another young woman who was in attendance, though, and paid Anika little mind when she served the dessert. Still, she found herself holding her breath as she stepped away.

Once the tables were cleared, and the guests were mingling, the Aita only required three or four people to serve drinks, which meant that they had some downtime in the kitchen to relax. Unfortunately, Anika had struck out and ended up with another tray in her hand, floating among the crowd. Carefully stepping around a young woman's voluptuous skirt, she walked around the room, the smell of wine heavy as people drank more and talked boisterously. She could feel the difference in the people; to others, it would be the subtle things, flushed cheeks, squinting eyes, slurring words, but Anika could feel more. The room was filled with thinning blood, and when the blood thinned, hearts beat faster to push it through the body effectively. She pushed the noise away and focused on not toppling over with the tray of full wine glasses.

A rather young woman, who looked like she hadn't yet learned the value in pacing her drinks, snapped her fingers, and Anika moved toward her, sliding lithely between guests. Michael stood beside her, watching as Anika approached. He watched her quietly as the woman took a new glass of wine, his face unreadable. She turned her back to them, grateful that he hadn't brought attention to her again.

* * *

Her feet were aching by the time guests started leaving. She shifted her weight back and forth to ease the discomfort as women were escorted from the hall. Some remained; the Aitas, Doctors, Liders, Komandantes, and even the Apaiza would occasionally stay up late into the night, drinking and talking. If this was the case, the servants were to leave them a selection of Reynard's favorite drinks and snacks, and only then were they dismissed.

John placed one last bottle of red wine on the table and nodded to Anika, her cue that she could finally leave. The timing seemed right. There were only a dozen people left, and the conversation had died down to a friendly buzzing. Shrugging her sore shoulders, she started walking toward the servant quarters.

Things were quiet in the halls. The others must have been tired and gone to bed early for once; normally she was the first to bed while the others stayed up for a drink. The emptiness was unsettling, and unease washed over her, like cold water running between her shoulder blades. She quickened her step, eager to get to her room.

Her breath caught in her throat as a door flung open in front of her, a man stumbling into the hallway. She willed herself to move and walked faster, eager to duck around him and not draw attention to herself. He staggered forward again, stopping in front of her. She paused, prickling as the man who had assaulted her earlier swayed in front of her, another bottle in his hand.

"Do you know who I am, servant girl?" he sneered.

"No," she whispered. She moved softly to the side, hoping that she could go past him. He dropped the bottle and reached out, grabbing her arm as she flinched away from the breaking of glass. His fingers dug in painfully as he pushed her backward until she hit the wall, the glass crunching as he stepped through it uncaring.

"I'm Morale's Komandante."

His putrid breath was hot on her face, and his dark hair matted with sweat as his eyes roamed over her hungrily. She nodded mutely, her blood pounding in her head as she tried to breathe, to think of what she could do to get away. He bowed mockingly, that terrible smile playing on his lips again as he rose and moved his free hand to her throat. She winced, pulling back, but he placed it gently on her, his fingers dancing over her skin.

"I'm glad you're relaxing a bit," he said. "It would be a shame for you to be so tense during this. You know, most women crawl into my bed and beg me for what I want to do to you."

"Please, Komandante, they'll notice I'm gone." The words were weak; she cringed at the quavering tone as his grip on her arm tightened. His pallid skin caught in the light, and she would have gagged if it weren't for his hand still at her throat. She closed her eyes to distance herself from the situation, wishing herself away but was dragged back as he pulled her chin straight, forcing her to look in his eyes.

He snarled and pushed her harder against the wall, his hips held firmly over hers as he let go of her arm. Instinctively, she grabbed his wrist at her throat, but he paid no attention as he pulled her shirt free. He grunted in excitement as his clammy hand found her bare skin. She tried to hold back the recoil and disgust. She knew she couldn't afford to anger him any more than she already had, but he was moving faster than she could think. She could feel the anger bubbling over, nearly spilling out of her at the unfairness of it all. She turned her face away, closing her eyes as she tried to block out his touch and slow her panicked thoughts. His hands roamed mercilessly over her as he pulled at her clothes. His hand left her neck, and she gasped, leaning forward slightly as he slapped her across the face. She yelped, hating the sound and sadistic smile that lit up his face when she did.

The lingering pain in her face brought her to focus. She knew he would take what he wanted, and he wouldn't stop until he'd used her and left her wishing she were dead. He cursed as he fumbled to unzip his pants and pull her skirt up, one hand still sloppily holding her against the wall. As his pants crumpled around his feet, he roughly turned her around, her face slamming into the cold wall, her head buzzing.

"You don't want to do this," she said, the words louder this time, desperation growing. He grabbed her hips and pulled her closer, her skirt rising as his hands moved between her legs, pulling possessively at the material between them. He chuckled in her ear, his breath sickeningly hot against her skin.

"Oh, but I do, and you'll like it."

He thrust his hips forward, and she grimaced as she felt the hardness against her backside. She felt his teeth against her neck as he pulled her underwear to the side, moaning as his fingers brushed against her.

"No!" She pushed away from the wall, and he stumbled back in surprise. She turned to flee, but he recovered quickly, slamming her into the wall again, his weight solid against her.

"Silly girl, did you think you could run? Did you think you could fight me?" His hands, rough and uncaring, gripped her hip as his other hand pulled her underwear aside again. She struggled, but he expected it now and held her in place as he ripped the fabric. She watched it fall to the ground and resigned herself to what she knew she had to do.

"No!" she screamed and reached behind her, grabbing his arms, her terror reaching its peak. Her eyes were closed as she felt out with her mind and found his beating heart. If she were in control of her emotions, she could have lowered his heartbeat slowly, safely, but she was drowning in his body, her senses overloaded, and instead, she pushed.

She pushed so hard that his heart ceased beating, and she felt the heat of his body fall away from her. She spun around as she pushed her skirt back down. Gasping for air, she tried to sense if the crumpled body on the ground was still breathing. She gagged, her power resisting the idea of helping him, even though she knew he was likely dead.

She looked around wildly, deciding what to do or where to run. A gasp from down the hallway pulled her from her planning, and she saw three Apaizas at the end of the hall, their robes billowing around them as they stared at her from the shadows in disbelief.

"Please..." She backed away from the body, her hands held up in front of her. One of the young men ran back in the door he had come through; he was yelling, but she didn't hear what he was saying. Another stepped into the light, but before she could see his face, he turned and said something to his companion. He followed the other man who'd raced away. As the last man turned back toward her, she trembled, seeing Michael looking at her in

6

confusion, worry creasing his brow as the Komandante let out a groan.

"For Aita's sake, you idiot, we have to run!"

The Komandante's stirring threw Michael into action as he darted toward her, grabbed her arm, and began pulling her down the hallway. Anika pulled her arm free and kept his pace, flying through a door into a room that she didn't know. He didn't look back to see if she was keeping up as he darted from door to door, shaking the handles angrily before spinning to look at her.

"You don't have any other secret powers that may come in handy right now, do you?" He didn't wait for an answer as he stepped back, bounding off his foot as he took a running leap at one of the doors.

"No," she gasped, "who are you?"

"This..." he backed up again, "is not really the time for discussion, Anika."

He threw his weight into it again, and this time, it burst open. He ran into the next room. She followed, feeling blind and shocked as he changed directions and ran down a hall.

She felt disoriented, but she kept up with him as he again changed direction, her mind too overwhelmed to even recognize where they were. Finally, they burst through a door, and the outdoor air hit her, cool and full of life. She stopped, hands falling to her knees as she hungrily swallowed the fresh air.

"Fool! Why are you stopping? They'll be on us in any minute. We have to get to the apartment."

"What apartment?" Her hands gesticulated wildly toward the lights of the city.

"Just keep up, will you?"

She bit back the retort at the tip of her tongue. Waiting for the order to find her was sure death; at least Michael seemed to have other plans. Seeing no alternative but to follow him, she swallowed one last gulp of air and began to run after him, dew filled grass wet against her ankles as she pushed toward the church gates and into the town square.

* * *

7

"Can we please stop so you can tell me what's going on?" she spat. He whipped his head back to look at her, scowling.

She crouched behind empty bins in the alleyway, the pleasant smell of the church gardens replaced by the stench of rotting fish carcass. He motioned her forward as he crept, stopping at a bare stretch of alley wall. He looked back and forth twice before jerking his head upwards. When Anika just looked at him quizzically, he rolled his eyes and gestured upwards again, even more frustrated than before.

"What in Aita's name are you pointing at?"

"Shh!"

She threw her hands up in frustration. "Did you lose the ability to speak when you left the church then?"

He glowered at her and pointed upwards again. Apparently, he didn't feel the need to answer her rhetorical questions either. She squinted but still didn't see anything as he shoved her aside. She stumbled back, confused, but then noticed that he had jumped to grab hold of a small handle above them.

There was a ladder inconspicuously and dangerously built into the wall. He let himself fall back to the ground, whispering in her ear. "I'm going to give you a boost, climb the rungs until you get to the roof. I'll meet you there."

"What?"

"Just do it."

He didn't give her a chance to refuse as he grabbed her waist and lifted her up. He was a tall man, and evidently quite strong as he didn't seem at all fatigued by lifting her. She grabbed the first rung and quickly pulled herself up to grab the second. When she got her weight settled, he pulled one foot away and yanked off her shoe, quickly switching her feet as he took the other. She looked down at him in confusion, ready to ask why but she stopped when she saw the look on his face.

"Go!"

She went, pulling herself up using muscles she wasn't used to. Without her shoes, she was able to grip the rungs as she moved higher and higher. She made a mental note not to look down as she continued climbing, too afraid to look for Michael below her and very aware of the wind buffeting her hair. When she was sure she could feel the void beneath ready to swallow her up if she so much as missed a toe the ladder ended, and she anxiously, precariously pulled herself over the ledge and rolled to lie on her back. Her breathing still heavy, she looked at the sky. Smog and smoke covered most of the stars, but it was still a beautiful and quiet night.

Michael jumped down from the ledge and crouched beside her. She opened her mouth to demand some answers, but he cut her off.

"We'll talk inside." He pointed to the end of the building where someone stood in a trapdoor, the light leaving them in shadow.

The man in the light jumped back into the trap door as they approached. He didn't bother using the ladder as he dropped the five or six feet. Michael, who seemingly left his manners at the church, followed him down, leaving Anika on the roof to hesitantly climb down the ladder.

"What's going on?" The man spoke firmly to Michael despite being a head shorter, smaller, and clearly weaker. His fluorescent red hair lay shaggily against his face, and he was pale and covered with freckles. In fact, he was so pale that Anika wondered if he was sick. "You weren't due to check in for another week."

Anika closed her eyes to quickly scan him and, despite his wildly beating heart, could detect nothing wrong.

"There was an incident at the church. I had to take her and run." Michael gestured at her. She bit her tongue as he shook his head in aggravation.

"Well, you didn't raise the alarm," the red-haired man said. "Rae is on the deck doing watch, she would have pulled us out if you had."

The red-haired man turned and walked into a small living room ahead of them. He sat down in a large chair and picked up his drink as Michael poured himself something from a bottle sitting on a sparsely decorated bookshelf. The room was nearly empty; the walls were bare, and the only furnishings were a few decrepit looking couches. She couldn't help but wonder how long they'd been staying there. Dust coated the empty shelves, and other than some tossed around books, there was nothing that could have possibly been used to pass the time. Michael sat down in the chair across from the man and tipped his head back, sighing as he savoured his drink.

9

"That's surprising," he said, swirling the drink in his hand. "We have a few minutes before we have to call in Rae and make a plan."

Jake let his head fall back on the sunken cushions and closed his eyes. The red-haired man took another drink and nodded, glancing at Anika uneasily. She stood in the doorway, waiting for someone to acknowledge what was happening, but they both sat in silence. When she couldn't bear it any longer, she stepped into the room and blurted, "Would one of you care to tell me what's going on here? Michael?"

Sighing, Michael opened his eyes and tilted his head to look at her. "Sit," he said, motioning to the seat beside him.

She scowled but did as he said, desperate for answers. Instead of finally giving her answers to her questions, Michael rose and poured another drink of what she assumed was whiskey. Lifting an empty glass her way, she nodded, and he poured another, passing it to her as he sat back down. He turned to face her, casually pulling one of his legs under him on the couch, all the formality of his role at the church disappeared.

"My name isn't Michael. I'm not an Apaiza in training. My name is Jake. This is Hcrib. Rae is on the roof patrolling. We are rebels." He paused, letting the information settle between them.

"You're rebels?" She asked the question, which wasn't really a question, as she lifted her glass and drank deeply. It was whiskey, and it wasn't good whiskey. It burned going down, and she coughed as she looked at Michael, *No, Jake*, she thought.

Hcrib looked to Jake uneasily. "Yes, and to be frank, I'm assuming that if you're here, and Jake is back, that means that his cover his blown. And if his cover was blown, I would assume that the alarms would be ringing at the church. Do we have time to discuss this?"

"The alarms should be ringing, but they aren't, and that scares me." Jake went to the window, opening it wider as he said, "Rae, can you hear me?"

"Sure can!" Her voice was feminine and soft. "Care to explain?"

"The alarms should be going off. She's a Naidisbo," said Jake, turning back to face Hcrib and Anika, resting his back against the wall. He shook his head in astonishment, equal to the look on Hcrib's face as Jake continued.

"She killed a man who tried to assault her tonight, and it was witnessed by two Apaiza who ran to raise the alarm. We escaped without incident."

"Not dead," she whispered, unable to find her voice, but they didn't pay her any attention as they continued.

"Why wouldn't they raise the alarms?" Hcrib said. He was looking at Anika, studying her, but she had a feeling the question wasn't directed at her.

"I don't know, but I'm sure they're looking for her. Reynard will want her."

"Why?" The wistful voice drifted through the window.

"I don't know exactly what he would do, but there are a few possibilities. He'll either keep her and convince her to use her powers for the order, or he'll kill her like the rest of the Naidisbo." Jake crossed his arms and lay his head back against the wall, closing his eyes. "And now we harbour the most wanted person in Hagio."

"Not just Hagio, Jake. We have the most valuable person in all of Torekan."

Hcrib went to the window, a hand settling on Jake's shoulder reassuringly as he looked Anika over again. He didn't say anything else as he spryly climbed out the window and slipped into the night. The one who Anika presumed was Rae slipped through the curtain feet first. She was smaller than Hcrib, slender and thin. She looked almost childlike in size. Her brown hair was long and wavy, settling just past her shoulders. Her skin was fair, but she didn't appear sickly like Hcrib. Anika was most taken with her eyes, brown and warm, and comforting as she looked Anika over without a hint of animosity on her face.

"Hi, Anika. I'm Rae." She strode forward and hugged her. Anika awkwardly squeezed the small girl's shoulders and muttered her hellos as she noticed Jake tighten his lips in impatience.

"We leave tonight. Let's pack our things." Jake didn't ask but demanded, and Anika was left sitting alone in the room as he and Rae left, whispering to one another. Anika took another drink and followed with a deep breath, holding back the tears that threatened to spill over as she thought back over the night and everything that had happened.

Before she had figured anything out, they were back. Blinking furiously, she tipped back the rest of her drink to hide the tears as she composed herself. Their backpacks were ready to go, their faces serious as Rae and Hcrib once again switched spots outside the window. She turned to Jake, who rocked back and forth impatiently as they waited.

"Where are we going?" she asked.

Jake just looked at her, and, for a moment, she thought he wouldn't answer, but he finally relented. "We have a camp. It's a long trek, but it's safe there. I know you're likely confused, but your best shot is to come with us. You heard what will happen to you if you stay here."

"Did I say I wasn't going?"

"No," his brow furrowed. "But you didn't say you were coming either."

"I'm not a complete idiot" She rolled her eyes, the tears threatening to rise again. "I know what I am. I've hidden it my whole life. But I have questions, about the rebellion, about you. I don't know if I can trust you people. I just met you."

He nodded as he picked up her shoes and threw them to her. "I don't know if we can trust you either, and I have questions for you too. We'll figure everything out when we're safely out of the city, and if you decide to leave before we get to camp, then you can go. You aren't our prisoner, but I won't let you jeopardize us either."

Hcrib came back in the room. He briefly studied the two of them before he climbed the ladder to the roof. Jake extended a hand towards the ladder as Hcrib disappeared and smiled grimly. "After you."

2

Cold Earth

"Follow me, keep close, and keep quiet."

Jake was crouched in front of Anika, behind the bins outside of the apartment. Rae was behind her, the three of them uncomfortably close. Hcrib was already gone. She didn't know when he'd disappeared or how he'd managed to vanish into thin air, but he'd left them there, waiting in the dark.

She didn't bother answering. Instead, she rocked back and forth on her feet, trying to keep warmth moving in her body. Her black top and skirt were comfortable for serving but too thin for the cool spring air that fell over the city at night. Worse were the servant shoes shoved onto her feet. She ached for her nursing shoes, her feet barking in pain already — and they hadn't even gotten out of the city.

Hcrib's whistle sounded, and Jake started to move. Anika launched forward ready to run with him, but Rae held her back.

"Always let the person in front of you run first," she whispered. "Make sure they aren't seen. Then, if everything is okay, go."

They kept to the shadows and close to the walls, moving slowly after each whistle from Hcrib. She did as she was told, darting across the road, holding her breath. Even though there was no shout of alarm, she felt naked and vulnerable as the light from the street burned behind her closed lids. She landed in the shadows, crouching beside Jake as her heart pounded in her chest. Rae landed behind her silently, patting Anika on the arm as they looked forward in anticipation.

The silence seemed to pulse, each noise and movement more noticeable as they continued waiting for the cue from Hcrib.

"Pst." Anika nearly jumped out of her skin at Hcrib's whisper. He couldn't be seen, but he was above them, somewhere. "There's a patrol ahead. Four men. I'll call when it's safe."

Jake grunted his agreement as Anika closed her eyes, relishing a break. How Hcrib managed to move so silently and stay hidden was astounding. Even more so was the anxiety swirling in her stomach each time he whistled, she didn't know how they could keep it up without being overheard. They sat there for a long time, her legs burning as the time passed slowly. Whatever and wherever the patrol was looking, they were making sure they did a thorough job.

Finally, Hcrib whistled, and they moved to the end of the alley, repeating the process as they crossed the open road. As Rae once again landed behind Anika, a shout came from behind them. Anika looked wildly between Jake and Rae. Jake ignored her.

"Rae, get on the balcony above us. Anika, don't move or make a sound." He pushed himself in front of her as she made herself as small as possible, willing herself to disappear into the shadows.

Rae nodded to Jake and jumped. Silently she glided above them, the wind in her wake buffeting Anika's hair. Anika squinted into the darkness, she could just barely make out Rae's form, perching on a railing above them effortlessly. Despite the immediacy of their situation her mind raced with what she had just witnessed, until she was pulled back to focus by the voices.

"I'm telling you, man. I saw something." The voice was close, just around the wall. The other person grunted; she could hear the reluctance in his response. "Well, we might as well look."

"Yeah, yeah, let's just get this over with. I'm done looking for someone we aren't going to find."

The two men stepped into the alleyway, their dark silhouettes masking their features. Jake tensed as the men debated which way they should explore first. They began to move toward them, lazily chatting as they wandered.

One of the men, who, thankfully, Anika didn't recognize, walked toward their hiding place, looking back over his shoulder as he continued talking to his comrade. She focused on him, fear hammering in her chest as he inched closer. Her attention was pulled when she heard the other man gasp, his hands going to this throat as he stumbled backward. The man closest to them finally turned, looking at his companion in confusion, but he didn't have a chance to so much as shout before Jake pounced from their hiding spot. He hadn't even reached for his dagger before Jake opened his throat. The man fell, his blood spurting out and darkening the stones around him. Anika jumped to her feet, fighting every urge inside of herself to go to him, to stitch the man back together. She looked away and watched as Jake approached the other man, who was still choking on seemingly nothing. He moved as silently as a cat hunting its prey; every part of him radiating deadliness. The man's eyes widened with fear, his hands scratching at his chest in desperation as Jake pushed him against the wall. There was no hesitation as Jake slit his throat, letting him crumple to the ground.

Anika realized that she was breathing loudly, a high-pitched noise escaping her as she tried to take in the scene, but she didn't care. Jake spun around to look at her, his emotions entirely unreadable as his head fell to the side, and he studied her. She wondered for a moment if she'd gotten herself into worse trouble than she'd have been if she'd stayed at the church and paid for her crimes.

"Get out of there," Rae whispered, landing silently next to Anika. "Help me drag this one behind the boxes."

Rae grabbed the man closest to them and started to pull him by his shoulders. Anika couldn't speak, and yet somehow, her body started moving, working on autopilot as she grabbed the dead man's legs and dropped him behind where she'd just stood.

She turned to see Jake and Hcrib waiting with the other body. They dumped the body on top of the other, and Hcrib disappeared ahead of them. Quicker than before, he whistled, and they moved forward.

They continued with their routine until finally, they made it to the countryside. While she knew she should have been on high alert the entire time, she had to admit she was trapped in her mind for the rest of their escape. *They didn't even think twice. We could have run; we could have just knocked them unconscious.* She was also realistic. She knew that the chances of those men staying quiet were slim, but she still struggled with what she had witnessed. *If I try to leave, they'll kill me without even a thought.*

Hcrib called, and they moved forward. They met him in the darkness, quiet and unmoving, only the light from the stars and moon illuminating him in the night. They gathered in a small huddle as Jake started doling out instructions.

"We have to move quickly," he said. "We should put as much space between us and Hagio tonight as we can. They'll assume that we tried to leave the city, and when they find the bodies, they'll know we did. Hcrib, you lead, then you, Rae. Anika, you walk with Rae, quietly. I'll be behind you."

She rolled her eyes with the mention of her being quiet, grateful for the darkness. Hcrib was already moving as Rae grabbed her hand, pulling lightly.

The pace outside of the city was hard and fast as they didn't have to worry as much about being seen. Anika's feet already ached and were tingling from all the crouching. As the hours passed, the tingling gave way to a dull unpleasantness. Hcrib's pace never let up. The only thing she had to be thankful for was that she was no longer cold. Instead, she was sweating.

Rae was slightly ahead of Anika as they veered onto a small, wooded pathway. The narrowness was made worse by the branches that invaded the space, scratching against her as she tried to duck around them. It was no use, though; wet leaves softly caressed her face in their place. As annoyed and tired as she was, she tried to enjoy the coolness against her burning skin.

She didn't know how much time had passed when they emerged from the grove. The sky was no brighter, and the moon and stars hadn't changed. She looked around, wishing for a break, but Hcrib and Rae showed no signs of slowing. She pushed forward, barely registering the rustling in the bushes around her. No doubt a small animal scurrying into the night; she didn't care to even look.

She continued, no longer trying to remember her surroundings and instead using all of her concentration to keep moving one foot in front of the other. Amid playing a mental battle with herself, debating whether she would just lie down on the ground and go to sleep or beg them to stop, she ran face first into Hcrib. He chuckled as she stumbled back. A light force at her back kept her standing upright, although neither Jake nor Rae had bothered to tell her they were stopping.

"I think we can stop here for the night," Hcrib said. He looked toward Jake for confirmation. "I'm going to do a quick scout of the area just to make sure there isn't anyone around us."

Jake murmured his agreement as Hcrib disappeared into the shadows. Jake and Rae kneeled, pulling sleeping rolls and blankets from their pack, neither bothering to talk — she hoped it was because they were as tired as she felt. Jake threw her a blanket, but she didn't react quickly, so it just fell to the ground, lying there invitingly. She flinched as she sat, the cold seeping into her bones. Jake ignored her fumble as he got to work building a fire. Anika snuggled into the blanket, gratefully wrapping it around her so that she didn't have to touch the cold earth. She lay down, eyes on Jake, and the small plume of smoke that he was blowing on, as she tried to find a comfortable place to lay her head. Despite her discomfort, she was asleep before the embers turned to flames.

* * *

The sun woke Anika before the noise of the others did. She lay for a moment, relishing in the warmth, stretching her stiff limbs and opening her eyes to a clear blue sky. She sat up, shoulders sore, and aching from the day before. The fire still smouldered, and the other's things were packed and organized. If they hadn't left their bags, she'd have assumed they'd abandoned her. Part of her was disappointed they hadn't. She stood, rolling her blanket up and setting it with Jake's things as Rae and Hcrib came through the trees. They were in deep conversation, but both seemed to be in good spirits.

"Good, you're finally up!" Rae went to her pack and pulled out a package of bread and cheese, handing it to her. Suddenly ravenous, she sat back down and began to eat, trying to slow herself down to savour it. "We convinced Jake to let you sleep before we kept going. He wasn't pleased, so he's on sentry duty."

"I can hear you," he said as he came through the trees. He didn't look as disgruntled as he had last night at least. "I think we should get going. There's no sign of anyone around us, so we can talk while we're walking."

Anika put the last piece of bread in her mouth and stood. She was stiff all over, but she knew walking would help to loosen her muscles, and worst-case scenario she could use her mind to relax them – although she refrained from using her powers on herself unless it were necessary. They fell into the same formation as the night before but with less distance between them and the pace more reasonable. They hadn't been walking long when Rae fell into step beside her. Anika looked at her warily from the corner of her eye. The girl seemed nice, almost jovial despite the circumstances.

"So, did you know that you're a Naidisbo?" Rae asked, glancing at her suspiciously.

Anika nodded. She'd known the questions would come up sooner or later. "Yes, I've always known."

"But you've never told anyone?" Jake asked behind her.

"Despite what you might think, I'm not a complete idiot," she answered smartly, looking over her shoulder. He raised his eyebrows, a slight smirk on his face.

"Do one of you want to fill Rae and me in on what happened last night?" Hcrib asked ahead of them, his red hair like a beacon of light in front of them.

Anika opened her mouth but was interrupted by Jake. "There isn't a lot to tell. I'd been to see Anika the day before yesterday for the burn I'd planned and — "

"You burned yourself on purpose?" she interrupted.

"Keep going!" he barked. "Of course, I did it on purpose. I had to get to know more than just the order while I was there. Anyway, there was a supper, which was particularly useful by the way, and afterward, I was going back to the Apaiza's rooms when, lo and behold, I stumbled on Komandante Andrew, trying to rape Anika here. I was trying to decide what to do — intervening would have blown my cover. An Apaiza wouldn't interrupt a Komandante. And not stopping him, well, that felt wrong. Anika forced my hand, though when she grabbed Andrew's arm... and killed him."

"Just like that?" Rae asked, snapping her fingers.

"Just like that." Jake's eyes met Anika's and he nodded. "I figured that the chances of him having a heart attack right before he raped a girl was slim, so I assumed she was Naidisbo. Turns out I was right."

"Not dead," Anika interjected.

"Oh." A look of concern flashed over his face, gone as quickly as she'd seen it as he said, "Doesn't matter."

"So, what were you looking for while you pretended to be an Apaiza?" Anika asked, hoping to change the focus away from her. She'd never spoken about being a Naidisbo, and it wasn't exactly an easy thing to start.

Unfortunately, he didn't take the bait. "I want to know more about you. Why were you at the church? Did you use your powers as a nurse? Where is your family? Does anyone know that you're Naidisbo?"

She sighed. "My mother died when I was young, and so my father took a full-time position as a steward in the church. I knew when I was little that I had a power; I could feel people's hearts beating when I was around them. I would become overwhelmed by it. My father taught me how to block out the sound. Usually, humming or singing worked if it was really difficult. He also taught me never to say anything about it. When I got older, the order trained me, and I stayed as a nurse. My father is still there. He's the only one who knows about me."

"I don't understand." Rae looked at her quizzically. "Weren't you tested?"

"Tested?"

"All children are tested when they are eleven, to see if they have any powers. The order visits communities, forcing children to touch trees, and if they respond, they take the children."

Anika shook her head. "Naidisbo's power doesn't come from the earth. It isn't linked to a tree. It's just there. It just is."

Hcrib's nodded. "That's true. The main properties, physical, fire, and water, are part of the person, handed down through generations. They don't need anything to wield or make their power stronger. But for us to use our powers effectively, we have to have the property on us that connects the power to the earth."

Rae nodded; her brows furrowed as though she was thinking about the differences.

"Are you all naturalists then?"

"Yes," Rae answered, although she still looked deep in thought. "The rebels are regular people and naturalists who haven't been killed."

"What are each of you?"

"Urki," Hcrib answered first. "It's what makes me a good sneak. I can manipulate sound, so people don't hear me when I'm beside them. I also have great vision, especially at night. Quite handy for my job. I have a knack for stealing, but I don't think that has anything to do with Urki. I think that's just me."

Anika laughed, relaxing a little. "And where do you keep your Urki?"

Hcrib stopped as she approached him and pulled up his pant legs, revealing two solid wood cuffs on his ankles. He winked and turned, continuing to lead.

"Makalak," Rae's voice was gentle and quiet as she pulled a necklace out of her shirt. A large, flat, wooden disc was attached to it. "I'm an airbender."

"That's what happened to that man?" Anika asked, unsure if she really wanted the answer.

"I can manipulate air to do what I want. It can help me move, or I can take it away from someone if I have to."

Anika nodded, looking at Jake quickly over her shoulder as they continued walking. "And you? What are you?"

He didn't answer right away, instead stepping up to join Anika and Rae. "Haltz." He pulled his dagger from his belt, gesturing to the wooden handle. "I'm a good warrior, even better with this element. I'm fast, and I'm strong."

"No other magnificent worldly powers?" Anika asked as she thought about that dagger that had opened the men's throats the night before. He smirked in response. Evidently, he thought his power was enough.

"What are you going to do?" He ignored her question.

20

"About?" She snapped back.

"They know what you are. There's no hiding it anymore." He was blunt and honest, but she knew she didn't have an answer to that question.

"Tell me more about your rebels. Do you think you have a chance?"

"Of course, we have a chance," Jake grumbled. "If we didn't think we had a chance, we wouldn't bother." He didn't offer any further explanation, and the conversation halted. Anika didn't mind; she was deep in thought, thinking about what she had learned, and what her options truly were. *They'd be crazy to trust me*; she thought. *I could be anyone, and yet they took me with them without a second thought.*

"What would happen if you were caught?"

No one answered. She looked to each of them in confusion. "Even people who brought naturalist wood into Hagio were killed. What would they do to you?"

"You're asking a question you know the answer to, Anika." Rae looked at her, face grim but stoic. "They wouldn't hesitate — we would die. There would be one less naturalist in the world, and the order would be one person closer to control."

She nodded and continued walking. Gradually, the landscape had begun to change, the hills becoming steeper, still lush and green in places, but the ordinary trees were beginning to thin. In some places, just the barren skeletons of burned power trees remained with the low regrowth of nature as it tried to regain the space.

"Stop," Hcrib commanded, and they all froze. Hcrib's hand hovered in the air, his head moving slowly to his left, listening for something that the others couldn't hear. He pointed to a cluster of ordinary trees beside them. Jake moved first with Rae and Anika following. They walked until they could just see the road. Hcrib was gone when they looked back. They all crouched as Jake turned to them. "Hcrib will scout. If he gives us the signal, then we attack. Anika, stay here, and keep out of sight."

The soft whistle from Hcrib came seconds later, and Jake nodded to Rae. They moved through the bush quietly, not sparing a second look at Anika. Anika stayed crouched and concealed as ordered, but the temptation to stand

and watch nearly killed her, until she heard the sounds of the fight.

Rae hadn't cut off the air this time, and from the sound of it, they'd gone straight into hand-to-hand combat with whomever was on the road. Anika winced as steel hit steel. She closed her eyes and blocked out the screaming, the gurgling noises of life ending. Eventually, the stench reached her, and she covered her mouth, supressing a gag; there was nothing quite like the smell of death.

"Come on." She jumped, startled as Hcrib stood behind her and offered his hand. She hadn't heard him approach. Taking his hand, she stood and followed him toward the road. Jake and Rae were both leaning against trees. Jake's hands were clenched together, his head down as he focused on his breathing. Rae held a hand lightly over her eyes; a deep exhale escaped her lips as she lowered her hand and looked up at the sky, shaking her head sadly. Between them lay three men, all dead, their blood turning the light soil around them to a dark brown. Jake looked up and met Anika's eyes. She wouldn't have dared mention it, but he looked lost and sad at that moment. He wiped his dagger along his pants and sheathed it, shaking his head as he gestured to the men.

"We should bury them. We're close to Santouri." He looked at them all expectantly but didn't move.

"No, we should leave them," Rae said, stepping forward and stretching. She pulled her arms overhead and swayed side to side, as though she'd just gone for a quick run rather than killed three men. "We aren't close enough to give away Santouri, but it will leave a message. Plus, that one was a Lider. He'll be someone of importance, and they'll notice he's gone. They'll know their route, anyway. Burying makes no difference."

Anika raised her brows. It was the first time she heard anyone object to Jake's decision, and she fully expected that there would be an argument to follow, but she looked at Jake, who still looked fatigued, and he nodded in agreement. She looked at Rae, waiting for her to appear shocked too, but instead, she shouldered her pack and turned to enter the woods.

"Come on. We should stay off the road. We don't want them to track us to Santouri." Jake gestured for her to follow, but she paused.

"Santouri is our base?" she asked. He nodded in reply. "Are you hurt?"

"No, but I would appreciate it if we could get moving."

She scowled but did as she was told, although she was certain his heart rate wasn't that fast before the battle, and it was racing now.

* * *

They walked for another hour before Jake finally fell behind them, grunting as he hit the ground. Anika was ready; she had been listening to his heart rate, bounding and quickening as they'd walked. Both she and Rae flew back to him, but he waved them off as he tried to stand. The effort seemed like too much, and he fell backward again, his legs useless.

"Your heart rate." She kneeled in front of him and tipped his chin up to look her in the eyes. He half-heartedly jerked away from her hands. "Where are you hurt?"

He grimaced and looked at his left leg, giving away the source of his pain. Without hesitation, she pulled up his pantleg but saw nothing unusual. Still, she could feel the heat radiating from him. She kneeled and twisted his leg, exposing the mangled calf.

"What do you think you're doing?" He pushed her hands from him and struggled to regain his footing, but he fell back. He lay on the ground, working to catch his breath and glaring at the mangled leg. "It will heal, and I'm fine. I don't need you putting your hands all over me, trying to fix me."

"Shut up. You're too stubborn for your own good." The gash was deep along the length of his calf. She spread her hands along the length of the wound and focused on the pulsation beneath her hands, ignoring the stickiness. "You'll bleed out by dawn if you don't let me fix you."

He grumbled and crossed his arms, the grimace never leaving his face as she slipped her fingers into the wound. She smiled at the harsh intake of breath and jerk of his leg. "Wimp, stay still, and let me work."

Closing her eyes, she saw him with her fingers. Saw the torn muscles, the serrated tissue torn by the dagger of the patrol soldier. She felt the energy move through her core and flow from her fingers to his wound. The tissues formed closer back together, and she moved her hand along the length of the calf, moving from within the wound to the outer layers of skin. She opened her eyes and watched in satisfaction as the skin joined back together. She lifted her hands and felt the energy settle back inside of her, slightly depleted.

"I should leave you with this nasty scar." She saw the side of his mouth tug up in response, a small smile escaping his guard.

"Please do." He didn't try to get up but placed one dark and muscular forearm behind his head and shut his eyes again. "I'll have a constant reminder of what it means to let my guard down, and if I want it fixed in the future, then you'll get what you want."

"And what's that?"

"Another opportunity to put your hands all over me." He laughed as he rolled over and stood up, much sturdier, much more himself than moments ago.

"Ugh, I knew you were actually a pig." She stood up and wiped her hands against her wrinkled servant clothes as she turned to Rae. "I don't understand him."

He laughed, and Rae joined him, answering, "I don't think he understands himself."

They started walking — apparently, resting wasn't an option. Jake's joking had been a welcome break to the tension that hung in the air. Despite her better judgment, hesitation, and full-body soreness, she found herself smiling. Working in the church had been monotonous. She did her job with Margaret every day, and she went to bed every night to wake up and do the same thing the next day. While she hadn't felt like she was missing anything, she also hadn't felt any excitement in her life. She wouldn't call the other servants her friends, Margaret was the closest thing to a friend that she had had.

Does Margaret even realize I'm gone? she thought sadly; she shook her head to reconsider. *Of course, she does. She'll miss the other hands while she is working, but did she care about me. Or did she care about what I did for her?*

She didn't have friends, but she did have her father. Sudden terror twisted in her chest, and she stopped walking, Jake stopped behind her and lay a hand on her shoulder. "Why did you stop?"

"My father," she stammered and looked over her shoulder. "When they realize it was me, they'll take him. They'll kill him. He kept my secret."

Jake nodded, his hand squeezed her shoulder, and he gently pushed her forward. She put one foot in front of the other and tried to ignore the tears in her eyes. Her breathing felt restricted; her thoughts raced out of control. She could go back and find him. He could be left alone, he could plead ignorance, or they could kill him. She let the tears fall. Rae reached out and took her hand, squeezing as they pressed on.

3

Margaret

Anika was never late. As much as Margaret enjoyed giving the girl a hard time while they were working, it wasn't because she disliked the girl; it was because she liked her. So, when Anika didn't show up for work that morning, Margaret found herself glancing at the doorway between each patient, her brow furrowing each time the jingle of the opening door rang through the room only to find another soldier in need of an elixir for their hangover from the night before.

She was berating a soldier when the ringing of the door pulled her attention away. She turned, a smidgen of hope rising in her chest that it would be Anika — only to be disappointed to see another soldier. This young man didn't look as haggard as the one sitting in her seat, she noted. He seemed generally well-kempt. She was pleased when he gave her a small bow and respectfully turned to his colleague.

"They asked you to bring her in immediately, Jared." His brows raised in irritation at the soldier she'd been attending to.

"I needed something for this headache before..."

"Regardless of the situation, particularly your situation," he stressed, "you're to bring this healer to the boardroom immediately."

Unease prickled at Margaret's neck as she looked between the two men, her chair inching back as she pushed away from them. "I'm sorry, could you explain?" she asked.

The tall soldier spoke directly to her. "Reynard and Edyta have requested your cooperation in an investigation regarding the other healer that works with you. You're expected in the boardroom immediately for questioning by the Komandante."

She blindly followed the soldiers as they made their way across the grounds. She tried to focus her thoughts on the dryness of the grass under her feet, or the burning of the sun as it broke through the clouds, but nothing worked. Instead, her mind wandered back to Anika, to when she had last seen her.

There hadn't been anything unusual that she could think of. Anika had helped her tend to the soldiers, had made a poultice, and restocked the shelves with supplies before she'd left. She hadn't seemed nervous or upset.

One of the soldiers held open the door to the church for her, and she walked into the boardroom where he nodded to the people standing at the end of the long table.

"Welcome!" A man that she didn't recognize smiled at her from across the room as he beckoned her over. She moved cautiously, not unaware of how unnaturally formal she should be behaving in front of the order, but she was still too shell-shocked to think straight.

"Please sit." A familiar servant pulled out a chair for her, an encouraging hand pushing her into it before she could answer one way or another.

The man across from her wore black robes. He smiled, but it didn't reach his eyes, eyes that she couldn't help noticing seemed cold and dead as he placed his hands on the table and leaned back. She looked around briefly; there were more people here than she'd have expected. Several men and women stood behind her, silent.

"Margaret, is it?" the man asked.

"Yes."

"Excellent, well.... The first thing I'd like to do is thank you for the tireless service that you provide to the order. You're a woman of many talents. I don't think anyone would disagree with me that you're vital to the running of smooth operations here."

The same unmoving smile was glued to his face as she answered, "It's my pleasure."

"Now, the second thing..." sighing in exacerbation. "Your assistant. We have reason to believe she may have been a rebel."

"Anika?" she exclaimed.

He nodded solemnly; the smile gone. "Sadly, yes. She absconded from the church last night with an undercover rebel. We, understandably, have some questions for those closest to her."

She agreed immediately, knowing that she really had no choice in the matter. It was a cardinal rule that you didn't say no to the church if they asked you for something. The man didn't wait for her response before he continued.

"Had Anika ever given any indication that she may be a rebel?"

"No." She could feel her heart beating wildly in her chest. She wasn't lying, but to not give them the answers they wanted, she could only pray they wouldn't think she was holding back.

"How long have you known Anika?"

"Almost six years now. I met her when I came to the church to be the head healer."

"And she was already employed as an assistant?"

"Yes." She pulled her hands into her lap, wringing them nervously.

"Did she ever seem resentful that she wasn't the head healer?" He leaned forward, his eyes, a bland hazel, boring into her.

"Never. She always did her work without complaint, she was professional, and she knew what she was doing."

She heard whispers behind her and turned to look. Two soldiers were whispering to one another, only to have a third elbow them to be quiet.

"Very good, and exactly what we've heard from the others," the man interviewing her said. She wondered for a moment how many other people had been interviewed. "And her healing abilities, how were they?"

"Excellent!" she declared, again more whispering from around the table, the tones quieter now.

"Did she ever give you any reason to think that she may be a naturalist, Margaret?"

Now she could hear the blood pounding in her ears. She straightened up in her chair and steeled her confidence. "None."

"Nothing?"

She swallowed, recognizing that they were now at the root of their investigation; this was what they really wanted to know.

"No, she never showed any signs of being a naturalist. She was a lovely girl. I'm sorry to hear that she's absconded."

"Margaret, if anything, and I can't stress this enough, if *anything* comes up, I need you to report it to us immediately. It's for everyone's best interest, and safety, that we locate Anika immediately."

She nodded, unable to speak as she stood and bowed briefly to her interviewer.

* * *

The silence seemed louder now that she knew Anika was truly gone, and the space felt void of her energy, leaving Margaret to wonder if perhaps she did have powers, her energy having cast over the space during their years working together.

She sat in her favourite chair, looking at the shelves of medicinal ingre-dients. She used to watch Anika from here, barking orders at her, to which the girl had nodded or smiled at Margaret before doing. She had been a good healer, a good assistant.

The knock on the door pulled her from her musings. She didn't know if she had even answered the knock when the door opened, and a figure ducked into the room, hood drawn over their face until they shut the door behind them and let it fall away.

"Stanton," she breathed.

"Margaret, I hope you're well." He sat, not waiting for her to answer as he hurried on. "I know they took you in for questioning. Please, if you knew anything, tell me you didn't give it away."

"I knew nothing." She shrugged.

He paused; doubt lined his face as he studied her. "Nothing, Stanton, I had no idea she was a rebel!"

29

Stanton's face crumpled briefly. "Margaret, she wasn't a rebel. She's Naidisbo."

Her ears rang. For a long time, Margaret studied him. She'd known him since she joined the church and had begun to work with Anika, but she'd never expected that the girl was a Naidisbo. She'd never shown any sign of being that kind of healer.

She stuttered, glancing at Stanton with disbelief as he nodded, head hanging down in sadness, his eyes wet with tears. "But... Stanton, I don't... she never..."

He nodded, his hands running through his hair as he slid his hood back. "She's hidden it her entire life."

"She couldn't have."

"She did. She knew before we even came to the church. She hid it for so long."

Margaret shook her head slowly back and forth. "How did she get caught? She never showed any signs of having power, and I worked with her every single day. If anyone would have seen it... it would have been me, Stanton!"

"I have no idea!" he declared, his eyes filling with tears again. This time he didn't rub them away, letting them fall over his cheeks as he took a deep breath. "She was so quiet about it. She never showed her powers."

"Did the soldiers give you any indication of what happened?" she asked.

He shook his head, his dark hair, desperately in need of a cut, swung around his ears as he held in a sob. "They said that she nearly killed someone, someone of importance, and when she was seen, she fled with the rebels."

"Why would she show her powers now after all this time?"

"I don't know!" He stood and began to walk around the room, his black servant robes swinging around his legs as he paced in the shadows of the setting sun. "You're asking me the same questions that the soldiers did, but I don't know the answers."

"Let me make you some tea." She rose from her chair but stopped when his hand pulled on her elbow, forcing her to look at him again.

"I have to go back; they'll be keeping a close eye on me." His eyes drifted to the windows, as though the soldiers would be coming for him already.

"Stanton, what can I do?"

He let go of her arm and moved to stand in the threshold of the door, his hand hovering on the handle. She could see the fear lining his eyes. The complete and utter exhaustion of the last day was wearing on him, and she wondered for a moment if he was making good decisions, or if what he was saying was truthful.

"Stanton, if you're tired you can rest here. We can talk about it more after you've gotten some sleep. Just tell me what to do."

He shook his head and wiped away another tear. She grabbed his falling hand and squeezed. Silently pleading with him, for some way to help him in this moment of need.

"They'll keep me here, Margaret, and if they don't find her, they'll kill me."

"Why?" Her heart was thundering in her chest, but she focused on Stanton.

"I kept a Naidisbo hidden in plain sight for years, in the church, under their noses. Margaret." He picked her hand up, trembling, and held her gaze, his brown eyes steady. "If they kill me, hang me in the square. Whatever they do to me, tell her she was worth it. Tell her I loved her. If I can't see her again, then I need you to do that for me."

"This is ridiculous, Stanton." This time, she pulled her hand away, trying to hide her own trembling.

He shook his head, a sad smile on his face. "I don't think I'll disappear immediately, but I couldn't wait to tell you that. Good night."

Margaret listened as his footsteps hurried away, his shadow falling over the window as he hurried by. It stopped for a moment, the darkness filling the room, and she wondered if he'd come back, but then he was gone. She looked around, at a loss what to do, overwhelmed by the information he'd just bombarded her with. She put the kettle on. When in doubt, she knew what to do: sit, have a cup of tea, and breathe.

* * *

The Naidisbo, working beside her for years. She still couldn't believe it. She wasn't sure that it was even true. Stanton had seemed nearly crazy with his grief, and she could have believed that he was mistaken if it wasn't for the small signs that she was starting to remember. It was like her memory had been triggered by the knowledge, and part of her wished that it hadn't been.

Like the times when soldiers, with wounds far too grave to be calm while being treated, seemed suddenly able to relax, or how the young girl that had burned her hand in the kitchen under scalding water had skipped away after Anika had held a cold cloth to it. She remembered thinking it odd that the girl hadn't needed to come back for any further treatment.

She didn't want to believe it.

Her cuppa, long ago refilled and again gone cold, sat discarded beside her as she stared at nothing and thought. The church was looking for information about Anika, but she didn't know if her memories were true. Suddenly, she doubted every interaction she'd ever had with her.

And Stanton, he was cleansing his own conscience, meeting his needs without even realizing what he was doing to her. She sighed and willed herself to stop grinding her teeth. He had no idea what he'd done by telling her that Anika was the Naidisbo. The soldiers wanted confirmation, and now she had the knowledge to give that to them.

And if she held that knowledge back, and then they found out? She swallowed — would they kill her too?

4

Makalak

They walked for hours until the sun set, and then they continued walking until finally Hcrib stopped, and they entered a cave. The cave was deep and cold, shadows seemed to curl away from the walls towards Anika as she settled herself in. Against the back wall, there were several bedrolls waiting, a stack of damp but thick blankets, and, most importantly, a ready to be lit pit for a fire.

Jake sat and immediately started trying to light the kindling that lay above the coals, cursing at the dampness, while Rae laid out bedrolls and passed Hcrib and Anika blankets.

"Ha! Got it!" cried Jake as he sat back and held his hands over the tiny, dancing flame.

"What is this place?" asked Anika as she lay down, kicking off her shoes. The thin mattress wouldn't have felt like much before, but after three nights of sleeping on the ground, it felt like a luxurious bed.

"We have locations about three days' walk from Santouri in every direction," Hcrib said, pulling his blanket over himself. "We keep them stocked, like this one, in case we need them. Times like this, it comes in very handy. Now, if you'll excuse me, I'm going to sleep. Getting you lot here isn't easy work."

Jake laughed and settled on his mattress, then cursed, sitting up. "Someone needs to go on first sentry."

Rae sighed and picked up her blanket as she moved to the front of the cave; no one objected. Anika thought about offering, but she hadn't done sentry yet, and she didn't know if they'd trust her to do so anyway. Before she could reconsider it, she was asleep.

* * *

Her dreams were vivid. The kind where the person wakes, knowing they feel disturbed but can't quite remember why. She remembered seeing her father and soldiers, herself, and her new companions. She smelled death.

She rolled over and rubbed her eyes, squeezing them tightly, trying to find sleep again in the darkness of the cave, but the few images she recalled plagued her. She saw her father struggling for air as Rae held her hands out, taking away his oxygen. She saw Jake behind him, dagger ready to strike.

Sighing, she gave in and opened her eyes. Rae was sleeping soundly across from her; light snores escaped her. It was still dark in the cave, and she knew sleep wouldn't come back easily. She stretched her arms above her head and breathed deeply as she rolled over to face the fire.

Her breath stopped. Beside Jake lay an outstretched cat. It wasn't a normal-sized cat. It was huge. It lay with its paws up and head facing the fire, at least seven feet long, black as night, and with teeth large enough that they jutted out over the animal's gums in its sleep. She scrambled to sit up, looking wildly between the entrance of the cave and Rae. How any of them had slept through a wildcat entering the cave was beyond her.

She pushed her blanket down, careful not to shift the bedroll as she tried to get up. Ever so slowly she shifted her weight and stepped towards the mouth of the cave, praying she had adopted some of Hcrib's sneaking abilities. The cat curled, nuzzling its head against Jake's back, and she heard a low purr escape it — Anika shook her head, baffled that Jake was sleeping. Rae rolled over as Anika stepped by her, the bedroll creaking as she settled. Anika hesitated, her breath hitching as one yellow eye slowly opened. Immediately the cat leaped to its feet when it saw Anika crouched across from it and

34

kneeled back on its hind legs to attack.

"Oh, Thor!" Rae exclaimed.

For a moment, Anika thought she was surely going to die by the beast's teeth, only to be hurled back when Rae's hands flew up, casting a wall of air between her and the creature. The cat hissed as its body hit the swirling air and it was thrown back towards Jake. It moved faster than any other animal she'd ever seen, rolling to its paws and beginning to pace, tail whipping back and forth, long teeth bared as the yellow eyes bore into her.

Jake, now sitting up, put a hand out. Anika winced, waiting for the attack but instead the cat went to him, pushing against his hand as he purred. Anika looked at them, utterly confused. Exacerbated, and too shocked to do anything else, she stayed on the ground, ignoring the cold beneath her and waiting for an explanation.

"Be good, Thor." Jake pushed his forehead against the cat's as it settled beside him. Thor draped his long front limbs over Jake's lap and put his head down, purring but keeping his yellow eyes on Anika the entire time.

"Would someone please care to explain to me what's going on?" She breathlessly asked the question to the room, her eyes never leaving the cat, who continued to stare her down.

"This is Thor, my hunting cat," Jake stated while scratching behind Thor's ears. "I couldn't bring him to Hagio, so he had to stay at Santouri. He must have tracked us down last night."

"Care to explain why your hunting cat wants to kill me?" she asked, inching toward her bedroll as the cat's eyes followed.

"He just doesn't know you," Jake said. "He won't kill you now that he knows you're with us. Will you, Thor?"

The animal purred in contentment and closed his eyes, as though under-standing Jake's words. She replayed his words in her head. She was with them — not a friend, not a comrade, but she was with them... it wasn't exactly reassuring. Nodding mutely, she lay back down. It was still dark outside, and she needed more sleep, though she doubted she would get any. Shutting her eyes, she tried to ignore the feeling of someone watching her. Grumbling to herself, she opened her eyes and turned over, suppressing the urge to flinch

35

away from Thor's yellow eyes still watching her in the dark. She shut her eyes again and tried to ignore the rising panic as she pictured him leaping toward her. She checked again and again, until finally the cat's eyes closed and they both slept.

When she woke, after a surprisingly restful sleep, she saw that Jake and Thor were packed. Hcrib and Rae were still there sleeping, the light filtering into the cave, dust dancing in the rays. Walking to the mouth of the cave, she met Jake who sat cross-legged, gazing out over the landscape before them. She hadn't taken much notice of the landscape the night before — she had been tired and ready to sleep — but she sat beside him now and took it in.

The land was lush and green. It spread out below them, hills and trees stretching as far as she could see. The only thing that marred the view were the fields of barren land where the order had burned trees down. There were two or three areas in the distance where she saw the smoke from a chimney, or perhaps a fire, but otherwise, it was serene. It felt entirely private. Below them was a small stream, gurgling in places, little bubbles giving away the presence of fish. Despite her reservations, watching Thor perch over the stream, his large feline shape ready to strike, made her smile. Though perhaps it was just because she wasn't on the other side of that coming strike.

With one paw in the air, he sat, completely still as he waited for the perfect opportunity. She jumped even though she'd known it was coming when the paw fell with claws out, and a large fish flew from the water. Thor turned and pounced, grabbing the fish and flinging it to the ground. Apparently, the hunting cat didn't play with his food.

She looked at Jake, who watched Thor with a smile on his face, the first one she'd seen since they'd left Hagio. Humming in observation, she said, "I didn't take you to be a cat lover."

He pulled his knees into his chest and shrugged, unashamed. "The other part of Haltz, which people tend to ignore, is the unique ability to communicate with hunting cats. Thor and I understand one another in a way that I have a hard time finding with people. Thor's been in my life for a long time."

36

He picked up the stick in front of him, idly making lines in the dirt. Anika looked at the creature and back to him. "How?"

"What do you mean?"

"How do you communicate?"

"Well, how does anyone communicate?" When she didn't offer an answer, he continued. "Thor can understand what I'm saying. He knows what I mean when I say you're a friend. He doesn't have to speak for me to understand what he says, I can tell more about him from his posture and body language than I can tell from most people. When you roll your eyes, I don't know if you're frustrated, trying to irk me, or who knows, maybe you're happy! But with Thor, I just know. I can't explain it, but I understand him."

"I get it." She nodded and looked at the cat, who was brushing his long body against the bushes on his way up the hill. Jake looked at her, incredulously. "No, really! I just know what's happening in someone's body. It doesn't sound much different."

"Huh, I guess that's true," he said, leaning back as Thor pushed against him, settling a large head in his lap.

"So, what exactly does he do?"

"Isn't that kind of self-explanatory?" He lay down fully, and the cat stretched alongside him, blocking most of Jake from Anika's view.

"Not really."

"We hunt, we fight together, we travel. Haven't you ever had a pet, Anika? Not that you're a pet, Thor." He patted the cat's head, and Thor gave a playful growl at the statement.

"No, we weren't allowed to have pets in the church." She looked at the cat, who stretched a paw out toward her. "Can I pet you?"

"You can," Jake's words floated over Thor, and she shimmied closer, a hand held out to Thor's face. Thor pushed against her. His fur, which looked coarse, was surprisingly soft against her skin. She hadn't been around many animals during her time in the church, other than the foxes, and those had been horrible creatures. She hadn't been around an animal that showed affection, or understanding, that she trusted not to hurt her for no reason.

She smiled as Thor purred in contentment, rolling with his belly in the

37

air, a large paw pulling her hand to his chin before she had a chance to stop scratching. Jake lay down, a hand behind his head.

"So, how are you?" he said, opening one eye to look at her. She shrugged her shoulders and avoided his gaze; she generally didn't do well talking about herself — yet that seemed to be impossible to avoid lately. Jake closed his eyes again and nodded. "You've been through a lot of shit in the last few days. I'm surprised by how well you're doing actually. I remember when I first joined, and I joined because I wanted to, not because I had to, leaving my home was the hardest thing I had ever done. Cutting contact with them, it was tough."

"Why did you cut contact with them?" she asked.

"It was the responsible thing to do; my family are strong, hardworking people. We used to have a lot of people who were power wielders, but even those who weren't, they could still fight better than any of your order soldiers."

"They aren't my soldiers," she interrupted with a glare.

"Sorry, you know what I mean. Anyway, during the last uprising, a lot of them died. We used to have a pretty large family, but most of my uncles were killed. My mum and dad survived and started farming in Rojos. They live a modest life now, one where they are safe, and not bothered by the order as long as they keep their heads down."

She nodded, looking over the vast landscape. She could see the appeal of being a farmer, with the space in the country. She expected that a family could live a comfortable lifestyle. It wasn't like the city where you lived on top of one another; in the country, you could breathe the clean air, walk for miles and only have yourself to talk to — it was what a lot of people dreamed of.

"I have two brothers, Matthew and Samuel — neither of them is a power wielder. They were never taught how to fight because my uncles were dead, and my father refused. I get why he refused. If we knew how to fight, then we'd be taken by the order and would become soldiers. If we refused, we would die."

He exhaled heavily and sat up. Thor stayed put, now snoring lightly. Jake wrapped his arms around his legs, looking forward at the land. "Like Rae said, at some time, the order comes around and takes children. They test them to see if they have power. My parents knew I had power. They'd kept one of my uncle's Haltz daggers." He stopped and looked at her for a moment, his eyes puzzled. "I was unnaturally fast as it was, so they kept me hidden. When the order came, I stayed in the woods, camped out and waited for them to go to the next farm. Every year, I did the same thing, and every year, I grew angrier that I had to hide, angrier that my power made me a freak, angrier that I had to pretend to be someone else to everyone outside of our house, angrier that my brothers didn't have the opportunities to become warriors like they should have."

Anika stayed silent, afraid that if she said anything, he'd stop talking. She cradled her head in her hand and watched him as he continued his story. "I first heard about the rebels when I was drinking at the tavern. Dad had sent me to get supplies from Langford, and Val was recruiting people. You'll meet her at Santouri. Anyway, she was talking about how we shouldn't have to hide who we are, and that resonated with me so loudly. I approached her after she was done, and I left the next day with her for Santouri."

"You never went back home?"

He shook his head, gazing toward the hills below them. "No, if they'd known I was leaving, then they'd have tried to stop me. If they had any idea I joined the rebels, they'd be at risk of telling the order, by force or mistake. It's safer for them not to know, to wonder what happened to me."

"I'm sorry."

He nodded and stood, stretching his arms overhead and shaking out his legs. "It was hard, but when we win this thing, they'll know. Hopefully, they'll forgive me. I'm doing this for them too."

She didn't know what to say, or if he was even looking for an answer, so she stayed quiet. The silence wasn't uncomfortable. They were just present, and for a moment, her anxieties seemed to drift away until Jake interrupted her thoughts. "Did they train you to spar there?"

She shrugged as she answered. "Everyone had some basic training. It was required. But I only had the minimum. I didn't need any more than that."

"All right, well, let's see what they taught you." He walked to the mouth of the cave and picked up two swords. "Supplies, never hurts to have some in the bases if you need them." He passed her one of the swords, handle first, and stepped back as she stood up.

She gingerly lifted the sword up and down in her hand. The weight wasn't completely foreign to her, but it had been some time since she'd properly trained. She knew she'd likely do poorly, but she'd done well enough in her lessons, and she knew how to defend herself should she have to. Widening her stance and angling herself slightly away from Jake, she nodded and held the sword at mid-level, ready.

He smiled back at her mischievously and stepped forward, his sword swinging in from the right, which she easily met and blocked. The feeling of metal hitting metal vibrated through her arm, and she stepped back slightly, allowing herself to get used to the sensation. Jake didn't give her much time to recover as he stepped forward. Swinging from the left, the sword arching in the air, she lifted her elbow, both hands holding the blade as she met his and held it against him, pushing him away.

Still smiling and undeterred, he was forced to step back, their blades sliding down as they separated. Feeling more comfortable, she lunged forward and feinted left, swinging her sword low on her right for his ankles, but Jake jumped, clearing her swing with ease.

He landed steadily, sword held confidently in both hands, and chuckled. Cursing, she stood up as he stepped forward, their swords meeting again as they danced faster. While Anika knew she wasn't challenging him, or even making him work, she was glad that she could withstand the pace he was setting. They shuffled back toward the mouth of the cave. Thor lay, yellow eyes moving back and forth from Anika to Jake as they moved in sync.

The dance continued, and Anika was surprised by how quickly the movements came back to her, but she also was tiring easily. Her feet, not fully recovered from the walking, were starting to ache, and she could feel her heart rate rising as she was pushed back by one of Jake's low swings. The step pushed her into the threshold of the cave, and Jake stepped back, sword held out to the side.

"I do love to win!" he yelled, pushing the sword's blade into the earth with exaggerated movement.

"How do you suppose you won?" She stepped forward, and Jake pulled the sword from the ground, his grin still glued to his face.

"You were pushed into the cave. I win."

"Rules don't count until you know them." She swung first, and Jake laughed, countering her attack with ease.

A cough behind them, clearly meant to break up their sparring, made them both turn. Rae, hair dishevelled, glared at them both. "Your fun woke us up, but seeing as we appear to have overslept, don't you think we should get moving?"

Jake grabbed Anika's sword as he walked to the cave, rolling his eyes to Anika as he did so. "My apologies, your majesty." He sarcastically bowed to Rae, which prompted a quick smack and a retreat into the cave for their things.

* * *

She took some satisfaction at the thought that Jake had seemed surprised with her ability to handle a sword. She didn't want to be over-confident, but she was fairly certain that she had been both well trained and gifted with some natural talent. Despite the easiness between them during their fight, Jake had quickly gone back to his seriousness, shutting down her attempts at conversation while they walked. Feeling defeated she fell into step in the middle of their group, talking with Rae and doing her best to ignore the weariness in her body.

"Where did you learn to handle a sword?" Rae asked her.

"We all had to have training." She shifted the backpack she wore until it was more comfortable. "It was mandatory if you worked for the order."

"That doesn't make sense. Why train a healer to fight?" Rae countered.

"Everyone had to," Anika shrugged. "You didn't ask questions. You just did what you were told. Asking questions led to dismissal, and without a job... well, things weren't always plentiful in Hagio. People starved if they

41

lost their work. So, you didn't question."

Anika was tired, but she was trying to put on a good show. She hadn't complained about the ache in her feet, or the growing throb in her shoulders. And while she knew she could simply use her abilities to make those aches and pains disappear, she only dulled them, unwilling to abuse her powers. She knew they were becoming more trusting of her, but still, she noticed the occasional looks of suspicion between them. As much as she wanted to curl up and go to sleep in the middle of their path, she soldiered on and tried to make small talk. "How did you know that you were an airbender?" she asked Rae.

"I always knew. I had to wait to use the power, but it was always there, like a fire bed waiting to be lit. When I got the Makalak, it was like something inside of me changed, like there had been something missing my entire life, and then suddenly, I was whole."

She held a hand up in the air, and Anika felt the wind shift, blowing against them softly. "There isn't a lot of Makalak left. When the order burned down all of the power trees, people tried to regrow them quietly and secretly, but Makalak is the most difficult. They are tall and thin, and while they can grow fast, not all the trees have the property that's needed to bend air. It seems to be entirely random, and, unfortunately, rare, unlike the other trees. When an airbender has Makalak, they guard it more than any other power wielder because we don't know when or where there will be more."

"How did you get yours?"

"My parents were airbenders. They left me at Santouri when they went on a raid. My dad was a great warrior and so he left his Makalak behind because he assumed he wouldn't need it. It was supposed to be a simple fight, but I think he knew it would be more than that. They both died on the raid. My mother's Makalak is gone, burned I assume, but I had his, and it allowed me to tap into my power."

"I'm sorry." Anika knew the pain of losing a parent, but to lose both, and to be raised by strangers — she didn't want to think about it longer than she had to.

"Thank you." Rae avoided her eye contact and continued walking. "Helena taught me everything she knew about being an airbender. You'll meet her at Santouri. She is one of the teachers. She helped me understand my power, and the rest I learned as I went. I'm the only airbender left that can fight, but we're very fortunate. We have a child who can learn, so I won't be the last one."

"Both your parents were airbenders — is it hereditary?" She stepped over a large tree in their path, startled when Rae used her power to jump and float over the barrier, landing delicately on the other side. "I think that seeing you do that will take some getting used to."

"We don't know if it's hereditary or not. We only know what the Hagin wielders can tell us. They know our history, remember our stories, and so they help teach us what we need to know." Anika must have looked confused. Rae continued, "The order has burned anything about naturalist magic. Our history is handed down mostly through stories and oral legend. We have only a few written stories at Santouri, and we guard them protectively."

"But it's history," she said. "Who cares about history?" The question sounded stupid as it left her mouth, but she couldn't very well take the words back.

"Smart people care about history, Anika." Rae shook her head in disbelief. "History is more than just a story. If people can read history, it can't be changed or denied, but if nothing is written, then the story of what happened, of who we are, is up for debate. The order can make people believe whatever they want about us, and how do we prove to people otherwise?"

"You show them the difference."

"You can't do that when you're forbidden to practise your power, let alone be alive, Anika." Rae jumped, and a gust of wind propelled her upwards until she was bobbing above the treeline. The wind buffeting her hair as it whipped away from her, and debris from the ground dancing in chaos from the force of the wind. Anika held up a hand to block the wind that was buffeting her face and resisted the urge to step backwards from the force of it. Suspended there, Anika could see the threat and intimidation from someone like Rae; she was simply terrifying. "If I did this around members of the order, I'd be hung and burned as an example."

Straight faced, she dropped to the ground and continued walking – the wind ceased to exist in her wake.

5

Crescent Moons

T he night sky was clear; stars twinkled above them. The crescent moons cast their preternatural light over where they'd stopped. Anika lay awake despite the long day of walking, distracted by the new ache in her shoulders. She rubbed her right, then her left, grimacing at the pain. It wasn't just physical discomfort that was keeping her awake; no, her thoughts were as much a problem as her body.

As a child, she'd grown up outside of the church, and her view of power wielders had been different — especially considering that she was a power wielder herself, but still, the order had been effective in their brainwashing. She had believed that those with power should be prevented from using it. The stories the church had told had been terrifying.

Stories about naturalists killing innocent people, entering Hagio, and slaughtering children. Were they even real? Or had they been made up to slander the people? Her father had always been quiet about rebels, never one to talk about things — especially people with powers. Silence had been sacred if they were to live.

That was another sore spot, something that made her uneasy. Her concerns for her father were justified, but there were things about him that she didn't know. He had worked for the order, and he was higher than a servant, but he wasn't a member. Yet she had seen him on many occasions, with high-ranking members, laughing and joking as though he were a comrade rather than just a worker.

She shook her head in a vain attempt to clear it. That would never make sense. If he were truly part of the order, then he would have surrendered her. If he'd believed the things that the order preached, then she'd have been killed when she first showed her powers.

She hated the thoughts that ran through her head. She hated her doubt of him. And as much as she wanted to be angry, as she wrapped her blanket tighter, she knew she'd have given anything to talk to him.

She sat up from her bedroll, frustrated and restless. Rae, Jake, and Thor were sleeping soundly. Hcrib sat farther down the hill, eyes focused on nothing but watching just the same. Pulling her blanket around her shoulders, she walked over to him and sat. He didn't even glance her way.

"Hey." She wrapped her arms around her knees and looked out over the dark landscape. Shadows clung to the trees, mist rolled over some of the fields, the night was silent.

"Hey," Hcrib looked at her and smiled. He looked tired. "How are you?"

"Good, how are you?"

"Tired," he said, confirming what she'd thought. He stood up, groaning as he stretched, "But I should do a perimeter check. Do you want to come with me?"

She nodded and stood, stretching her tired arms as she followed him. He moved quietly and quickly, stepping a few paces at a time and stopping to check his surroundings. They continued this pattern of starting and stopping as they circled around the camp. Hcrib's ability to sneak was impressive. While her feet crunched on the crisp earth, and she pushed away branches, he was silent. She had no doubt that the only reason she could still detect him was that he chose to stay close enough for her to know he was there.

He stopped, and she stopped. He glared at her as she crunched a branch. He held a finger to his lips, telling her to be quiet as he looked around them cautiously. She listened but heard nothing, noticing that Hcrib had now closed his eyes. He remained still, hearing something she could not. He motioned for her to get down, and she crouched, peering ahead into the night, but whatever he was seeing was invisible to her. He pointed into the darkness, and she waited, watching the direction he'd indicated. Eventually, a light started bouncing below them, moving slowly across the landscape.

Breaking the silence, Hcrib looked at her and said, "It's fine. It's a farmer checking on his livestock." He stood and started walking back around the perimeter, Anika behind him.

"You could see him that clearly?" She asked in awe.

"Almost as clear as I could see him during the day."

"That's amazing," she sat, shifting the blanket underneath her to protect her from the dew of the earth.

"It's hugely useful, but it can be a pain. I constantly sneak up on people without even realizing it. And I never get passed up for sentry, because who wouldn't want their quietest, best eyes, and best ears on duty? I don't think I've ever gotten a full night's sleep unless I was at Santouri. Even then, I'm the first to get woken up." He looked at her and sighed. "Sorry, I'm just complaining because I'm tired. I do that."

"Well, I can't sleep anyway. Why don't you go sleep now?"

He chuckled and ran his hands through his hair. "Have you ever done sentry before, Anika?"

She hesitated. "Well, no, but you can tell me what to do. And if something comes up, I'll wake you."

He shook his head stubbornly. "No, it will be Jake's turn in another thirty minutes anyway. But you should talk to him about doing sentry. That would be really helpful."

She nodded and feeling both dismissed and pleased that he thought she should do sentry, she went back to bed and finally was able to go to sleep.

* * *

The brief stop for lunch had been short-lived as they'd quickly made a soup from their dwindling supplies and Thor's earlier hunt. Nonetheless, it had been enough to get them through the final leg of their journey, which had been steeper and more difficult than before.

Jake had let her know that it would be arduous as they approached Santouri, but she hadn't really expected it to be as intense as it were. The elevation was extreme, and she felt winded, while the others seemed fine. Worse, she was sure; she was breathing loud enough for everyone to hear, so she closed her eyes and focused on her lungs, expanding the tightened airways to increase her airflow. She hated relying on her powers, but she thought that collapsing as they reached the top of the hill might be even worse.

"Kane!" Anika looked up in surprise as Rae began running. Below them lay an open field, a garden blooming at the edge of a river, and beyond it Santouri. She laughed as Rae jumped, unnaturally clearing the river and garden and landed on the other side, vaulting toward a tall man. The man, bare-chested, covered in tattoos, with dark hair that fell about his shoulders, turned and grabbed Rae as she jumped into his arms. Anika flushed as their embrace turned into a passionate kiss — turning, she caught Jake rolling his eyes in their direction.

Santouri was larger than she thought it would be. The church, cold and sterile, had never felt like a welcoming place. But the moment she laid her eyes upon Santouri she felt a sense of peace and solitude. Seemingly undisturbed by the difficulties that made life in Hagio so strenuous, Santouri instead seemed a haven. Small rock walls divided the land into plots of gardens, which people were tending to. In Hagio, and the church, people moved from place to place without so much as looking up, always eager to get to the next task at hand. Here though, it seemed as though the people were enjoying their time, children could be heard laughing, and the pleasant sound of easy conversation drifted towards them. Even the buildings seemed welcoming, small log-sided cabins were scattered among the grounds and in the centre of the clearing was a rather large building, its entrance decorated with flowers and lazy vined plants that framed the door.

"It's cozy," she said to no one in particular.

Jake nodded, seemingly lost in his own thoughts. "Come on. Val will be anxious to meet you, and we need to get you settled in before the team debrief tonight."

* * *

"So, you're a Naidisbo then." Val was about a foot shorter than Anika, and yet made her feel small and insignificant as she looked up at her, judging her. Her face screamed distrust, and Anika thought that it was likely she could have chosen to hide it should she have liked to. Anika felt like a fish out of water as Val started to step around her, examining her. She focused on Val's black hair pulled back into a tight and long ponytail that swayed as she stepped. She examined her with just as much judgment, taking note of the muscular arms and fish tattoo that stood boldly white against the dark skin.

She looked to her left. Jake stood beside her, keeping a respectful distance as Val finished her round, the look of disdain ever-present and speaking volumes more than her words would have.

"How did you find her?" Her eyes lingered on Anika, but her words were spoken to Jake.

He told her, albeit briefly, about their journey from the church to Santouri. Val nodded, her eyes never straying far from Anika.

"I have no reason to doubt her. I've seen her power twice now. She healed my leg on the way here after a run-in with a patrol. I could have died if she hadn't healed me." Jake spoke surely, his eyes avoiding Anika's as he admitted what she had known that day on the trail.

Val scoffed. "Perhaps you shouldn't have been so careless as to get hurt then."

Anika felt herself start to smile but quickly pursed her lips as Val's eyes narrowed in response. "And so, what do you think of your situation? Are you prepared to join us, or are you merely here to stay alive?"

"Can it not be both?" She met Val's eyes with determination, ignoring her racing heart. She appreciated strength, but she suspected she would have to prove herself to be respected by Val.

Val nodded. There was no hint of a smile or break in her composure. "She may stay, Jake, and she may join us, but should she betray us, or become a burden, then she is your responsibility to dispose of." Jake pursed his lips in frustration but did not retaliate. Anika raised her eyebrows in shock. She hadn't seen him present meekly before. "You will have to train, help out around Santouri, and not cause trouble. I don't trust you, but he vouches for you, and that will do for now. We are a team, and we trust in one another, but if that is broken, we do not give second chances. I will not have anyone endanger the lives of my family."

Anika nodded, gobsmacked as she followed Jake out of the room. She hardly took in her surroundings as they walked, instead dwelling on Val's words.

"This is the dining room. We all eat together in the evenings." She feigned interest as he pushed open a large door. They stepped into an enormous room with long tables and benches, bare at that time but still cozy. "You won't have to help in the kitchen. It's fully staffed right now; Rae is often in here working. She loves to cook. Kane helps out here too. He says it's because the other staff can't carry the weight or tinker, but it's because of Rae."

They moved out of the dining area and made their way down the hall until they hit the end. On either side of them ran the two wings she'd seen from before. She turned with him to face the left as he pointed out the many doors, all sleeping quarters. Anika's mind was still on Kane, the large man with all the tattoos, and so she asked about him.

"Well, he's from the south, a family of fishermen mostly. Kane's a tinker. He can change his size whenever he pleases. It's quite helpful when you're in combat. He goes from being under five feet tall, surprising enemies above him, to seven and a half feet, towering over them." Jake's hand arched through the air. He pulled it back, making a whipping motion. "Kane loves his shoge though. He's in his glory when he can really use it."

"Shoge?" She hadn't the slightest idea what he was talking about.

"It's a sort of chain, and on the ends are knives. It's incredibly effective in battle, and he also knows how to create weapons. He's... clever." He held a door open for her, and she passed under his arm into the dark and musty stairwell leading down into greater darkness. "Hold up, we need some light."

She waited as he lit the lantern, and they descended the steep stairs in front of them; she carefully put one foot in front of the other as they made their way down. At the bottom, he squeezed past her, leaving a wake of dust and crumbling stone. With the narrow space, it was difficult, he awkwardly pulled the latch at the top of the door, before bending to pull the latches that secured the door to the ground. Whatever was behind the door was kept under tighter security than most things in the church had been.

"Do I want to see what's in here?" she asked to his bent forward back. He grunted in response and stood, shouldering the door open. She followed, dodging falling debris as she stepped into the musty room.

"This is my favourite place in Santouri." He held the lamp up, and in front of them was a small wall of books, neatly stacked and carefully arranged. "It's our history, or what remains of it. We try not to read the books very often; once they are gone, there won't be anything left."

He ran his hand along the books, quiet until he found the one he wanted and passed it to her. "Here, you should read this one." She took the book, but her thoughts were preoccupied. She had thought that a library would make her feel more at home, but the remnants of what they had, so heavily guarded and touched so little, made her feel sad for what their world had come to. That an entire history had been repressed, and was hidden like a prisoner, felt wrong.

They made their way back to the courtyard, Anika nodding in agreement to the things Jake was saying but not really listening.

"You're quiet." He placed a hand on her back to guide her down a path between the gardens. "Are you upset?"

"No." She watched a middle-aged man pull carrots from the ground and wave at her. She half-heartedly waved back, her smile forced. "I'm just taking it all in."

He nodded and pointed to their left. "This is where we train. It isn't anything special, but it's enough."

In front of her, there were four squared-off areas that she guessed measured no more than 10x10. Three of them were currently in use. People sparred, some clumsily, some impressively, but she noted that they all seemed to be doing so happily. A man and a woman were taunting one another, their movements almost coordinated as her sword fell to meet his long knives in a clang of metal, her laughter following it.

"Ah, this must be the Naidisbo then." She followed the voice to see a tall man, skin smooth but weathered and tanned from time outside, who stopped beside her. A bow and arrows were slung across his back and he was covered in a full suit of daunting looking leather armour, yet he appeared to be relaxed. "Come, Jake, are you not going to introduce me?"

Jake chuckled under his breath as he held a hand out to introduce Anika. "Roth, this is Anika. Anika, this is Roth. Roth is — "

"That's quite alright, Jake. I am quite capable of introducing myself."

Jake laughed and shook his head, excusing himself to get them a drink, leaving Anika to shake the outstretched hand of Roth. His grip was firm but not painful. She couldn't help but think of her father as the man smiled, a twinkle in his eyes as he looked down at her.

"You should watch out for Jake. He is a humorous but high tempered young man," he said with a kind smile that reached his dark eyes. "I'm Roth. I protect Santouri. I never leave this place. I'm sure that Jake has filled you in of my duties by now, though."

"Err, well, no, not exactly. In fact, he hadn't mentioned you."

"Scoundrel!" He winked at her and turned, nodding to the small building to their right. "I'll assume he considers the children to be of enough importance to mention then. There has to be someone who is present to watch over them all, especially when the others are gone on..." He paused, glancing at her, "excursions."

He nodded his head toward the young man and woman sparring in the ring. "That would be Mae and Edric; they are core members here. Mae is a shapeshifter, although she hardly ever uses the power. She prefers to augment."

"Augment?"

Roth's eyebrows raised, but he did not scoff at her lack of knowledge. "She can increase or decrease the powers of others with ease. It makes her quarterstaff more deadly than her foes suspect."

He nodded toward the sparring pair in the ring; in perfect timing, Mae's quarterstaff collided with Edric's arm in a sickening snap, and he stumbled backward. Mae stepped forward, her height equally large, her long blonde hair pulled tightly into a braid swayed back and forth as she raised her quarterstaff above her, Edric's hand raised in defeat, Anika could hear the slight chuckle as she offered a hand to Edric, raising him to his feet.

"He is so... pale." The small amount of Edric's exposed skin seemed to glow in the sunlight. "Is he unwell?"

"Ah, quite the opposite, Naidisbo —"

"Anika, please."

"My apologies." The hint of a smile played on his lips. "Edric is from the far north. They have little light, and so the people are fair. Edric's family especially are known for their light skin, and their eyes are particularly mesmerizing. Not unlike how Reynard strengthens his soldiers, Edric has more physical strength than he should. Mae is teaching him control."

"So, he is new too?" She felt slightly uplifted at the idea of not being the only new person at Santouri, but Roth chuckled and shook his head.

"I am afraid not. Edric's ability to control his strength has been improving, but it is slow and has taken years to get this far. When he first arrived, we had to segregate him from the others. Northerners are a bloodthirsty lot, you see, and he joined us with one goal."

The sound of Mae's quarterstaff meeting Edric's skin resonated with a dull thud before them. "And what is his one goal?"

"To be considered a true soldier of the north, you must kill a priest with your bare hands. When Edric completes his goal, he will return home to his brothers to protect the lands."

"There is a lot of information to take in." She lay her hands against the fence in front of them, watching Mae and Edric spar with only their hands now.

"Jake will be a good resource; he will not deceive you. Should you find yourself in need of assistance, you may find me and ask." He bowed deeply at the waist and left her, walking toward the schoolhouse, where children were beginning to pour outside, laughing and playing with one another as they ran to keep up with Roth, two pulling on his sleeves as they walked. He playfully picked up one of the shrieking children as she watched, slightly perplexed by the formal, yet kind man.

Val jumped into the other ring, tossing her blade aside. As their eyes met,

53

she nodded and turned to her opponent, who closed the gate behind him. He was tall, his hair a dirty blonde, and in desperate need of a haircut. He carried a hammer casually at his side. In his other hand, he held a bag, which he dropped, the contents spilling to the ground; various sizes of rocks scattered around him.

They faced each other, Val holding a wooden sword while she stood, her stance wide and crouched. As the man lifted his empty hand to his side, a rock rose to hover by his side.

Jake rejoined her, handing her a glass of water. "Val is an impressive fighter." A primal yell escaped her as she lunged forward, her body moving back and forth as the man's rocks flew in her direction. She leaped into the air, dodging the rocks with ease. Her sword before her landed with a crack against his shoulder, and he fell to one knee with an audible inhale of pain. "She trains with all of us. The one she's fighting with is Brennan, by the way."

"How does she do that? It's impossible to escape all of those," she asked as Val gave a hand to Brennan so they could start again.

"Val has foresight. It's an old power, and it drains the user of their energy quickly, but it allows her to see what will happen in the immediate future. It makes her a skilled fighter." This time Val rolled to the side, lithely jumping against the wall to propel toward Brennan from the side.

"Oh!" Anika exclaimed as Brennan successfully dodged the assault, and Jake laughed.

"She's letting him dodge." Anika watched as Val's sword landed against the back of Brennan's knees in a teasing smack as she ducked a rock that flew in her direction. Brennan spun, exposing his back to Val, and threw a cascade of rocks at her over his shoulder. Val, with no hesitation, bent backward at the waist, and the rocks hit the wall behind her, clattering to the ground. Jake gestured for Anika to follow as they moved toward the schoolhouse and back into the main building.

"You can have this room…" He pushed the door open in the wing they had walked by earlier. "It's empty and clean. I'll drop your things outside your door. You'll want to get some rest before dinner."

She nodded and stepped into the room. It was small and not much different than her room had been in the church. "When is dinner?" she asked, turning to face him.

"Six sharp." He paused in her doorway. "You'll want to be on time. We will have a debriefing tonight. I expect that you'll be involved."

The door shut, loudly, and she sat on the small twin bed. The rectangular window above it provided the only light the room had. Her mind buzzed, and suddenly, the weight of the day, of all those that she had met, and been introduced to, hit her like a dead weight. She lay her head against the pillow, barely registering the sound of her things scraping against the door as Jake set them down, and she was asleep.

6

Layers of Skin

"I should have known you'd miss dinner." Rae shook her shoulder and pulled her to a seat. "Here, you'll need to eat this quickly. You don't have much time until we have to meet for the debrief."

Anika shook her head, trying to clear the sleep and focus on the plate of food that Rae had placed in her hands. Rae sat lightly in the chair of her desk and began to twirl her hair around her finger, waiting patiently as Anika finally began to eat.

She was hungry, and yet she hardly tasted the food as she ate it. Her brain knew that it looked delicious — it had to be. Her plate was piled with potatoes, meat, and roasted vegetables. It made every meal she'd ever eaten at the church look like garbage.

She was grateful that Rae remained silent, observing her eat with a thin smile on her face. Her hands kept busy by playing in her hair, a habit which Anika would have assumed to be nervous if Rae hadn't been so composed while doing so.

Finally, when she finished, her mind more awake, her body less fatigued, and her appreciation for the food greater, she stood and followed Rae as they walked back toward the main hall.

"Where does the debrief happen?"

"The development room. Did Jake not show it to you earlier?" Rae asked as they stopped in front of the same door where she'd first met Val.

"No, we were here earlier. He just didn't tell me what it was." Rae nodded in response and pushed the door open. Inside, a small group of people sat chatting in a semi-circle. She recognized all but two. A woman directly across from her met her gaze with piercing blue eyes. Her skin was smooth, and Anika immediately felt drawn to her; the short pixie hair, dark as night sat against her fair skin in sharp contrast. Beside her sat a woman. Her very presence exuded kindness in a matronly way as she chatted with her neighbor amicably. Her hair, long and white, lay braided on one side.

It was then that Anika realized the room's natural conversation had ceased and that Rae had taken a seat next to Kane, away from her. Standing, somewhat uncomfortably now, feeling tiny beads of perspiration begin to form on her back, she waited, the air tense.

"Is no one going to offer this young lady a chair?" asked the woman with the white hair.

Val stood, stretching her back and twisting, a series of cracks followed as she groaned. Facing Anika, she nodded to her chair, and Anika sat quickly.

"Thank you, Helena." Val walked to the desk and board at the front of the group and perched against its edge. "Should you have not come to Anika's rescue, she may have died of fright." Val smiled, and a few around the room chuckled.

Helena winked at Anika from her seat as Val continued. "We might as well get started with the debrief then..."

"Hawk isn't here, Val." Jake raised his eyebrows in the way that Anika was becoming familiar with.

"Sulking, I would imagine. She is not pleased with the news of our newest addition," she remarked, nodding toward Anika. A casual flick of the hand and eye roll indicated they could move on as she stated, "Jake, provide an overview of what occurred during your station in the order."

As Jake ran through the series of events that had occurred during his time in the church, she watched the faces of each of the people around the group, studying them. At the beginning of the semi-circle, Rae and Kane sat together, their chairs closer than the rest, with one of Rae's legs draped casually over Kane's lap, her hand forever twirling in her hair while his hand

57

rested on her small leg with ease. Beside them sat Jake, bent over, speaking with little animation, quite like a soldier providing an update, she thought, his eyes intense, his voice steady and focused. Helena and the girl with black hair were next, listening intently. Between Anika and the girl with black hair sat Brennan, his eyes wandered often to the girl with black hair, who sat with her body turned slightly toward him, occasionally meeting his glances with a subtle smile.

On the other side of Anika sat Hcrib. He said little, and beside him Roth, who looked unnatural sitting at all. Anika thought he exuded an energy, a need to stand to attention when around his peers. Lastly, Mae and Edric sat. Mae's foot tapped while listening to Jake, while Edric leaned forward in attention, his eyes glinting at the talk of the priests.

"And that's when I found Anika in the hallway..." He looked at her and smiled. "I watched as she dropped a man with a mere touch. I abandoned all plans right then and there, and I took her and ran. Then we came back here. We were intercepted once on the way. I took an injury, Anika healed me, and we made our way back to Santouri."

"There were no survivors from your attack?" Val remained rigid in her questioning. Jake shook his head in response. "And you are certain that Santouri's position was not given away?" Again, he shook his head, which earned him a sharp exhale from Val and a nod of satisfaction.

"Well then, it seems we have a Naidisbo in our midst." Val looked up and held Anika's gaze, steadily, intensely. Anika questioned if she waited for her to say something, but there was nothing to respond to, so Anika remained quiet, the tension filling the air.

Val picked up a small knife on the table and pushed it into the skin on the top of her arm, blood swelling and dripping as she pulled the blade down, her face unmoving and focused, giving away no sign of pain. She set the knife down on the table and met Anika's gaze, eyebrows raised in invitation. "Show us you are what they say you are then," she whispered.

Anika's heart was sprinting now. All eyes in the group fluttered between Val, who remained standing, arm held out as blood dripped to the floor, and Anika, who suddenly felt that the chair was not under her but attached to her.

"Well?" Val asked.

Hcrib's hand found hers and squeezed, and she loosened the grip that she had on her knee. Feeling encouraged by his smile, she stood and walked to Val. Everything in the room came into clearer focus as she stepped: the grey rock floor beneath her shoes uneven, the light casting sunbeams through the room, leaving specks of dust floating. Yet, despite her heightened senses from the anticipation of this moment, nothing compared to the overwhelming noise that filled her mind; with each step forward, the pulse became stronger, louder. Her eyes grew heavy as she reached Val, her hands reaching out to close over the wound.

The blood was sticky, but she hardly noticed. Her hands guided her over the cut pushing away the wasted blood and finding the muscles. As she pulled each layer of skin together, bonding it, she felt Val's breathing shift. She became more tense, as though resisting the urge to pull away from Anika's touch.

Running her hands over the top layer of skin, she opened her eyes and watched the last of the cut close. The loudness of the pulsing decreased, and she backed away, her hands sticky and the scent of iron strong in her nose.

Val met her gaze for a moment, and Anika thought she saw a flicker of excitement. She unsteadily returned to her seat, Hcrib winking at her as she sat, holding her blood-covered hands in front of her carefully.

"Meeting dismissed." Val used the hem of her shirt to wipe at the remaining blood on her arm. "Tomorrow after breakfast, we will reconvene to discuss our plans going forward, training schedules, and Santouri's defence. Goodnight."

With that, she left the room, leaving the door open behind her. After a moment of heavy silence, the others followed, chatting easily to one another. Anika sat, her hands still held in front of her as they filed out. Hcrib paused beside her, about to say something but moved on as the girl she didn't know stepped in front of her.

"I'm Florence. Let's get you some hot water to take to your room so you can wash up. You look horrible."

Before waiting for a response, she was striding to the door, her tall willowy body moving with grace, and Anika followed, her own gait feeling sloppy and weighted. Florence stopped briefly at the kitchen to ask for the hot water to be brought to them.

Anika had just been wondering how Florence would know which room was hers when Florence stopped at her door and opened it, stepping inside without hesitation. She sat on the chair and waited until Anika sat on the bed.

"You are tired," she stated bluntly, her brows slightly furrowed while watching Anika.

"I am."

She nodded, thoughtful and silent. It was several moments before she spoke. "You are also sad. What would make you happier now?"

A knock came to the partially open door, and a young lady with messy blonde hair dropped a bowl of steaming water on the table. She looked to Florence. "You're welcome, Flo."

Anika's unease was being quickly replaced with confusion. Florence stood and they traded places, and Florence again asked her what would make her happy. Anika placed her hands in the bowl; the hot water was warm enough to sting but not so much that she couldn't tolerate it.

"If I could fit my entire body into this pot of water, I'd feel happier," she said, laughing as she looked over her shoulder at Florence. Florence only nodded, her face stern as she closed her eyes.

Anika gasped as the heat moved from her hands. Travelling up her arms, it spread as though she were submerging herself in a bath. The heat consumed her, filling her with pleasure and distraction from her last few days of travel. Her joints loosened, replaced by the relaxing feeling of submersion.

And suddenly, it was gone.

Florence watched her as she opened her eyes, her face unchanged, and Anika sat back suddenly and heavily into the chair, trying to form her words to Florence, to ask, how and what she had just experienced.

Instead, Florence stood and said goodnight, leaving the room with Anika watching, her questions still unformed, her mind still overwhelmed, and her body exhausted.

And so, she slept, dreaming of hot baths and sticky blood.

* * *

The knocking on the door came loud and quick, the three raps jolting her from her sleep. Sunlight filtered through the small window as she sat up and groggily put a hand to her head, noting that she hadn't even managed to get under the blankets before she had fallen into the deep sleep she'd just been rudely awaked from.

Three more knocks came as she sleepily mumbled a greeting to whomever was at the door. Mae poked her head inside and shook her head. The long blonde braid that she had adorned the day before swayed as her brows furrowed. She stated, "Get up. It's time for breakfast."

The breakfast was more than she had expected: scrambled eggs, buttered homemade bread, sausages, and potatoes diced and spiced with an aroma she couldn't identify. Mae sat across from her, stabbing her food and eating quickly, eyes lowered, conversation lacking.

"So, I've been learning that everyone here is very individual in their skills. What should I know about you?" Anika asked, her voice as loud and direct as she could muster. Mae looked up from her meal, and Anika was sure she held back a glare before conceding to the discussion.

"I'm a shapeshifter and an augmenter. I'm sure you've already been told that." She stabbed a sausage and took a large bite before continuing, "but my real love is hand-to-hand combat. There is no greater feeling than watching as you cut back a foe with nothing but your skill."

"Don't scare her, Mae." Rae sat down beside Anika, and they were joined by Kane and Brennan. "She's not as nasty as she appears." She smirked at Mae, who scowled and pushed the rest of the sausage into her mouth, "but she is just as good at hand-to-hand combat as she'd have you believe. She will be a good one for you to train with."

Mae scoffed and continued to eat, clearly not thinking the conversation worthy of her ongoing devotion.

"So, are you ready for today?" Rae asked kindly. Anika smiled uneasily, unaware of what today exactly was. "Val will want to see if you have any amount of skill today. We've been taking bets on if she'll get in the ring with you or make someone else train with you. I hope you're feeling rested." Rae smiled; Anika swallowed nervously.

"Well, to be honest, I'm not."

Rae laughed, the light sound friendly and in no way condescending. "I'm sure you're exhausted, but that is perhaps the best time to show your skills. I've seen you, remember? You don't have much to be afraid of."

Anika smiled, thankful, albeit worried about what the remainder of the day would look like. Rae put her bread down and nodded to someone over Anika's shoulder. "Speak of the devil. Here she comes now."

"Finish your food and meet us to discuss our plans going forward. Following that, we will need to re-discuss the training regime to make room for you, Naidisbo..."

"Anika," she interrupted, turning to look at Val behind her. "My name is Anika."

A slight uplift of her mouth was the only indication she had heard Anika as she continued. "I'll see you all in ten minutes."

Mae left with her, and Anika turned back to see Rae smiling at her incredulously. "What?"

"Ballsy." Kale and Brennan both nodded in agreement. "But she didn't smack you, so I guess that's a good sign."

* * *

"Keep your shield up!" The wooden edge of Val's sword struck her left shoulder, rendering the arm numb and even heavier. "Up!" the wooden sword was pulled back again, and Anika used her right arm, sword in hand to push the left higher, blocking the movement and shifting to the right as fast as she could, letting the shield absorb the blow. She parried farther to the right and, lunging forward, brought her sword down to Val's thigh, only to have Val block it easily.

With seemingly no effort, Val was behind her, and Anika's knees were buckling under the sword for the third time as she landed against the dirt with an audible smack, her muscles groaning in response to the repeated abuse.

"I thought you said she had skill," Val called from behind her as Anika closed her eyes in frustration.

"Perhaps if you gave her a shot, she'd have a chance," Jake yelled from the ring.

"She won't have a chance against real swords, Jake, but sure, if you want to 'give her a chance,' get in here and teach her something useful."

Settling her increasing breath and biting back retorts, Anika stood, leaning heavily against the wooden sword as Jake entered the ring.

They settled into their stance, and with the first strike of his sword, they fell into an easy dance, each of them moving as though knowing what the other would do, meeting each other's jabs, moving backward and forward.

"Good." He pushed forward and moved his arms faster. Letting his power show, he suddenly overwhelmed her, his sword landing blows before she had time to recognize he had even launched them.

"Not fair!" she gasped, again on the ground. "You didn't say we were training with powers!"

He laughed and reached a hand out to help her up. She accepted, dusting her pants off again as she stood, "but what is the point of powers if you aren't trained to use them in battle?"

"You're sure she's a Naidisbo then? She's terribly whiny."

Anika looked to her left. Standing at the edge of the circle was a young woman, one she had not yet met. Her hair, a deep brown, and rather untamed, was loosely pulled back from her face as she leaned, almost in boredom, against the ring wall, her bow strapped to her back, her gaze intensely on Anika, with no sign of a smile. She radiated unease and frustration, a crease between her brows deepening as she held Anika's gaze, as though they remained locked in a war of quiet contemplation of one another.

Jake turned, leaning easily on his wooden sword. "Hawk, I see you've deemed us worthy of your presence again."

Hawk's face remained impassive as she gave him a curt nod in greeting. "Well, get back to it. She isn't going to train herself, is she?" Hawk turned and began to leave as Anika looked to Jake, mouth gaping in silent question.

"You'll get used to her, I promise. She's young, she's brilliant, and she's a pain in all of our asses, but she's a good person." He threw the sword up and caught it in his right hand. "She's also right; let's get back to it."

* * *

Each day encompassed training, training that left her muscles stiff, aching, and bruised come nightfall. Each evening before bed, she soaked in the warmth of the tub, being mindful there was only one for everyone, rubbing out her aches and pains, gently massaging the bruises ranging from fresh and black to old and yellow. Her training had progressed nicely over the weeks, and she was able to spend time with each person in the ring, learning how to combat hand to hand, as well as begin to understand and appreciate everyone's unique powers.

She gazed at the ceiling, the rock face dented with imperfections. A thin film of condensation from the steam of her bath coated the surface, threatening to drip back down into her tub at any moment. Despite the physical toll training had on her, she felt fulfilled in a way she hadn't experienced when working as a healer for the order. At times, her hands itched with the need to make a paste or feel someone's blood move through their body, but despite the odd scrape or cut, no one was seriously injured during her time there, something that would be wrong to feel disappointed about.

She gingerly stretched her legs forward, wincing as her calves screamed in protest. She had trained with almost everyone now. Brennan had taught her the art of being aware of her surroundings as he manipulated stones to fly in her direction from every angle as he attacked her front with his hammer. Edric taught her to be quick with his brute strength, which he had a hard time controlling once unleashed; she smiled as she remembered Jake's anger when Edric had snapped her sword in two during their first practice. Edric had merely apologized and stalked off, leaving Anika to think she had done something wrong, until Jake had explained that Edric was temperamental, at the best of times. She had even become quick at dodging Kane's shoge, and Mae had slowly begun to warm up to her, practising with her quarterstaff in the ring, and agreeing to show her what it felt like to have her powers augmented in the future. She had asked to experience it now, but Mae had merely smirked and said she didn't think she was ready to 'handle her.' Roth had been kind and patient in the ring, directing her with precision and accuracy to improve her fine movements during their hand-to-hand combat.

He had even convinced Val to fight in hand-to-hand combat with him as a demonstration; they had been equally matched, Val using her foresight to meet the guard's flurry of action in his weapons. Part of his training for Anika had been to have her witness Florence — Flo, as she had been corrected — fight against the others. He had pointed out each moment that Flo was in the ring with someone in hand-to-hand combat, they fumbled or left cursing. Flo had winked at her from the ring as both Jake and Val had faced off with her at the same time; however, she spent little to no energy disarming them both before turning and raising an eyebrow to Roth in invitation.

She had watched, perplexed, as Roth stood his ground with Flo. He remained steady, with no signs of mistake, frustration, or the quick ending to combat that the others had shown. Roth explained afterward that he was gifted in a not so obvious way. His skin, hard and resistant to the cut of a regular blade was a benefit, but his true gift, he said, was his mind, which could not be penetrated by anyone, even a gifted mind manipulator such as Flo. He had recommended that Anika spend some time with Flo to experience mind manipulation. She stretched her back in the tub, the satisfying series of cracks that radiated down her spine providing some relief to the sore muscles, and shook her head. She wasn't sure that she was ready to have Florence manipulate her like that, again.

The only person who had not trained with her, no, she corrected herself, *had refused* to train with her, was Hawk. She claimed that it was pointless. She was a sniper. She did not fight hand to hand unless it was necessary, but Anika felt there was more. The girl stayed a healthy distance away, answered her in conversation only when absolutely necessary, and, for the most part, looked like a teenager who had been grounded for her bad behaviour the night before.

* * *

"Please, let me get that for you." Anika bent to pick up the large basket overflowing with colourful vegetables. Helena nodded gratefully as she stood. Using her wooden staff for support, she patted Anika on the shoulder and began walking, slowly but without any falter in her step, toward the main building, to the kitchens.

"How are you adjusting to life here, Anika?"

"I'm adjusting," she said while walking toward the main rooms. The sky, blue above them, sun blazing, matched her mood as she glanced at Helena, whose white hair and smooth skin, tanned from her time at Santouri, had grown used to the outdoor elements.

Helena nodded and grabbed a carrot from the basket. She wiped the dirt on her gardening apron before taking a bite off the end and loudly chewed as they made their way in the stifling heat of midday.

"It can be difficult," she said, "especially when bringing such strong personalities together for a common cause. It will get easier, and you will feel less like an outsider soon, I hope."

"I hope so too," Anika said. "I'm just not sure how that will happen if there is no opportunity aside from training to gain their trust. I can only spar so often, and while I don't doubt the benefits, I think I could learn more here."

"There is always more to learn," Helena said. "For instance, you have not asked me about my powers." Anika looked at her, incredulously. "Yes," said Helena, "I can do more than garden, Anika."

"What are your abilities, then?" Anika asked, smiling at the elderly woman's wit.

"I am the only known Skao left. It is my job to ensure that the children here in Santouri learn as much as they can about the naturalists so that our future is preserved in the coming generations."

"So, you are a storyteller?" Anika clarified.

"Amongst other abilities, yes." Helena opened the door for Anika as they entered the main building. "But I am also a poisoner. Through my touch, I may manipulate objects or people leaving no trace of poison and no possible antidote. The only drawback is that once the individual has perished, their excrement is black. Should an observer recognize this, they will become privy to the fact that the individual had been poisoned, by Skao."

"That seems like an incredibly valuable tool to have on our side," Anika observed

"Incredibly powerful indeed," Helena responded. "Unfortunately, with incredible power, there are often repercussions beyond that of normal warfare. Val and I have agreed, that given my age and as the last of my kind, it is unnecessary for my skill to be used against the church. We have also agreed, though, that this power is a secret worth preserving to be used when the time is right."

Anika nodded.

"Wash them and chop them," Helena stated.

"I'm sorry?" Anika asked.

"The vegetables, dear." Helena threw her long white braid over her shoulder as she shuffled towards the door. "Supper will not make itself, and you're looking terribly sunburned. I think it's best if I finish the gardening."

"Wait!" Anika started forward as the elderly woman stood in the doorway. "How old are you, Helena? If you don't mind my asking."

"The Skao's hair turns white when they reach their full power and ability. Our skin doesn't age, and so it is hard to say how old we are through observation alone."

"So, how old are you then?"

"I'm a hundred and four next month, dear. Now get to work on the vegetables. Don't chop them so finely this time either. I like my stew chunkier than last time."

She winked and left.

Anika smiled as she began washing the vegetables. She took her time; it was just after noon, so supper wouldn't need to be ready for some time yet.

She had spent a great deal of time with the elderly woman while gardening and preparing meals over the last few weeks. She had slowly gained her trust, and Helena had spent much time educating her about the ways of the naturalists, remaining guarded of her own characteristics. Anika appreciated what it felt like to have a companion there, someone she could speak freely with.

Anika had been aware of the naturalists during her time at the church, that they had powers connected to the earth. But she had been unaware of the intricacies that this contained until Helena had taken the time to educate her. Within the naturalists, there were bloodlines or families, and while many held their own family names, the power wielders often adopted the name of their power's bloodline. She had taken the time to explain that Jake's family name had likely been something else, but as he now went by Jake Redla, she could determine that his power was pulled from the Haltz tree. In fact, she had learned that each bloodline was connected to a different tree, and while power wielders did not need to have the tree's wood on them to yield power, holding the wood that gave them power would enhance it greatly.

Helena seemed to use Jake as an example often. She had divulged that the Redla family were mostly located in the Rojos region, which is where the Haltz tree had grown most heavily, or it had done so, before the order had moved through the region, burning trees, and killing those who resisted them.

But the order had been unable to fully destroy all trees, and what magical wood was left was nourished by passersby and taken only as necessary. Anika hadn't yet spotted everyone's wooden accent, but she had noticed several. Jake's sword handles were a deep ebony wood that glistened, deep grooves worn into it from where his hands held firmly while he wielded them. Brennan's hammer handle looked black, but upon closer inspection was a grainy wood; Edric wore multiple rings of pale clean wood, Kane's dagger handles, Mae's quarterstaff, ribboned in decorative honey brown wood, and Rae wore a long necklace, a wooden teardrop pendant on the end, which she could be seen twiddling between her fingers when lost in thought or listening intently.

She hadn't figured out the rest of them yet; Flo, Hawk, Helena, Hcrib, Roth, and Val remained a mystery to her. She smiled to herself as she chopped the carrots in larger pieces, as per Helena's request. An unusual contentment running over her as she sang softly.

* * *

"Pop quiz, whoever answers the most questions gets an extra slice of pie tonight made by yours truly." Flo stood at the front of the classroom, arms crossed, looking down over the six children who sat on the floor. Two lay there looking disinterested. A younger girl sat cross-legged and entranced by the dark-haired woman's voice. The other children were listening in the half-listening way that children do.

Anika stood at the back of the classroom with Helena, observing the lesson briefly. It had been her suggestion, that should she wish to understand and know more about their people, she would pop into the classroom between training and helping out around the camp.

The children looked more attentive with the bribery of pie, one boldly requesting the type of pie, earning a glare of silence from Flo as she stated, "Where do the Ralpop people primarily come from?"

The cross-legged girl raised a hand eagerly. "Ferreya!"

The boy beside her grumbled his discontent as Flo nodded. "Urki power wielders, such as Hcrib, are excellent spies — why?"

The girl raised her hand again. "He has night vision!"

Flo nodded, looking to the other students. "Half point, Jane. He has more than night vision that makes him a good spy. What else? Paul?"

The boy who remained lying on the ground lazily looked at Flo and sighed, muttering, "He can manipulate sound. He makes it louder, or quieter, depending on what best helps him sneak."

The cross-legged girl flipped her braid over her shoulder. "That's not fair. He's half Hcrib himself!" she stated indignantly.

"Multiple point question." Flo held up two fingers. "The Elpam are known to be large people, but they are also known for two very important abilities.

Name them."

One of the girls, who appeared incredibly uninterested, ran a hand through her hair and rested her face on her hand, mumbling, "Mae doesn't mind her sweets, but I'm guessing you mean shapeshifting and augmenting."

Flo smirked at the girl's brazenness. "Careful, Lana. I'll let Mae know you said that if you don't start paying attention."

Helena leaned over and whispered, "Lana is Mae's little sister. She is quite discouraged that she is so much smaller than Mae, and her shapeshifting isn't skilled enough to change her size on a regular basis."

Flo had moved on to the next question, not having received a satisfactory response from the children. She nodded at one of the boys who hadn't yet answered, and he shrugged his shoulders in response. Finally, when Flo didn't give in or move on, he stated, "The haunt." Helena laughed and gestured to the door. Anika followed as they left the small classroom in companionable silence.

"Helena, can I ask you a question?"

"Mm, go on then."

"What is the haunt?"

"Ah, you mean the cwn annwn, Anika." She stopped and turned, gazing at the mountain range to their east. "The Skao reign from Vidal. I am thankful that Santouri is in my home region, but the mountains are where my people come from, where they thrive. The cwn annwn, or the haunt as most people call them, are the animals of my bloodline."

"Why have I never heard of them until now?" Anika gazed at the mountain range. Peaks and valleys sharply jutted into the horizon, meeting the sky in a violently, and yet majestic, picture.

"Like my people, there are few left. During the last uprising, when the rest of my bloodline perished, their haunts perished with them. A haunt is a pack of large dogs; they are white," she touched her own white braid lovingly, "with glowing red eyes. They are bound to no one but the Skao people. They do not make themselves present often, preferring to live in the mountains, away from people, but if called upon, or if a Skao person is in need, they are known to show up."

"What do they do?"

"They are magnificent in battle. Many of them perished with my people on the battlefield. They are said to be the keepers of hell; the church spent a great deal of time convincing common people that should they see a dog of the haunt, their souls would be taken there, but if they joined the church, that would not be so."

"And people believed that?"

"People will believe anything should they hear it long enough or see something that convinces them. When the haunt fought with us, and only responded to the commands of the Skao, it was enough that people began to believe the stories. It's why I don't call to them. They will come to me if I am truly in need, but until then, I prefer to know that my companions live in peace in the mountains, safe from those who believe in the tales of idiots."

"How many are left?" Anika looked at the elderly woman who remained gazing at the mountains, a sadness reflected in her eyes as she shook her head unhappily.

"I don't know."

7

Santouri

L ife at Santouri was serene and fulfilling. Spending time training, although physically exerting, was rewarding. Spending time with the children, Flo, and Helena left her feeling assured, something she had only experienced when healing people in the order. She had proven to be somewhat useful, although she didn't think Val would ever admit to it, during the various cuts and scrapes, and by helping in the gardens, classroom, and kitchen.

She had even started feeling as though she could call some of the others her friends. Her only true remaining barrier was Hawk, who disappeared for days at a time, scowled when she was spoken to, and made frequent gestures of frustration in response to Anika.

Last week, Anika and Jake had been sitting together, listening to the evening music in the main hall. They had been sipping a sweet wine that Rae had proudly served after announcing that she spent the last three months perfecting it, when she noticed that Hawk sat two tables away, slouched in her chair and glaring in her direction.

Anika had checked to see what she could possibly be doing wrong but could find nothing. She was seated beside Jake, Rae, and Kane across from them, drinking their wine and laughing as they strained to hear one another over the music.

She had tried to get back to the music and conversation. Ignoring Hawk seemed to be the best course of action until she looked up to the sound of approaching footsteps to find Hawk standing at the edge of their table.

"Well, can I sit?"

"You don't have to ask if you can sit, Hawk." Kane kicked an empty chair out from under the table, and she sat, her full mug of beer spilling slightly as she leaned forward, gazing intensely at Anika.

Rae shrugged her shoulder at the group and tried to move on with the conversation, but the mood was dampened by Hawk's intense behaviour. Finally, Jake sighed and snapped his fingers in front of Hawk's gaze. "What's going on with you, Hawk? Are you wasted, or is there some other reason that you're assaulting Anika with your eyes?"

"Have you ever killed anyone?" she asked Anika, ignoring Jake entirely.

"What? Why would you ask me that?"

"Well you're a Naidisbo. I would think that given your great and mystical power, you'd easily have killed at least a few people while you were working as a *healer* in the church." She took a deep drink from her mug and chuckled to herself. "I mean, you are supposedly on our side. If I'd been working for the enemy that long, I would have been trying to make a difference where I could."

"Hawk, what's your problem?" exclaimed Rae. "Why are you being like this? Val trusts her. Isn't that enough for you?"

Hawk turned and glared at Rae. "Does she trust her, though? She does nothing here but train and cook. It seems to me that she is just learning about us; she isn't actually helping us in any way."

"Hawk." A warning from Kane.

"Well?" Hawk turned back to Anika, ignoring Kane and Rae.

"I..." Anika looked for the words but knew in her gut that it didn't matter what she said. It wouldn't convince Hawk of her intentions. She shrugged and was about to leave when Jake spoke up.

"Back off, Hawk. Get off your high horse and grow up." Jake sat a hand on her knee and squeezed. He didn't come to her defence in training. He always pushed her harder, but he jumped in now, when she needed it most.

Hawk rolled her eyes and haughtily left the table, a slight sway in her

73

stomping.

"What was that about?" Rae lay her head on Kane's arm and chuckled. "She's even more temperamental when she drinks, not that I'm surprised."

"What do I have to do to convince her that I'm not a spy or an order sympathizer?" Anika asked. Jake squeezed her hand under the table, lingering for a moment as she met his gaze.

"Actually, I have an idea. I think we should talk to Val about what you can do to assist before the next meeting. If Hawk sees that you are actively helping, then she may be more inclined to like you," he suggested.

Kane and Rae both nodded as Hcrib joined their table. He ran a hand through his red hair, sipped his beer and interjected, "Sorry to interrupt, I have to report the orders movements at tomorrow's meeting. I think we need more information about their current movements. Let's volunteer Anika as part of the team."

"Am I ready, though? I don't want to be a liability out there." She lowered her gaze; she wasn't so proud that she couldn't admit that she wasn't a great fighter yet.

"You've improved so much, Anika." Rae reached across the table and grasped her hand in support. "If there's minimal chance of combat, you wouldn't be a liability, and even if there was a scuffle, you could hold your own."

Jake had remained silent; he met Kane's gaze across the table. Anika often wondered if the two best friends could communicate telepathically. Finally, he took a sip of the sweet wine and nodded. "I'll talk to Val tomorrow before the meeting. I'm going to bed. If we're suggesting this tomorrow, I'm going to need all the sleep I can get."

His hand slipped from Anika's, the loss of his warmth leaving her watching as he left the room.

* * *

The next morning, Val called a meeting with the main members before Anika had even finished eating breakfast. Sighing, she left the half-eaten plate of steaming sausages, eggs, and toast behind and followed the others to the development room. Val took her place behind the desk, leaning, as always, against the wall, one foot casually lifted and resting on the table, hands crossed, face neutral as the rest filed in. Edric and Brennan were still complaining about their interrupted breakfast when Val raised a hand, her motion making the room fall silent.

"I'll call this meeting to order. Hcrib, give us your update." She nodded to him and took a seat at her desk, legs casually outstretched and ankles crossed above it.

Hcrib nodded. Anika couldn't help but notice that he was more tanned from his week away, his hair a little less fiery than before. "The order's patrols have been on the move. I followed one of the patrols south. It was the usual series of events. Stop in at the villages, drink, flash their money at the people, get some new recruits for the order, and move on. Until we got to Stuart, just south of the Ferreya border, they still had some feasible farmland and trees to their west. One of the patrons of the pub mouthed off to a soldier, and a fight broke out. It was chaos... I left then and observed from a distance. They burned trees, and they burned homes."

"Fuckers!" Hawk shook her head in indignation and crossed her arms, glaring ahead at nothing.

"Language!" warned Helena.

"Anyway," Hcrib continued, "I followed them back into Ferreya. I figured that they would continue to stop at each village and recruit, but I was surprised to see that at Heathson, they didn't do any burning. Instead, they set up a medical tent."

"A medical tent?" Mae questioned.

"A medical tent," Hcrib confirmed. "Yeah, they have a Doctor on patrol, and two priests, a good target, to say the least. He provided medical service to the village while he screened the children for powers. The next village they burned again. This time, I don't know why, maybe resistance. I couldn't get close enough to hear the rationale."

Hcrib twisted uncomfortably in his chair and cracked his back before resuming. "So they continued going northwest, until we finally got to

Langford. I thought it was worth the risk being in the pub during their recruitment, so I sat, drank, and listened. It was the usual spiel: why the order is wonderful, how it will save you, blah blah, blah. I was just beginning to think it wasn't worth it when I overheard that they planned to go to Bancotta next!"

Anika looked around in confusion, wondering if anyone else was missing something. Luckily, Rae and several of the others looked confused as well. Finally, Rae shook her head stating, "But that isn't Reynard's territory. He is only Aita of the south. The north belongs to Edyta. Why is he moving into her district?"

"I don't know why, but I did manage to hear some rumours of unrest in the order. It sounds like there has been tension between Reynard and Edyta. Recently they had strong words about the 'management styles' of their districts. Apparently, Reynard confided in the Doctor that it would benefit the nation if Edyta were 'displaced.'"

"Displaced?" Val nodded, thinking.

"That was what the soldier said. I don't know what he's planning, but he is moving into her territory. I'm not done..." He put his hand up to stop them. "That night the Doctor was, well, wasted, and decided he didn't want to bother checking the children as he does in each village, instead...." Hcrib paused and looked at his hands, his focus shifting away from the room, "instead, he had the soldiers kill all the children, without checking them for natural power."

The anger in the room was palpable. Anika felt it rising around her, heart rates skyrocketed, temperatures rose in response, and suddenly, the room felt as though it might explode. She realized that she wasn't in focus, that she had become lost in the sensation of it all when Roth set a gentle hand on her wrist and squeezed, bringing her back to their space.

She nodded gratefully and looked around. As far as she was aware, no one had said anything yet, but Hawk was standing, vibrating as Flo went to her, guiding her back to her chair with a gentle but firm push as Jake looked to Val. "So, what are we going to do?"

She didn't answer him, instead looking to Hcrib. "Are you finished?"

"No, almost," he nodded sadly. "They are moving north to Bancotta. They plan to take the central passage rather than the west due to flooding in the mountain barrens. They are going to cut close to Santouri."

"Why the fuck is no one saying anything!?" shouted Hawk. Flo sat another hand on her shoulder. She remained seated, but her anger did not diminish.

"We need to discuss what to do." Val looked at her calmly. "Get it together, Hawk. We can't just rush in and kill them all. We'd compromise ourselves, and we wouldn't bring back those children. Then they may realize that Santouri is close. We have to think."

"There's nothing to think about," Edric interjected from where he stood, his albino skin nearly glowing in the light of the room, fists clenched and rage simmering from him. "This is an opportunity to make change. We make change by killing their priests, their Doctor, their soldiers."

"Edric, we can't just kill them. We have to figure out why they are moving north. We need to figure out if it's worth it," Kane stated, still sitting.

"They are killing innocent people!" Hawk yelled but remained seated. More quietly, she said, "I don't see what the big debate is. We can't let them kill more innocent children. Innocent people, Val!"

"I have to agree with Hawk." Jake nodded in her direction, both Hawk and Flo nodding in appreciation. "We can't let them kill more innocents." He looked to Val and scanned the room. "But we also need to know why Reynard is moving into Edyta's territory. This is an opportunity to gather intel."

Exasperated, Kane stood up and faced Val. "You can't possibly think attacking a patrol is a good idea. We'd compromise everything. Attacking a Doctor is basically saying we are ready to take the order to war, Val!"

Edric stood behind him. Anika could feel his heart pounding. "Idiot!" he spat. "Coward! You just want to stay here, comfortable, living your little life with Rae." He jerked his chin at her, still seated as the tension in the room rose.

"How dare you!" Kane turned and lunged forward. Edric did not hesitate as he jumped to meet him. As they were about to collide Rae held up her hands and pushed her palms forward. Suddenly, both men hit an invisible barrier, knocking their steps backward, their faces angrier as they both whipped their faces sideways to find Rae with a small smirk on her face.

"You're both acting like hot-tempered fools. You're jumping to conclusions. Sit your asses down and shut up, or I'll put you both in tornados so you can't hear anything until this meeting is over."

Edric sat, his face glowing red from anger and chest heaving, while Kane sat beside Rae, who patted his forearm in comradery and turned to Val.

"What a lovely spectacle. Don't worry, Edric. You'll get to kill your priest in time." Val uncrossed her legs and pulled herself into the desk. "Here is what I propose. We need to increase security measures for Santouri, but we also need to gather more information about Reynard and Edyta before we move forward with any large-scale pushbacks."

She held a hand up as Hawk stood from her chair, Flo quickly pulling her back down. "I'm not saying that we stand idly by, Hawk. Don't get all haughty right away. I think we send a patrol of our own; they can gather the intel and remain in Bancotta, maybe follow them to the other villages, and observe. If the Doctor orders them to kill the children, or anyone for that fact, we act. And we will act with a plan," she stressed. "Unfortunately, whoever is out there will have to make that plan depending on the village."

"We need to vote." Jake turned to Val as he crossed his arms.

"I don't think we should interfere," Helena finally spoke from her chair in the corner. Anika was shocked the woman didn't die right there after the glares that were thrown in her direction. "I'm not saying that we should stand idly by forever; but Santouri is at risk. We need to protect it, and we need to protect our children. Should Reynard and Edyta go to war, they may resolve half of our concerns as it is. Let them kill one another off; our job will be easier in the long run."

"She has a point." Roth winked at Helena.

"Okay," Val stood. "We vote. All those in favour of sending our own patrol, raise your hands."

Anika counted: Edric, Jake, Hcrib, Mae, Brennan, and Hawk all raised their hands immediately.

"And in favour of remaining uninvolved?" Helena, Roth, Flo, Rae, and Kane raised their hands.

"Anika?" Val was looking at her with impatience. "You didn't vote, vote."

"Oh," she faltered in her response, "I'm sorry..."

"Don't be sorry. Just vote." Val exuded annoyance.

Anika looked at Jake. His hands were clasped together, casually between his knees as his gaze met hers, and he nodded. She didn't know what his nod meant, but she knew her answer: "Intervene."

"Alright, that is seven to five for intervening. Let's make a plan." Val walked to the paper and turned to the group with expectation.

In the end, they managed to make a decent plan. Although they couldn't plan how to intervene should the Doctor order kills, they could figure out whom to increase camp security with, and who to send on the patrol. They decided to send Hcrib, as he already knew their location and history; Brennan, because he was good muscle; and Kane, because, well, more muscle. They had also agreed that the rest would begin doing more security shifts. Val had even made a point that Anika would begin security duty, to which Hawk had snorted, earning a glare from Jake and Helena immediately.

As they left the development room, Anika grabbed Jake's arm. "I have questions."

He looked over his shoulder but didn't stop. "Well, that's good. I can't talk now though; I have to take Thor for a hunt, or he'll kill me in my sleep tonight. I'll find you when I'm back."

* * *

She was starting to memorize the ceiling of her room; the imperfections in the rock stood out with a glaring intensity. She could almost imagine the ceiling was like a map — ridges and hollows were mountains and valleys, smooth areas were grasslands, the dampness near the window was swampland.

She was still thinking about the ceiling when the knock came at her door. Calling them in, she sat up, making room as Jake walked in. He must have just returned from Thor's hunt. Smears of dirt streaked his ebony skin. A small cut trickled blood on his cheek, and he looked dishevelled.

"Did Thor drag you into battle?" she asked, making room for him on her bed.

"He may as well have. The bastard dragged me halfway to Hagio chasing a deer." A thump and hiss on the other side of the door set her into laughter as he cursed under his breath. He sat and leaned against the wall rather than join her on the bed. Running a hand along his cropped hair, he casually wrapped his arms around his knees and turned to her saying, "So, you have questions about the meeting?"

"Wait." She sat forward, kneeling, and moving closer to him. He froze as her hand rose to his cheek, question in his eyes. She paused in response. "Your cheek is bleeding. I was going to heal it."

"Oh." The air was heavy as they both remained frozen. Finally, she moved, ignoring her own racing heart, and she laid a hand against his cheek. Her breathing felt off, and her power felt foreign as she felt his skin beneath her palm, warm and soft. She stroked her thumb up, noticing that he took a deep breath as she met the cut on his cheek. He smelled like the woods, like fresh earth.

"Do you not want me to fix it?"

His words were fractured. "No... no, I do. Keep going."

He straightened his legs in front of him, and she leaned over him. They were closer than they'd ever been before, and she felt very aware of his body below hers, of his dark eyes watching her with a quiet intensity.

She pushed her thumb to the wound and closed her eyes. The skin wasn't damaged terribly, and in moments, it was stitching back together: a thin red line was all that remained as she removed her hand and settled back to her wall, where it was safe.

Their gazes met, and for a moment, they just observed one another, both waiting for the other to speak first. Finally, he broke the silence. "So, your questions."

She exhaled, strangely aware of her body. "Right. Why is everyone so excited about the Doctor being on the patrol? The Doctor is just second in command to Reynard. In the church, he hardly has a function. But Hcrib said he was checking the children for power. How?"

"He has a very important function for the church. He carries a piece of wood for each power. They are concealed on him at all times so that soldiers don't sell them off to villagers, and so villagers can't use them to augment their powers. When the patrols stop in villages and cities, they round up all of the children who have turned eleven and the Doctor 'tests' them. He makes each child touch each piece of wood; he can tell if the child has power while this is happening."

"But how?"

"I don't know," he replied, shaking his head. "But I do know that each child that shows their powers is usually taken back to the church. We don't know what happens to them after that."

"But this time was different." She finished the sentence for them. "Why kill innocent children, even if they are not power wielders?"

"Did you ever see them come to the church with the children they rounded up?"

She glanced his way, wondering if he was gauging her knowledge or asking out of genuine curiosity. "There were rumours; they rumoured that in the basement of the church, they held books about naturalists, and one of the girls was adamant that she had heard people in there."

"They used to take them back to Hagio, but we don't know what happened to them after that."

"They can't possibly have kept them all hidden. What purpose would they have for that?"

He ran his hands up and down his arms and nodded mournfully. "I agree. They would have executed them all. But why take them to Hagio in the first place if they were going to kill them, and why start killing them in their villages now?"

"Are you asking me, or are you wondering out loud?" She gave him a half-grin and shrugged her shoulders. "I guess there is really only one way to find out. They need to see if they can collect more information when they follow them."

He nodded, although he seemed absent-minded, not really listening to what she was saying. "Do you have any other questions?"

"Someone needs to train me on how to do watch." A statement rather than a question, purposeful. She didn't want anything to go wrong and end up being blamed.

"Don't worry about it," he said. "We will have you paired up with someone in the beginning."

She chuckled to herself and looked up to find him gazing at her inquisitively. "Well, as long as it isn't Hawk, I think we should be okay. If you pair me up with Hawk, she may make me disappear... and make it look like an accident."

"She isn't as bad as she seems," he cut her off. "She has her reasons for being skeptical of newcomers."

"Oh?"

"I don't think it would be fair of me to tell you her story, but you have to know she isn't a bad person." He smirked at her incredulous glance. "No, really, she's hot-headed but well-intentioned. When you get to know her, you'll see what I mean."

"If."

"Sorry?"

"If, if I get to know her. It seems more and more unlikely."

"Well, maybe she should train you for watch." He chuckled at her widened eyes. "No, I'm serious. She's experienced, she's a sniper, she has refused to train with you, but she may be up for showing you the ropes of watch."

"I doubt she will want to train me if she refuses to spar with me, Jake."

He nodded. "You're right, she won't want to. But she also won't say no to Val."

"You're really going to force me to do this, aren't you?" He nodded, and she sighed deeply. "Why can't you just show me how to do watch?"

She shuffled her outstretched legs on the bed, crossing one bare leg over the other as his hand reached forward and clasped her bare ankle, his thumb running slowly over the bridge of her foot. Her breathing tightened, and she felt his heart rate accelerate in their touch. "I don't think it would be wise."

"Why?" She knew perfectly well why, but she pushed his boundaries; she wanted more than a physical tell of his feelings toward her.

"I don't think it would be wise for you and I to do watch. You're...

distracting."

"And why's that?" His hand stayed on her ankle, a thumb sliding over her smooth skin leaving goosebumps in its wake.

"I lose focus around you." He lifted his hand, her skin feeling cold and empty beneath it. Standing, he placed a hand on the doorknob and turned to her. "I think you know why, and I think we can both agree it isn't a good idea to lose focus. Goodnight, Anika."

"Goodnight, Jake." The door closed, and she grinned at the sound of Thor meowing at Jake in greeting, his footsteps fading as he made his way to his room.

* * *

Training with Hawk went poorly, to say it positively. In fact, she wasn't sure what she had even been trained to do. Hawk had spent the majority of their training walking, perching in places (whether or not these were the places she was supposed to sit and watch from, she couldn't be sure. It could have just been where Hawk preferred), and glaring in Anika's direction.

When she tried to ask questions, Hawk had somehow managed to glare at her more intensely than before and had shushed her. So, they had wandered the perimeter of Santouri in angry silence for two hours before finally giving report to Rae and Jake, detailing that they had seen nothing of interest. After that, they had reported the same thing to Roth, and without so much as a curt nod in her direction, Hawk had stalked back to the main building and left her, with much less tension, standing with Roth.

He chuckled and sheathed the blade he'd been sharpening. "I'm sure next time will go much better for you and Ms. Hsa."

But it hadn't. In fact, each time they had 'trained,' it had gone entirely the same way with Hawk remaining in sullen silence, blatantly ignoring Anika's questions or concerns. Fortunately, Anika did begin to piece together what was expected of them on watch. Hawk always maintained the same pattern. She remained at each watchpoint for fifteen minutes, scanning the horizon, before moving to the next one. If there was anything worthy of investigation, she took the time to do so. It only happened once, and it was only a deer rustling in the bushes, but she still reported it in great detail to the next watch as well as Roth.

After two gruelling weeks of doing a nightly watch shift with Hawk, she finally completed her first shift on her own after a terse nod from Val. Surprisingly, Hawk and Jake had agreed that she seemed ready for the task independently. Val had asked Hawk, not Jake, if she felt Anika could be trusted. Anika had thought that surely, she would receive a strong no in response, but Hawk had nodded her approval and left without a look in her direction.

She had smiled broadly at Jake as he left, throwing a congratulatory wink in her direction as he did. And, although it had felt like a win at the time, the feeling quickly evaporated when she completed her first shift, alone, and found herself missing Hawk, not for her less than stellar company but for the presence of another person during the silence of the night.

Two more weeks passed, with Anika completing nightly watches, helping in the kitchens, gardens, and continuing to train, but unfortunately not make any steady gains, on her hand-to-hand combat. Val hadn't forced her to show her powers again, and for that, she was grateful as she knew she needed to focus on her weaponry. She was still sub-par with a sword and dagger. Her initial pride in her abilities had been shattered after she realized they'd all been going easy on her during their training sessions.

It was during one of her training sessions with Mae, in which the tall woman was helping her up for what felt like the millionth time, that they had both turned in surprise at the sound of a happy scream from another ring. Rae jumped over the stone closure and bounded down the hill, her air carrying her farther than physically possible. Anika shielded her eyes and smiled at the sight of three people, two tall and large, one short and slight, making their way to the camp. She and Mae, with a look of mutual agreement, agreed to postpone their training and walked to the gate, waiting for Hcrib, Brennan, and Kane. She was pleased to see that they all appeared to be in good health, and she couldn't help but notice that Flo had left the schoolhouse, moving more quickly than her normal calm gait usually allowed to meet Brennan, his hand lingering on her back as he let her go.

Kane, still indisposed by Rae's embrace, yelled through her hair, the words garbled. Hcrib winked at Anika, followed by an obvious eye roll in the two couple's directions. He nodded to Mae and clarified, "We need to call a meeting right away. Where's Val?"

"She and Jake were meeting in the development room last I saw." Mae turned and began walking toward the main building. Hcrib grabbed Anika's forearm, squeezing and pulling her in the same direction.

"How was it?" she asked, noticing that he walked faster and with less careful stealth than normal.

"We gained valuable information, and I'm tired as all hell." He squeezed her hand as he held open the door for her. "I'm glad to be home."

* * *

"There's no need to have you all here." Val was looking at Anika but addressing the room. "Jake, Hcrib, Brennan, Kane and Rae, you stay. The rest of you can go."

"I thought we agreed to discuss things as a team when they returned." Helena stood in the corner, idly stroking her long white braid.

"We did, and we will. You don't need to be present for the debrief. I'll call a meeting when it makes sense for you all to be here."

Helena shrugged and left the room, followed quickly by Flo, Hawk, and Mae. Anika stood, unmoving and feeling confused.

"It doesn't make sense. Why wouldn't we all hear what they have to report on?" She looked at Val, her confusion quickly replaced by frustration.

"That's hardly a concern for you." Val dipped her head toward the door, and Anika left, her frustration growing.

Roth was ahead of her, heading outside so she ran to him. Slowing to a steady walk beside him, she commented on her annoyance of being excluded. She assumed that as protector of Santouri, he would share her feelings, but he remained silent as she proclaimed her anger, until finally, she said, "I don't understand. Why you aren't frustrated, Roth!"

His gait did not falter as he continued toward his post, near the gardens at the front gate. "There is always a reason for Val's decisions. She would not leave us blind to necessary information. You just need to trust, Anika."

"Well, it would make more sense to just include you now, and me, rather than repeating themselves later."

"Have you many friends, Anika?" He stopped then and turned to her, hands crossed casually in front of him.

"Well, I had friends in the church." She furrowed her brow; this was not where she had hoped this conversation would lead.

"If they were truly your friends, you would know that it does not matter if you are excluded from time to time. If you do not see them for months or years, your relationship remains the same, like a familiar place that you feel welcomed. You do not question its integrity. You trust that it is right."

She laughed, a thinly veiled attempt at covering her true feelings. "But surely, as the man who protects this very place, you must wonder why you, of all people, Roth, weren't invited!"

"Someday, you will understand the importance of trust, friendship, and patience, Anika." He swung a leg over the barrier of the ring and stretched his arms overhead, twisting his torso from side to side. Anika stood on the other side, watching him silently, his words reverberating in her head.

"Well, let's train then." He pulled a longsword from his belt and swung it in a low arc, gesturing to the ring. "Your frustration could be a useful tool to improve your skills."

"Or it could make me sloppy," she stated as she climbed over the stone wall, a cascade of rock and dirt falling as she slid over the edge.

"Patience does not come naturally, and this is one of the best ways to learn it."

Sighing, in defeat, and at the same time shivering with the excitement of the upcoming physical exertion, she grabbed a dull sword, making sure to point out that he was holding a weapon of much greater finesse.

"Irrelevant." He held the blade forward. It glinted in the bright sunlight, as she jeered. "I'm serious. A blade's edge is important when you strike to injure someone, but for combat, the weight, the fit, and the balance of the blade is much more important."

She held her blade up. "Maybe so, but you know that blade much more intimately than I know this one."

"Put that down." He playfully pushed her blade aside with his own, and she silently questioned him. "You are fine with a longsword. I've watched you train. Pick up those wooden daggers."

She did as instructed and paused watching him, waiting for him to drop his blade and pick up daggers as well. He leaped forward, his blade swinging for her from the left, and she ducked, the air shifting over her head as she cursed and spun, only to see him coming forward, his blade pointed straight toward her torso. She again spun to the side. This time, as he turned to face her, she held her daggers tightly in each fist, waiting for the next assault.

The blade whistled as he ran forward, pushing against the rocky wall as he somersaulted to the side, the blade coming low toward her shins as she dove, ungracefully, and fell in a heap. Her chest heaved as she looked up to see Roth standing again, casually leaning his weight against the blade.

"What the hell was that!?" She pushed herself off the ground, wiping rocks and dirt from her legs as she stood.

"I was helping you train," he said simply.

"I have daggers. You have a longsword! How is that helping me train. That's not fair!" She threw the daggers to the side, chest still heaving as she yelled at him. The anger, not just from their practice, but from everything else bubbling over as she released herself upon him.

"Do you think it will be fair in battle?" He twirled the blade's handle where he stood and chuckled. "You need to be able to respond to whatever the enemy throws at you, Anika. You have to trust that your training is sufficient for you to handle an enemy, no matter what weapon they possess."

She scoffed. "Again, with the trust."

"It's perhaps the most important thing."

She picked up the daggers and faced him. "Fine, let's try again, but can you at least give me a chance?"

He lifted the blade, chuckling again. "The enemy won't give you a chance, Anika. I wouldn't want to do such a disservice to you."

She groaned. "Bastard," she said and raised the wooden daggers again.

He smiled and lunged forward, his blade making a resounding clunk in the ground as she cheered in success as her dagger hit his abdomen, and the other found his shoulder. He turned, smiling, as she threw her arms up in success and laughed.

"Well, now that the two of you are done, I need you both in the development room so we can discuss our plans." Anika looked up to see Val and Jake leaning against the ring, casually watching, for how long she did not know. She shook away the creeping feelings of frustration and followed them back in silence.

8

Conditions

"Edric's gone to get Helena. In the meantime, the patrol is still heading to Bancotta, meaning they will pass by us quite closely."

"So, what do we plan to do about it?" Hawk was sulking against the back wall quietly, her bow slung across her back, the tail of an arrow sticking through the frizz of her hair.

Val raised an eyebrow, to which Anika smirked when Hawk seemed to huff even harder than before. Val paused as some of the others joined them. Mae stretched out her legs as she sat and nodded to the others. Edric came in, Helena holding on to his arm, although she didn't need the physical help, it was a sign of their enduring friendship. Helena acted as a mentor Anika suspected, or a surrogate mother or grandmother, while Edric was away from his large family.

"After careful deliberation, we have decided it is essential to use this opportunity to eliminate the Doctor travelling with the patrol. Although they will be travelling close to our base, the opportunity is unlikely to arise again," Val stated.

Jake nodded, continuing for Val. "We discussed how we could possibly eliminate the Doctor yet not make it known that we had purposefully done so."

Roth interjected with resounding support, his main goal to protect Santouri achieved. Jake continued, "To do this, we need to eliminate the Doctor so that it looks like an accident, and it doesn't become linked to us."

Val continued, "While we are talented, and our abilities are strong, they are also obvious. If, let's say, Mae drew the Doctor away from the patrol and took his head off with her quarterstaff, it would be obvious."

"I'd love to, though," interjected Mae, smiling and lazily crossing her arms.

"No doubt!" declared Edric, now sitting beside Mae.

"Of course, we would all love to take him out personally, but, as I said, it would be too obvious. We need someone who can cause-effect, without it being noticed." Val's eyes turned to Helena, who was sitting, a hand remaining on Edric's arm, as though she knew this was coming and was prepared for his upcoming response.

"Helena, you can poison, and no one would have any idea how, when, or where that poison came from." Jake remained passive as he watched her.

"Absolutely not!" Edric exclaimed. He made to jump from his chair, and Helena's hand tightened as she pulled him back to sitting.

"Of course," she looked to Edric, "it makes sense."

"I'll be damned if it makes sense!" Edric shrugged her hand off. "It doesn't make sense at all; we can't risk Helena going against the Doctor! She's the last Skao. She teaches the children. She keeps Santouri alive. Use Mae. Have her shapeshift!"

"I think it's up to Helena if she wants to do the mission." Flo cut Edric off; Anika suspected they knew this would spiral out of control.

"Flo is right, Edric. This is my decision." Helena stood, pushing her white hair from her eyes, taking her sunhat off as she moved toward the door. "I will do as you ask. I'd like to tend to the gardens now and be left alone."

She looked at Edric; he eventually nodded in understanding as she closed the door behind her. He waited a moment, most of the eyes in the room on him as he stood. "Don't take any unnecessary risks, and don't even think about trying to get me to stay behind."

Val nodded as he left the room. She turned to the others. "We have discussed who is going to escort Helena. We assumed Edric would demand to go. Kane, Jake, and Rae will accompany them. They will pack tonight and leave in the morning. Meeting dismissed."

Helena slipped back in as the others were leaving the room, pulling Anika to the side and waiting until it was only Jake and Val remaining with them. She smiled, and Anika thought she saw sadness in her eyes as she turned to them, a hand planted firmly against Anika's back as she said, "I've taken a moment to think of this request. I have one condition — Anika joins us."

"Absolutely not." Val shook her head immediately. "She isn't ready."

"She is. If this is truly something you want, then she comes along."

"Why?" Jake interjected.

"It's time." Helena shrugged her shoulders and let go of Anika as she made to leave again. "I'll be packing. Anika, you should go pack too, love."

Anika nodded deftly, processing the words.

Val, still scowling, snapped at her, "Well, go pack then. Jake, make sure you prep her. And Anika, don't be a fucking liability for me."

* * *

"Here, I brought you some supper so you can pack." Jake left the door open as he entered her room. Thor followed, settling in the doorframe, black tail swinging back and forth in the hallway, yellow eyes watching them casually.

"How long are we going?" She folded one of her few shirts and added it to the meagre pile of pants on her bed.

"A week likely." He sat down the plate, still steaming.

"Well, I guess I'm done packing then..." She sat on the edge of the bed as Jake perched against her small table, the light reflecting on his ebony skin.

"Do you feel ready?"

"I don't know. I wasn't expecting to go. I feel worried. Val will gut me if I mess anything up..." She leaned against the wall casually, stretching her legs forward on the bed. "Do you think I'm ready?"

He stood, the pause heavy and filling the room with uncomfortably weighted silence. "No. I think it's too soon."

Anika nodded, surprised at the level of overwhelming disappointment that she felt from his words. He moved to the door, calling Thor on his way, but the large cat merely let him pass, looking at him with those slanted yellow eyes that Anika thought could pierce her soul.

"Thor, let's go get ready." Jake whistled, but the large cat continued to look at him, tail lazily drifting back and forth as he remained curled up in the doorway. "Fine, stay then. There will be music in the kitchen when you're done packing."

Anika smiled back as the large cat looked at her. She could have sworn he rolled his eyes as he jumped onto her bed, taking up the majority of the space as he pushed her to the edge, his furry black head pushing under her arm.

She wrapped her arm around his neck, pushing her face into the coarse hair and breathed deeply, the cat purring as she scratched behind his ears. Her breathing felt a little softer, the idea of going on the mission, a little easier as his purrs reverberated through her.

"Why did it bother me so much to hear him say I'm not ready, Thor?" She pulled him closer, hand scratching under his chin. Thor closed his eyes in bliss, his purring getting louder. "Why do I even care what he thinks?"

Thor rolled onto his back, his head burrowing into her belly as his front paws pulled her head down into a hug. She laughed as he rolled back up and jumped off the bed. She stood gingerly and followed him to the kitchens.

Things were in full swing, music playing, children and adults dancing in the open space, tables pushed to the far sides of the walls. She caught Jake's eye, and he waved her over. Thor walked ahead, jumping up beside him on the bench. He gave the cat a scowl as he scratched behind his ears. Rae patted the seat beside her, and Anika sat, feeling hyperaware of Jake's presence on the other side of Thor.

"Are you all packed for tomorrow?" She poured Anika a glass from the pitcher on the table. Anika nodded as she sipped, surprised to find it a pleasantly cool cider. "Good, I think you're ready for your first mission."

Anika looked up in surprise, noticing the look that Jake shot toward Rae, which he clearly hadn't intended her to see. The crushing disappointment quickly clouded what she had felt from Rae as she nodded, solemn.

"No, I really do." Rae patted her hand and refilled her already half-empty glass again. "You've been training a lot, and Val didn't see you on our way to

Santouri. She will cool down once she realizes that you can handle yourself."

"Thanks, I really appreciate it." Anika took another swig from her glass. The drink was easy to go down.

"It's true." Rae shrugged and turned to Kane on her other side. "Let's dance!" She grabbed him by the hand and pulled him up. They were soon twirling to the sound of fiddles and guitars in the kitchen.

Anika drank them in, laughing to herself as a cluster of children ran past, one grabbing Thor's tail as he went. Thor lightly swatting him as the child let go, shrieking playfully. Hcrib joined them and sat beside Jake, the two of them chatting easily. The gnawing feeling of still being an outsider weighed heavily on her mind as she looked around the room, so full of energy. She refilled her glass from the pitcher and continued to drink. Anika was surprised to see Val walk in and find a seat with Mae and Edric, a smile on her face as she watched the dancing.

The tempo of the music shifted to a slow rhythm. Anika looked around for the source, her eyes finally falling on Flo who sang a soft and sweet tune to the room, the chatter around them dying down as her voice, deep and smooth, mystified them all.

"Have you heard this before?" he asked.

She looked over in surprise. Jake, now alone, idly scratched Thor behind the ears. The room, now dark with the setting sun, was lit only by the lamps scattered around the room and the blazing fire near the kitchen.

"No." She looked back at Flo, her hands moving quickly over the guitar, the firelight dancing against her flawless skin.

"It's the story of her people. It's rare for the Swey to have children, so when they do, they are fed the liquid of the Hagin seeds. It's why she looks so young. Flo is one of the only people I know that still knows the languages of Ferreya and the stories of her people."

Anika nodded, unsure what to say. She drank deeply again and then almost fell out of the seat as the air filled with sparkles. Golden animals moved around the room, floating majestically in front of her.

"Oh, my Alvar!" She let go of her glass, squeezing her eyes shut. She opened them again, but the animals and sparkles remained. One of the

93

kids laughed as she fell over, a deer prancing around her as she shrieked in happiness.

"Flo is a mind manipulator, remember?" Jake leaned into Thor, rubbing his face into the cat's neck as he watched the dancing animals.

"She's manipulating everyone here right now. How?" Anika reached forward, her hand passing through a golden rabbit as it bounced over their table.

"She's incredibly powerful. She just doesn't showcase it often."

"It's beautiful." She turned to him as the animals faded from view and Flo's voice drifted to nothing as she was replaced by a livelier tune.

"Come on." Jake stood up and Thor jumped down on the floor. He held out a hand to her and pulled her to her feet. "You should go to bed; it's going to be a long week."

The room swayed in front of her as she stood, her eyes feeling heavy in her head. She must have stepped forward involuntarily because Thor pushed against her legs, pushing her back, and Jake had grabbed her arm, steadying her where she stood. "How much of the cider did you drink?"

They walked toward her room, the music fading as they ambled, Jake's hand remained firmly on her arm. Each step felt heavy, her limbs weighted and dragging. "Okay, the fact that you didn't even answer tells me that you definitely drank too much. I can't believe Rae didn't warn you."

"Warn me of... huh?" She stopped as he pulled her arm back in front of her door, realizing she would have likely walked right past it.

"Alvar, you're wasted. That cider isn't just a normal cider. It's strong. You might as well have been drinking whiskey."

"Oh, Alvar..." She leaned her back against the door and turned the handle. He was still in front of her. His arms reached around her. His body heat surrounded her; he smelled like woods, strong and deep. She felt overcome by the sensation; the same electricity filled the space between them as before. She reached up, touching the faint remaining scratch on his face.

He flattened her hand against his cheek, his hand remaining over hers as he turned his face in, his lips surprisingly soft and gentle as they brushed against her palm.

He pulled her hand down, his eyes dark and brazenly watching her. She felt the room swaying slightly as she pulled him backward, stepping into her room but he stopped. A faint smile was on his face as he pulled her closer with a hand firmly planted behind her neck.

His forehead leaned against hers, his breath warm against her skin as he chuckled, "You are drunker than I even thought. Get some sleep, Anika. You're going to need it tomorrow."

He turned her around and gently pushed her into her room, pulling the door shut but not before she caught the look he gave her. Her lids heavy, her face flushed, she sat on the bed and kicked off her shoes.

"Ugh," she groaned and laid her head back, the ceiling spinning as she shut her eyes and welcomed sleep.

* * *

Their journey was long and uneventful. They shared sentry duties nightly, developing an easy pace and level of comfort with their reports to one another. They sat around the fires, flames always kept low, telling stories, and chit-chatting during the evenings. Rae and Kane added a level of comfort among the group, their easygoing banter with one another welcome, especially with the energy between Anika and Jake.

She wondered if the others could feel it; the heaviness in the air between them felt static and real to her. His eyes avoided hers often, and she looked his way frequently, fleeting looks, hoping to catch his gaze, darting away when she did. Each night, they unrolled their blankets, Jake always opposite hers, the fire strategically placed between them. Each night, she gazed into the flames, willing to be able to see through them, thinking back to the first night they had sat under the stars, cursing herself as she remembered her drunken body language the night before they left.

"Get up!" She woke, taking a moment to orientate herself to her surroundings, the hiss of water hitting the coals of the still-simmering campfire as Kane looked toward the mountains. Semi- crouched, he looked prepared to fight.

"Get up!" he repeated, and she finally moved. The others were already packing their bags. She was embarrassed to see that even Helena already had her bedroll tied to her pack. Edric took it from her and threw it over his shoulder before giving her a hand up. She fumbled with her own, hoping no one would notice the haphazard job she did as she shoved it into her bag and unsteadily jumped to her feet, following the others as Kane led the way deeper into the wood.

No one spoke, a known understanding that they were to remain silent until the sentry told them otherwise. They walked, carefully holding back branches for one another. Edric provided a hand to Helena whenever necessary, at one point picking her up and gently setting her on the other side of a felled tree.

A little out of breath from the incline, Anika was grateful to Kane when they stopped. They gathered together in a small circle, and at last, Rae broke their silence.

"What did you see?"

"They are close to us. We've made good time. They will pass by our site in just a few hours. I think they've changed their strategy since we last scouted them though. They shouldn't be this close to Bancotta yet. I think they've put a rush on things and are travelling at night."

"But why?" Rae stood across from him; arms crossed in front of her.

Jake answered before Kane had the opportunity. "I bet Reynard is behind it. He'll want the Doctor to get to Bancotta before Edyta hears he's crossed into the northlands."

"If that's the case, we're looking at the possibility of a civil war in the order. Edyta is a stronger woman than people give her credit for. She won't be pleased with Reynard," Helena said, a steadying arm held against Edric.

"I think we need to revisit our plan. If you're right, Helena, we have a golden opportunity to spur this on." Jake was looking at Helena, the seriousness lining his face illuminated in the moonlight.

"Oh?"

"If we can do this, without it being known that it was us, we could also make it seem like Edyta is taking retribution against Reynard for encroaching on her territory. If we could get them to pair against one another, they may do a lot of our dirty work for us."

"That's brilliant," Edric exclaimed. "But are we sure there is no opportunity to kill a priest?"

"Edric, we've been over this!" Rae declared.

"You'll get your kill man!" Kane cried at the same time.

"Fine," Edric pouted. "Wasted opportunity this is, though."

Anika remained silent despite her confusion. It wasn't the time or the place to dissect Edric's impatience. They agreed to remain where they were, sending scouts out two at a time to scope the patrol, with one person monitoring their own camp as they moved toward Bancotta. It would mean little sleep, especially with Helena being unable to do watch, but it would ensure their safety, and given the complexity of the plan, it was essential that they be both safe and Helena be rested.

That night, Jake kept watch of the camp, having volunteered almost immediately for the solo job. Anika and Edric lay in the shadows of the foliage above the patrol. Edric's energy was high; Anika could feel his heart rate, elevated, the entire time, and she had been forced to throw pointed glares in his direction on multiple occasions as he squirmed or made unnecessary noises.

They had watched for two hours, but nothing had developed. The patrol had a similar routine as their own group. Sentry changed every hour, but they had more members to spare to perform the duty. They travelled in a group of twelve. So far, no one had seen the Doctor take sentry duty, and he had the luxury of sleeping in a tent, rather than under the stars.

The rustle of leaves from behind them caused both their heart rates to increase even more, Anika was pleased to feel, as they turned to see Rae and Kane emerge from the trees, with a quick "No movement." From Edric, they switched spots and started the trek back to camp.

She waited what she felt was a safe distance, and even then, she spoke quietly. "Are you okay, Edric?"

He held a branch for her, and she nodded in appreciation as he looked at her, stumped apparently, by her question. "I'm fine. Why?"

"You seem on edge."

He scoffed, the moonlight catching his pale skin as they passed through an open area. "I miss my family. I've been waiting for an opportunity since I left them to prove myself, and now one is present, but I'm not allowed to take it... it makes me frustrated."

"Why do you have to prove yourself?"

"My family, the Repinujs, we like to fight. In fact, stories say that people used to avoid the northlands, specifically Greyfork, for fear of running in to 'the white men.' That was during the last rebellion. To reach manhood, you must prove yourself to be strong, to have mastered the art of fighting, but the only way to do that is to kill a priest or someone of high rank in the order. I'm the last one."

"The last one?" She was grateful his back was to her so he couldn't read her expression. She wasn't sure she could hide the repulsion on her face.

"I have seven older brothers. I'm the only one left here. The others have all become men and returned home, but I am still a boy, and I will continue to be until there is an opportunity."

They stopped, Edric gazing at the sky for a moment. The night was clear, stars and the half-moon shining light on their surroundings. "It's dark for twenty-three hours of the day in Greyfork. It's why we are all so pale and why I have to stay covered from the sun. Coming south is difficult. It's painful not to just be away from our family, but the heat, the physical discomfort, and the emotional toll of being the last one here are extremely difficult. I will soon be a failure."

"But your brothers can't have all killed priests, Edric. I worked at the church. Surely, it would have been talked about if priests were being killed that often."

"Do you really think Reynard would go around broadcasting that his priests were dying?" Edric scoffed before continuing. "He wouldn't. I'm sure he pretended that priests died of 'old age' or 'illnesses' when they were killed in the communities. But they weren't — it was us."

* * *

"Alright, let's review before we move in." They sat in a small circle. In the valley to their west lay the small town of Bancotta. They had scoped it out earlier, Rae giving her a detailed overview of the buildings from a distance. They hadn't been exaggerating when they said it was small. A tavern, a store, and a blacksmith were the only businesses in the town. The rest of the buildings belonging to residents. Rae said most of them were farmers who travelled east to the area, which still had feasible land.

Jake continued, "The patrol has stopped here for two nights, less than their usual three, given the small size of the community. Tonight will be reserved for rest after their journey. We can assume they will spend the night at the tavern, ideally drinking, followed by a late start tomorrow morning. The Doctor will not see tomorrow morning."

Edric scowled, but he didn't say anything as Jake continued. "Edric and Helena, you will enter the valley and the tavern. You are mother and son, travelling south from Morales to Hagio. You need treatment from the healers."

"When you enter the tavern, you'll sit nearest the entrance and order supper, acting as natural as possible. Rae will follow within twenty minutes. My hope is that they are sitting at the bar and drinking. If that's the case, she will join them. If they are at a table, she will interrupt them. Rae, you'll need to serve as a significant distraction. Talk to them about the land, farming, flirt, whatever it takes to keep them looking at you. During that time, Helena will excuse herself to go to the washroom. As she walks by you, she will touch his cup, poisoning it without him being aware that anything has occurred."

"During this time, Kane, Anika, and I will be close enough to respond if necessary. If all goes according to plan, you two will get a lovely supper, Rae will get some decent ale, and we'll be heading home the day after tomorrow." Jake smiled at them all, but Anika detected some nervousness.

They broke apart, Edric and Helena heading downhill to the tavern. The four of them sat there in silence, watching the pair, so different and yet so alike, walk toward the tavern. Finally, Kane turned to Rae, gathering her hands into his own and kissed the tops of her knuckles. He lifted one tattooed hand to her cheek and smiled tenderly at her. Rae returned the look, head pushed into his palm.

Anika felt a pang of jealousy toward them: their comfort, their love for one another evident in the smallest of touches. A few whispered words into her ear, and Rae started down the hill as well, her step light, although not as carefree as usual.

The three remained in silence for a while longer before finally, Kane nodded to Jake stating, "I'll watch from the northeast."

Jake nodded. "We'll go southeast then."

"You know, I could be of more use than being your shadow." She followed him as they moved farther south, staying just inside the trees.

"No need." He didn't so much as look her way as he continued to make his own path. Trying to dampen her simmering frustration, she followed until they finally stopped, the tavern not far from them.

They could hear the rumbling of people in a busy place; things sounded as though they were going well. The crash came from nowhere, the sound of splintering glass and wood, followed by a deep yell.

"What..." exclaimed Anika, but then she was cut off by the screaming.

9

Helena

"Mom!" The little girl threw herself on to her mother, her long brown braid hitting her mother's face as they toppled to the ground. The girl sat up, straddling her mother's torso as she playfully planted a loud kiss on her cheek, saying, "Hi."

Her mom, tall and slender, with hair white as snow, squeezed the little girl tight and rocked forward to flip them over, pinning her to the ground as she planted an equally loud kiss on the girl's cheek and whispered, "Hello, my love."

They untangled, the mom pulling the girl to her feet and walking into the kitchen hand in hand. The little girl pulled away to push the step stool to the counter, where she climbed up and joined her mom, chopping vegetables for their supper.

"What are we having?" she asked, eyeing a carrot hungrily.

Her mother, all-knowing, handed the carrot to her, and she happily crunched into the sweetness of it, the taste of earth still clinging. "Soup," she answered as she pulled a pot out off the shelf to the side of them.

"Again?" the girl whined, rolling her eyes at her mother's back.

"Yes, don't roll your eyes. It's rude." Her mom turned back around and smiled at her. "Go find your dad outside, and tell him I need the chicken."

She didn't dare roll her eyes again. Her mother, even though she insisted she didn't, had some sort of sixth sense that let her know every toe that the girl put out of line. Instead, she jumped off the top step of the stool, earning a soft tut of disapproval from her mom, and ran to the front door of the cabin.

The cabin was small. Wooden walls surrounded just three small rooms. One room was her parents', one room was their bathroom, and one room served as their kitchen, dining, living, and the girl's space all as one. The little girl didn't love having to sleep in the living room, but she didn't complain about it because she liked falling asleep with her friend and cuddling in front of the wood fire.

She pushed open the front door, yelling for her father as she stepped out into the pattering rain. The air had a chill to it, and she shivered as she dodged the dripping raindrops off the roof and looked for her father. She skipped one foot in front of the other as she made her way to the small barn by the cabin, knowing her father would be in there tending to the livestock. Sure enough, she opened the door, the smell of manure familiar and comforting as she walked into the barn.

And was nearly bowled over by the large white wolf. "Elora!" her father shouted, and the wolf bounced on to all fours, its tongue leaving a trail of wet slobber on the girl's face as she struggled to her feet.

"Did she have the babies?" she inquired, looking around eagerly for signs of the pups that her father had promised would soon be born. He nodded happily and took her hand, leading her to the bale of hay against the back wall. There, nestled among the hay, lay four newborn pups. The girl reached out, but her father pushed her hand back gently, holding it firmly in his own.

She looked up at him. His hair was white as her mother's, but his eyes were a stunning green. He smiled kindly as he explained, "You must wait, my love. They are so new that it would be a disservice to them to disrupt the first hours of their life. Elora needs time to bathe them and give them milk. When they've grown stronger, you can play with them. Like everything in life, we must be patient, and give them the conditions necessary for them to flourish."

She looked back down at the pups, holding back every urge to pick them up, but she did as she was told. "Can we name them?"

Her father looked at Elora, who had curled around the pups, her white tail wagging happily as the pups latched on to a drink, and he nodded. "One of these pups will be yours, if Elora allows it."

"Really!"

"Shh," he reminded her, gently squeezing her hand. "It's too soon to decide, but when they are older, one will speak to you more than the others, and you'll know you're meant to be together."

She nodded, mesmerized by the wiggling pups in front of her. She knew that someday she would be able to speak with them, but imagining them, each so small and helpless, being her companion was difficult. Her eyes were drawn to the all-white one, so much like her mother, Elora, but she kept her thoughts to herself, aware of her father sitting beside her.

"Ahem!" her mother said from behind them, and the girl spun, suddenly remembering her task. "Is anyone going to bring me chicken, or are you planning on having supper today?"

They had supper as a family every night, and despite her excitement over the puppies, tonight was no different. She held out her bowl, and her mother ladled soup into it. A simple nod of the head was all that the girl needed to put both feet on the floor.

"My love, your father and I have been meaning to talk to you about something." Her mother ran her hands over the girl's hair, and she squirmed away, soup dripping as she brought it to her mouth. "There is a war coming."

"War?" Her spoon remained frozen in her hands. Something about the word — even though she didn't know it — made her feel apprehensive.

"You know that your father and I, and someday you," she added as an afterthought, "are gifted with a deadly power, and with the gift of companionship with the haunt. But we haven't told you everything there is to know about being a Skao. Now, we think it's time you know about it all."

The girl nodded; the soup was forgotten as her mother launched into the tale of their people.

* * *

"Come!" She followed the shout with a shrill whistle as she walked back to the cabin. Her wolf, no longer a cub and now fully grown, bounded through the woods, her energy as high as it had been when she'd first chosen the girl as her partner. The girl scratched the wolf's ears as they walked along the riverbank, earning an affectionate lick along her arm. It was early in the morning as they made their way back. The dew was still heavy on the ground, the air thick with the lifting condensation of nighttime.

She had been gone for almost a week, which was perhaps the longest that she'd been away from her parents, but they'd insisted that she spend time with her friend in the village, to get to know more people. It wasn't that she was a loner, she had a friend after all, but she was just as content to spend time with her wolf, her best friend, Phoebe. Phoebe ran ahead, chasing a swooping swallow as they got closer to home, and the girl picked up her pace, excited to get back to the comforts of her cabin.

It wasn't even that she didn't like other people. She just felt that their company was *inferior* to the company of Phoebe and her parents. No one really understood her on the same level that they did. Others may have understood her words or actions, or feigned interest for the sake of being polite, but there was no superficiality with her family. Every word they spoke was genuine; every time Phoebe nuzzled her hands on to her head, it was sincere.

So, this morning when she had woken up, the makeshift bed on the floor of her friend's room horribly uncomfortable beneath her, she had gotten up, and without so much as a goodbye, had walked out of her friend's home and begun the journey back to hers. It was an hour by foot, and the time passed quickly once Phoebe joined her. The girl was thankful for each time she could use Phoebe's strong back to lift another foot over another fallen branch.

The sun was rising in the sky, and the dew was nearly gone by the time she got back to the clearing where her cabin was. She pulled her hair out of the ponytail. A deep chestnut brown, it swung nearly to her waist, but most often stayed up, out of her way. She pulled her fingers through it, longing for a warm bath with some of her mom's homemade bath salts when she noticed Phoebe.

The wolf stood in front of her, pushing her back toward the way they came, her white fur bristling around her neck as a low growl filled the silence of the clearing. Warning signals started to fill the girl's mind as she looked for anything amiss.

Everything *looked* okay. Chickens clucked in the yard, and the food and water troughs were full enough, but as she tried to take a step forward, Phoebe again pushed her back. She knelt, placing a hand on Phoebe's back as she drew her hand over the quivering muscles.

"What is it?" she whispered, and she closed her eyes, listening. The information flooded through her hand, and she stood. "They're here then."

She swallowed and looked down at Phoebe, who returned the look with great concern. The girl spoke as much to herself as to Phoebe. "We'll check the cabin first."

But they didn't have to. The door swung open, and a man stepped into the yard. Oblivious to her or Phoebe's presence, he stood with his hands on his hips, thrusting them forward as he stretched them in a long lazy circle, the smoke from his pipe matching, lazily curling upwards. The girl stayed utterly still as she took in the red uniform and the sheer confidence that the man exhibited. Sensing her hesitation, Phoebe didn't move either. He still stood, not noticing them as he puffed happily on the pipe; whatever had occurred inside her cabin had evidently ended.

She didn't know how he couldn't hear her heart hammering in her chest as she looked for any movement, any flicker of her parents, as she prayed that they'd been out hunting together when the man arrived.

Finally, the man opened his eyes, and at the moment Phoebe bristled, lips curling back in a snarl as his gaze fell on them, and he smiled, all teeth and no heart behind it. He didn't jump or seem surprised as he said, "Helena, I presume?"

Put off by the man's strange reaction, she nodded slowly as Phoebe pushed against her legs, urging her back toward the forest. Her hand floated to the back of her waistband, where her small knife lay in hiding, always on her, as her parents instructed. The man set his pipe down calmly, taking a moment to knock the glowing ashes on to the ground.

Helena grimaced at the sight of the burning ashes on the grass. Thankful it wasn't a dry year, she shook her head, willing herself to focus as the man turned toward her again. Phoebe's pressure against her legs was not forgotten as she fought every urge to run.

But she knew that running would accomplish nothing. He'd chase her down and catch her, for whatever purpose. Then she'd be subject to whatever he intended and likely at a worse calibre than if she stayed and tried to talk her way, or fight her way — she thought with a hand on her knife — through it.

When she remained silent in answer to his question, he nodded, as though taking it as a yes, and drew the sword from his belt. Her heart started racing as she saw the redness stuck to it. Her eyes darting wildly to the door of the cabin, but still, there was no movement. The soldier held the sword in hand and casually tapped it against his leg. "Helena, I don't want to make this painful for you; it can end quickly if you submit."

Phoebe growled deeper and bared her teeth as he took a step forward. The man chuckled, looking at the wolf and swinging his blade in a long arc, as though he were showing off. "Your wolf won't save you from this, Helena. I'll even let her live if you surrender without a fight."

She paused looking at Phoebe, but she wasn't experienced with soldiers, she hadn't ever spoken to one, let alone fought a man that wasn't her father or someone to train with in the village. The soldier took the opportunity to run forward, blade raised to his shoulder, and he leaped toward her.

Phoebe jumped to meet him, paws landing against the man's stomach as her teeth found his ribcage. The soldier released an animal-like howl as he pulled away from her and spun back. Blade still in his hand, he used his arm to staunch the wound at his side as he spun to face Phoebe, who moved him away from Helena.

"Stupid fucking wolves!" he screamed as he lunged forward again, the sword missing as Phoebe dodged to the side, her teeth snapping at the man's leg as he jumped away. He finally had his back to Helena as she gripped the knife. Hands trembling and filled with adrenaline, she stepped forward, the knife raised overhead. She plunged it down into the space of his shoulder. The man tried to scream, but only a gasp came out as she pushed her weight into his back, pushing him to his knees.

She pulled the knife free. Breath racing, she stepped back as the man clutched his chest. Her father had told her that a well-aimed stab to the lungs would kill the strongest man, even an enhanced soldier of the order, but he'd never said it would be slow. He'd also never said the man would get back up, but the soldier got one foot firmly planted on the ground and started to rise, leaning heavily on the sword as he turned to face her.

His face was grimaced in pain, and blood dribbled from the corner of his mouth as he lifted the sword. From behind him, Phoebe jumped again, this time paws landing squarely on his back to push him forward, but the soldier spun as he went to the ground, blade connecting with Phoebe's side.

"No!" Helena rushed forward, the soldier nearly forgotten as Phoebe's fur began to bleed red, but she staggered to her feet and pushed in front of Helena, pouncing on the soldier before he could struggle back to his feet, her teeth sinking into his throat and tearing.

The blood spilled faster then, wolf and man mixing together as Helena scrambled forward, pulling Phoebe from the man's chest and cradling her in her arms. Weeping, she scratched behind her ears, hand cradling her face as the wolf nuzzled into her embrace and closed her eyes, her body going lax as her spirit left her.

Helena didn't know when the soldier died; she didn't know how long she sat there, weeping, swearing, willing Phoebe back to life. As her sobs subsided, she pulled her close again, kissing her snout as she stood, straining to lift Phoebe with her. She wouldn't leave her with the soldier. Dead or not, she would honour her wolf.

The cabin. She hiccupped, realizing that it had been still, that no one had come, soldier or family, when she cried, that no wolf had aided them. She knew, as she stood facing the cabin, with her best friend dead in her arms, what would lay beyond that door, but she had to see it to believe it. She sat Phoebe down at the threshold and stepped inside, her heart plummeting further still.

Elora's body was in the living room. The soldier must have killed her first, her white fur, so like Phoebe's was coated in blood. She stepped over her childhood wolf's body, tears blurring her vision. She wiped them away and

107

stepped into her parents' room. They had been well-trained fighters, they would have woken to Elora's cries of death, but they hadn't had time. Her mother, still naked, lay in the bed, an arm reaching for the floor where her father lay, his own knife not far from his hand.

She fell to her knees. Filled with grief, she slammed her hands down on to the wooden floor and screamed; she continued screaming until her voice was gone, replaced with tiny sobs. When she finally opened her eyes, the floor, the walls, everything but her parents and her wolves' bodies were covered in a thick black poison that leaked from her hands. She stood, grief making way for anger as she stepped into the poison; she willed it to take her, but it moved away from her, making space for her steps as she moved to her parents' bodies, readying herself to bury them.

She caught sight of herself in the mirror and paused. Her hair was stark white. She'd reached her full power.

10

Unanswerable

"Stay here!" Jake ran toward the tavern as the banging and yelling continued. She sat on her heels, eyes straining, willing herself to be able to suddenly see through walls, but instead, she was forced to listen and watch as Jake stopped by the front door, trying to look in inconspicuously.

A moment later, Kane reached him, leaning against the other side of the door, shoge in hand already. She blinked twice, forgetting his ability as he grew another foot and a half before her eyes. She couldn't hear them, but she could see them nodding to one another before Jake drew his weapon and they ran into the tavern.

The noise continued, escalating further when Jake and Kane entered the building. She stood, pacing back and forth on her feet as she watched, waiting for someone, anyone, to leave the building. But the door remained empty, and the yelling continued. She tried to rationalize. There was no more banging, just raised voices now. She stepped forward toward the tavern, stopping, knowing that she should likely listen to Jake, and yet remembering the last time when she had merely sat by, a quiet spectator to their efforts.

"I am not useless," she mumbled to herself. She went to sit back down, but the sound of another crash and more shouting caused her to step another foot forward. Throwing all caution and sensibility to the wind, she found herself running.

She hesitated, but only briefly, when she made it to the doorway. Taking a steadying breath and pulling out her short sword, she stepped into the tavern. In front of her, a fight had escalated, Edric and Helena were backed into a corner. Edric, covered in blood, held a hand in front of Helena, whom she noticed had blood streaked through her now very unravelled braid. The woman strained against Edric's arm as he met the blade of another soldier pushing in their direction.

Jake, Kane, and Rae were all engaged in combat, all taking on multiple soldiers at once. Anika looked around, finally noticing that the Doctor, distinguished by his robes of royal purple, remained seated, watching the fight unfolding around him, seemingly unfazed.

As though he felt her gaze, his eyes met hers, a widening look of realization dawning on him as he stood and took a step toward her. For a moment she saw only surprise in his eyes, but it was quickly replaced with something else, some thirst to take her captive written on his face. She stepped back, her mistake, her foolishness becoming immediately obvious to her; although she had been just a healer, he would have known her face from the church, and he had recognized her.

The clash of metal against metal continued as the Doctor took another step forward, his recognition forming on his lips as she was pulled in the direction of Jake's voice. "Anika, for Alvar's sake, run!"

His blade entered the stomach of a soldier with a solid thump as it pierced cloth and flesh. She turned to do as told but not before taking one last look at the scene in front of her. Rae turned from the soldier she had just felled, fear lining her face as she threw her hands forward, wind bursting from her toward the soldier whose blade found its way past Edric's arms at the same moment and into Helena's chest. In that moment, silence fell. Helena's eyes widened and was broken a breath later as a shattered scream erupted from Edric; the wind from Rae had knocked him and the soldier, whose hands still held the knife in Helena's chest, to the side.

She turned as Edric's hands found the soldier's throat, the sickening snap of bone following her as she fled.

She hit the treeline in seconds, with the others not far behind her. She didn't dare look back, terrified of what she may see. Terrified of the possibility of Helena's body, terrified of the despair on the faces of her friends. She wouldn't even allow herself to tap into her power, knowing that the confirmation that there was one less life in their group would bring her to her knees. They stopped running only when Edric finally begged them to. Anika finally allowed herself to fall to her knees and buried her face in her hands. Edric stopped beside her, and she looked away as he lay Helena down on the ground. His sobs filled the clearing. Rae walked to him, kneeling and wrapping her arms around his neck as he leaned into her and continued to cry, leaving blood everywhere he touched.

Anika struggled to control her breathing as she crawled forward and placed a hand on Helena's ankle. Even though she already knew her friend was gone, she shut her eyes and listened, but there was nothing; no sign of life remained. The woman, once so full of wisdom and kindness, was no longer with them. Anika, holding back sobs, shut Helena's eyelids and straightened the long white braid over her shoulder, hiccupping as she moved back from the body.

They gathered around her body, no one speaking, each lost in their own world of thought. Finally, Jake placed a hand on Edric's shoulder and squeezed. "Come, we should bury her."

Another sob broke from him as Kane and Jake began to dig into the soft earth of the clearing. Edric watched for a moment, eyes darting to Helena's body, but finally, he gently pushed Rae away and rose to help dig the grave, arms shaking the entire time.

Her burial was hurried and less than what Helena deserved. They stood, each reflecting on their own memories with the elderly woman in silence. Jake held her staff in his hands, eyes heavy and red-rimmed. He lay it down across the grave and stepped back, head bowed. Immediately the earth began to shift, the soil sinking and from it a small green bud emerging. Anika watched as it emerged, her despair burying the surprise of the preternatural Skao sapling that was now in front of her. Jake turned and faced the others. "We should continue on before nightfall."

No one responded, an unwanted agreement rang between them. As they left the clearing, they each looked once more to the small Skao sapling, Edric leaving last. As they walked, with the sun setting on the horizon, dusk settling around their shoulders, a distant howling could be heard throughout the mountains, and Anika smiled. The haunt had come.

* * *

The journey back was tense. Rae and Kane had gone back to keep an eye on the remaining soldiers and Doctor, with a plan to push ahead harder and catch up with them closer to Santouri. They needed information on what happened next. Edric, in his grieving, was unable to perform sentry duty, and so the task had fallen to Anika and Jake to share.

But each hand off was strained, with a different energy than before. Finally, three nights after their failed mission, she had just finished letting him know there was no sign of problems when she turned to him and exclaimed, "I'm sorry, okay!"

He turned, slowly, hesitantly. "Why?"

"For whatever reason you're treating me like this! Like I'm useless to you!" She pulled her arms in tightly to her sides, shivering despite the warmth of the night.

"Fuck... Anika... You're a fucking liability!" he exploded, stepping toward her and then backing away as she stepped back. "You don't even realize it, do you?"

She remained silent; he wasn't looking for an answer.

"If you had just stayed where I told you to stay, then the Doctor wouldn't have seen you. Now they know you're with us! If you hadn't followed, Alvar. I hate to say it, Anika, but if you'd just listened, then Helena would still be alive!"

"Do not blame me for Helena's death!" She stepped forward this time, her arms raising in anger. She could feel the threat of tears burning in her eyes as Jake shook his head, resentment lined his eyes.

"No, I don't blame you. I blame myself. I knew you weren't ready, and I conceded to Helena's wishes. Alvar knows why she wanted you to come along so badly anyway; it ended up costing her life."

"Alvar, you're an asshole." Anika turned and made her way to the fire, throwing herself down on to her bedroll and turning away from him. Edric didn't so much as acknowledge them, even though he lay there staring into the fire, lost in his own thoughts.

During their argument, they hadn't been watching for visitors, and so when Kane and Rae walked into the clearing, she and Jake both shouted in surprise. Rae, significantly shorter than Kane, whom Anika assumed was still taller than his natural self, raised her brows in bewilderment and finally said, "Sounds like you two have been getting along well since we left you."

"We're fine." Jake leaned against a tree casually, his darkness bleeding into the night around him. "What's your report?"

"So hasty, my man." Kane walked past him, giving a light and encouraging slap to his shoulder. "They changed their plans after our meeting. There were only four soldiers left and the Doctor. They were heading south, toward Hagio when we left them."

"They didn't bother to check the children or finish their business in Bancotta." Rae joined Edric on his bedroll and ran a hand over the broad shoulders. He released a shuddering breath at her touch.

"Why didn't they try to follow us any longer?" Anika asked. Her voice sounded flat. Any gumption she'd once had deadened from Helena's death, and Jake's explosion.

"Let's just count our blessings, shall we?" Jake barked at her, earning a glare from both Rae and Kane. "Pack up. We need to get back to Santouri."

* * *

"I think Jake punished Anika enough on the journey back, Val." Rae sat forward, elbows resting on her knees, Kane's hand casually rubbing her back as they debriefed.

"I don't give two flying fucks what you think here, Rae. Helena is dead. One of our people, our family, is fucking dead. DEAD!" Val screamed in response.

"I know." Rae held Val's gaze steadily. "I was there when she died."

When they'd gotten back Val had called an emergency meeting. The tension in the room was heavy. Anika looked around, trying to gauge the reactions of the others. Mae wore her emotions on her face, lined with anger. Flo and Roth sat in solemn thought; she couldn't read what they were thinking. Hawk had thrown her bow down in anger and stormed out immediately upon having the news delivered. Hcrib followed her, his shoulders slumped in sadness. Brennan had gone to Edric and enveloped him in his embrace. He remained beside him, a comforting arm around his shoulders.

But the energy in the room, the anger, was directed at Anika. Listening to Jake relay the events had made it evident that he felt the outcome would have gone differently had she listened to him. She willed herself to disappear into her chair and closed her eyes as Val smashed her fist against the desk she stood behind.

"There's more. Rae and I did manage to collect some information about the patrol's plans before we joined back up with the others," Kane reported.

"What do you mean?" Jake responded. "You told me there was nothing more to report."

"It wasn't the time to bring it up," Rae muttered.

"That wasn't your decision to make!" Jake fumed.

"Well, it's done now. The Doctor recognized Anika when he saw her. For a healer, you certainly made yourself known at the church. He told his second in command that they needed to return to Hagio immediately to report to Reynard that the Naidisbo had been spotted. They know she is with the rebels, and they want you." Kane said the last piece to her, sadly, his gaze holding hers.

"They knew I was Naidisbo the night I left the church though. This can't be new information to them. They would have suspected I was with rebels when Jake disappeared," she defended. "It can't possibly be new information."

"Well, apparently it is. Maybe they didn't link Jake to us, but now they have," Rae piped in.

Val's head hung low, chin resting on her chest, eyes closed as she struggled with the information. "So, you mean to tell me that not only did your actions result in the death of Helena, the last of her kind, our friend, our glue... but now, because you couldn't listen for one goddamn minute, you've risked the rest of us too."

"Val," Jake started but was cut off.

"No, I can't look at her right now." She pointed to the door. "Please go. We'll figure this out later."

Tears burning in her eyes, she fled. She stopped briefly at the door and looked back, hopeful that just one person would reach out to her, to show some kindness. Their eyes avoided hers though, no one so much as glanced her way, and so she went to her room, wiping away the tears that threatened to consume her.

Sitting in her bed, she looked up as Thor pushed open her door and jumped in the bed, the deep rumbling of his purrs comforting. He nuzzled his head under her chin, and she let the tears fall into the coarse dark fur.

She was crying for so many reasons. She was overwhelmed with it all. Her life had been uprooted in a single evening. She had been confident that she was ready for the mission, Helena had even said so, and yet she had failed and caused her death. The people that she had come to call friends were understandably angry and now at risk from her actions.

She didn't know how long she lay there; time passed with irrelevance as she wallowed in her thoughts.

"I should just go, Thor." The words muffled against the cat's fur.

"No, you shouldn't."

Anika started. Val stood in the doorway, leaning in a false attempt at seeming casual. She pushed her long dark hair behind her shoulder and twisted the bracelet on her arm, gazing at it sadly. "Helena gave me this before she left."

"Why?"

"Damned if I know. She had a reason for everything. She would have had a reason for demanding that you go along too." Val entered the room and sat at Anika's desk, putting her feet up on Thor, who groaned in response. He swatted at her in annoyance and with a huff of impatience when she didn't remove her feet, leapt from the bed and left them alone.

"She couldn't have had a very good one." Anika looked away as she whispered the words.

"Well, we can't know what it is now. Helena was like a mom to a lot of us. You aren't solely to blame. Jake made me see that." She continued to twist the bracelet on her arm. "Don't tell him that, though. I hate being wrong."

Anika scoffed.

"We are going to need to figure something out, though. I don't know what the solution is yet, but we will figure something out." She pushed her chair back and stood, getting ready to leave as suddenly as she had arrived.

"Wait, I don't understand!" Anika stammered, "You have foresight. Why wouldn't you use it? Couldn't it at least provide us, me, with some direction?"

"You're a weapon of war now, Anika. You are the only known Naidisbo. Your powers, if harnessed, could lead to the complete control of anyone the order desires." Val sighed. "I've already used my foresight, and I hate relying on it. What I saw, the potentials, they're scary, Anika."

"Well, what is it?" She pushed herself up on the bed, wiping her tears away. She wouldn't have admitted it, but for a minute, she felt excited, hopeful.

"I can see two possible scenarios. The first, you stay with us, you help us work toward peace and freedom for the naturalists. The second, it's much more detailed, which scares me."

"Why?"

"Detailed often means it's more likely, at least that's what's been proven in the past." She sat back down and nodded, to herself, rather than Anika, an unconscious decision to divulge what she had seen. "In an effort to gain control of you, the order finds Santouri. I don't know when, but they do. When they attack, we are overthrown. Reynard himself is there, and you join him, voluntarily."

"No!" Anika exclaimed, "I would never!"

"But you do. Reynard makes it very clear that your father will be the one to be punished if you don't, and so you go."

"I wouldn't," Anika starts.

"I can't see any further than that," Val cuts her off. "It is a possibility; my gift isn't wrong."

"Well, this time it is," cried Anika.

"There are always two scenarios, sometimes more. I can't predict which one happens. But Anika, I've also learned that my foresight changes. Tomorrow, I could see something entirely different, based on you, based on the events that transpire or based on the order. There is a constant evolution."

"I wouldn't join Reynard. I'd die first." Her fist clenched the sheets below her.

"That's easier said than done, and I don't know if you're strong enough to actually die for us, Anika."

Anika closed her eyes and tried to bring her attention to focus. Her head was spinning with information, information that she was incredibly afraid of. She took a deep breath and opened her eyes. Val was gone, and her room was empty once more.

She lay her face on her pillow and screamed in frustration.

She sat for what felt like an eternity after Val had left, thinking about what she had said. The ceiling, which she had so clearly memorized, seemed to taunt her, as she made out the faces of people in the stone.

"You okay?" Jake pushed the door open with his foot. She turned her head and looked at him, a tug in her low belly as she took him in. His expression was guarded as he stepped into the light, his eyes dark, concealing his thoughts from her.

"No," she answered. She turned and looked back at the ceiling.

"Anything I can do?"

She smirked. "Anything you want to do? You made it pretty clear how angry you are with me; I doubt you want to help me right now."

"I am angry my friend is dead." He sighed and sat on the end of her bed; she pulled her knees up to her chest in reflex. "I'm sorry I took it out on you, though."

"Thanks." She smiled, with little sincerity behind it, "but you don't have to apologize. You're right. I wasn't ready."

"No, you weren't ready." He casually placed a hand on the back of her calf, patting hesitantly, her leg tingling as he pulled his hand away. "I should have pushed harder for you to stay back."

"Did Val tell you?"

"About her vision?"

"Yeah."

"Yeah."

They continued; the conversation weighted but easy for the first time since Bancotta. Jake sighed, continuing, "What do you think?"

"I don't think I'd ever join the order. That's not me."

"Do you want to know what I think?"

She nodded in answer.

"I think you don't know who you are, any more than we know who you are right now. You've been part of the order. Even if you were just a healer, there is a part of you that still identifies with them. Your father is one of them, and I don't know that if they used him, that you would stay with us."

She nodded, unsure what to say. "To be honest, you haven't proved that your allegiance is to us. And if I'm being strictly objective, you could have sabotaged our mission on purpose."

She didn't answer, the tone of the room shifting with Jake's accusation.

"I'm not saying that's what you did, Anika, but if I were an outsider, looking at the situation, I'd think it was possible."

"But you aren't an outsider, Jake." She sat up and rubbed her stinging eyes. "What do you think for real, by knowing me?"

"I think you wouldn't leave us unless you had to, but I think it's possible."

"I guess you don't know me very well then." She got up and strode out the door, unsure where she was heading.

* * *

The next few days she spent time with the children. The loss of Helena had affected them all greatly. They looked to the mountains often, as though they thought she was there, or as though looking to the woman's homeland gave them at least some form of comfort after her loss. One of the children, the small girl with blonde braids, like Helena, Anika thought, had asked her what had happened.

118

For a moment, it had stumped her, and she had sat, wondering what the right thing to say was. Finally, she had said, as truthfully as possible, "The bad men killed her." The girl had nodded, a quick understanding and acceptance of Anika's words, and she had said nothing more on the topic.

Spending time with the children did little to ease her guilt and grief. And it didn't help that things were uncomfortable with some of the others. Hawk seemed ready to explode in anger anytime Anika walked into the room. Mae, Brennan, and Edric seemed distant, hesitant to resume their previously comfortable relationship. She and Jake spent their time making superficial pleasantries, attempting to avoid the uncomfortable tension between them; what had been physically charged before now lay in emotional tension between them.

Flo really was the only one whom she found to be helpful. Days later, after supper, and after everyone but her had left, she had sat at the long bench and gazed into the kitchens where Rae and Kane were cleaning up. Once Helena would have been there with them, throwing orders out in her matronly way. Now her absence was more heavily noted to Anika in there than anywhere else.

"You look like you could use a drink," Flo said, sitting across from her. Her blue eyes always set Anika back in surprise, their intensity unsettling, as though her very soul was available for Flo to dig through.

"Do I?" She spun the empty glass in her hands, wishing it were full again.

"Perhaps you need to talk instead."

"No, thanks."

"*Talk to me, Anika. Your silence protects no one, including yourself.*" Flo's lips hadn't moved, and Anika realized with a start that she had inserted the sentence into her mind.

"Please don't do that to me." She held a hand up as though she could block the manipulation.

Flo smiled and nodded. "Well then, I guess you'll have to talk to me, won't you?"

Anika sighed as the smooth-skinned hand of Flo reached across the table and ran a thumb across the back of her hand patiently.

"What do you want to talk about? I know how you felt about the mission in the first place. You voted against it. And then it happened anyway, and she died."

"Yes, but that doesn't mean that I'm angry you went." She pulled her hand away and sat perfectly straight, listening intently to Anika.

"I don't understand why she insisted I go. I wasn't ready, and she insisted I go anyway, and then I ended up being the reason she was killed." She looked away, unable to meet Flo's gaze.

"There is never only one reason that someone is killed. Everything that happens in life is a series of events. Everything happens for a reason."

Anika scoffed. "Please don't feed me bullshit like that. I hardly believe everything happens for a reason, Flo."

"No?" She paused and looked toward the kitchens. "Do you think that it is just chance that we have all come together? That Rae and Kane love each other and found each other in Santouri? Do you really think it's chance that Jake found you in that hallway at the church, at the very moment you revealed your powers?"

"I don't think you want me to answer." Anika met her gaze only briefly before looking away. "I think it was chance."

This time Flo scoffed. "We can agree to disagree, but Helena liked you. She thought you were the answer. She had a reason for making you go on that mission; do you have any idea why?"

"No."

"Do you want to see something, Anika?" Flo smiled warmly.

"What?"

"I think you need to see what you looked like when you first came here, all those months ago, and what you look like now."

"I fail to see how that will help me."

"Trust me." Flo held out a hand, and cautiously Anika took it, closing her eyes. Suddenly, she was watching Jake lead her into the gates of Santouri. She looked to her left. Helena had stood beside whom she presumed was Flo as they had arrived. Anika was surprised by her appearance. She had known she looked nervous, even apprehensive as she walked through the gates, but she was shocked to see the colour of her skin. She looked unwell; dark circles lay under reddened and sick looking eyes, her hair hung flat against her shoulders, desperate for a wash, and she looked thin.

"You looked awful." Anika opened her eyes and laughed at Flo, who sat with raised brows. "I'm sorry if that's harsh, but you looked downright awful!"

"Is there a point to this conversation?" She laughed.

"Yes, close your eyes."

Anika watched as she entered the garden. The sun was high in the sky, and beamed down on Helena, who was pulling carrots from the earth. She threw a welcoming wave in Anika's direction, and Anika heard a muffled hello ring through the vision. Anika watched the duplicate of herself as she made her way toward Helena. She looked much more vibrant. Her hair was fuller. It held shine to it, and her skin had lost its pale sickliness that it once held. Her eyes were once again bright, and most importantly, she looked healthy.

"Quite a difference, huh?" Flo removed her hand and stood up at the table.

"Why show me that?" Anika stood up with her, and they made their way to the hall.

"To show you that this place is worth it, and that Helena knew how it had changed you, for the better."

"Goodnight, Flo." She stopped at her door and nodded to the mysterious woman, as intimidating and yet friendly as ever.

* * *

Despite the loss, a new normalcy settled over Santouri with time. The children and her friends returned to their duties. The gardens continued to grow, and people began to heal, as did their relationships. Anika thought that Helena would have liked the way things had settled following her death. Her presence, while still very much felt, did not mean sadness, and instead, she was remembered with joy.

Except for Edric. Edric had spent the last few weeks in solitude, exiting his room only for the most necessary of needs, at times, not even that.

They had taken turns going to him, trying to convince him to eat more than one meal a day, but he had remained steadfast in his grief. Jake had assured her that despite this, he would have little physical repercussions. His power was brute physical strength, and she had been astonished to see that despite weeks of little food, and broken sleep, he remained as muscular and large as ever.

What had changed had been his heart. He had once been passionate, engaged, energetic, but since Helena's death, he had become withdrawn, morose, and lacked the drive that had once made him a valuable member of the team. They had even stopped going to see him individually, instead going to see him in pairs, teaming up to motivate or guilt him into leaving his room, but nothing had worked.

* * *

She leaned against the rock wall, breathing heavily as Roth chuckled. Although she had improved immensely since arriving at Santouri, she still found herself easily fatigued when sparring with him. Once she would have been horrified for him to see her so spent but she had grown closer to him, finding his physique and attitude to be less intimidating than when she had first arrived.

"Any idea what to do about Edric?" she asked between panting breaths.

He spun his sword around and smiled grimly. "I believe it is best to let the man process in his own time. Everyone responds differently to death. It isn't our place to push him."

Anika nodded and picked up the two short swords. Squaring off with Roth again, she saw Jake and Val approach from a distance as she met Roth's sword with a grunt of fatigue, before spinning out of his way as he lunged forward.

They parried back and forth for a few moments, Jake and Val now watching from the perimeter of the ring. Finally, uncomfortable with the audience, Roth and Anika nodded to one another and sat down their weapons, turning their attention to Val and Jake.

"Don't stop on account of us." Val nodded at their discarded weaponry.

"It's fine. We were done anyway."

"Well, in that case, I'm calling another meeting. We've had news."

* * *

"Okay, well, I suspect that Edric won't be joining us, so let's get on with it. First off, welcome back Hcrib and Mae. They have brought exciting and confusing news." Val looked over them all, her gaze lingering on Anika. "The news that the Naidisbo is with the rebels has shaken things up, but unfortunately, it seems to have also halted our hopes of a civil war, at least for now. It does mean, though, that Reynard is eager to find our dear Anika, and he has left the confines of his church."

"He's travelling?" exclaimed Kane, leaning forward expectantly.

"Yup, according to our friends here, Reynard has joined the Doctor and is travelling south, stopping in villages in their search for Anika, and also recruiting new members to the order, convincing them with their new rumoured powers."

"What, enhanced soldiers, Reynard's fire and Edyta's water aren't enough?" Brennan laughed dryly.

"It sounds as though they are convincing locals that their powers have gotten bigger, grander somehow." Val paused. "We don't have all of the details yet, but it's working. People are joining them. What's more, despite Reynard sending his men into Bancotta, Edyta has sent patrols to the northern villages, recruiting and spreading the word of their powers as well."

Jake stepped to the large map on the wall in front of them. "Val and I have been discussing what the best approach is. Reynard and the Doctor are travelling in a small group, which leaves them a vulnerable target that's difficult to pass up."

Rae cut in, "Which is likely exactly why they are doing this, to draw us in and expose Anika."

Jake held up a hand, halting her. "Perhaps, but we also think we may be ready to face them, even if that is the case. We propose that we break into two teams. We send a team north to tail Edyta's men, gather intel, gather a few rebel recruits, and at the same time, we send a group south. If there is an opportunity to overthrow Reynard, then we take it, and if not, then we gather recruits and intel as well."

"I want to go north," Hawk interjected.

"Why?" Val asked.

"I have my reasons; I want to go north."

Val's silence filled the room. Finally, she conceded to Hawk with a nod. "Fine, Hawk goes north. We also plan to send Mae, Brennan, and Edric with her."

"He isn't ready," Flo's smooth voice cut in.

Val sighed. "He needs to get ready. There are several priests in the group. I'm hoping it motivates him, and it would do him well to get back to the northlands."

"I'll tell him." Flo sighed and sent a knowing look to Roth who smiled grimly.

Jake thanked Flo and continued. "Flo and Roth will stay here to protect Santouri. Hcrib, Rae, Kane, Anika, Val, and I will head south."

"No, we discussed this. Anika stays here in Santouri," Val insisted.

Jake's eyes met hers, his face serious. "We need to bring her. She's ready."

"She's exactly what Reynard is looking for; we're setting ourselves up for capture," Val stated.

"I have to agree. It seems foolish," Rae exclaimed.

"Yeah, seems like we're walking into a trap," Kane agreed.

"Do I not get a say in this?" Anika spat the words, hardly having thought of what she was saying. She wished she could suck them back in but they were out there, and part of her was sick of feeling as though she were invisible. Val looked at her but said nothing as she whipped her head back to look at Jake.

"We've been over this. Her actions on the last mission were grossly inappropriate. She isn't ready to go out again. It's just that simple," sneered Val.

"Those actions are also the reason we have this opportunity to begin with,"

Anika interrupted. "Reynard would still be scooped up in that church if he didn't know I was with you."

Val was silent as she considered. Her gaze was heavy on the desk in front of her, and without even looking up she nodded. "Don't mess this up."

"I won't."

"Anika goes south." Val cleared her throat. "Everyone pack your bags. We leave at sunrise."

11

Firsts

Anika didn't sleep well; she tossed and turned, distracted by the immediacy of their new plans. When the sun finally began to rise, she was out of bed and on her way to the gates before the others had begun to stir. As Roth and Flo waved off the two groups, one with a pale and sickly looking Edric lagging behind, she looked at Santouri, the sun rising over it, casting it in a spectacular red light, and gave her thanks that she'd found the place.

As they walked, she remained mostly alone, reflecting on her time with the group, her knowledge of Val's foresight, and what it meant for her. She nervously considered the possibility that Reynard was looking to capture her, reassuring herself that he wouldn't kill her when he wanted her powers.

They walked hard, pausing only for a quick lunch before pressing onwards. They had planned to move south as fast as possible, ideally being close to Reynard without his knowledge, possibly getting to infiltrate villages immediately afterward to gather intel and find those who refused to join the order.

The first night was uneventful. Their fire was kept low and, on the coals, to suppress any suspicion. As the second night approached, they made the decision not to have a fire. They thought that they were likely too close to Reynard and his patrol by now.

On the third day, the sun was blazing overhead. Despite the upcoming fall, the humidity became thicker, and walking became more strenuous. The sweat trickled down her back, her face wet to the touch. She continued, determined to say nothing.

Just as they had reached the hollow of another hill Rae bent at the waist, panting and demanding that they stop to rest. Anika sighed as she let her pack fall and eagerly made her way to the bubbling creek, discarding her clothes in the shelter of the bushes, and wading in the river in her bra and underwear.

The water was cool enough that it bit into her skin as she ducked her head under, but she welcomed the pain as it washed away the sweat that suffocated her. As she resurfaced, pushing her long hair away, she looked toward the sky and admired the stillness of the clouds, the brilliance of the blue, and for a moment, she forgot her troubles.

She felt his presence the same moment she heard his feet wade into the water. Their eyes met at the same time, both of them glancing away as he made his way to her.

"I hate to admit it, but I'm glad Rae called us to stop."

Squinting one eye open, she lazily looked him over as she floated, letting the sunbeams bathe her. "Mmmm, this feels so much nicer than walking."

For a moment, it was quiet. Only the rustling of the woods and bubbling of the creek filling the void between them. Jake groaned as he shifted positions in the water. "Anika, do you hate me?"

"What?" She pulled her head from the water, tossing her hair back as she pushed down the panic rising in her chest. "Why would I hate you?"

Looking for his words he moved closer, the space between them stretching like a terrible void she wanted desperately to cross. "I was awful when Helena died. I blamed you, and that wasn't fair."

She nodded, fighting the urge to close the distance as she inched away. "I don't hate you. I agreed with you. I still agree with you."

The reminder made her feel sick with guilt, so she looked away, breathing in the fresh air and focusing on the feeling of water against her skin. She slowed her racing heart with a thought and her eyes opened to find him closer again. "I am sorry, though. I was wrong. I was angry, and it wasn't fair to take it out on you."

"It's okay..." She hesitated. Part of her screamed to put more space between them, but something else inside of her moved her forward, ready to cross some invisible line they'd drawn. She let the current move her closer, the water suddenly feeling warmer than before. "Do you think I'm ready this time?"

"I'm scared of what Val saw. I'm scared that if we get too close to you, that if we lose you..." He inched closer again, their knees bumping gently under the water, "I don't know what I would do if we lost you."

"You won't lose me," she breathed.

"Do you promise?" he almost whispered the words. His eyes gave nothing away as he waited for an answer.

Finally, she nodded, and with an exhale of relief, he reached for her, his arms finding her waist and pulling her in. Any thought, any hesitation, flew from her mind as her legs circled his waist, losing any space that had been left between them. His lips found hers, his kiss claiming her promise. His teeth scraped against her as he eased her mouth open, slowly exploring her with his tongue. She smiled as he softly murmured her name. The warmth of him had her moving. Her hands ran along his back, following the lines of muscles, taut with hours of hard labour. Anika didn't hesitate as she let her hand find the back of his head, the bristles of his hair, making her skin feel more alive than she had ever felt. Suddenly, he pulled away, separating himself from her as her hand gently touched her swollen lips, and she ached for more.

"I'm sorry!" he exclaimed, running his hands over his eyes and looking at the sky as he turned away from her.

"Why?" Her knees sunk into the riverbed's sandy bottom, scraping against her sensitive skin, leaving goosebumps.

"You have enough to think about without me ambushing you." He turned, moving toward the shoreline.

"Jake," she called. "Wait. You didn't ambush me."

He turned, the sunlight catching the droplets of water against his ebony skin as he moved toward her again. "Can I kiss you again?"

She went to him, slowly sliding her body over his, settling into him as he wrapped his arms around her, strong and secure, and lifted a hand to his face. "Your heart is racing," she whispered.

"Are you surprised?" He chuckled and pulled her in again. This time the kiss was softer, a gentle exploration of her lips. She gasped as he left her mouth, planting a kiss against her jaw, moving toward her ear and neck as he whispered, "I don't need to be a Naidisbo to know your heart is racing."

"If you two are done in there, we should probably keep going." Kane stood at the shoreline, a smirk playing on his lips as the two of them broke away. Anika was suddenly very aware that she wore nothing but her bra and underwear.

* * *

"Where are we exactly?" she whispered to Rae, who knelt beside her in the bushes. They looked down on the small village below them. The patrol was giving an animated speech in the square. There was no sign of Reynard or the Doctor with them.

"Rojas," Rae replied, continuing, "they must be staying hidden at their base camp, making the soldiers do their dirty work."

"Do you think they're actually looking for me?" Anika sunk lower, feeling suddenly exposed in the light of day.

"Honestly?" Rae looked at her, the hint of a frown playing at her lips as Anika nodded silently. "Yes, they likely were this entire time."

Anika sighed, watching as two young village men walked with the patrol, heading east, to what they presumed was their base camp, and where Reynard and the Doctor remained. "At least they haven't tested the children."

"Maybe our attack scared the Doctor. If he isn't here to test them, then at least they are safe," Rae replied as they slowly started crawling back to their camp.

They gave their report, Val and Jake nodding enthusiastically. It was quickly decided that they should continue surveillance, and if there was no sign of the Doctor or Reynard, they would go in, try to gather information, and encourage people to join the rebellion, or at least remain far away from the church.

Anika had suspected that she wouldn't be one of the ones going into the village. If Reynard were indeed looking for her, then they would be playing into his hands. Val pointed out that it was also idiotic for her to remain there alone; if Reynard knew where they were and cornered her while the rest of them were gone, she'd have no chance. So, it was decided that she and Hcrib would remain at the site, while Jake and Val went to the village first, followed by Rae and Kane, each pair with their separate missions.

Hcrib sat, twiddling with the hot coals of their dead fire, as Anika lay on her back, gazing at the blue of the sky, watching the fluffy white clouds roll past on the heavy wind. She pulled her sweater tighter, cutting out the wind and thinking about Jake.

Their relationship was hot and cold, full of ups and downs, emotionally charged at the best of times and left her feeling confused and lost. It was one thing to be filled with lust and another to have a relationship with someone, and she had no idea what Jake wanted. She sighed; she had no idea if Jake knew what he wanted either. His moods were intense, their interactions even more intense than his moods.

But their kiss had been something she hadn't experienced before, the possessiveness of it. The force had overwhelmed her, every sensible thought and doubt driven from her mind just by the touch of his lips. It had felt right when she had wrapped her body around his, relishing the control she felt over him.

She didn't realize how long she'd been lost in her thoughts, hardly aware of the wind or Hcrib's restless pacing when Rae and Kane came back into the clearing. Kane hadn't said a word since he'd interrupted them, and she had no idea if he had told Rae or not. She hadn't said anything either. He was keeping his distance though, face serious as he and Rae sat and chatted with Hcrib amicably as they waited for Jake and Val to return.

It wasn't long after that they did, and if they had hoped Reynard wouldn't know their location, they did little to conceal it. They crashed and banged their way into the clearing, both red-faced and nearly spitting at one another.

"What in Alvar's name happened to you two?" Kane demanded.

"Jake's an idiot!" Val shouted in his direction as Rae hissed at her to be quiet. Jake sat across from Anika, furiously staring straight ahead as Val continued her onslaught of criticisms. "We were asking around, being inconspicuous..."

"Nothing inconspicuous about shouting, Val," Rae interjected.

"Right, sorry, anyway, we were asking about what Reynard's men wanted. There was one mention of them looking for a girl, and Jake totally derailed the conversation. It was so obvious that Anika was with us! If that gets back to Reynard and his men, we're fucked!"

"Slow down," Hcrib stated. "What do you mean?"

Val took a deep breath and shook her head, shooting Jake a glare as she rephrased. "The villagers mentioned that the soldiers were asking if there was a healer who had recently passed through, and rather than continue to gather intel, Jake grilled them about the healer, asking for more details."

"Well, were there any more details?" Rae asked.

"No, they're just asking if there is a healer passing through the villages, and they have a description of you, long black hair, blue eyes, the whole bit," Jake finished.

Anika ran her hand along the soil beneath her hand, anchoring herself to the earth as she accepted the confirmation of what they'd expected.

"Well, all we know is that they are going to continue south. They suspect the rebel camp is in Moises somewhere, and so they are going to head toward Roland next. We should keep following them," Val stated, confident and firm in her decision.

"Wait, now we know for sure they are looking for Anika, wouldn't it be stupid for her to stay with us?" questioned Kane.

"Just as stupid to send her back alone," observed Jake.

"But we risk exposing her. They could take her," countered Rae.

"Not if we're smart about it!" exclaimed Hcrib.

"Do I not get a say in where I go or what I do?" Anika interjected. She stood and squared off with the group of them, hands held against her hips to hide her trembling. When no one answered, she continued, "You're making it out to be more complicated than it is. I'll come with you to Roland and stay behind, same as this time."

Slowly, they all nodded and started packing their things, ready for another painful walk.

* * *

The terrain changed gradually, from the lush green forestry of Ferreya to the barren felled forests of Moises. They moved as fast and as quietly as they could manage, with little cover to shield them. Jake had told her in a whispered conversation that the land had once been rich with the Errauts tree, but the church had burned them all and continued to come back, ensuring that the tree remained dormant and unable to provide their magic to the land. He let it slip that Hawk was from the area. She didn't talk about her power often, or her people, and none of them knew her story.

They didn't talk about the kiss. Both of them skirted around the topic, hyperaware of the space between them, both afraid of what the slight touch of a hand may lead to. She couldn't help noticing that even though they made efforts to talk to the others, they still found a way back to each other. Anika did notice that Kane watched them, scowling each time she noticed, and only receiving a sly smile in answer.

They finally received a welcome break from the sun and the vulnerability of being in the open when they entered a grove of non-power-wielding trees. Stepping carefully over a felled log, she stopped suddenly when Jake, only steps in front of her, froze. His hand slid to the knife at his waist as he slowly pulled it free before dropping it and himself to his knees laughing. Thor grumbled as he bounded from the bush and tackled Jake, rubbing his head under his chin before walking to Anika and pushing himself against her legs with a happy purr. She caught herself as she started to stumble back from his weight and leaned down to scratch his ears.

"What are you doing here, buddy?" Jake asked as Thor went back to him, crouching low and butting Jake's chest with his head as they hugged again. Anika watched as Jake looked into the animal's eyes, and they spoke to one another in whatever way they communicated.

"Right, well, let's eat and keep going. We don't have time to waste," Val said as she tapped her walking stick on the ground impatiently.

Lunch was quick. Val grumbled about the hold up until they started moving again. Anika waited until the others moved ahead, eager to talk to Kane, whom she had been avoiding. She steeled herself, knowing she was already blushing before she'd even said a word. She fell into step beside him, admiring the tattoos running over his torso, opening and closing her mouth but not finding the words. She didn't know if he noticed or took pity on her, but he glanced her way, the sly smile there, and said, "Did you know my family originally came from the south?"

"I didn't." She quickened her pace to keep up with him.

"Mmm," he gestured to the barren landscape, "it looked a lot different then, but we came from here. There were a lot of us, especially in the communities near the ocean."

She raised an eyebrow, waiting to hear more. "Fishermen. Unfortunately, most of the men died during the last rebellion, but the women continued on. Most of the boats are owned by fisherwomen now. They work just as hard as the men, they say — I say even harder."

"Women are stronger than we give them credit for," she stated neutrally.

"No doubt about it, but the church has always made them out to be inferior. Even with Edyta in power, they still managed to make women seem like they were lesser than men. Not the Ecurps people, though. They honour women. Women are stronger than men." He gazed affectionately at Rae, who bounced along ahead of them, seemingly untouched by the heat and fatigue wearing on the rest of them. "She's the perfect example of that."

"She's amazing." Anika paused. "Do you have family left?" she asked carefully.

"My mum is still alive, and I have a younger sister who lives in Balin. My sister took over the fishing when she turned eighteen, and my mom stays at home, keeping house and helping with the few Ecurps children that are left. My father died during the last rebellion."

"I'm sorry." She reached a hand out and touched his forearm briefly, softly.

"Thanks." He continued to walk, not quite meeting her eye contact. "That's why I'm here, for him, for all the other kids that are taken because they are naturalists. Because it isn't fair, and it needs to stop. And then I can go home."

"And Rae? Will she go with you?" she asked timidly.

"Hmm, I hope a lecture isn't coming on relationships. You don't seem to be in the place to give one." He laughed.

"Oh, Alvar, no. I'm sorry I didn't mean to pry!"

"No, it's okay. Rae and I have an understanding. We don't know what will happen, if we will succeed in this lifetime, and so it seems senseless to plan that far ahead."

"That's terribly morbid," Anika said with unease.

"It might seem that way, but it's also realistic. We can't just leave the rebellion, and unless we succeed, or die, there isn't a way out of this life." He jumped easily over a puddle, continuing. "So, I guess that means you're really stuck with us too, unless you run off with the church."

Her breath hitched as she began to panic, until she noticed the smile and she breathed, returning the smile shakily as she murmured her agreement and let Kane move ahead of her.

It took two days to get to Roland. Anika had never been. It was much smaller than Hagio had been, but it also looked busier. People moved along the streets with horses. The buildings were close together with orange thatched roofs, unlike the dull brown ones of Hagio, some in an obvious state of disrepair, others clearly belonging to the wealthy villagers. A high wall surrounded it, stark and intimidating. She couldn't tell if it was to keep people like them out or to keep the residents in.

She stood up as her friends disappeared within the walls and walked back to their belongings, picking up her short blade and spinning it in her hand. She smiled. Her abilities had improved, and she felt less clumsy with the knife; her hand felt more natural, holding the handle made for her grip.

Thor meowed at her, her assigned companion while the others were gone, and swished his tail from across the clearing where he lay on Jake's belongings. She lunged forward, practising a low thrust as the cat turned around to go back to sleep, ignoring her feeble practice. She spent the next while practising against an unfortunate tree, one which she hoped wasn't power-wielding, Thor occasionally opening a large yellow eye to watch her lazily, unintimidated as ever.

She became uneasy when they still hadn't arrived back, and the sun was beginning to set. She sat next to Thor, her blade long since abandoned, sticking out of the tree she had conquered in her practice, and lay across him, wondering aloud where they were. He continued to seem unfazed, rolling onto his back and demanding his belly to be rubbed.

She had dozed off at some point against the large cat, waking to the arguing of the group as they rejoined her, with a vicious, "Good way to get yourself killed falling asleep, Anika!" from Val before she rounded on the others.

They continued to bicker at one another, Anika struggling to make sense of what had happened. Finally, as Hcrib cursed in frustration, she interrupted, "Could someone please tell me what happened?"

"Sorry, Anika." Rae sat down heavily beside her. "Things went very poorly."

"Why?"

"I'm going for a walk. I'll be back soon." Hcrib waved them off and melted into the trees.

"Hcrib had been tracking the order, but we got closer than he knew, and somehow they figured out where we were or at least that we were close. They got to the city first and made sure to tell everyone that if they were caught talking to us, they'd be executed. Every door was slammed in our face, and to make it worse, we don't know where Reynard and his patrol are, because we lost them."

"The fuckers skirted us." Val threw a rock at Anika's victimized tree.

"No need for that language," Rae piped in. "We just need to get eyes on them again."

"You don't see, do you?" Val rounded on her. "They clearly have eyes on us. They knew where we were. They knew we were coming in to get recruits. We need to figure out where to go, how to throw them off our track."

"Well, when Hcrib's back, we can make a plan," Kane interrupted.

"We can't wait for Hcrib while he's out there nursing his wounds. It's obvious what we have to do. They won't expect us to head north to Hagio. They won't look for us in the capitol, or at least it will throw off their scent," Val said with finality.

"Or they will expect us to change our trajectory and head back north. So, we continue south, get to Balin, and finish recruiting while they head north. Then they won't have time to put Balin off joining the rebellion," Kane offered.

"I know you want to get home." Rae stood, laying a gentle hand on Kane's arm as she pulled him close. "But I think Val's right."

"I am right. We go north."

"Val, you can't just pull rank!" Jake said angrily. "We're a team; we need to make the decision together!"

"I vote south," Kane said, he pulled Rae in closer, looking for support.

The whistle pierced their small clearing, with a dull thud as the arrow found its mark on Anika's victim tree. Around them, soldiers moved forward in the clearing. Anika did a quick count. Six of them, each grim, each with their weapons held steady as they circled them.

"I must give you some praise for your efforts." The Doctor walked out of the trees, clapping his hands mockingly. His white smock was spotless, his face ecstatic as he looked at each of them. Thor stood snarling at the soldiers, turning on the Doctor, who looked at Jake knowingly. "Tell your animal to back down unless you want it to die."

"Thor, down." Jake nodded. Thor growled one last time before returning to Anika's side, sitting on his hind legs, quiet but on edge and ready to pounce.

"Good." The Doctor ran a hand through his greying hair, cracking his arthritic fingers as he sarcastically opened his arms to the group. "This really is quite simple. While you believed to be tracking us, we have been tracking you. I don't think it's a stretch to assume it is your lot that attacked us in Bancotta."

He walked to Rae, hand still clasped in Kane's, and pushed a wisp of her hair behind her ear, to which Kane growled. "Careful now!" exclaimed the

Doctor as he placed his hand over theirs. "There's no point fighting, young man. Your fate was decided the moment you killed my men. You are threats to our order."

He walked away from them all, rejoining the circle of soldiers. "Kill them," he said carelessly.

"Like hell you will!" declared Jake as he pulled his sword from his belt. Anika sat frozen beside Thor, her heart thundering in her ears as she watched her friends take stance for battle.

"Now, now, Doctor, I think we can pause for just a moment. We don't need to be nearly so hasty with our friends." Anika felt her spine tingle uncomfortably as Reynard walked into the clearing. He looked as he often had at the church. He wore a deep red coat and black pants, a ghastly combination with his fair skin. His voice, silky and manipulative by nature, thundered, "I think it's high time we work with our rebellious friends."

He looked at each of them for a moment. The clearing fell silent as he raised a hand for order. His gaze stopped on her as he smiled. "Anika, love, how wonderful to see you!"

She couldn't answer. She couldn't so much as speak, the thundering in her ears growing louder.

"We've missed you at the church. What a wonderfully skilled healer to lose. Such a shame you thought that revealing your powers would make you a naturalist. Your ability is far greater than theirs." He paused, placing a hand over his heart. "You, my love, have one of the pure powers."

He walked easily toward her, kneeling so his face was level with her own. Thor moved in front of her as Reynard held out a hand. "You must realize that your power, so like mine, would be rewarded?" In his outstretched hand, a flame appeared, the orange tendrils licking the air, the heat already caressing her face. He closed his hand suddenly, the flame disappearing, and Anika felt Thor relax as Reynard stood and walked away from her.

He stopped by the Doctor and clapped him on the back. "We've discussed you in great detail, Anika, and we think you could do powerful work with us." He turned back to look at her. "Join us?"

She heard Jake exhale sharply, but she looked to Val, whose face remained ferocious, and yet her eyes appeared sad, as though this perhaps was the very moment that she had seen. She looked back to Reynard and shook her head from side to side.

"Well, perhaps I can appeal to the side of you which seems to commiserate with these lowlifes, Anika. Your friend Hcrib is with us." He looked to Val. "I offer you a simple exchange, Val. You and your friends walk free, with Hcrib, in exchange for Anika."

"That's up to Anika, not me." Her voice was steady.

"An interesting approach for a so-called leader." He looked to Anika. "Well, what do you say then? Your service, in exchange for your friends' lives? Your *leader* clearly doesn't care."

Before she had the opportunity to speak, to even know what her own answer would be, Jake spoke up. "Don't answer, Anika. If you go with him, he'll kill us anyway."

Reynard smiled. "Quite right, young man." He turned to the Doctor. "Kill them, but be quick about it."

Everyone moved. She reached for her small blade as Thor bounded forward, teeth and claws sinking into the belly of a soldier whose sword fell to the side as he screamed and crumpled under the weight of the cat.

Reynard whistled, and Anika's eyes widened in shock as two foxes jumped over the bushes, circling Thor, embers spitting from their mouths as they hissed.

"Anika, you can stop this right now!" cried Reynard as he walked away from the clearing, melting into the trees behind them.

Anika charged toward a soldier who was lunging toward Kane. She angled her blade upwards into the man's flank, gasping at the resistance of the man's body, at the spasming he made as Kane's shoge collided with his skull, a sickening splatter sounding as the man's head hit the ground. She jumped, narrowly avoiding the splatter as she turned her back to meet Kane's, seeing Rae fall from above on another soldier, her sword penetrating his shoulder from above, burying itself deep inside of his chest as she used her air to propel away from him again.

She looked around, feeling panicked. Kane charged forward to another target, Val stood over a fallen soldier, and finally, her eyes found Jake, engaged with the Doctor in an equal display of power and skill.

"Anika, this is your last chance," called Reynard from the clearing.

12

Puppet

The sound of lives ending filled her ears, of blades slicing, of blood spilling, and at the same time, her head grew quieter with each life that was ended, the absence of another heartbeat, the silence of another's breath.

With each one, Reynard's words grew louder in her consciousness. She could barely see him now. He stood within the trees, darkness surrounding him. She looked around again, blood dripping from Thor's snout, Jake still fighting with the Doctor as her other friends felled soldiers, focused on saving their lives.

She could end it all. She could get Hcrib back if she could do something about Reynard. With the beginnings of a plan in works, she walked into the clearing, moving toward him as confidently as she could muster. He watched her walk toward him, the hint of a smile playing on his lips.

She focused on him, searching for his heartbeat among the others. Once she found his, it was obvious; his was the only one that remained slow and steady, disengaged from battle, calm and confident in his upper hand. She maintained his eye contact, willing herself to remain confident as she pushed against his heart, slowing it by only a beat or two, hoping he wouldn't notice.

As she got closer, she pushed further, dropping his heart rate by another few beats. With only a few feet remaining between them, he calmly said, "Enough. I know what you're doing."

He raised his hands and looked past her. She turned in fear, watching as the tree Rae was pushing away from for leverage burst into flames, causing her to stumble and fall, rolling away from the sword that met the ground, intended for her.

"I can end them all right now. Stop."

She obeyed, turning to face him again, the realization dawning on her that she had willingly gone to him, like a fly in a spider's web.

"Anika, don't!" Jake's yell reached her as she swallowed nervously. Reynard faced her, still smiling as another one of his foxes moved forward, brushing against her legs as he reached a hand out to her.

"We both know how this ends, Anika." He curled his fingers in, urging her to reach forward. "You could save everyone there with one word."

"No," she whispered.

"Very well." He swept a hand low to his side. Anika stumbled back as the woods burst into flames to her left, then stumbled again as the trees to her right burst into flame. The flames moved quickly toward the clearing. Reynard looked calmly on, uncaring about his own men still fighting with her friends.

She heard her friends shouting, the realization dawning on them as the flames surrounded the group. Reynard smiled at her, and a wall of flames rose between them, completing the circle. She stepped back against the heat, the tendrils of flame kissing her skin as she was forced back toward the clearing, turning to face her friends, each panting.

Jake ran forward, grabbing her arm and pulling her toward the rest of them. She tripped over a body, noticing briefly the white robe of the Doctor as he caught her weight, pulling her upright as the circle of flame pushed closer.

Rae stepped ahead of them, facing the shadow of Reynard beyond the wall, and raising her arms, she pushed the air around them. While encapsulating them, the wind from her powers pushed the flames back. But Reynard was strong and continued to push the flames forward as he backed farther into the clearing. Rae, straining, pushed the wind around them as they stood helpless. Anika watched as the flames grew taller. Rae began to shiver, and finally, she fell to her knees, Kane wrapping his arms around her before she fell to all fours. Reynard smiled as the flames died to nothing, leaving a ring of embers around them.

"If you wish to see your friend again, you'll meet me at the mill outside of Roland in the next two days. I'll see you soon, Anika," Reynard called through the flames, and then they were gone, the fire dead, smoke drifting away, as he left their sight.

Jake rushed to Rae and Kane, Anika watching, feeling each of them to assess their injuries. She checked Jake first. He appeared to be fine other than a few cuts and scrapes. Her mind wandered to Val, also fine, and finally to Kane, where she paused. Kane was not fine. His blood was pooling in his side, leaving him faster than his body would be able to keep up with. She moved toward him quickly, placing both of her hands on his torso, to find his shirt sticky and soaked with blood. He grunted in recognition of her touch and then relaxed, leaving Jake to support Rae as she closed her eyes and slowed the flow of blood, stitching the damaged vessels inside.

As soon as he was healed, she moved to Rae; her breathing remained laboured, but she had no extraneous injuries. Anika closed her eyes, looking for something she could fix, but she found nothing. "I don't understand. She isn't injured!"

"She used too much of her power. It's an old magic. The more magic used, the more pulled from her lifeline. It's a direct exchange and usually has time to rebuild, but she pushed too hard." Kane knelt beside her again, caressing her hair as he pulled her head into his lap. "She just needs time."

Anika looked wildly over her, reaffirming what Kane had said, but she found nothing she could repair. Nodding in defeat, she sat back, as Thor padded by her to Jake and sat, seemingly unhurt in his battle with the foxes.

"How could you be so idiotic?" Val hissed behind her. Anika turned. Val leaned against the still smoking tree, sweat lined her limbs and face, taut with anger. "You went after Reynard. What were you thinking?"

"I thought I could have spared your lives!" She stood up, impatience prickling at her senses.

"Right, as though you could take on the Aita, like he was another common soldier?" Val sneered. "You made him turn back, made him show his hand!

142

If you had stayed here, fought like the rest of us, then Rae wouldn't have had to drain her power!"

"Or he'd still have encircled us with fire and killed the lot of us," Kane piped in.

"No, Val's right. Anika left the group again. She put us all in jeopardy, not just Rae." Jake shook his head, avoiding her eye contact. "You went to him without a second thought."

Anika winced. Jake's words hurt more than Val's. She knew Val was angry and hot-tempered, but she thought she could count on Jake to show some level of care for her.

"Time and time again, you prove that you're not ready, that you're a liability, and now look where it's gotten us." Val gestured to Rae, limp on the ground. "We should send you back to Santouri before you cause more damage."

Anika trembled, pushing the anger down, but it was bubbling over. Giving in, she grabbed a discarded blade from the ground and turned to face Val. "I'm sick and tired of hearing about what a liability I am. I'm sick and tired of you blaming me for every misfortune. Why don't you take some responsibility and realize that you didn't assign anyone sentry? You're the reason Hcrib's gone!"

Val drew her blade and swung it low, hitting Anika's, the clash of steel ringing in the clearing as Anika stepped back, and Val pushed forward, bringing her blade down again and again, with Anika meeting it again and again. Anika pushed forward, swinging her blade low toward Val's legs, barely missing, as Val used her leg to trip Anika.

She hit the ground, wincing as she scurried back to her feet. Val stood a few feet away, blade still raised in defence as Anika lunged forward again, only to have the butt of Val's knife collide with her shoulder, throwing her balance off as she fell to the side gracelessly.

She regained her balance and lunged again, but Val was far more skilled, even without her gift of sight. A quick push of her sword threw Anika's blade to the side. Anika lunged forward, with no weapon, and Val tossed hers to the side, meeting her fists with her forearms, blocking the assault.

Anika huffed in frustration as Val once again took her feet out from under her, and she landed on her tailbone, the impact making her see stars. Her head filled with noise as she stood, the clearing spinning as she moved forward again, the fight doing little to bring down her anger.

But arms found her shoulders and pulled her back. Kane stood between them, arms outstretched. He stood taller and larger than his normal self. She pushed the hands on her shoulders away, turning on Jake who released her as he backed up.

She listened as Val left the clearing, storming through the brush. She made no effort to be quiet as she could be heard cursing and smashing branches. They listened until they couldn't hear her anymore, and finally, the quiet settled on them again.

"Come on, help me start a fire. Rae will need it to heal, and there's no point hiding. They know where we are." Jake started picking up twigs around the body of a dead soldier. "Kane, can you move the bodies, put them in the bush?"

Kane nodded, adjusting Rae's head on Thor's torso, who wrapped a paw around her still body and got to work dragging the dead men from the clearing.

Anika watched for a moment, feeling slightly sick as one body left a smear of blood on the ground before she turned and started to pick up kindling.

* * *

Rae slept deeply. They each watched her chest rise and fall. Thor stayed close, a soft pillow, and Kane lay behind her, sleeping lightly, twitching awake each time she or the cat moved.

Jake and Anika sat arm's length from one another, Jake poking the fire with a stick as Anika stared into the flames, thinking about the fire that Reynard had brought from nowhere with such ferocity and power.

"Why did you go after him?"

"I thought I could stop him."

"Really?" he laughed and looked at the starry sky. "You thought that with

144

your little training, and with your unrefined skills as the Naidisbo that you could take on Reynard, the Aita?"

"Mmm," she answered, lying down on her blanket and turning her back to him. She stared into the trees, remembering how it had felt when Reynard had called her name. She couldn't describe it, the pull that she had felt deep inside of her, the way when he had called her name, she had felt it not just in her mind but throughout her entire body.

She had felt more than fear when he had revealed his power. When he had thrown the grove of trees into flame, she had been overcome by a desire to feel that same level of power course through her blood, to hold the world in the palm of her hands.

She took a deep breath, pushing the thoughts away. Her rational mind knew better, knew that she wanted to stay with her friends and help them, knew that their cause was true and made sense, but the other part, that tug from somewhere deep inside of her, a place where she dared not go, was powerful and dark, tempting her more than she cared to admit.

Val didn't come back until late that night. Anika woke to hear her lay out her bedroll. She didn't say anything. Whatever was to be said could wait until the morning.

* * *

"I had another vision..." She woke to Val's whispered words. She shrugged off her blanket and sat up, still shaking off the fog of her brain. "Your path seems to have altered a bit after our encounter."

"How do you mean?"

"It's more extreme than before. I see two scenarios: one you are with us, we are victorious, and the other... the other you're victorious with Reynard, as his puppet."

She shook her head, the pull back in her gut. "What do you mean, his puppet?"

"You're with him, partners, or so he says..." She kicked dirt on to the simmering coals. "You rule, together. Edyta, she's gone."

"Oh," Anika replied, noticing Jake's gaze watching them, she shook her head and held his look. "Well, how are we going to get back Hcrib?"

13

A Trade

"I think it's obvious what needs to be done if we are going to get Hcrib back." Anika looked over them. Val still looked tired, her expedition from the night before kept to herself. Rae, now awake but still quite weak, lay watching them all, her head in Kane's lap as she listened. If she felt the tension, she didn't say anything.

"Oh, do you?" Val wrinkled her nose. "Well, please share then."

"Reynard wants me to join him. He'll trade Hcrib for me." She looked to each of them, saying what they already knew. Jake's brow furrowed deeper as he threw a rock into the trees, falling back with his hands behind his head, Kane and Rae both remained silent, but concern lined their faces, while Val stared at her with intensity, unreadable.

"And what if he decides to kill Hcrib when you go to him? Or what if he's decided that he'll kill you when he gets you?" Jake interjected.

Val, though, was slowly beginning to nod. "Anika and I will meet with Reynard while the rest of you work on getting Hcrib out of wherever they are holding him. Obviously, we will scout the area out first." She held up a hand to Jake, who had been about to interrupt. "Once we get Hcrib out, Anika talks to Reynard, she goes with him if necessary, and then leaves when the opportunity arises."

"Why wouldn't he just kill her or take her prisoner? You're acting like she is going to be accepted by Reynard." Kane shook his head.

"Kane's right. He isn't going to just believe that Anika suddenly wants to join the order," Rae said quietly.

"Reynard wants me to join him. He needs me to cooperate if he wants my powers, so he won't kill me."

"But he could take you prisoner. You're acting like there will be some simple opportunity for escape," Jake finished.

Anika nodded, "I think that's a risk we have to take."

"Or is it a risk that you want to take?" Jake asked, eyes gazing at the sky. Anika saw Val's brows rise in surprise.

"I want to get Hcrib back."

No one answered. Finally, with a huff, Val began to roll up her bedroll.

"Let's get moving," she finished.

* * *

The old mill where they met Reynard looked quiet from the outside; the only inclination that someone was there at all was the one lonely guard at the entrance, the red uniform an extreme contrast to the peeling paint of the mill.

They were not naïve enough to think that Reynard would have Hcrib with him, so Jake, Rae, and Kane were tasked with finding him in the surrounding areas. Val assumed that he'd be with the patrol, and should that be the case, they wouldn't be far from Reynard in case he needed backup.

Val and Anika, together but silent, stepped over the remnants of fallen trees as they made their way to the mill where the soldier stood stiffly, hand on his sword as they approached.

"You know why we're here," Val greeted him with a scowl, nose scrunched up as she looked him over.

He jerked his head at the door, letting them pass. The building was old and decrepit; wooden beams ran across the ceiling, thick webs clinging to the rafters. The floors creaked beneath their feet, and in her periphery, Anika glimpsed the tiny scuttling movements of creatures that she didn't wish to see any closer. Ahead of them, Reynard leaned casually against a door; a sly smile played on his lips as they approached.

"Welcome, ladies, I see you were wise enough to come alone." He gently patted the door as he stood, his movements as carefree as if he were having his afternoon tea. "Your dear friend Hcrib is waiting for you as agreed."

She fought the rising panic and urge to whip her head toward Val, but Val only met Reynard's gaze with an equal nonchalance as she nodded. Anika had to give Val credit as nothing on her face indicated their miscalculation in presuming that Hcrib was elsewhere.

She ignored the voice in her head that wondered if Val had hoped for this mistake to conveniently relieve them of the liability she so clearly thought Anika was. She didn't bother to try and slow down her galloping heart. Instead, she focused on Val and Reynard's. She could have screamed to hear the steady, confident beating from them both, no sign of nervousness present, only sheer confidence. Regardless of her reservations she knew what had to be done, that she couldn't walk out the door and leave without getting Hcrib back to the group safely.

"Well, there's no point in delaying things then, is there?" She tried to hide the tremble in her voice, but the words tasted like poison as she spoke to Val. "I've been thinking about what Reynard said, about my potential. I do want to hear more of what he has to say. I need to know what I'm capable of."

Val's face didn't give any sign if she had even heard Anika. "Let Hcrib out, and we'll leave then."

He instead looked to Anika. "I have your word you'll come with me?" He reached into his pocket and pulled a key out.

"As long as you let them go without harm," she answered.

"Very well." Hcrib stumbled forward as the door opened, turning as soon as he could and backing away from Reynard until he met Val's steady hand against his back.

"Anika, what are you doing?" Cheeks flushed and eyes wild, Hcrib shook his head.

"Hcrib, Anika's made a decision, and we have to live with it." Val avoided meeting her gaze, her voice deadpan as ever.

The tension was tangible as they stood looking at one another, no one knowing what to do or say next. Reynard flippantly gestured to the door, dismissing the others and without so much as a goodbye from Val, and a loud, but quickly killed protest from Hcrib. The door shut behind them, leaving Anika and Reynard alone.

"So, either you have come with me for the sake of your friend, or something I have said to you has piqued your interest, Anika." He gestured to a rather dilapidated chair in which she sat, grateful that at least by sitting she was less likely to vomit her dinner all over the dusty floor. "I certainly hope that you are not here out of gallantry. They wouldn't deserve it."

"No?" Her heart quickened as she spoke back to him. "Why do you say that?"

"I wanted you to see how easily Val would trade you for Hcrib; if they valued you, there would have been some commotion, some trepidation. I was right, though. I posted one soldier at the door, and she dispersed your other comrades. Did you think she actually thought that I'd hold the sneak elsewhere?"

"I don't know what Val thought." She crossed her legs and arms, willing herself to be ignore the resurging voice at the back of her head.

"I think you do know, though; I think you realize that Val has had difficulty with you from the start. Did she tell you that we know each other?" He grinned at the look of surprise on her face as he continued. "No, I didn't think she would have told you. Val and I know each other well, but I won't bore you with our story. I know though that she wouldn't enjoy having someone as powerful as you within their little group."

"That makes no sense," Anika interrupted.

This time it was him that looked surprised. "Please, darling, let me finish before you say something you regret."

"Don't call me darling." She spit the words out before she had time to think them through.

He smiled. "Such a fiery soul you have, and yet you questioned that you should come with me. I admit I am surprised. But then again, I suppose you did feel some sense of loyalty to them after that awful incident at the church. Escape was really unnecessary, you know; I wouldn't have punished you."

She remained silent.

"I regress, darling — ah, sorry. I'll refrain from calling you that." His smile didn't falter as he leaned forward, elbows relaxing on his knees, and for a moment, she wondered how genuine he was. "Val enjoys her power. She enjoys being the leader and being in control just as much as I do, but there is a difference between Val and I. Val has never been willing to share her power. She desires control above all else."

"And you don't?"

"Heavens, no. I just want what is best for the people that live here. I want safety, I want security, I want our people to know that there is nothing to fear. Sadly, the naturalists have proved time and time again that their powers, while impressive, are difficult to control, and they've hurt our people, repeatedly putting them in danger. I suppose they've told you something different, though."

"They have."

"Well, if you'll come with me, you'll hear our side of the story, and you'll find them to be quite different; I know you'll come to a conclusion of your own, and I'm confident that you'll see the light."

"Is the light fire?"

He laughed, a great booming sound which made Anika jump in her seat. "You're as clever as I imagined you to be! Anika, I only want to do what's best for our people, and unlike Val, I'm not so arrogant to think that I should be the only person in control of this country. I would happily share the power if it meant that our people were safe and secure."

"Are you not already sharing with Edyta?" She relaxed her arms as he leaned back again, nodding in agreement.

"Certainly! I hope that by having the most skilled and powerful people at the helm, we can steer this nation to be the most proficient it has ever been."

"Then why have you been crossing into the north?"

Reynard had the decency to look impressed as he chuckled. "I promise it is not as sinister as it may seem, Anika. I'm sure you have many more questions you want answered, but I need your word you'll come with me as we journey back to Hagio."

She took a shaky breath, and unsure if her answer came from the reality that she was his prisoner and had no choice, or from a dark place of curiosity, she whispered, "Yes."

"Excellent." He held out a hand to her as he stood. "Let's go."

She took it.

* * *

His men were standoffish and seemingly uneasy to her sudden appearance. Reynard had dismissed them quickly, barking orders about sentry duty, ensuring that the remaining men were well versed in their plans to head to Hagio, and demanding that he and Anika be brought their supper as soon as it was ready.

A young man, who looked as though he hadn't yet been enhanced for the duties of soldiering, handed her a steaming bowl of stew and backed away, withholding eye contact, his head tucked down.

"They have such respect for you already." Reynard watched the young man retreating and leaned back on his plush blankets. "The legends of the Naidisbo family are not unlike others, exaggerated but built on truth. It's right that they respect you."

"Do they, though? Or do they fear us?" She stirred the contents of her bowl, impressed that it did look and smell rather delicious.

"Respect and fear are healthy companions, Anika; often both are required to be a true leader."

She nodded noncommittally as she tested the stew and found herself surprised at the richness of it. More surprising however, was that she found herself comfortable with Reynard. His words, which with she did not necessarily agree entirely, had yet to seem incredibly outlandish.

"I do owe you an apology, Anika." He sat his bowl aside. "When you were a nurse at the church, I certainly had noticed you. I won't pretend that I didn't, but I didn't see your potential. Did you know you held such power?"

She hesitated. "I knew that I had an intimate knowledge of the human body. I knew I could heal people, and I suppose I knew I was Naidisbo, but I didn't exercise my abilities."

"Have you tested the limits of your power yet??" He leaned forward in anticipation.

"No." She lowered her eyes to drink, grateful for a moment of reprieve. "I have only used my powers to heal when necessary."

"But of course! I didn't mean anything sinister. I understand that your father remains at the church, a loyal worker if I ever did know one."

Her heart quickened. She had feebly hoped that they wouldn't have made the connection. She swallowed, willing her voice to remain steady. "Is my father okay?"

"Of course, we wouldn't want any harm to come to the father of the Naidisbo." She jumped involuntarily as Reynard smiled and snapped his fingers. The bushes to her right rustled as a fox slinked from beneath them, going to Reynard and curling up, amber eyes fixed on Anika as its red tail swished back and forth. Reynard scratched the fox's ears affectionately, and the creature breathed heavily, small sparks dancing from its nostrils. "This is my sweet girl Piper. She's been my loyal companion for many years."

"She's magnificent," Anika whispered, Piper's eyes remained fixed on her as she set her bowl aside, suddenly nauseated.

"Anika, may I be straightforward with you?"

She nodded, hoping that whatever he said wouldn't result in her nausea worsening.

"I am hopeful that you will see this as an opportunity. I am looking for more than just a Naidisbo; I am looking for a companion, someone to rule with me, to be my partner, my lover."

No luck, her stomach turned, the nausea growing worse. Every part of her conflicted.

"I know that that is forward, and I know that we don't know each other well, but there is something between us, and I believe you feel it too. There's a pull, a connection."

He stood, pulling her with him as she tried to use her power to settle her now churning stomach, but he was disrupting her focus. He put a hand beneath her chin and lifted her face, so their eyes met, and she did everything in her power to not look away.

"Please say yes to trying this, Anika. We could be magnificent." His thumb stroked her cheek and she found herself thinking that only a man who relied on others to do his dirty work could have hands as smooth as his.

She stepped back and cleared her throat. "This is all a bit much for me right now. I don't know what to think."

His hands dropped to his side, his eyes narrowing. "This can be very easy for you or very difficult, Anika."

He stepped forward, grabbing her forearm and turning her to face him again. "I'm not lying about what there is between us. I think you feel it too, but I do expect you to obey. It would be easier if you allowed yourself to enjoy your power."

"I don't want to hurt people." She pulled away, but his grip remained tight.

"I've asked you to hurt no one, but I will ask you to show me your powers." He let her go and reached down beside Piper, who remained unfazed. Frozen where she stood, nausea suddenly forgotten, she watched as he picked up the knife and with excruciating slowness pushed the blade into his thigh, groaning as he pulled it down, blood spilling from the gaping wound.

The knife fell to the ground, and she watched as he gasped, trying to catch his breath. Finally, blood still spilling, he stood at his full height and pulled her toward him. "Heal me. Show me your power."

"N... No," she stammered, panic overwhelming her.

"Do it!" He placed his hands on her shoulders and shook her. "You claim you don't want to hurt people. Well, heal me!"

"This is not the way to convince me." Her breathing was jagged, uncontrolled. He groaned suddenly, the deep rumbling of a man in pain. She cried out as he pulled her to him, his mouth crushing hers in a rough kiss. She didn't move; she didn't dare let herself respond to him as she internally fought the assault. He stopped, leaning his forehead against hers, his breathing becoming more and more laboured as they stood forehead to forehead, his pants growing louder as his blood started pooling into the earth.

Her body trembled as she quietly sobbed, pushing away as his hands pulled her closer and he rained possessive kisses over her cheeks and jaw. His hands drifted to her back as he pulled her in, slumping his weight onto her as the stickiness and warmth of the blood began to cover her thigh.

"Heal me."

As suddenly as he'd pulled her in, he pushed her away and slapped her, the sound rebounding around them as she cried out and fell to the side. He wavered and finally sat, Piper continuing to watch the two of them as Anika held a hand to her burning cheek.

"Heal me, Anika. I don't want you to be my prisoner."

She knelt beside him, a sob escaping her throat as she gave in and placed her hands on the wound. When it was done she lurched to the side, finally releasing the contents of her stomach on the ground. She wiped her sleeve against her mouth and watched through her tears as Piper slinked away. She was still wondering how the animal could find her vomiting to be the thing that finally phased her when she saw Reynard's unsettling smile. Shakily, she tried to return it.

* * *

They journeyed toward Hagio by horseback, Reynard quiet and distant as he led the men on his large Camarillo horse. She was inexperienced at riding, and her muscles ached after hours on the much smaller horse she'd been given. She had done a count of the men around her, twelve in total, and other than the poor boy who seemed stuck with the menial tasks of on the road housekeeping duties, she didn't wish to meet any of them in battle.

On their second day of riding, in which Anika was starting to feel as though her thighs and back may break in two, Reynard gestured her forward to him. Her horse, strong-willed, pushed against her as she steered it to meet him.

"Today you will ride with me, Anika." He didn't so much as slow down as her horse unhappily fell into step with his own. She remained there in silence, unwilling to start whatever conversation he was seeking. "Have you had time to reflect on my proposal?" He didn't wait for her to answer. "I am hopeful it will make you realize it is better to work with me than against me."

She took a deep breath. "It has." It wasn't like she could say otherwise.

"Please explain why you hesitated to heal me, Anika. I have heard that as a nurse, you never hesitated; your kindness has been spoken of by many of my soldiers."

"I never healed with my powers. I healed the soldiers with herbs and remedies, as did the other nurses."

"Why hide such power, though?"

She snapped her head to the side, glaring at him as she reigned in her sudden flare of anger. "Why would I risk showing my power? I thought I'd be killed."

She jumped as a hiss came from her other side, and she turned to see Piper slinking alongside them, sparks jumping from her nostrils as she glared at Anika.

"Piper, my love, Anika is speaking her mind. I welcome her to do so." Reynard smiled collegially at her. "I won't pretend that your fear isn't justified. The rumours and what is necessary to keep peace have made it seem as though you would be at risk. But, Anika, none of the naturalists have your power. You must understand, you are not one of them."

"No?"

"No, your power is not linked to the earth, to the trees. Your power is innate. It comes from inside of you, from your lineage and your people. Like mine, you need nothing to call your power. And your power is pure because of that."

"But what about the naturalists' power is impure?" She willed her voice not to shake as she asked, knowing the question held some accusation. He remained silent, looking ahead and stroking his horse affectionately as he considered her question.

"I concede, it isn't only a matter of purity, Anika. You'll have heard the version of history given to you from the rebels, but the last rebellion happened because the naturalists were using their power to destroy our people. With so many powers, so many abilities, the naturalists were causing our people distress. No one was safe, and no one knew who would have powers and how they could have been manipulated. Imagine if you were a simple farmer, powerless, and you employed a young man to help you. That man though, to his unawares, is a Swey, and as he works, he gathers more and more Hagin, until his power is larger than he can resist. That farmer is suddenly being manipulated by the Swey. His thoughts are no longer his own, and before he knows it, his farm is no longer his."

"You speak from experience?"

"Yes, but it is just one of many problems that the naturalists caused."

"But how can you tarnish all naturalists with the same brush?"

"Anika, the naturalists have been controlled for a reason, and peace has fallen on our people because of it. Our ancestors were right to do what they did, and who are we to question it or interfere with it? The rebels wish to cause us unbalance, to throw our society into chaos once again. It's my job to prevent that, to keep the peace."

"And you believe peace cannot be achieved without the repression of an entire people?" She felt the heat of Piper's breath against her leg but continued to look to Reynard, knowing her question was brazen but feeling the need to ask regardless.

"Remaining complacent, even idle, Anika, leads to unrest. When leaders let their guard down or show even an ounce of weakness, those waiting to take control will pounce at the opportunity. I do not claim that everything we have said about naturalists is true, but wiser leaders than I have stressed that even the smallest lie can be believed when it's repeated often enough." He looked at her, and she wondered for a moment if there was sadness behind his smile. "You and I, Anika, we could rule like no one before."

She nearly fell off her horse, and quickly tried to conceal the squeal that came from her as Piper jumped on to her horse's neck. Her horse started to rear up in protest but the fox jumped again, body lithely landing in front of Reynard as it curled up into a perfect circle and idly watched her from the slit of one eye as Reynard caressed her head in affection. Anika let the horse fall slightly behind Reynard's as it shook in fear, her equally unsteady hand trying to calm the animal as they continued in silence.

They stopped that evening for supper, Anika eating alone as Reynard talked to his men in hushed tones. She noticed with satisfaction that none of the men made eye contact with her, and when forced to converse, they looked away and hurried to leave her.

Reynard approached her, his confidence – which only came across as misplaced arrogance - exuding as he held a hand out to her.

"Care for an evening walk?" he asked as he pulled her to her feet.

"Alright." She left her hand in his, terrified of how he might react if she were to pull away. His mood was as about as predictable as a sun bear – which could flip from jovial to violent for no apparent reason.

They walked in silence, Reynard holding back branches for her. Finally, the wooded area ended, and she realized, unhappily, that he had led her to a rather small and isolated lake. It would have been peaceful if she were there with anyone else. As it was, with the rays of sunlight catching between the trees and the heat on her skin, it instead brought Jake to mind. For a moment she could feel his hand slide to the back of her neck, and she yearned for how his lips had felt on her skin. It felt like a lifetime ago that they'd been tangled together in the water.

"When I was a boy, I used to come here." His words pulled her from the memory.

"Here? We're in the middle of nowhere."

"No, just a half an hour walk east, and you'd step on to my grandfather's land. I used to come here to think." He released her hand and sat on the sandy ground, patting it so she would join him. "That was during the last rebellion. I remember feeling so angry that the naturalists would try to ruin the peace we had fought so hard for, but I would come here and remember what I was fighting for, for my people, for happiness."

He patted the ground beside him and she sat, drawing her knees in to her chest. He laid a hand on her arm, and she turned to him, keeping her face carefully neutral. He looked at her, calmly, and she, for a moment, saw no ill intention in his gaze. He truly believed in his cause.

"Anika, I owe you an apology. Again, I am sorry for being harsh with you, for forcing you to use your power. I do not wish to rule over you; I wish to rule with you. Sometimes it's hard to draw the line when you're the one in

158

charge."

"It's okay." She wondered if part of her meant the words.

Before it had registered that he had moved closer, his hand found the back of her neck, and he pulled her in, his lips meeting hers, this time with surprising gentleness. Instinctively, her hand lifted to press against his chest, and she pushed away, but he pulled her closer, finishing the kiss with a peck on her lips. She raised a hand to her lips; confusion, intrigue, and repulsion filled her all at once.

"I apologize. I should have asked."

"Yes, you should have." She cleared her throat and stood, brushing the sand off of her pants. "I'd like to go back to camp, please."

She avoided his eye contact as he reached for her hand, but she saw him nod in her periphery. "Of course, Anika, there is something here, though. I know you feel it. We could be happy."

She kept her eyes low and followed, scared at what she felt stirring inside of her.

14

Kane

Sometimes she pushed his buttons more than he liked to admit, but he kept his mouth shut, looking to Rae for reassurance that he needed to bite his lip, to go with the flow, and let her and Jake bicker it out. Still, he hadn't even voiced it to Rae, but he sometimes wondered if Jake should be the one in charge instead of Val.

He threw another rock into the trees, branches breaking from the strength behind it as he lay back and stared up at the blue sky. He needed a breather, and Rae had known it when they'd stopped. She'd ushered him to the side, and with a kiss and a confident pat on the arm, she sent him on his way, with a gentle reminder to breathe.

Val hadn't done anything that should have upset him; logically, he knew that. Her approach bothered him sometimes, the way she dictated everything they did, pretending to take what they wanted into consideration. At times, even though he was surrounded by people, most importantly, Rae, he felt lonely, and he didn't know how that was possible.

He scowled, annoyed by his own annoyance. Rae said he thought too much about their social interactions, but he wasn't like Brennan. He wasn't socially inept. He knew how to talk to people, how to joke and laugh. No, he corrected himself, Val just got under his skin. It's what happened when you spend too much time with people.

"Grossly inappropriate," he mocked Val as he rolled his eyes, speaking to no one. He recognized that yes, Anika was new, but she wasn't this hard on other new members. He felt bad for her. He knew the others didn't like how Val was treating Anika either, but no one said anything, and he didn't really know why.

Rae said it was because she was the leader, not elaborating beyond that, as though being the leader was the end of the discussion and what she said went. Kane knew it was because Rae didn't know what else they could do about it, or if they should do anything about it. He paused; even he wasn't sure if they should do anything about it.

That's when the guilt started seeping in. Val was a good leader. She was authoritarian because she had to be, because she wanted to keep them alive, and he felt the all too familiar sensation of remorse build as he came to the same realization that he always did.

Pushing himself up from the ground, he stood, dusting the dirt off the back of his pants as he stretched, back cracking from lying on the uneven ground. He may have gained some clarity, but he wasn't ready to head back to base, so he went in the opposite direction, trying to avoid ruminating on everything he'd been thinking of. Instead, he focused on what he'd get for his next tattoo.

As he walked, he held both arms in front of himself, examining the swirling black patterns that ran up each side. Each swirl contained images small enough that from a distance, they were barely noticeable, but up close, they told a story. He had started on the left arm, recording everything he could remember from when he was growing up: his younger sisters and him playing in the kitchen, learning how to sail, fishing, joining the order — his entire story stretched from wrist to wrist. He flexed his arm. In the swirl of his right bicep, there was the story of how he'd met Rae, which made him pause and smile.

He continued walking, not needing to duck as he shrunk in size to go under a tree that would have blocked his stature otherwise. His power had become second nature at some point in his life, but he couldn't remember when. He'd known it was in him all along, but he hadn't been able to access it really, not until he'd gotten his shoge, a hand-me-down from his mother. The handle was delicately carved wood, and when he held it, his power coursed through his veins like water.

Testing his abilities, he closed his eyes and opened them again. He'd shrunk himself down to the size of a child. He could never be as quiet as Hcrib, but this allowed him to move through the woods with less noise, his footstep smaller, his body lighter. He could hear the river getting closer now as he continued walking; he'd stop and get a drink of fresh water and then head back to base, literally and figuratively cooled down, he hoped.

He reached the clearing and stopped; voices drifted his way.

"... surprised?" He knew that voice. He looked up the river and stopped in his tracks, completely silent. Jake, shirtless, Anika, also shirtless. He was relieved to see that she was at least wearing a bra as Jake pulled her into him, the water noisily splashing between them as he kissed her. It didn't look like they were going to stop anytime soon, so he grew to his normal height and walked up the river toward them. Anika's head tipped back as Jake found her neck. Kane coughed loudly before he spoke.

"If you two are done in there, we should probably keep going." He turned but not before seeing the two of them break apart, panic on both of their faces. Anika's arms crossed to cover her chest.

He walked back ahead of them. He knew that what he and Rae had was real, had never doubted what they felt for one another. And it wasn't that he was surprised by Jake and Anika, but it could be problematic, especially if they parted ways and it turned ugly. Then again, he corrected himself. He hadn't seen them together often. No, he'd have to talk to Rae about it before making any decisions. She'd know. She'd been with them from the start.

* * *

Anika and Jake had both avoided him when they'd come back, sheepishly going to their belongings and walking with the group, staying away from one another to the extent that it was obvious something had happened between them. It was especially noticeable how much Jake was ignoring him. They'd been friends for years. They were brothers when it came down to it. He ignored the part of him that was hurt Jake hadn't come to him about this.

He dropped to the back of the group. Rae looked for him from the front of the group and, knowing him, knew he would need to talk. She jumped, a blast of air propelling her into the air as she used the current to float back toward him, landing lithely beside him and falling into step as she grabbed his hand.

"What are you thinking about?" she asked.

"Us." He smiled. He wasn't lying. He was thinking about them.

She squeezed his hand in response. "What about us?"

"How we just knew, you know?" She nodded, but he continued anyway. "I've never wondered if something would happen. Not once did I think it wouldn't work out."

"Me neither." She smiled and stopped him, using her air to lift her up by a foot and kiss him quickly on the lips. "But why are you thinking about this?"

He chuckled. "I ran into two of our little group getting hot and heavy in the stream today."

"No!" she gasped, fighting to keep her voice down. He watched her look from member to member, eyes lingering on Anika and Jake. She looked back at him, brow raised in speculation as he nodded.

"Anika and Jake," she mused. "That's good."

"It is?" he pondered.

"Why wouldn't it be?"

He fumbled over his words. "Well, she's the Naidisbo. What if they break up and then...?"

Rae held up her hand and cut him off. "We don't know what's between them, and they're both adults. If they broke up, I hardly think Anika would kill everyone around her out of vengeance."

"No, that's not what I'm saying," he spat.

"Sounds like maybe you're put out that Jake didn't tell you." She leaned her head against his arm and smiled. "It's okay, love."

He scowled but didn't disagree; she knew him too well for him to try and defend himself. And before he could figure out what he wanted to say, Val had turned around looking for Rae, and she'd leaped into the air and back to the front of the group, leaving him alone in the back again.

He noticed Jake, who was away to the side of him, glance nervously over at him. With Rae's words ringing in his head, he jogged to meet him. Jake didn't look at him right away. He glanced nervously between Kane and Anika, waiting for him to speak first.

"You want to talk about it?" Kane asked.

Jake sighed, running a hand over his cropped hair as he looked at Kane. "I don't know, man," he started, gaze shifting to Anika. "What is there to talk about?"

Kane shrugged. "I don't know what there is between you guys, but sometimes it helps to spitball off of each other."

"You never had to spitball about Rae," Jake pointed out.

"True." Kane nodded, thinking. "But this is complicated. Rae and I are both rebels... you rescued Anika, but you rescued her from the church, where she was living, willingly."

Jake nodded, lips pursed. "Exactly."

For a moment, Kane thought he wasn't going to say anything further, but then Jake kicked a rock as they passed and swore under his breath. "She's the fucking Naidisbo, you know? And I know that shouldn't make any difference, but it does."

"You have a lot to consider."

"Yeah." Jake didn't offer anything more. Kane didn't know what to say. They weren't good at this, at the deep discussions.

"So, how was it?" he asked, grinning.

"Fucker," Jake said, but he laughed as he said it. "It's good."

Kane had never seen his friend smile like that before.

15

Flickering Flames

The wind was starting to turn crisp as she pulled her blanket closer around her, gazing up at the star-speckled sky. The camp was quiet, the only sound the crackling of the fire and the occasional snore from sleeping soldiers. She knew that there were at least two men on sentry, but they were silent, blended into the trees. Reynard's tent swayed slightly in the breeze, and she felt, for a moment, envy at the thought of being in an enclosure, safe from the elements.

She startled at a sound in the distance, a brief cry for only a moment, followed by the deep silence she had grown used to. Instinctively, she felt her heart begin to race, and she breathed deeply, slowing it. Then the feeling started to creep into her, the awareness that something around her had changed. She hadn't bothered to count the heartbeats, but it felt as though there were a new heartbeat or a different heartbeat than before moving toward her back.

She sat up and turned quickly, sensing the person more strongly. She nearly screamed when she saw Jake crouched in the trees, bloody knife in hand and a finger to his lips in warning. She nodded, not moving a muscle.

A soldier on the other side of the fire grunted as he turned over, mumbling incomprehensible words in his sleep as he settled back in slumber. With a nod from Jake, she silently rose from her blankets and made her way to the edge of the clearing. She gave a start to see Hcrib pop up with a smile as he enveloped her into a hug and exclaimed, loudly, how excited he was to see her.

"You'll wake them!" she whispered.

"He's enclosed us, we're in a bubble, and they can't hear us." Jake raised a hand to her and dropped it back to his side before he made contact. "Are you okay?"

"I am," she answered honestly, but it felt like a lie. She looked back at the campsite, the sleeping men, the tent swaying slightly in the wind, and felt mixed emotion.

"Come on. The others are waiting for us. They're dying to know how you are." Hcrib squeezed her hand and started moving through the brush. She followed, trying to ignore the sensation of eyes on her back as she left the camp.

They didn't need to walk long before the trees began to thin, and they were walking over open land with only the moonlight to guide them. The others waited for them at the edge of the clearing, each with their blankets wrapped tightly around their shoulders in the absence of a fire. She couldn't pinpoint why, but as Rae embraced her, she felt nervous. Val nodded to her seriously, and Kane threw a mocking salute in her direction as they settled to the ground with them.

"Finally," Val said. "Tell us everything."

Anika did, without question. She told them what had happened since she had left them, but she left out Reynard's kiss, glancing guiltily at Jake as she skirted past the topic. When she finished, the group looked at her silently, the silence eventually lasting longer than she was comfortable with before she asked, "What is it?"

"Well, did you decide?" asked Rae.

"Decide what?"

"Decide if you want to be with him, if you believe him?" followed Kane.

"Are you kidding? I know exactly what I want. If I didn't before then, I do now even more. I am with you all, 100%... and... and I don't know how else to prove it to you." She sat in frustration, looking at Jake in hopes of some sort of validation but receiving none as his gaze lingered to the trees.

"Good. Let's rest for an hour and then get moving before Reynard's men wake. Jake... you take first watch with me."

"Val, we hardly need..."

"Jake, we both take first watch."

* * *

"Come with me." Val shook her shoulder, jolting her awake from the slumber she had quickly fallen into.

"Okay," she grumbled, getting to her feet groggily. She looked around, slightly disoriented until Val impatiently coughed from where she waited for her. "Where are we going?"

"I need to see you do something, Anika. You've said time and time again that you are on our side, and yet, something always happens that makes me question it. I need to see you use your powers against them."

"How?" She wiped her eyes as she ducked under the branches of a low tree. "You'll see. You also need an opportunity to use your powers to practise. You could have done so much more before, but you didn't. Your powers, they aren't refined."

"I can't practise on you, Val." Her thoughts were becoming clearer as she woke up and her brain registered what Val was saying. Val came to a sudden stop and Anika nearly ran her over, that was, until she too froze at the sight in front of her. In the clearing was a man, awake and straining against his bound hands and wrists, eyes bulging as his gaze fell upon her. Jake sat beside him, calmly twirling a dagger in hand. He nodded to Val as he stood and avoiding Anika's eyes left the two of them with the captured man.

"Val... how?" She didn't recognize the man from those that she had been with.

"It doesn't matter."

"Val, I can't. He's defenceless."

"Kill him."

"Fuck Val, you're acting just like him." She took some satisfaction at the glint of fear in Val's eyes as she stepped back in disgust "Using me for my power, like I'm your slave."

"Don't. You know that's not what this is."

She knew in her heart that she couldn't kill the man but then, part of her wanted to use her power. Part of her wanted to feel what Reynard told her she was capable of. Part of her craved to know her potential. Conflicted, and exhausted she cursed at Val, closed her eyes and reached out for his heartbeat. The beat was fast, panicked. The moment she'd try to slow his heart she pictured his face, and she couldn't bring herself to do it. She opened her eyes, affirming her vision as the man strained against his bindings. Val grabbed her arm, taking her by surprise as she pulled Anika closer to the man.

"Hold it in your mind, damnit!" She stood only a foot away from the man now, close enough that she could smell his fear. Anika focused on the sensation and knowledge filling her chest. The warmth of it was like a small flame burning in her heart; she knew she needed to foster it, focus on its strength so it would grow.

"Focus!" Val stepped back to give her space. "Look at him and feel it!"

The man lay behind Val, his mouth gagged, but his eyes pleaded with Anika. He strained against the ropes that bound his hands behind him as he whimpered.

The flame flickered as she grew distracted by the man. She closed her eyes again, letting herself enter his body and feel the shallow breaths in his lungs. She strained her face, picturing his inhale breathing life into her as a flame, and then she felt it, the momentary lapse in his breath. When she opened her eyes, Val stood between them, a smile on her lips as the man's eyes widened in panic as his breath was cut off.

She let the flame inside of her heart go out and watched as he caught his breath, the moment of relief temporary as Val stomped forward in frustration and kicked him in the stomach.

"I'm sorry." It sounded weak. Val wasn't facing her, but she knew that she could hear. Huffing in her frustration Val lashed out at the man again, kicking his back this time. He arched and Anika looked away as his eyes filled with tears. Val flipped her knife open in her hand, the blade glinting in the setting sun. The scent of urine filled the clearing as Anika backed away from the man who was whimpering at the sight of Val's weapon. "I want to learn, I do, but I can't kill a man for practise."

Val turned and looked at her, her silence louder than words. She looked at Anika and the man fleetingly. "Do you think that this is just some innocent man we picked up in a village we passed through?"

"How am I supposed to know when you don't tell me anything?" She sat on the ground cross-legged, the three of them now making a rather unlikely triangle, the gagged man silent except for the odd hiccup as he listened.

"We don't tell you anything because you aren't ready, Anika. You need to learn to yield your power effectively."

"I can yield it," she said louder.

"No, you can heal, but you have the ability to do so much more... you can kill. Your ancestors wiped out troops with their powers. They cut off their air, stopped their hearts where they stood, Anika..." She stood and walked to the man, pushing the tip of her knife into the small of his back. He arched away from her, moaning as she slowly pushed the blade down, holding him in place. "They could have drowned this man in his own blood if they wanted to."

"That's horrific!"

"It's horrific? Anika, this man..." she grinned as she jumped to her feet and placed her foot on his neck, pressing hard as he strained under the pressure, "he works for Reynard. He stands by when they kill children!"

Anika nodded. She couldn't say the words, but she had witnessed the children coming into the church. She had seen the tear-streaked faces of those young ones who had been ripped from their families. She had watched them be taken to the basement, some returning to work in the staff, most never appearing again.

"Do you know what they do to them?" Anika shook her head, still speechless. "They don't just take children from their homes, Anika. They test them with the roots of their trees, and if they show their gifts, they give them to the foxes. Then the foxes take their time. They are cruel animals. They play with their new toys, they burn them slowly, and when they are done playing, they incinerate their bodies. This man... Anika... he supports

169

that."

"What do you want me to say?" Anika hadn't moved despite desperately wanting to run anywhere that would get her away from this situation with Val. But Val just stared at her, relentlessly probing her with her eyes.

"Kill him!"

"I CAN'T." Something inside of her was breaking as she stood and stepped toward Val whose foot hadn't moved from the man's neck. She could feel the heat building in her body, centred and flowing from her, pulling in the heartbeats of Val and the man. She breathed deeply and saw them both. She felt the life inside of them, and she pushed against it. She pushed their hearts away, relishing as she felt them start to race.

"Anika!" Val screamed her name, bringing her attention back to the moment. Gasping, her own breath rapid, she saw in astonishment that Val was now kneeling on the ground, clasping her chest. Val was pointing to the man who was flopping like a fish out of water, bending against the tautness of the ropes, his eyes squeezed tightly shut. She broke the connection between their bodies and waited for Val's anger.

Val looked at her, but instead of anger, she smiled and nodded as she worked to catch her breath. "Good, that was good. You need... to... focus... focus on him... the enemy... you can do it."

Anika's eyes closed, and she shook her head in denial, the anger that had driven her fading away. She could feel them both and differentiate between them now, but she was drained from the energy her outburst had required and scared by her power when she was out of control. "Not now, Val."

Val nodded and stood, her breathing more settled. "Fine, you worked hard. We need to keep moving, and unless you want to carry him, then I suggest you help me bury him."

"We can't bury him alive, Val!"

"Obviously not." She picked up the knife that had fallen aside and stepped over the man so her feet were on each side of his shoulders. She leaned over and pulled his head up, his eyes making one last desperate plea to Anika. Val swiftly drew the blade along his neck and pushed him onto his stomach, watching Anika as the man's blood pulsed into the soil. His body writhed on the ground, slower and slower as his life left him. Val walked to their things and pulled out two spades, throwing one to Anika. "Dig."

"Was that necessary?" Anika caught the spade and turned to Val, the last beat of his heart sounded, and Anika wiped away a silent tear that had escaped her.

Val glanced at the man, no emotion betrayed on her face. "Yes," she declared, and she struck soil.

16

Temptations

"So, while being held captive by Reynard's men, I had the opportunity to learn a little bit of their plans..." Hcrib stated to the room.

Anika sat, lost in thought. She knew what Hcrib would tell the group. He had already briefed them on their way back to Santouri. He had overheard a plan to augment Anika's powers, making her stronger and more capable than ever. The soldiers had said that Reynard talked of her wiping out all the rebels without pause and then, ultimately, the destruction of the rest of the trees that held power.

She had spent most of the walk back thinking about what Hcrib had said, wondering how truthful Reynard's account of events, his desires, were. She wasn't the only one who had wondered why Reynard would augment her powers. Those who could augment were naturalists, and thus, a threat as Mae had pointed out, being an augmenter herself.

"Rumour has it that there is a group of rebels gathering in the south. They have a leader, a cousin of Kane's actually, who has gathered a few men from their community and some men and women from neighbouring communities. I guess when the last patrol went through and killed a resisting mother, they decided enough was enough."

"Who is it? I'll write to them," Kane interjected.

"If you think it will help," Hcrib continued. "Apparently, the patrol has also been working against Anika... letting people know that we have a Naidisbo and that being associated with Anika would mean certain death."

"There have also been rumours from the north, that Edyta is losing control and her soldiers are becoming dissatisfied, some even leaving their compound," said Val.

"Where are they going?" asked Edric.

"We don't know, but to leave the order would mean certain death if they were caught, so we have to assume they are gathering elsewhere in secret," Val answered, looking around the room before continuing. "I know we haven't had time to rest, but there is a level of urgency here we need to attend to. We have an opportunity, an opportunity to show that Anika is on our side and could be of help to these rebels in the south. And we need to investigate what's happening in the north. I propose that we split into two groups."

"And leave Santouri defenceless?" Roth interjected.

"No, you'll remain here, as will Flo," Val answered, receiving a satisfied smile from Roth as Flo nodded in agreement.

"Anika goes south, to show the people she is on our side. Kane, you'll be necessary as well... your cousin is more likely to talk to you than anyone else." She looked around the room, deciding in the moment whom to send. Anika watched her eyes settle on Jake for a moment before looking back to Anika. "Hcrib, Brennan, and Hawk will join you. Jake, Rae, Edric, and Mae will join me as we journey north to investigate."

Rae raised a hand. "Wouldn't it make sense for Jake and me to journey south? We've just been and..."

Val held up a hand to halt her. "No, I've decided, and we can't have any distractions. We leave tomorrow."

"Val, we just got back..." Jake said as he stood.

"We don't have time to waste." She shook her head. "It isn't up for discussion."

Kane scowled, arms crossed and fists clenching as they left.

* * *

Anika picked her still dirty clothes off the end of her bed, folding them and placing them back in her backpack with a heavy sigh. She pulled the blanket off her bed and began to roll it, turning to the knock at her door. Flo stood, as regal as ever, and for a moment, Anika thought that she looked like a queen. Her ebony hair framed her face, which Anika sadly saw was full of confusion.

"What?" she asked, concerned.

"Do the others know?"

"Know what?"

"That Reynard kissed you, that you've struggled with what you feel for him. That..." she paused, breathing deeply and closing her eyes for a moment, "that part of you questions which side you are on."

"Did you look into my mind?" Her heart thundered.

"I did." She hesitated but rushed on before Anika could interrupt. "I know I shouldn't have, but you've practically been broadcasting it to the world. I couldn't not see it."

"It wasn't your place to look, Flo!" She threw the blanket she was holding down and sat on the end of the bed, exhausted.

"Reynard kissed you?" Jake stepped into the doorway, looking from Flo to Anika. His ebony skin flushed. She could see the heat rising on his cheeks as he pushed past Flo and walked to her, stopping just out of reach as though there were an invisible wall between them. Anika saw Flo mouth 'sorry' as she slipped away. Anika hoped she could hear her cursing her in her mind as she fled.

"Why didn't you say anything?" he asked.

"Because it didn't mean anything."

"Right, the classic line that everyone says."

"Jake..." She paused, unsure of where she was going or what she wanted to say. "I only didn't tell you because there was no point! I couldn't very well stop him. I needed him to think I wasn't working against him. Do you think I could have just slipped away in the night if I'd denied him?"

"That's not the point, and you know it." His hands curled up and down into fists. She sat back on her bed and patted beside her for him to join her. Taking his hands in her own, she sighed.

"I won't pretend that I'm not confused. Since you rescued me, my entire life has turned upside down, but I do know what side I'm on in all of this. And I know what I felt when you kissed me..."

He stopped her abruptly, a hand raised to her lips, and she thought for a moment that he would kiss her as he cradled her cheek in his hand, but he stared at her instead, his face giving away nothing. Finally, he swallowed and leaned in, his lips softly caressing hers. She leaned into him, but neither of them pushed the moment further. Instead, they broke away from each other, bodies separated in tense silence.

"Something's different now," he whispered, eyes downcast.

She thought for a moment that he would kiss her again, but instead he stood, still avoiding her eyes as he fumbled for his words. For a moment, she felt like she could see the future, where he decided that it was too difficult to be with her, where she didn't want him, that she wanted power. She saw what he must be seeing: her, standing with Reynard, crown on her head, controlling the people with her power, and she knew that he must feel smaller than he'd ever felt before.

So, she stood, and without thinking, she pulled him to her, her hands clasped behind his head as she brought his mouth down to hers with as much passion as she could muster. He remained frozen, but as she pulled him back toward her bed, he didn't pull away. As though he just came alive, he pushed her back, her legs wrapping around his waist as he crushed her lips with his own, their breathing becoming ragged, their hearts thundering in her head. She gasped as he pulled away from her lips, his own moving over her jaw and down her neck. She struggled to control herself as she pushed her hips against him, a hand running down his tight muscled back.

His hands possessively worked their way up her body, a hand finding her covered breast. She moaned as his thumb caressed her nipple through her shirt.

"Ahem," someone said loudly.

They broke apart, both slightly out of breath. Anika blushed as she realized that the door had remained open the entire time. Edric and Mae stood there, Edric grinning and Mae looking like a nun who'd walked in on an unholy scene.

"Doors exist for a reason, and supper's ready," she spat.

"Yeah, looks like you've worked up an appetite," Edric said as they left, grunting as Mae elbowed him in the stomach.

"Edric apparently regained his humour while we were gone." Anika grinned at Jake, the tension slipping back in as the others left.

"Apparently," he smiled back, and for a moment, it felt like everything was okay between them. Anika reached for his hand.

"You'll be safe?" she asked.

"Promise you'll be safe?" he retorted.

"I do. Come on... let's go eat. I'd hate to see what Edric would think if we didn't come to supper."

"I'm tempted to let him think whatever he wants." He pulled her in as they stood, softly kissing her forehead. With his hand warm and heavy against her back, she pulled him to the door, and they went to join the others. Every part of her wanted to shut that door and keep going, but she wanted to be with her people before they left. *Her people*, she reminded herself, and she smiled.

17

The Wings

They journeyed south at an impossibly fast rate. Brennan and Kane, who had fallen into their roles as the leaders of the group, moved alarmingly, and exhaustingly faster than she had thought possible. The first night, when they had finally been permitted to stop, Anika had needed an hour to catch her breath as she bathed in the stream, washing off the sweat and dirt that she'd accumulated during the walk.

As she had lain in the stream, enjoying the sound of crickets chirping and the crisp air goose-pimpled her exposed flesh, she had thought of Jake and their goodbye. There was little doubt that everyone knew what had been happening between them; Val especially had seemed perturbed when they had separated ways, ensuring that Jake and Anika hadn't had a moment alone. Edric had merely smirked as Jake nodded to her, a mumbled "Be safe, okay?" given before he had turned away.

The night before had left something unfinished between them. She longed to have a few moments to talk to him, the longing growing worse the farther south they journeyed, knowing that he journeyed in the opposite direction. With no way of knowing how he was, a small knot of anxiety had formed in her stomach and refused to move, keeping him in the back of her mind always.

When she returned to camp, she found Hawk, Kane, and Brennan chatting excitedly. Hawk was holding one of her arrows in the air. Anika was surprised to see that the girl was smiling as she twirled the arrow through her fingers with ease.

"What's going on?" she asked.

Hawk's smile faded, but Anika was pleased to see that it wasn't entirely gone as Kane answered with excitement, "Brennan's come up with an ingenious plan!"

Brennan chuckled, running a hand through his shaggy blonde hair. "Hawk's a good shot." She nodded in appreciation. "But an arrow doesn't always finish the job, so I poisoned them!"

"How?" Anika looked at the arrow, still spinning in Hawk's hands.

"Pretty simple really. When she hits someone with these arrows, the wood splinters out and the poison leaks from inside the arrow into the person, so even if she shoots someone in the leg, they'll be dead in..." he paused, thinking, "sixty seconds!"

Anika nodded, still not quite used to Brennan's attitude. It seemed a gruesome and terrible way to die, but she also was impressed by his ingenuity. Hawk cocked an arrow in her bow and landed it into the rabbit they had laid out for supper. True to their word, when she pulled it from its body, there were three obvious points where the wood had separated, and a purple liquid was oozing out of the animal's flesh.

Brennan cheered, but Kane groaned. "Why'd you do that, Hawk? That was supper!" She shrugged her shoulders as she threw the arrow into the dead fire pit.

"Fine, go find us something else to eat, but for Alvar's sake, please don't shoot it with your poison arrow!" he exclaimed.

Brennan, suddenly overcome with out-of-place laughter, lay down on the ground and held a hand to his chest as Hawk smirked and made her way into the trees. Anika, slightly perplexed by the entire situation, made a decision in that moment and followed Hawk.

"Hey, wait up!"

Hawk turned, wincing as her curly hair caught in a branch. She pulled it free and turned away from Anika. "Hey, can you wait?" she asked again.

"What do you want?" She continued walking, not looking back at Anika.

"Can I come with you?"

"I guess, but don't scare anything off." Anika breathed a sigh of relief. Not a complete no was impressive coming from Hawk.

They walked in silence, Anika unsure of what she was hoping to achieve with Hawk, who had never exactly welcomed her with open arms to their group. Hawk held a hand up, and Anika stopped, carefully remaining quiet as Hawk silently plucked an arrow from her sheath and pulled it back. Anika searched the bushes but saw nothing, not even a movement, and then, as she was becoming convinced that Hawk had, in fact, seen nothing, a rabbit jumped out from behind the bush. It had hardly moved before Hawk's arrow speared it through the torso, already dead as it hit the ground.

"That should do for tonight," she mumbled, more to herself than Anika.

"That was amazing!" Anika declared. "I didn't even realize there was a rabbit near us."

Hawk scoffed. "Well, that's no surprise."

"Excuse me?" Anika asked Hawk's back as she pulled the arrow from the rabbit, wiping the blood from the arrow on to her pants. Hawk turned to her, an eyebrow raised.

"It's no surprise," she repeated.

"Why?"

She picked the rabbit up and silently bent over it for a moment before returning to their conversation. Anika wondered if she had been praying, leaving her feeling a bit more generous toward Hawk before it disappeared. "Well... you came from the church. You have no idea what it's like to be out here with us."

"Hawk, I've been here for months now," retorted Anika.

"Months may as well be days, and anyway, it doesn't matter, Anika. It isn't about how long you're with someone. Someone could be with us for a day or two, and they would be more in line with us than you are." Hawk stepped by her as they headed back in the direction of their camp.

"Why do you say that? The others don't seem to feel that way."

"Because they are more trustworthy. But you, Anika... you're a Naidisbo..."

Anika interrupted her. "I've tried time and time again to make you trust me; I don't know what I have to do!" She stopped. "You know what, Hawk? Maybe you just don't trust anyone!"

Hawk turned, and Anika nearly ran into her. "Yeah," she answered, "I don't trust anyone."

"Oh," Anika mumbled in response, not having really expected to get a response at all.

"Going south, through Moises, it makes me want to puke my guts up, Anika." She sat abruptly on the ground, and Anika joined her. "Val knows what going south does to me, and she made me go without her."

"Well, we're all here," Anika said weakly.

"Val rescued me when the order slaughtered my entire family. She's the only reason I'm alive." Hawk stared ahead, Anika getting the sense that she was looking through her.

"I'm sorry," she started.

"Don't. Val pulled me away from the house as I was about to go inside. I had to listen to their screaming the entire time, but she knew it was too late for them. I knew it was too, but I'll never forgive myself for running."

"I..."

"I should have died with them. My little sister, she was better at everything. She was better with a bow, she was kinder, she should have been the one to live, but instead I lived, and I didn't deserve to." Hawk stood up and held a hand out for Anika to do the same. "So, no, I don't trust people. Because even though Val saved me that day, she also showed me the truth, that you can't trust anyone or anything in this world. If there were anything to trust in, my family would be alive."

"Hawk, can I ask you something?"

"What?" She flipped her matted curls over her shoulder and readjusted her bow.

"You're so angry, but you don't want to kill."

"That's not a question," she answered.

"No, but you know what I'm asking."

"I don't think that killing is the answer. To revenge death with death won't solve anything. But I'll do what I have to do for Val. I have to believe I'm alive for some reason."

"I think that's what we all have to believe," Anika answered. Hawk merely nodded as they started walking again. Anika felt as if she knew a little more about her comrade and a little more about why she acted the way she did.

* * *

Anika hadn't been at Santouri long enough to really see Kane and Brennan's friendship, but she quickly realized that the two men were more than just friends; at some point in time they had become family. They spent the majority of the time joking with each other, an easy banter flowing from them to the rest of the group. Hawk even joined in on their fun occasionally. At one point, when the two men had started duelling with fire-lighted sticks, she had snapped her fingers, extinguishing the clearing of any light, a power that Anika hadn't been aware existed.

Unfortunately, the two had only cheered at the added challenge and began to clash their burning sticks together with more vigour. With a disgruntled sigh, Hawk again snapped her fingers, and they all stumbled as the camp lit up as though struck by lightning, causing Brennan to fall down, cursing as he rolled away from the still burning stick.

Hawk had grinned, and Anika had nearly died from the shock.

On their fourth day, Brennan held up a hand and beckoned Kane forward, where they whispered together before turning, motioning for their small group to huddle together.

"We're here," Kane said. "If Ezra is the leader, then he will let me talk to him. I think it would make the most sense for just me and Anika to go in."

"No, they're on our side. We all go," Hcrib interjected.

"If we all go in and something goes wrong, then we're all dead," Hawk replied, staring at the dilapidated barn. "I'll stay here and be the eyes."

Kane nodded, throwing his pack on the ground, the others following suit. A quick wave, and Anika was following Kane, Brennan, and Hcrib as they made their way to the building. A young man, chest puffed out, clearly trying to make himself seem larger and not succeeding, stopped them as they made their way to the door.

"Business?" he asked gruffly.

Kane nodded. "We're here to talk to Ezra. I'm his cousin Kane."

Anika noticed the man's heart rate escalate briefly. "Ezra is no longer with us. Janna leads us now." He looked at each of them, studying them for a moment before pushing the door open. Kane, puzzled, led the way.

Inside was as dark and dilapidated as the rest of the space. To Anika's surprise they seemed to have walked into a brothel. Anika tore her eyes away from the nakedness, feeling her face flush as she saw a woman blatantly pleasing a man on the couch. She moaned as her head bobbed up and down, the man pushing his hips higher as he met Anika's eyes. She turned away, blushing.

"Suppose we could have warned you," Brennan chuckled.

"You think?" she asked.

"Yeah, that's why I said it." He laughed again, Anika rolling her eyes, used to his literal sense of humour.

"Hear you're looking for Janna?" A girl approached them. Anika breathed a sigh of relief, noting that she was at least clothed, although scantily so; she wore a thin strip of material over her breasts and a skirt, her long brown limbs and a thin exposed waist noticeable.

Anika didn't register who answered her, but they were soon led into a separate room where a group of young men and women sat in heated discussion. As they entered, the room fell into a hushed and tense silence.

"Ah, so it's true." A young woman at the centre of the group stepped forward. Her long dark hair hung unwashed and uncombed around spindly shoulders. Anika thought she could have been pretty if she took care of herself and bothered to smile, but as it was, she looked downright unapproachable.

"Where's Ezra?" asked Kane, ignoring her.

"Dead," she replied without missing a beat. "Killed when the last patrol came through. I'm Janna. I lead this group now."

Kane stood frozen and silent. Brennan laid a hand on his arm and continued for him. "We're here to discuss your activities. We come from Santouri."

"I know who you all are." She cut him off with a wave of her hand. "Sit. I want to know more about you, especially her." She shot Anika a look.

It was clear from the discussion that they were on the same side, but it was also apparent to Anika that they were very satisfied running as an independent group; she felt in her gut that they were unlikely to convince them to join. She was sitting, lost in thought, when she realized that the group had gone completely silent and were looking at her in expectation.

"Ugh, sorry?"

"You're the Naidisbo, correct?" asked Janna.

"I am," she answered hesitantly.

"I've heard rumours about you." She crossed her legs, her gaze intense, unsettling.

"Oh," Anika responded weakly.

"The Naidisbo, working in the church with our enemies and never making a move to change anything until all of a sudden, she becomes a self-proclaimed rebel and joins our side." She scrutinized her, her hands idly tapping the arms of her chair. "Funny, all that time there, the perfect opportunity to end our people's suffering, and you never took it. It makes me wonder..."

Anika clenched her jaw and tried to prevent her face from contorting in rage, anger at this woman blossoming as she accused her. "You don't know me or my situation..." she started.

"No, I suppose I don't," Janna interrupted with a slight smile. "But if I were your comrades, I'd certainly be wondering how sincere you are, and I'd wonder if perhaps you were a spy. Reynard's lover perhaps? There seems to be many gaps in your story. I think it would be necessary to fill those in before letting you get too close to us."

"Janna," the young man to her left spoke up. Anika glanced at him. Pock-faced and young, he looked and sounded timid. She waved a hand and cut him off.

"We won't be going with you. If she isn't willing to give us some answers, then I don't think I can risk my people working with you."

"There's nothing to tell you. There is no story here." Anika willed her voice to be less aggressive as she responded.

"So, you've said, but it proves nothing." Janna nodded to Kane, Brennan, and Hcrib before her gaze fell on Anika again. "Good evening. Safe travels back, Naidisbo."

Dismissed, Kane and Brennan mumbled their thanks while Anika followed Hcrib as they left, dejected and questioning.

Hawk stood as they approached, her anticipation difficult for even her to disguise as she swayed from foot to foot. "Well, what did they say?" she asked.

"They said they couldn't join us," Hcrib answered.

"Why in Alvar's name not?"

"Because of me," Anika answered as she brushed past them all, leading the group as they started their journey north, each disappointed, each filled with questions of what and where to go next as the sun set on the horizon, casting them all in the darkness that reflected their spirits.

* * *

"We haven't seen a patrol in the last two days. Let's just stop and eat somewhere. There's no wildlife, and I'm starving!" complained Hawk as they were walking past a small town. Hcrib rolled his eyes and looked to Kane, who finally shrugged his shoulders.

"Fine," he sighed, "but Anika, put your hair up and wear your hood. We don't need you to be recognized."

She did as told and followed the others as they entered the tavern. It was dark inside, and Anika had to squint as she adjusted from the brightness outside. People were happily mingling, laughter and conversation ringing through the room. The bartender gave them a stern nod toward the table in the back corner that was still empty, and they filed in, Anika remaining in the corner with her hood up, nodding in thanks as the waitress pushed a mug of beer in her direction.

It had been a long time since she had had beer, the sweet liquid a welcome reprieve from the heat outside that had descended on them midday.

"There's rabbit stew today or mystery loaf," said the waitress, impatiently tapping her fingers against her crossed arms.

"Mystery loaf?" asked Hcrib.

"Yeah, could be goat, cow, horse, could be all of them. Just depends on what the chef has back there," she answered, smacking on whatever she was chewing in her mouth.

"I think it's safe to say we will be taking five stews," laughed Hcrib.

The young woman threw them an uncaring nod and walked away, as Hawk's brows disappeared beneath her hairline in disbelief.

"I don't know. Mystery loaf didn't sound half bad." Brennan chuckled as Hawk groaned.

"What are we going to tell Val, you guys?" Anika put her head in her hands and shook it.

"The truth," answered Brennan, clapping a hand on her shoulder.

"Great." She leaned back and sighed. "Another reason not to trust me."

"You didn't do anything this time, and for all we know, Reynard has been spreading lies about you. It would make sense, make people not trust us."

"People like Val," she retorted.

"Hey," Hawk interjected, "Val knows the difference. She will trust you if there is reason to trust you."

"Do you think there is reason to trust me?"

"What I think doesn't matter." Hawk nodded with thanks as the woman returned with their stews. As she delivered the last bowl to Hcrib, the front door burst open, light flooding in only to be promptly cut off as a man ran to the bar.

Breathless, the young man said to the barkeep, "Pa, they just came back with the news. Jane is on her way home. She and Drake are safe, but the streets are flooding with people, and the guards are literally cutting down the crowds in Hagio!"

"But they are safe?" the man answered, his hands stilled on the grimy glass he'd been cleaning.

They stopped listening, Hcrib turning to look at them all, the corner of his mouth lifting in eagerness.

"Unrest in Hagio, it seems," murmured Kane as he looked to each of them. Anika could see the eagerness in his eyes as he smiled. "Perhaps it would be worth investigating?"

"We don't even know why or how true it is." Hawk shook her head in disagreement.

"Exactly. If Val hears that we knew there was trouble and we didn't find out what it was about, when we were passing right by, we would be doing a disservice." Brennan slurped his stew loudly.

"Hawk's right. If people are fleeing the city, then we shouldn't get too close. Plus, Anika is a very wanted person. This could be a trap," Hcrib spoke up.

"Or it could be that finally the people have had enough with Reynard and Edyta and are doing something about it." Kane looked at Brennan, who smiled broadly. "We have to at least go find out what's happening. We'll keep Anika out of sight and hunker down at the apartment."

"No, too risky," interrupted Hawk.

"Let's vote," Anika finally spoke up, her heart thundering. The group nodded in agreement, Kane and Brennan raising their hands to head to Hagio, Hawk and Hcrib voting to bypass and get back to Santouri.

Kane looked at her, glee dancing in his eyes. Brennan too looked more excited than a boy receiving birthday presents. She swallowed, unsure how or why she was making the decision that she was, but she mumbled, "We go."

Kane and Brennan high fived across the table as Hawk and Hcrib looked at each other, both displeased, but neither spoke up.

* * *

Getting to the apartment in Hagio had been no easy task. As the young man had said in the tavern, the streets were flooded with people when they arrived. Rather than waiting for the sun to go down and sneaking in, they had walked in, in broad daylight, staying on side streets and dodging out of sight of soldiers.

But it hadn't been like they had expected it to be. Instead of people angry and full of energy, the crowds of people seemed subdued, as though they were waiting for something. Anika couldn't help but shiver at the atmosphere. It seemed like everyone was defeated, as though they had lost hope as they waited for some monumental announcement that the five of them were unaware of.

Anika ducked under a lowered tavern sign as they slipped down the alleyway of the apartment. She followed Kane, having only been there on the night of her first escape from the church months ago. She watched in surprise as he pulled his knife from his pocket, looked to ensure they were alone, shimmied out a brick from the wall, flipped it over, and popped out a key.

He opened the door, gesturing for each of them to go inside. Anika silently cursing Jake for making her climb that wretched ladder all those nights ago. She ducked under a hanging curtain as they made their way up the stairs. The entryway smelled stale, evidence that no fresh air had touched the space since they had last been here. Kane squeezed by them, unlocking the second door and pushing it open to reveal the apartment.

The last time she had been here, Anika hadn't been able to fully appreciate the apartment. Although it was sparsely decorated, it was at least cozy. Pillows and blankets were scattered over the furniture, a mishmash of décor that leant to the homey atmosphere. Hawk went to a window, pushing the blinds to the side as she peered through the crack into the street. Hawk's face was all hard lines and usually bore a frown, but the beams of the sunlight made her appear youthful and soft. For a moment Anika thought she looked like the carefree girl she should have been, until she frowned at whatever she saw. Hcrib threw his bag on an armchair and lay on the couch, groaning as Brennan went to the fridge, grunting in dissatisfaction that it was empty.

"Well, did you really think there'd be anything edible in there?" asked Kane.

"A man can dream," he answered, shrugging.

"Anything out there that you can see?" she asked Hawk.

Hawk nodded and turned to face them, letting the curtain fall back in to place and darkness settle over the room again. "Yeah, it looks like they are going to be making an announcement soon. The doctor and a priest are setting the stage. We could see better from the roof, though."

Anika looked at the plush green armchair across from Hcrib in longing but, with a sigh, nodded in agreement and followed as Kane climbed the ladder and held open the door for them to follow. The air outside was crisp and fresh and the sun shone with excruciating brightness on the roof.

Hawk hadn't been exaggerating about the centre square. The execution platform was surrounded by people, all silent and waiting in expectation as the doctor and a priest whom Anika vaguely recognized sat in silence.

A soft murmur ran through the crowd as they shifted their attention toward the church. Anika could just make out the outline of Reynard, his shoulders broad and straight as he made his way to the stage, surrounded by soldiers.

A young man accompanied him, someone that Anika didn't recognize. He was only slightly shorter than Reynard, but his features couldn't have been more different. For Reynard's dark hair, the young man was blonde and fair, the pockmarks on his face visible from a distance, a sore sight compared to Reynard's smooth features.

The young man sat in the chair by the doctor, a place normally reserved for Edyta. Anika noticed that his hands gripped the arms tightly as he sat waiting. Finally, Reynard looked to the crowd and smiled. "My darling people of Hagio, your attention tonight is greatly appreciated, as I come to you in both mourning and celebration." Anika looked at the others, noting their similar looks of confusion.

Reynard bowed his head. "It is with great sorrow that I announce Edyta's passing." Gasps waved through the crowd, Reynard nodding along with the people. "Rebels ended her life in the north. Just another example of their evil seeping into our world, making it unsafe for us."

Anika looked at the others in disbelief. "What is he talking about?"

"I have no idea." Kane remained transfixed on Reynard. "Val wouldn't have done anything to Edyta without talking it over with us as a group first."

"Unless the opportunity was too sweet to pass up," said Brennan.

"Sadly, Edyta left this world before her goal of a peaceful continent could be achieved." Reynard held a hand to his brow, taking a moment of apparent grief before he continued. "But Edyta would have wanted us to continue striving for peace, striving to ensure the rebels don't ruin the progress we have made toward unity as a continent! Tonight, we will celebrate Edyta's life and the addition of this young man joining us."

He walked to the young man and pulled him to his feet, an arm wrapped around him. "I present to you Grayson."

Reynard continued talking as he moved both himself and Grayson to the centre stage, but Anika's attention was pulled to Kane who, staying low behind their barrier, was whispering urgently to Hawk.

"What are you arguing about?" she asked.

Hawk and Kane looked at her, Hawk scowling as she angrily whispered, "He wants me to assassinate them."

Anika paused, looking again at Reynard and Grayson, who continued to address the crowd. Kane was right. From this vantage point, Hawk had a clear shot and could likely get both Reynard and Grayson if she were quick enough.

"You can get them both before the soldiers even know what's happened!" urged Kane, echoing Anika's thoughts. "Please, Hawk. Val would want you to end this war right now if she were here."

"You don't know that!" exclaimed Hawk. She pulled an arrow, cocking it into the bow, peering over the ledge at the still speaking Reynard, whose lingering embrace on Grayson seemed cold and artificial. Hawk's head was bowed, and Anika noticed her hands trembling as she moved to them. Staying beneath the ledge, she placed a hand on Hawk's arm and gently pushed the bow down. Hawk looked at her, tears in her eyes.

"Hawk, you don't have to do this," she whispered. Her heart was beating wildly as she said the words, unsure what had come over her. But she knew it didn't feel right, forcing Hawk into assassinating Reynard and Grayson, Grayson, who hadn't done anything wrong, and Hawk who looked as though she were ready to collapse.

"What are you talking about, Anika?" Kane pulled her hand off Hawk in anger. "We can't waste this opportunity!"

"We have to." Anika scrambled to organize her thoughts, to determine a reason that Hawk shouldn't assassinate Reynard. "If we kill them now, we will all die. The city is swarming with soldiers. And even if we kill Reynard and Grayson, do you really think that doctor isn't waiting to take control? We will have forfeited our lives, and Val and the others will have to continue the war against a new leader."

"Or Reynard and Grayson die, and, in the chaos, we escape! Hawk, please take the shot!"

Brennan and Kane both started encouraging her while Anika remained silent, watching Hawk, who just stared at Reynard and Grayson in silence, not listening to the two men reasoning behind her. Anika wasn't one to pray, but she silently prayed that Hawk would make the decision that wouldn't leave her emotionally destroyed. Finally, Hawk shook her head. Putting the arrow back, she went to the door and looked back at them all, her eyes remaining glued to Anika. "I can't do it. It isn't honourable to kill a man this way."

"There's nothing honourable in war, Hawk. You're being ridiculous!" declared Kane, moving toward her, but she simply shook her head and climbed down the ladder, shutting the door behind her. Hcrib, who had remained silent during the argument, stepped forward and placed a hand on Kane's arm, telling him to let her go. From above, they heard the door slam shut beneath them. Anika, peering over the edge, watched as Hawk's bushy hair disappeared beneath her hood, and she melted into the crowd.

18

Shifting Power

"Where's Hawk?" Val put her feet up on the coffee table and crossed her arms indignantly. Hcrib and Anika exchanged a knowing glance as Kane began telling Val what happened.

Finishing the story of Hawk leaving them two days ago, he asked, "How did you know we were here?"

She sighed. "We didn't. We came for the same reason you did, to get information."

"You'd have wanted her to take the shot, wouldn't you, Val?" asked Brennan from the chair.

She looked at him, her silence stretching on, Brennan seemingly oblivious to it as he leaned forward in hopeful expectation. "It doesn't matter. What's done is done."

Anika was puzzled. Val never minded providing her opinion, and for her to dismiss the question, something she would no doubt feel strongly about, was not like her.

"So, what did Reynard announce?" Jake asked from the kitchen island where he'd leaned silently since they arrived. His eyes had dark circles underneath them and Anika wondered how much sleep he'd had since she'd seen him.

Willing him to meet her gaze, she answered, "That Edyta died in the north, killed by rebels." Val scoffed. "That Grayson was replacing her, that's all."

"That's not all," Hcrib interjected as Val and Jake both started to speak, cutting them off. "He announced that with his fire, Grayson's water, and the Naidisbo, they would finally be able to achieve peace and safety from the naturalists."

"What!?" exclaimed Anika.

"While you lot were busy bullying Hawk, I was listening." He glared at them all.

"Alright, well, this makes the decision pretty easy actually. We need to get more information on what happened to Edyta. I think it goes without saying that we didn't kill her, and we also need to get Anika out of here before she's spotted by anyone in the order." Val looked at each of them: Anika following her gaze as she studied Jake, still leaning in the kitchen; Edric and Mae sprawled in front of the fire lazily; Kane and Rae, reunited and wrapped around one another on the sofa; and Hcrib in the chair, arms crossed in frustration with them. "Anika, you'll have to stay here, out of sight. We will use the next forty-eight hours to gather as much intel as we can. Hcrib, I know it's a lot to ask, but I'll need you out there the entire time. The rest can take shifts to watch your back."

Hcrib nodded. "I assumed as much. I'm going to have a nap now then."

Her stomach dropped. The small space, overcrowded with people, even if they were her friends, was suffocating. Anika couldn't imagine spending the next 48 hours inside, unable to escape.

"There's something else you should know, something we discovered on our way into Hagio." Val was speaking directly to her. Jake attempted to cut her off before Val held up a hand silencing him. "Your father was imprisoned and then honourably released from the order."

"Honourably released?" she asked numbly.

"Yes." Val nodded morosely. "Given who you are, I think he should have been killed. The only reason I can see him being released is to either draw you in to be captured again, or he's given information about you to Reynard in exchange for his life."

"There's no information to give," she mumbled.

"I agree. This means more than ever that you need to stay here, stay hidden.

If you wander, if you try to find him, the order will be watching."

"We don't know it's a trap," she said, but the words were weak and unconvincing even to her ears.

"Nonetheless, you stay put." Val sighed heavily and stood. "I'm going up to the roof to get some air and to get away from all of you."

"Pleasant," scoffed Jake after her, earning him a flipped finger in response.

That night, as the fire hissed and snapped in the hearth, Anika lay awake, under her thin blanket on the floor, and was consumed by a wish to be outside. She knew that part of it was because she shouldn't leave the apartment, but the other part of her longed for fresh air and freedom. She looked over at Jake, lying nearer the front door, knife clasped in his hands, and wished that she could speak with him privately, to hear about his journey north, to tell him about their journey south.

If she were being honest, she just wanted to talk to him, and yet it had seemed like he was keeping his distance since he got back. She wasn't sure if it was because of the others or because of her, but either way, it left her feeling insecure and uneasy.

She sighed, hyper-aware of the number of people around her, the sounds of their bodies echoing in her head, louder and louder as sleep evaded her. She went back to her tried and true trick of counting the imperfections in the old stone ceiling above her but even that failed her. Her eyes landed on Jake, and she found him staring back at her. With a nod of his head, they both stood and tiptoed quietly to the stairwell outside of the apartment.

The space was cramped but at least private; he stood a few steps below her as she entered behind him. "Hey."

"Hey," he answered. "How are you?"

"I'm okay," she responded, then shook her head as she tried to rid herself of the discomfort in the air. "This feels awkward! It shouldn't feel awkward. Why does it?"

"I missed you." He ignored her, reaching up and taking her hand in his. In that touch, she felt the awkwardness melt away.

"I missed you too," she breathed, her hand clasping his. "I want to know everything that happened while you were north. Oh! And have you heard anything from Roth or Flo? I'm dying to know how Santouri is."

"Roth managed to get us a letter on the way here. Roth and Flo are fine. The children are fine," he added, seeing that she was about to ask, "but I want to know about you, about what happened when you went south."

She started to tell him, but he cut her off. "Wait, let's walk. We won't run into Hcrib and Mae," he again anticipated her objection, "and I could use the fresh air."

"But Val was clear. I'm supposed to stay put."

"She won't know if we are gone for..." he silently calculated, "thirty minutes, at most!"

She nodded, uneasy, following him down the stairs and into the alleyway where he looked both ways before stepping into the street and waving her to follow. The night was quiet. Most residents were inside, as there was an imposed curfew by the order. At each corner, they looked both ways before ducking into the shadows of the next alley, enjoying the silence and the moonlight as they walked, basking in one another's presence. His hand grazing hers ever so softly as they walked.

Jake nodded to two discarded barrels; she took a seat on one as he claimed the opposite and they fell into hushed conversation. She listened with rapt attention as he described their journey north. Similar to their own south, they had had very limited success. They were unable to discover anything worth the journey, and Edyta and the soldiers were scarcely seen.

"In fact, it seemed as though things were almost peaceful in the north. It was strange, but people were content. It wasn't like here at all."

"Where was Edyta then?" she asked, hesitantly.

"We never found out, but I assume Reynard is behind her disappearance.... death," he corrected. "Where do you think Hawk went?"

She sighed deeply. "I don't know. Honestly, I wasn't telling her not to take the shot for any reason other than I thought it would be stupid exposing ourselves like that... but she was upset, and I don't blame her. We tried to force her hand."

He nodded, looking down the alley where they heard a shuffle of feet. Jake jumped to his own, followed closely by Anika. They sank behind the barrels and into the shadows. Silence followed for a moment as they both sat, holding their breath. Jake, the moment that he began to move into the light, sank back as a figure appeared at the end of the alley. The person, hunched over and hooded, walked with a limp, as though they were elderly or injured. She pushed Jake's arm down as he unsheathed his knife from his belt.

"Please, put down your weapons." The shape held up a hand, not as weathered or old as Anika would have expected.

They both froze where they stood, confused and dampening down the urge to run from whomever approached them.

"Anika, you really don't recognize my voice?" the hooded man whispered.

She gasped, the sudden realization hitting her like a punch to the stomach as she jumped from behind the barrels and into the light. Jake, even, unable to hold her back. "Dad, what are you doing? Why are you hunched over like that!"

"I need to stay out of sight, and I needed to make sure they didn't follow me. Anika, you have to get out of Hagio." He embraced her, standing straight as he tucked her hair behind her ear and gazed at her affectionately.

"Dad." She held his shoulders, looking at him in shock. "How did you know where to find us?"

"There's no time to explain, Anika. They are trying to trap you. Reynard, he wants to use you to end the naturalists. I'm safe for now, but you need to get away before they catch you. You and your friends." He nodded to Jake, who stood still, dagger in hand. "You need to leave now. Reynard's men, they killed Edyta because she wasn't falling in line with his vision."

"Dad, I'm sorry you risked leaving to tell us this, but we already knew. We are leaving soon."

"There's more." He stepped away from her and let his hood fall back. Anika contained her gasp at how much he had aged since she had last seen him. "There are things I never knew about your mother, things I didn't want to know in case they could ever be used against me. You need to go to the northlands and find Dorothea. She can tell you the story of your mother. She can tell you more than I'll ever know."

She stepped forward and clasped his hand in hers, shaking her head in confusion. "Dad, I need you to explain everything to me. Come with us!"

"Anika," Jake hissed.

"There's no reason he can't!" she cried.

Her father patted her hand tenderly. "I'm afraid I wasn't a great father to you when we were in the church, Anika, but if I go with you, they will notice, and they will be searching for you all within the hour. I'll stay here. It's the safest option."

"It's not safe for you!"

"No, but I wouldn't be able to live with myself if I didn't give you a chance. You need to find Dorothea. She can help you. Please, go tonight!" he urged. He placed a hand on her cheek, a soft caress, his hand colder than Anika liked, and turned, the limp gone as he fled to the end of the alley. With a last glance of longing towards her he turned, disappearing from their sight.

"Anika, we have to get back. We have to tell Val." Jake took her hand, which had fallen to her side numbly. She nodded, letting him lead her through the alleys, lost in thought, wondering what on earth someone could possibly tell her about her mother that would change the tides of her future — and cursing herself for not even thinking to check if her father had needed healing.

* * *

"You left." Val shook her head. "After I explicitly asked you, only you, Anika, not to leave the apartment."

"I understand that, but what my father said is so much more important than that, Val." She fought the urge to swing her hands in the air as she spoke.

"I made her leave." Jake put a hand against her arm gently and turned to Val. Anika caught Mae rolling her eyes at them as she pretended to be disinterested. "It was my fault."

"How heroic of you," drawled Val. "Anika's a big girl. Maybe I should be more concerned about her easy level of influence than anything else."

She yelled at Edric, who was in the fridge, rattling dishware, telling him to bring her a drink. "Something strong," she said, to which he grunted in reply.

"Val, whatever this woman knows could help us. My father wouldn't send me on a fool's errand. He may not have been the most transparent man, but he wasn't dishonest either."

"No?" she asked. "He didn't keep your identity hidden, working in the church that entire time? Anyway, it doesn't matter. The reality is that this is a trap, Anika."

"It isn't!" She raised her voice slightly, earning a stern look from Mae, who continued to pretend to be absorbed in the flames of the fireplace. "You weren't there. He was scared."

"He was, Val," Jake interrupted again.

"Do you really think the soldiers would let your father out of their sight? This is part of their plan, Anika. Send you north, away from the rest of us, and pick you up there again, but this time you won't just walk out of their camp."

"I have to agree," Rae, quiet as always, piped up from behind them where she was levitating a bowl in the air, carefully using the wind to keep the contents inside delicately balanced, preventing them from tumbling to the ground. "It's too convenient, Anika. It separates you from us all."

"He never said I had to go alone!" she stressed.

"It doesn't matter. Either you go alone and get kidnapped, or you go with a group, and we're ambushed," Kane said, walking up behind Rae and wrapping an arm around her shoulder lazily. He knocked her off balance. She cursed as some of the contents of the bowl spilled.

"Well then, send me, Jake, and Thor," she countered, looking back to Val, who pursed her lips in frustration. "Edric can tell us what we need to know about the northlands, and then we will meet you back in Santouri when we've found and talked to Dorothea."

"Absolutely not!" Val shook her head, looking away from Anika and fixing her eyes on Jake. "This is not happening. I hope my second would at least have the sense to see that this is a bad plan."

"I think we need to go — if not for us," he held up a hand to stop Val, who had been about to speak, "then for Anika. You've said repeatedly that you don't think she knows what side she is on. You've said that we don't know if we can trust her. Well, maybe it has something to do with the fact that she doesn't know anything about her past. Maybe if we get her some answers, then she will know for sure where she belongs in this war, Val."

"Idiot." She shook her head and looked away. "I'll have no part in condoning this. If you go, Jake, you'll no longer be my second."

He nodded his head sombrely, saying calmly and surely, "You say that, but you can't afford to lose me and Hawk, Val."

"Alvar, you're an asshole, Jake." She stood and grabbed her coat and bag, throwing them on. "I'm going out. Do as you please, but don't expect any support from Santouri if you end up in trouble." She paused, looking at Jake. "I'm disappointed in you. You're picking her over the cause."

"I'm doing this for both her and the cause," he countered. Val shook her head as she slammed the door behind her, disappearing into the stairwell.

Nobody spoke, but Mae huffed her displeasure and Edric sighed, grabbing Val's untouched drink from Brennan who'd happily picked it up after her departure. "Well, come on, then." He tipped the drink back and winced. "Let's talk about the northlands. Not sure I can tell you anything you don't already know, but at least we can stop sitting around in silence."

19

Truths

They left at first light, sneaking away like thieves in the night. Val remained absent, not having shown up after storming off the night before. The others said goodbye with mixed emotions in the air. Hcrib had stopped in from his intel gathering to give Anika and Jake quick hugs before ducking out again with Edric, who had longingly looked north as he wished them well. Mae had scowled and questioned them to make sure they were entirely sure about their decision to go. Brennan had nodded in polite disregard of events, while Kane had made amends with Anika due to a swift kick from Rae when he'd muttered that he had been right asking Hawk to take the shot. He'd then told them to behave and winked at them both, getting another elbow from Rae, who kissed them both and sent them on their way.

They had moved quickly, staying in the shadows and avoiding the rising sun as they left Hagio. Hoods up and heads down, they worked their way north as fast as they could, both quickly out of breath in the harsh elevation. Thor had even once given her a gentle nudge behind her knees when she stopped, gasping for air. She was sure his soft purr and the affectionate rub of his head against her was the only thing that kept her moving.

They moved to fast to have idle chit chat. They both knew the urgency that was needed to get away from Hagio and into the mountains where they could safely hide.

The elevation was growing harsher, and the sky rumbled with the threat of impending rain as Jake stopped. Anika grunted as she walked straight into his back, nearly knocking herself backwards as he laughed and caught her arm, holding her steady.

"I think it's safe to rest here." He moved into a small alcove within the hillside, groaning as he sat, and stretched his legs in front of him. Anika followed suit. Thor padded over and lay down between them. She laughed as the cat blew air from his nose, and she wondered if he was groaning in solidarity with them.

"What are you thinking?" She looked at Jake, who was watching her and Thor. She couldn't read his expression in the darkness.

"I was thinking that somehow you still look beautiful after spending all day walking and sweating." He looked shocked at his own words and shrugged his shoulders as though it could take away what he had said.

"Thanks," she replied quietly, "that never hurts to hear."

"Hey, can I ask you something?" he followed up.

"Of course." She stretched her legs out and lay down, gazing at him as he shuffled his feet back and forth in the dirt in front of him.

"What do you remember about your mom?"

"Not a lot." She looked away.

"Is that why it's so important for you to go talk to this woman?"

She nodded slowly before answering, collecting her thoughts and memories. "I remember she had long black hair, I think the same colour as mine, but she always wore it twisted up at the bottom of her neck because it would get in the way when she was working..." She paused, reflecting on the image in her mind. "She smelled like rosemary and lavender."

"You smell like rosemary and lavender," he pointed out.

"I know. She used to rub it into my temples at night to help me sleep. I still do it. It reminds me of her, and it works." She rolled on to her side and smiled at him. "She was so warm. I used to crawl into bed between her and Dad, and even though Dad was snoring, she would hum and run her fingers through my hair until I fell asleep."

"She sounds lovely," he sighed. "How did she die?"

"We lived in Langford when she was alive. She and Dad fished for a living, and one day, she drowned. Dad came home and told me we were moving to Hagio so he could get a job."

"He couldn't keep fishing?"

"Not alone, and he couldn't afford to hire someone to help..." She pictured their home, thatched roof, and wooden siding. It had been warm and cozy with a fire burning in the hearth all the time to keep the winter chill out. "He changed after that."

"How so?"

"The day my mother died, he died with her. I think if I hadn't been at home waiting, he would have thrown himself into the ocean to drown too. I think he resented me for keeping him alive."

"But now he's trying to help you," Jake countered.

"Yes, I suppose he is." She lay silently lost in thought. "But shouldn't he have tried to help me years ago?"

"How?"

"He told me to contain my powers, to make sure no one knew or noticed that I was different. In a lot of ways, he repressed who I am. He robbed me of my identity and made me hide under the nose of the church."

"Maybe that's how he was protecting you."

"I don't know if he was protecting me or himself. I wouldn't say it in front of Val, but I don't know if my father's intentions are good, Jake. She could be right. It could all be a trap."

"Or you could be wrong, and we could find something out that changes the entire tide of this war." He stood up, dusting the dirt off his pants and held out a hand to her. "Come on," he said, pulling her to her feet, "we can make it a bit farther before we stop for the night."

"Slave driver," she muttered as she stood. He didn't let go of her hand until Thor's tail swatted them both, and they separated, keen to keep going, tempted to stay where they were.

As they walked north, the landscape changed. While there were few trees on the outskirts of Hagio, the land became more and more desolate as they walked. There was less foliage, and the terrain had become drier and colder.

The first night, they had slept comfortably. The second she had felt the chill deep in her bones when she woke. On their third day, finding cover was nearly impossible, and the air was becoming so crisp that she could see her breath in the air, like tiny plumes of smoke as they walked.

By the end of the third day, they stopped, both exhausted. "Do you think it's safe enough to start a fire?" she asked, pulling her blanket tightly around her shoulders.

Jake was rubbing his hands together, blowing his breath on them as he nodded. "I think we have to risk it."

She sighed in relief. Looking around them, they couldn't see anything for miles. The ground, barren, stretched on in every direction. "Do you think it's much farther?"

He nodded. "We'll get there tomorrow night if we keep up this pace. Thor, if you can, can you please find us something to eat?"

Thor huffed but conceded, stretching his long black paws in front of him, his hindquarter in the air before sauntering off, and in a few moments, he was running, becoming a smaller and smaller black blur in the distance.

"Grab the matches for me, would you?" Jake asked as he pulled a few small branches from his pack. He took them from her and tried to light them, but the cold wind put out the flame as soon as it appeared. Finally, cursing, he pulled a book from his bag and opened its cover, staring down at it but not reading the words on the pages.

"What?" Anika asked.

"I need kindling, but it feels wrong to tear up books." He sighed and closed his eyes, pulling a few pages from the book and bunching them up to place under the sticks. The flame caught for a moment before it fizzled away again, leaving the charred pages swaying sadly in the cold wind.

"Let's try to get some sleep." Anika pulled her blanket tighter and lay her head on the ground, her teeth beginning to chatter as the cold seeped into her head. She let her powers push away the headache that was already consuming her as she tried to focus on what little warmth she had.

"Anika, come over here." She looked up to see Jake leaning on one elbow with his hand placed on the ground in front of him, and she nodded. It felt like they were about to cross a line, a boundary that once broken couldn't be replaced and so she hesitated before she lay down in front of him. He again lifted his blanket for her and beckoned her in. She laid down, quickly forgetting her reservations as she was embraced by his warmth curled behind her.

His hand settled on her hip and stilled, frozen as they danced this unmoving tango of their relationship. She wondered if he felt as hyper-aware of the situation as she did. She wondered if he too, could feel every place that their bodies connected, like a fire burned where they touched. He lay still, not speaking, but she could feel his heart racing in his chest as she rolled to face him, close enough she could feel his breath on her lips.

"Thank you," she said. "Thank you for coming with me."

His hand tightened on her hip. "You're welcome."

"Jake?"

"Mhm," he slowly started moving his hand up and down her side in long gentle strokes.

"This feels right." She closed that last inch between them and pushed her mouth to his, hesitant but wanting. Her hands drifted up to find his face as she pulled a leg over his hip.

And then his hands were pulling her up and over so that she straddled him, their blankets falling away, their skin oblivious to the cold as they let their hands roam and their mouths explore one another, as the last three days of temptation finally exploded between them.

She groaned as his hand found her breast through her shirt. Suddenly desperate to feel his skin against hers, she pushed it down and under her clothes. Jake moaned as he found her breast, her nipple taunt between his fingers as he lightly pulled at it, earning a gasp from Anika as she placed a hand over his, stilling him.

"What's wrong?" he asked, looking up at her.

"Nothing, but I'm afraid if we keep going, we won't stop."

"I don't want to stop." He used his other hand, low on her back to grind his hips to hers as she moaned.

"I don't either," she whispered as the cold air bit against her flaming skin.

He pulled her down, their mouths meeting with more intensity as he rolled her over to lie between her legs, pulling the blankets around them both as he kissed her neck, teeth scraping. Her hips rose to meet his as he pushed her farther into the ground. She could feel how hard he was, how ready he was for this to happen.

His hands fumbled with her pants, pulling at the buttons and laces as he moved to lie beside her again. They stilled for a moment as she pulled back to look in his eyes, taking in the smirk on his lips as he gently began to move his hand. Forgetting her thoughts, her desire to feel him as well, she let her body take over as her hips rocked. Everything around them faded into oblivion as she moaned, her head falling back as his thumb circled outside of her, pushing with the perfect amount of pressure to bring her to the edge.

"Come for me," he whispered in her ear, his teeth nipping her earlobe as she gasped, her body arching and shaking as waves of pleasure flowed through her and she tipped over the edge.

"Let me return the favour," she panted as the world came back into focus, her hand pulling at his waistband. She wanted to be closer, to have more of him inside of her. She wanted to make him feel as utterly shattered as she did, but his hand found hers, and he pulled it instead to his lips.

"You have no idea how much I want that, but Thor is waiting to come back. I don't think he's overly enthused by us right now."

She flushed with embarrassment. Cold and forgotten, Thor huffed in annoyance as he ambled up to them, lying on the other side of the failed fire.

"Let's sleep," he whispered. She nodded in agreement, turning over to face Thor, who was glaring at them with his yellow eyes. She mouthed that she was sorry, quickly succumbing to warmth of Jake behind her, their supper forgotten.

* * *

"This is Greyfork?" she asked Jake and Thor as they looked down at the so-called capital of the north. She'd expected more.

"Yup," Jake answered.

"It's so... barren," she answered. The landscape had changed during their last day of walking. What was once a rocky desert had quickly become icy tundra, the sparse vegetation frosted and limp. She had thought her breath was cold before, but now when she breathed, it turned to fog, and crystals of ice had formed on her eyebrows and eyelashes.

She held her hands over her eyes, protected by thin leather gloves. She waited for the frost on her lashes to melt before looking down on the village again. Smoke plumes curled from the chimneys of most of the homes, the windows boarded with wood.

"Windows let the cold in. They board them up this time of year," Jake said, answering her unspoken question.

"They must be miserable," she muttered, rubbing her arms and pulling the blanket she now wore around her shoulders tighter.

"Edric says they are content. It's all most of them have ever known, and when they venture south, they find the heat unbearable."

"I can't imagine it."

"Come on. Let's go find Dorothea." He started down the hill, Thor padding along beside them until Jake turned and regretfully told him to wait, fearing he'd scare the villagers. Thor grumbled but turned away as Anika looked at Jake wildly.

"Oh, but he'll be so cold!" she exclaimed.

"He has fur! And look," he pointed to a barren tree in the distance, thick twisting trunks matched the grey and white of the landscape, "I guarantee when we come out, he'll be sitting in that tree watching us and likely enjoying any reactions he gets from the villagers who notice him."

The largest building, with a door that was continuously flung open with people wandering to and from seemed to be the most logical place to go to, so they did. Jake pushed the door open, Anika following closely behind.

She hesitated as she followed. There were so many people milling around, layers of fur covering most of them. The skin that was showing was a delicate white and nearly glowing in the darkness of the tavern they'd entered.

Jake nodded to a few people as he approached the bar. Anika couldn't help but notice how much of an outsider he appeared here, with his ebony skin, compared to their blue-tinged complexion. Apparently, Jake didn't notice, or he chose not to acknowledge the stares as he sat at the bar, asking for something to warm their bones from the barkeep.

The man nodded, looking at them both suspiciously, but poured two steaming mugs for them, nonetheless. Anika sipped. It was tart with a nip of alcohol, strong but pleasurable, warming her bones almost immediately. Jake complimented the barkeep, who gave him a side smile, still not fully engaging him in conversation as they sat, waiting for an opening to converse. Finally, the barkeep had moved on to others, in the packed bar, flitting past them occasionally, glancing at their mugs to see if they needed refilling. As he passed by again, Jake raised a hand, and the man stopped.

He was pale, the same as all the others here, but Anika was captivated by his eyes; they were the lightest blue she had ever seen, and when his gaze fixed on her, she was reminded strongly of Edric. His eyes were the only ones that she had ever seen that came anywhere near to this man.

"Are you related to Edric Repinuj?" she blurted out before shooting a panicked look at Jake. They hadn't discussed acknowledging their association with Edric. She had said the words before even thinking that there could be dire consequences for themselves or Edric's family if their conversation was heard by the wrong people.

"I'm his cousin, luckily enough for you." He raised a hairless brow. "Has the bastard killed a priest yet? I suppose not since he hasn't come home," he answered before giving them the time to respond.

"Would you give us directions?" Jake asked, ignoring the scoff from Edric's cousin.

"Where are you going?"

"We need to find a woman named Dorothea," he finished.

"Dorothea," he paused, tapping long fingers on the bar in front of them. "Don't know why you'd want anything to do with that old witch. She's cursed, ya know."

"We need to see her," Anika pleaded.

"You'll have to keep heading north. She isn't far from here, but she is outta the village. I don't know that she takes kindly to strangers, especially southerners showing up on her doorstep."

Apparently, that was the end of the conversation as he moved on to serve another patron. Jake threw a few coins down on the bar as they left, receiving a few glances from those milling about. Anika wondered what they must have thought of her and Jake, opposite of them in every possible way.

* * *

It was exactly as Edric's cousin had described: the small cabin, somewhat run-down, paint peeling from the walls, roof slanted slightly, was dreary. Anika, stared down upon it from the small hill they stood on and almost felt sad for the woman she'd yet to meet, thinking of the isolation and unhappiness that must come with living in such a place.

Their knock on the door, with its peeling white and grey paint, was followed by silence. She shrugged her shoulder to Jake in a silent question. He nodded at the curling smoke from the chimney. Someone was home. Finally, she raised her hand and knocked again; they both winced hearing the disgruntled groan that came from inside.

The woman who opened the door had certainly seen kinder years. Her skin, weathered, looked sickly with her unnatural complexion. She took them in, her grey eyes contemplating them.

"Could we speak with you, Dorothea?" she asked, smiling kindly.

"You look like your mother," she answered, the door still open only a crack as she eyed them. She made no gesture to open the door wider or welcome them in, but Anika could feel the heat billowing out of the crack, and she resisted the urge to push the woman aside for just a touch of warmth.

"You know who I am?" she asked.

"Yes." She pulled back the door and beckoned them inside. "Not sure who the man is, but I doubt you'll mean me harm."

"We won't. We just have some questions." Anika pushed past Jake in her haste. Dorothea, a rather short and thick woman, pushed her silver hair behind her ears and motioned to the couch. The inside of her home was as shabby as the outside. Odds and ends were strewn about with no obvious purpose. The central focus of the room, the fire, roared with concerningly high flames, which Anika ignored as she sat, hands and feet outstretched as she welcomed the heat and ignored the fact that she was quite certain that the house may catch fire before they left.

"My father sent me," she started, before Dorothea held up a hand silencing her.

"Your father was always a dimwitted man. I heard he joined the order." She shook her head and sat on the other end of the couch, leaving Jake standing awkwardly behind them.

"Sit," she ordered, and he moved to the chair beside them, his discomfort evident as he remained on the perch, ready to bounce into action should he have to. But Anika felt oddly comfortable with the woman, who evidently knew who she was and had known her mother. She suspected that her short temperament was off-putting to Jake, but she found the woman radiated a maternal way about her, a warmth in the room that wasn't only from the fire. It made her long for some semblance of normalcy again, her mother, Margaret, anyone who would have embraced her.

Dorothea studied Jake, an eyebrow raised in her assessment before turning back to Anika. "So, I assume that you are here to find out about your mother?"

Dorothea didn't wait for a response before she continued. "I've been alive for over a hundred years. I lived through the last rebellion, and I don't know that I've ever met someone as conflicted as your mother was. You may not like what I have to say about the woman, but you're here, so I'll tell you it all. The last war nearly destroyed us, the naturalists. In fact, when the Naidisbos were taken down, we stepped back, recognizing defeat." She paused, taking a drink of water. She hadn't bothered to offer them anything. "I only heard of your mother years after the rebellion ended. She was with your father at the time. You were born already."

"How did you find out about her?" Anika asked.

"That's not the question to ask. It's not important. I suppose you don't know how your mother's family died?" she asked.

Anika shook her head. Dorothea nodded sadly as she continued, "Your grandparents were leading the last rebellion. They were magnificent leaders, confident and ruthless. That's what I liked best about them. Your mother was the middle daughter of three girls. Your grandfather made no bones about it. He wanted a boy, but your mother continued to give birth to girls. At least your mother looked Naidisbo, with her jet-black hair and bright eyes, whereas her sisters were lighter...the order slaughtered them all. It was nasty business."

"How did my mother escape?" she asked, breathless and at the edge of her seat. Some deep part of her ached for the family she'd never known but she pushed the thought away as Dorothea continued.

"They didn't realize she had escaped for a very long time. No... your parents' best friends were their neighbours. They had a young girl as well, older than your mother and best friends with your aunt. She was at the house that day, and your mother was at their house when it happened. The order never even realized. They counted three dead girls and assumed it had been right."

She stood, the audible cracking of old bones filling the room as she slowly walked to the kitchen and set the kettle on. "Either of you want tea?"

They both said no as she nodded. "Your mother found them. I never heard her version of the events, but I heard what others said. They'd left your grandfather and grandmother until the end, made them watch as they'd slit the throats of the children before they finally ended it. Apparently, your grandfather fought hard."

"I don't understand," Anika interrupted as Dorothea poured her tea. "They were Naidisbo. Why didn't they use their powers?"

"Ah, the question no one knows the answer to." She sat back down and sipped from the steaming cup. "They say it nearly drove your mother mad with wondering. Finding them all and wondering why they hadn't just stopped the hearts of the men that killed them. They said she vowed revenge right then and there, as a child."

"Did she ever find out?" asked Jake.

Dorothea shook her head. "No, she was raised by the friend's family, adopted in the place of their murdered daughter, and always resented for it.

209

They stopped talking about her powers, taught her to keep them subdued. If it hadn't been for their friendship with your grandparents, I think they'd have cast her to the streets. They risked losing their son and themselves if the order had found out. Your mother changed her name and moved on with her life."

"But she continued to fight for the naturalists, didn't she? She vowed revenge," Jake answered.

"She did, but she never got it. Instead, you came along, she settled down with your father, and she changed."

"How do you mean?"

"You'll know of Silas, correct?"

The name sounded familiar but she couldn't place where or when she'd heard it before, so she shook her head. She sat further back in her seat, willing herself to stay silent and listen, but she felt sick from all they'd learned in the minutes since they'd stepped inside.

"Alvar, they don't teach anything of history anymore, do they?" Her shaking head reminded Anika of Margaret — the lecture feeling oddly similar. "Silas, Edyta's brother, I'll assume you know who she is, yes? Alright, well, Silas was head of that family at one time. Silas and your mother grew close. There were rumours that your mother was siding with the order, but just as many rumours said she was infiltrating them through Silas, gathering intel, and waiting to get her revenge."

"Which was it?" Anika felt cold again, nausea threatening to overtake her. Her mother had had the same wavering conflict that she did.

"We never found out, and she never said. Silas was killed by the naturalists during the last stand of the rebellion. Your mother left with the rebels, presumably on their side, given that they didn't kill her as well. And then she had you."

The room felt as if it were closing in on her. She could still hear the crackling of the fire, but she suddenly felt very far away, dread washing over her as tears threatened to overtake her eyes.

"Anika's father sent us here," Jake started before Anika held up a hand, cutting him off.

"Say it clearly," she whispered.

"Your birth father was Silas, water wielder. Your father raised you with your mother, yes, but your blood carries more than just the Naidisbo legacy."

She sat, quiet, the words repeating in her ears, her face flooded with heat. Jake, behind her, ran his hands over his head again and again, no doubt thinking of all the questions, consequences, and possibilities this could bring. She heard him curse but couldn't bring herself to look at him, fearful of what his eyes would betray, of what he must surely think of her now.

"I need a minute," she gasped as she stood and walked to the door, leaving her thin blanket behind. She hardly felt the sting of the cold air as she stepped outside, instead it felt like a welcome wave washing over her as her mind raced. She stumbled forwards, not thinking of anything, and yet completely unable to slow the thoughts that threatened to completely overwhelm her.

She focused on her breathing as she looked across the landscape, stark and white. She began to count in her mind, willing more oxygen to her lungs, slowing the near hyperventilation as her mind and body settled and she began thinking of what this could mean. Could her mother have turned to the order in the end, or was she truly trying to gather intel for the naturalists? She knew what she wanted to believe — that her mother had fought for equal rights for all people — but part of her was uncertain. She cut off the doubt; her mother would have wanted revenge for her family, and she had been a healer. She wouldn't have become pregnant with a child and been unaware. It would have been purposeful. She squeezed her eyes tightly, pushing back tears. Had she wanted the pregnancy? Had she been forced into the situation with no way to get out? Again, she dismissed the thought. Her mother could have aborted the baby, her, with her powers if she hadn't wanted her.

And what did this mean for her future? She held the blood of both sides, the order and the naturalists. She corrected herself. She wasn't a naturalist. They had sided together in the past only because they shared the same moral values — as Reynard had said, her power was different... pure. She stood between the two tides of war, unsure of what side she was meant to join, or which side was right, if either. She wondered for a moment if this was how her mother had felt, the gut-wrenching twisting of indecision, of the inability to think clearly or decisively.

If she had been on the side of the order, why abandon the revenge that she had sought for years, and if she had been a naturalist, why become pregnant with the enemy's child?

Why put her child in this position?

She heard the creak of the door behind her but didn't turn, still lost in thought as the familiar footsteps stopped behind her, the silence heavy in the air. Finally, he said, "Are you alright?"

She rubbed her arms, the chill not entirely from the weather as she answered, "No." She relayed her thoughts and concerns, turning to watch his face as she did. She waited for the inevitable reassurance that most people would give, but he stayed silent, solemn.

"Before you make more decisions, before you get lost in the possibilities, let's get the rest of the story. Then you can freak out." He reached a hand out and laid it on her arm, gentle and comforting.

She placed a hand over it, nodding as she pushed past him, ready to face the rest of Dorothea's story.

20

Stanton

The cells were ungodly hot, which shouldn't have surprised Carter. He was sure that Reynard enjoyed the thought of cooking his prisoners alive with his power. The sweat clung to him, occasionally dripping from his nose to the concrete ground. He'd stopped caring long ago, days, or weeks, when he realized that he'd just keep sweating. At least they left him a pail of water every day. He wouldn't die of dehydration, yet.

He rolled over to his other side. His cell, no more than six by six, didn't leave much in the way of comforts: no bed, no pillow, just a pail of water, and a pail for his shit and piss. He reminded himself he was alive, before wondering if this was even a life worth living anymore. He'd thought about killing himself for the last two days but didn't want to give them the satisfaction of his death — and he also wondered if anyone would even notice. Would it be worth it?

He tried to keep track of time, but there were no windows. Since he had gotten here, he'd determined the guards came twice a day, he assumed morning and night to swap the pails and scrunch their noses in disgust at his sorry state. Still, he'd lost track of how often that happened, and so time meant nothing.

The other cells around him were empty. He thought there would be more political prisoners in the church, but it was just him, unless they held the other prisoners elsewhere. He'd known that when he refused the soldiers, he'd been making a political statement, even though his wife had begged him not to. At first, he'd thought that it didn't matter. Nothing had happened, until the Lider came in the next night and demanded a pint — he'd asked if he planned on paying, and the Lider had smiled cockily. Alvar, Carter hated when they acted like the entitled pricks that they were.

That had been when he'd decided enough was enough. He knew his wife had thought he'd gone mad — and maybe he had — but he'd said no. Said no to a Lider and all the soldiers there, told them that they were arrogant, conceited, found every foul word he could and threw it in their face. His wife had stood away from him in the bar, a hand held over her mouth as she quietly sobbed.

He hadn't fought when they'd dragged him out of his pub. He hadn't even been rational enough to tell his wife he was sorry or tell her to tell the kids he loved them. Part of him knew he'd snapped. He'd left his wife without anyone to run the pub, and she was just a woman — the locals would take advantage of her sex eventually. He cursed himself as he rolled over; the time to reflect, the sweating, had cleared his head.

But he'd reflected enough, and still nothing had happened. He didn't expect to be brought to Reynard himself, but he anticipated he'd be hung in the square like all the other political prisoners, maybe used as an example. He didn't know what they were waiting for. He closed his eyes and begged sleep to find him.

When he woke, it was just as hot, just as unbearable. He groaned as he rolled back to the other side, facing the stairs. He sat up. The door at the top of the stairs opened, and light flooded in. For a moment, he was blinded as he held a hand up, squinting, hoping that they weren't just going to empty the pail. He needed a change. He'd even prefer execution at this point.

Two soldiers slowly walked down the stairs. They'd left the door open, and the light washed over a large figure they carried between them. The soldier coming down the stairs first cursed as he tried to hold his balance. The person's head cracked against the wall — Carter hoped they were unconscious. The soldier holding the person's feet grimaced. He looked younger than the lower soldier and scared. As the younger soldier dropped the person's feet, they hit the ground with a heavy thud, no resistance. He fumbled with the keys as he unlocked the cell beside Carter, and the older soldier dragged the body in by their shoulders.

He was about to call out, ask for something, when he was silenced by the state of the man whose hood had fallen back. No, Carter didn't need a change that badly, especially if he would end up looking like that poor soul beside him. The soldiers locked the cell, and without even a glance toward Carter, they walked up the stairs, shutting the door behind them.

It took a few minutes for Carter's sight to adjust to the light as he sat up, sliding to the bars and peering through them at the man. Dark hair but pale skin, he looked near death. The man's eyes were blackened, the nose bent at an unnatural angle, and dried blood soaked the front of him. Carter winced, a little more grateful for his own circumstances.

"Pst, you okay?" he said. What a stupid question, he thought. Obviously, the man wasn't okay. The man didn't move, but Carter could see him breathing, and for now, that was all the distraction that he needed.

* * *

Eventually, the man woke up. Groaning and stretching, he'd gasped in pain as his hands had flown to his nose, scraping the dried blood off his face and spitting on the floor. He'd looked around wildly, taking in his surroundings, eyes washing over Carter as they flew to the stairs, hope dying as he saw the closed door.

Slowly, the eyes travelled back to Carter. He nodded to the pails behind the man saying, "Should be water in one of them. Don't drink it all at once. They don't fill it often."

The man turned, leaning over the bucket and drinking greedily. The slurping, which made Carter think of his dog, continued for longer than he'd have recommended, but he didn't say anything. Finally, the man sat back, wiping his face and covering his eyes. Carter saw his chest heave.

"What did you do?" he asked.

The man looked at him from behind his hands and shook his head. Curling up in a ball, with his back to Carter, he didn't answer.

215

The guards didn't stay away as long this time. The door opened again, and Carter looked up in anticipation.

"More water?" he asked as the two men stepped on to the ground in front of him.

The soldiers ignored him as they unlocked his new roommate's cell. The man was backed into a corner, shaking his head back and forth, mumbling to himself as much as them, "I don't know, don't know, don't know."

"Let's go." One of the soldiers pulled him to his feet, keeping a hand tight around his arm as the other locked up and followed them up the stairs, the man's head hanging the entire time.

Carter wondered why he didn't fight.

It wasn't long before they brought him back. This time the man was shaking uncontrollably as they locked him in the cell. Carter didn't bother to ask; he didn't think the man would answer anyway. He took his hood down, and Carter grimaced, the burn — a perfect handprint ran over his cheek, his ear. Black fingers burned into the man's scalp as he rocked back and forth, cradling his own head in his hands.

Carter couldn't help himself. "The water, man. It will help."

The man didn't respond, but he must have heard as he crawled forward, whimpering now, and dunked his head into the pail. Carter thought he heard the wound hiss. Yeah, he was definitely going crazy.

When the man finally pulled his head out of the pail, he turned to Carter, shrugging off the robe and spreading it out on to the ground, lying carefully on the unburned side. He stared at Carter for a moment before finally, he said, "Thank you."

"No problem. Reynard do that?" he asked.

The man nodded; Carter couldn't help but notice the tears in his eyes as he gingerly touched the burn on his face.

"Fuck, looks sore."

"It is."

"What did you do?"

"Nothing."

"Must of did something. Reynard doesn't personally see to the prisoners."

"It's what I didn't do." The man sat up, grimacing. "What's your name?"

"Carter."

"What did you do?" the man asked.

"Wouldn't serve some of his soldiers at my pub." He raised a shoulder, shrugging the act off. "Who are you?"

"Stanton."

"So, what didn't you do, Stanton?" Carter moved closer to the bars to hear him better.

"Guess there's no shame in saying it. Everyone knows." He paused, but Carter didn't say anything to change the man's mind. He needed some form of entertainment in this godforsaken place. "My daughter is a Naidisbo. I hid her here, in plain sight for years. They just found out."

Carter thought he might stop breathing. "The Naidisbo are dead." Matter of fact.

"Nope." Stanton shook his head and sighed.

"They wouldn't have left you alive." Again, Carter was matter of fact. Clearly, Stanton was crazier than he was if he thought his daughter was Naidisbo.

"They need to find her, and they think I know where she went." He moved to push the hair out of his face, wincing as he felt the burn again.

"But you don't? Or she's your kid, so you just won't say?" Carter found himself inching closer to his cage. The man was more intriguing than he could have hoped for. For a minute, he forgot how sweltering it was.

"I don't know. I really don't know..." He paused, thinking. "They say she left with rebels. I didn't even know that she knew rebels."

Stanton lay back down and closed his eyes. Carter was surprised by how quickly the man fell asleep. He must have been in an incredible amount of pain, and even more exhausted.

They took him again the next time, right after they'd emptied his piss and shit pail and filled the water pail. Each time they switched them, he thanked them for not switching the pails around. One nasty guard had done that. His drinking water had tasted like shit for ages.

This time Stanton had pleaded to stay in his cell. The soldier had slapped him on his burn. The shrieking had reverberated in Carter's ears for a long time after Stanton left. He never knew how long Stanton had gone. It could have been minutes or hours; he had no concept of time. Each time he came back a little worse for wear. Sometimes he wouldn't have any new visible injuries, but he'd be clutching an arm, a leg, and he'd started moaning in his sleep.

But when he was awake, he told Carter about his daughter, Anika, the Naidisbo. Carter had started to tell him about his kids, a boy and a girl, four and six, respectively. He hadn't expected to begin feeling sane while he was in the cells. It was the opposite of what he'd expected, but he missed his wife; he missed his kids. Talking about them with Stanton made him remember a time where he wasn't deluded by thoughts of soldiers.

The fourth time they took Stanton, he had begged Carter to do something. He'd said he couldn't bear to be tortured again. Carter had just sat. He couldn't do anything. He was just as powerless as Stanton, even less so since he was still in his cell.

Stanton had apologized when he'd come back, had said he was desperate. He knew Carter couldn't do anything about it. He'd told Carter he wished he were dead, taking it back quickly when he thought of his daughter, and holding on to the hope that he'd see her again — that she'd live.

"Why do you think they're keeping you alive?" Carter asked. It had been some time since they'd taken Stanton. He wondered if they were giving him a break or trying to increase the psychological torture of wondering when the next visit would be.

"I think they want to use me; I think if they find her, then they think she'll turn herself in for me."

"Do you think she would?"

"I hope she wouldn't." He shook his head. Carter had never seen a man so defeated. "I hoped she'd never have to use her power."

"A Naidisbo could change everything, Stanton." Carter reached a hand through the cell and found Stanton's, squeezing it reassuringly — their first moment of contact, a friendly gesture from one prisoner to another. Stanton stared at the hand for a moment and pulled away.

"Anika," he corrected Carter. "Anika could change everything."

"Anika," Carter agreed.

The next time they took Stanton, Carter had found himself standing, hands clasped on his cell bars, found words on the tip of his tongue, but he couldn't bring himself to say anything. It didn't matter. Stanton shook his head, a silent warning for Carter to keep quiet.

This time they'd broken his face; Carter was sure of it. One of Stanton's eyes was closed over. Blood trickled from his eye socket as he wiped fresh blood on to his robe.

"Alvar, the pressure's terrible." Stanton held his hands against his temples. Carter couldn't see all the colours of the bruises, but he suspected he had the whole spectrum. Stanton was a tougher man than he was.

The next time the soldiers came, they didn't open either men's cells. The soldier stood at the base of the stairs and watched, watched and listened. They curbed their conversation, but they still spoke to one another, the silence unbearable, the loneliness more than either could take. When the other soldier joined them, keys jingling as he opened Stanton's cell, Carter couldn't help himself as he stood again, this time saying, "Please."

He didn't even know what he'd have begged for; he didn't want to switch places with Stanton, didn't have anything to bargain with them. It didn't matter anyway — the soldier sneered at Carter as he led Stanton up the stairs.

He hated when Stanton was gone — the silence was unbearable. But this time when they brought him back, he just rolled over. He didn't talk to Carter, didn't tell him how they'd tortured him. Instead, Stanton had quietly sobbed until he'd fallen asleep, and even when he woke, his breathing was hitched with pain. He'd kept his back to Carter.

The soldiers came within hours. Carter couldn't say for sure, but it hadn't been long. He sat at the bars, wishing he could reach Stanton to give him a reassuring handshake, anything to make him feel better.

Stanton stood and followed them. He didn't look Carter's way. He didn't fight. He just slowly hobbled up the stairs, his limp worse than when he'd first arrived, head hung low and defeated.

Carter's first clue was when they didn't shut the door behind them.

Apprehension filled him when the shadow of the soldier flooded the doorway again. He scooted to the back of his cell as the soldier walked calmly down the stairs again, keys jingling as he unlocked Carter's cell.

"Come on," the soldier ordered, holding the cell open.

He didn't move.

"Come on," the soldier repeated, shaking the door in agitation.

Carter slid up the back wall of his cell nervously. Finally, the soldier cursed and strode in, grabbing him by the arm and pulling him out. He pushed him ahead and into the stairs where Carter painfully fell forward, his shins screeching in agony at contact with the concrete. He willed himself to be quiet, reminding himself of the torture that Stanton had been subjected to since he'd been imprisoned.

He summoned his courage and stood tall, walking up the stairs toward the light with as much pride as he could muster. He stepped into the light to be greeted by another soldier, one of the young ones. He squinted. Being so long in the darkness made him sensitive to the lights above ground. They didn't walk far before the young soldier opened a door and gestured Carter inside.

He'd heard about the lavish ballroom of the church before, but it was even more spectacular than he'd ever imagined. He looked around in awe: large marble posts connected to the ceiling, golden décor strung between them, glinting spectacularly.

He lost his breath and every ounce of courage he had when he saw Reynard sitting in his throne at the front of the room. The man radiated power, a flame dancing in the palm of his hand as he lazily looked Carter over. Carter's heart thundered in his chest. *Everyone must have been able to hear it.* Each step closer, he was consumed with more fear, until finally he saw the steps in front of him, and the soldier pushed him to his knees in front of Reynard where he remained, head bowed in respect.

"Carter, is it?" Reynard drawled.

Carter dared to look up. Fear boiled in his belly as he took in all of Reynard, the red coat, the same colour of blood, the darkness of his hair, which seemed to ripple off him like darkness, darkness and fire combined. Carter willed himself to nod, not daring to speak.

"I've decided your fate, Carter," Reynard continued. "Your crimes are punishable by death."

Numbness flooded him.

"But I'm not an unfair man." Carter looked up in hope. A smile played at Reynard's lips. "I will give you a chance to win your life back."

Those were the words he'd longed to hear, the hope he'd been silently building with Stanton in those cells, the longing to see his children again. To see the smile on his daughter's face, or feel his son jump into his arms — Stanton had given him hope, had pulled him out of his insanity, to remember he had a reason to live. But now, his hope was tainted. He didn't miss how sinister the words were out of Reynard's mouth.

"Stanton!" Reynard shouted. He looked to his left, Carter following his gaze as his friend limped out of the doorway, his head still down.

"Stanton," Carter echoed, confused. Still, Stanton didn't raise his gaze. He clenched his hands in his robe as he walked forward, stopping at the end of Reynard's podium, waiting for Reynard to address him.

"Stand, Carter, and fight for your life."

"What?" He looked at Reynard in confusion, eyes darting to the soldiers on either side of him and then to Stanton standing at the end of the podium.

Reynard smiled and tossed him a knife. It clattered on the ground in front of him. "Fight for your life, Carter."

He turned just in time to see Stanton pull the blade from his robe as he stepped behind Carter. Pulling his head up and back, he felt Stanton's tears wet his face, saw the sadness in his eyes as he lowered his lips to Carter's forehead and whispered, "I'm sorry."

He drew the blade across Carter's neck quickly, faltering only at the end when he let the blade fall to the ground, the sound faraway as Carter's hands found his throat, desperately trying to hold it together. Watching as his blood spilled forward, as his hands lost feeling, as he fell forward, as slowly, the world began to blur, and the darkness consumed him.

* * *

"You may return to your room, Stanton. You are not permitted to leave the grounds of the church. I'll be in touch."

Stanton nodded and limped toward the servants' barracks. One step closer to freedom and to hell.

21

A Gift and a Curse

"So, people believed her to be a naturalist, even after I was born?" She clutched the teacup in her hand, having finally relented and taken one after standing in the cold, shivering for as long as she had.

"Some doubted, until the end."

"Why then?"

Dorothea ignored her question, anxiety slithering in Anika's belly like a snake, but she kept quiet as the old woman spoke. "Your mother and your father — the one that raised you, that is — they never loved one another, but it was a good arrangement for you. Your father, that man, what is his name again?"

"Stanton."

Dorothea scoffed. "Dreadfully common name in those parts. It's no wonder I forgot it. Anyway, we never knew why he raised you, or if he even knew you weren't his, but he knew your mother had been involved with Silas at the least. When they killed her, because there is no doubt, he joined the order out of necessity."

"They killed my mother?" Jake had inhaled sharply behind her as she said the words.

She nodded. "There was no doubt. They made it look like an accident, of course, and it came at a completely unprovoked time. They had long crushed the rebellion. They drowned your mother while she fished with your father,

223

made it look like an accident, a rope wrapped around her foot while her body bobbed in the water."

"How did they know it was the order, and why would my father join the order after they murdered my mother?" So many questions burned at her lips. Her confusion grew with her frustration as the place they'd sought answers turned into more mysteries.

"What safer place to hide, then, with the enemies who wonder if you know of their dirty deeds?" she retorted.

Anika sat silenced, thinking over the information Dorothea had dumped on her. Aware that while people had speculated her mother's death was a murder, they didn't know for certain. Dorothea had made her mind up, but this only added to her confusion, and she wondered what side her mother had truly been on. She pushed down the questions about her father, why he'd bothered to raise her if she wasn't his blood. She burned to know why Dorothea claimed they hadn't loved one another, but she wanted to hear from him what their story had been, not from a stranger.

"Idabel was a good woman; I have no doubt she acted the way she did for good reason."

Anika's head snapped up. "My mother's name was Marion."

Dorothea shook her head slowly. "No, my dear, your mother's true name was Idabel Naidisbo. Marion Dian was a farce, created when you were born."

Another lie, another uncertainty in her past that she would have to take time to process. The few memories she had with her mother, of her father, affectionately singing her mother's name, what she thought her mother's name had been, Marion, suddenly tainted.

"In our history, they speak of Idabel's death," Jake murmured, "that when the church killed the girls, they saved Idabel for the last, for she had been rumoured to be the most powerful and dangerous Naidisbo the future would ever know. They made her father watch as they cut her apart piece by piece until her skin was ribbons, the throbbing of her blood leaking from her body, the very torture that they say killed her father."

"But that girl was actually a friend... not my mother," whispered Anika, Dorothea nodding at her statement, not really a question.

"Thank you," she said, calmly, more calmly than she truly felt as she stood.

"Sit back down, girl," Dorothea motioned for them both to sit. "I am not just a history book. You have questions, doubts about your mother's intentions, and now of your own. You made the journey; I might as well tell you what I see."

"You have foresight?" Jake asked.

"A gift and a curse, I'm afraid." She pulled her legs beneath her, surprisingly agile for a woman of her apparent age. "You've been told by someone else that you are wavering, that there are two possible sides that you could end up within this war, but there is more that I see. I have toyed with telling you. I don't know that it would help to know. In fact, I think it could destroy you. But his mind tells me that he believes you're pure, that you will make the right choices." She fixed her eyes on Jake. "You have unwavering doubt in her. Perhaps you should try telling her so."

"I..." he started before Dorothea cut him off, undeterred by Jake's interruption.

"IF you survive, because there is the possibility you'll die in this war, then you'll rule."

"I've heard this before. You don't surprise me." Anika dismissed her comment, but the old woman held up a weathered hand and continued.

"The future is forever evolving, changing, based on the events and decisions you make. One decision impacts all the possibilities."

"Then what good is it to know, when it could change at any time?" asked Jake, standing to leave. His entire frame rippled as he paused and Dorothea answered.

"Because knowledge is power. Anika, your mother questioned her role and the necessity of the ongoing rebellion. You will face the same challenge. I can see many paths for you; all are possible. I can see you tapping into the power of water, ruling with Reynard after he kills Grayson, keeping Reynard alive. I see you leading the rebellion, dying among your comrades, hand in hand with your lover," she nodded to Jake, but he remained where he stood, stiff and quiet. "I see you, Anika, I see you bridging the order and the naturalists, shifting the world, the first of a new kind of people, a united people. I see you overwhelmed by decision, hiding the remainder of the days away in solitude, afraid to face your potential."

"How will I ever know which path is right?" she whispered.

"This could all change tomorrow, with one decision. These visions change. Really, this is a curse. There is no certainty, even with foresight."

"You are cursed," Jake interrupted, his behaviour changed, agitated by something the old woman had said. "Anika let's go. You don't need to listen to any more of this." He strode to the door and waited as Anika rose.

She stopped and looked to Dorothea, who sat calmly, eyes focused on the fire in her hearth. "Thank you. Even though it can change, I think I'd rather know. I want to know that I don't turn into a monster in each possible future, Dorothea." She paused, finding her words. "Is there no future where the rebellion wins, the order finally falls?"

Dorothea didn't move her eyes from the flame as she answered, "No, as it stands in this moment, there is no chance of success, but just one decision could change that."

* * *

"Why would Val not share the fact that we can't win this war?" huffed Anika as she slid down a snowy slope. They slowly made their way back to the village, each desperate for some shelter and warmth.

"As Dorothea said, the future is constantly changing. Maybe Val hasn't seen it."

"Do you really believe we can't win?" Anika asked, taking his offered hand as she stepped over an old rotten log.

"I think the visions are useless. It doesn't do us any good to know the possibilities when we can't predict how our decisions will change them anyway."

"But if it gives hope, or a path to work for, it is good," she demanded.

"Or it instills fear, makes you question each step and decision you make in this war, Anika. She made it sound like the only possibility was for you to work with the order and that the rebellion would fail, and you would die with it. What good does that do for us?" He avoided her eyes.

"I suppose foresight exists for a reason," she muttered in reply.

"For battle, to know what moves your foe will make against you." He shook his head. She could feel the anger simmering off him. "Clearly, a gift that is meant to be used for short term advantages. She's abusing it by looking so far ahead."

"That isn't fair. Val uses it to look ahead too."

"Val uses it for battle. At least she has common sense. At least she knows what she wants!" His voice rose and he kicked the snow in front of him, soft plumes drifting through the air.

"How can I not wonder!?" she exclaimed, shouting despite the silence around them as they entered the village again. "You heard what she said about my mother... about my father!"

She stopped, and he turned to her. The smoke from the houses below them rose behind him as he hung his head. He stepped forward and took both of her hands in his own, so cold, but she warmed to his touch.

"I'm sorry. I'm sorry I have this power, a power I can't touch, didn't even know about. I feel... dirty." She trembled as she looked down at their hands, wondering if they'd ever reach a place where they could move past the uncertainty of who she was.

His thumb found her chin and tilted her face up to look at him, his own gaze softening as he softly traced her lips and shook his head. "It doesn't change anything. It doesn't change what I feel when I'm around you. It doesn't change who you are or what you believe in, Anika. You're a good person. You could use this to your advantage, to the advantage of us in this war."

Her gaze drifted to his mouth as he spoke, and she wished only for some distraction from the worries that occupied her. "What do you feel when you're around me?" She stepped closer to him, pulling his hands to her waist as she lifted her face to his, his breath warm on her skin as he leaned in, their mouths nearly touching.

Jake sighed, leaning his forehead against hers as he laughed. "Hello, Thor." He turned, Anika following his gaze as the cat jumped down from the tree

227

and stalked past them with a low growl as he left.

"He says he's sick of us," chuckled Jake as he turned back to her, his mouth finally lowering and meeting her lips with a gentleness that she wasn't used to from him. The tea Dorothea had given them lingered on him as he softly nipped her bottom lip before pulling away. "Come on. We should go as far as we can by nightfall."

"Or we could stay here, get a room in the tavern?" Anika feigned a look of innocence, her hand halting him as he'd started to walk away from her.

"Thor..."

"Could stay in the stables," she finished.

* * *

The room left a lot to be desired, she thought to herself as she sat on the bed and pulled off her shoes. Her feet were nearly frozen within them, her socks wet and crunchy from the walk. Jake took them and lay them in front of the fire with his own. He hadn't argued and hadn't said a word when she had asked the barkeep for one room, with two beds, which they didn't have. She'd said one was fine, despite the lingering gaze the keep had made on her left hand, with no signs of a wedding band.

"I do sort of feel bad for Thor." She sighed as she rubbed her feet, willing warmth into them as the fire steadily grew.

"He was fine. In fact, he was thrilled he could cuddle the horses for the night. But I think that poor stable boy is terrified that he'll just eat the horses by morning." Jake sat in the chair near the fire, the distance between them cramped in the tiny room.

"You are confusing," she whispered, just loud enough for him to hear. "Two nights ago, you wanted me. Today you kiss me again, but now you're over there."

"You aren't the only one who's confused." He stood and walked to the tiny window, staring at the swirling snow outside. "Dorothea said that we die as lovers, and she said that you rule with Reynard as lovers."

"What do you want me to say?" She stood, walking to him and wrapping her arms around his waist. Her head leaned against his back, the steady beat of his heart beneath her ear.

"What if you don't choose me?" He turned, a hand cupping her chin to look up at him.

"Wha —" she started, but he cut her off.

"Some part of you doubts that there is anything between us, anything worth fighting for. If part of you wasn't interested in Reynard, as you've said before, then there would be no future where you rule by his side as his queen." The words were strangled as he pulled her hands from his waist and pushed past her. He paced around the room, a hand running over his unshaven face. "What if you end up with me, and it's some second best for you? Will you always wonder if you could have been happier, could have been more powerful?"

"You're getting caught up in these visions now after you told me not to! Alvar, I probably turn into a hermit in one of the visions!" she declared.

"I don't want to be your distraction while you wait to make a choice." He stopped in front of her. She was surprised at the anger that flitted into his eyes. "I don't want to keep playing this game with you if it just leads to one of us getting hurt."

"Dorothea said every decision leads to a different outcome, a new future. You're making it really easy for me to make a decision right now," she huffed, eyeing the door. "You don't trust me, fine. I knew what vision I wanted when she talked about them. I knew that I would rather die with you in battle then be queen with Reynard."

She went to the door and turned the handle, prepared to storm out, sleep in the stables with Thor if she had to, but he dashed forward, pulling the door shut. The doorknob pushed into her stomach as he stood behind her, his breathing ragged as they stood frozen, each waiting for the other to move first. She refused to be the one who made the first move when he so clearly was caught up in his head. She knew that he needed to make this choice, to prove to both himself and her that he was worth choosing. Tortuously, he ran his hand down the nape of her neck, his mouth finding her earlobe and gently nipping at her.

She shrieked, on the edge of pleasure and pain as she spun to meet him. She found his lips, all the gentleness of their earlier kiss gone as he lifted her up, her legs wrapping around his waist as his hands anchored themselves to her ass, squeezing. She pushed her hips against him, and he growled, his hardness between her legs growing.

He pulled his mouth away from hers and studied her, not voicing whatever thoughts he was drowning in. Her entire being was consumed by him, in his smell, his warmth. Anika's breath hitched as he found her lips again, the knob painfully digging into her back entirely ignored.

He backed up, his hands holding her securely as he turned toward the bed and sat her down. They both ignored the creaking of the bedsprings as his hands found her shirt, pulling the layers off as she struggled with his buttons. She fought for restraint as his hands found her bare skin. Her back arched as his hands moved over her, and then he pulled away. Stepping back, he gazed down at her and shook his head.

"What?" she asked, breathlessly.

"You're beautiful." His hands brushed down her shoulders, her skin vibrating under the calloused touch as he cupped her breast, his hand full. "You're so... soft."

She laughed, only to have it disappear with a groan as his thumb stroked her nipple, his fingers pinching lightly, teasing as she arched her back to his touch again, willing to give him everything.

"So pale," he murmured as he lowered to his knees in front of her, his mouth finding her nipple hard as she gasped, pulling his head in closer, the light from the flames dancing on his dark skin. He moved to her other breast as she writhed, her breath quickening from his touch as she pulled him closer.

His mouth was still ravaging her, her legs circling his waist to pull him closer until she finally whispered to him, "Please."

He grinned. "I like hearing you beg." But he wasn't dissuaded as his kisses started moving down her stomach; she trembled as her hands ran over his shoulders, his long-muscled arms.

"Jake," she whispered.

"Sh," he responded, his hands pulling at her waistband as he slid her pants,

230

her underwear over her hips, pulling them off each leg as his gaze remained on hers, steady and unwavering. He paused, kneeled in front of her, like a knight before his queen.

She repeated, "Please."

His shoulders spread her legs as he lowered his head, his breath hot as he licked her, parting her as she arched beneath him. His tongue left her shaking as her hips rose to meet him. Her hands fisted in the bedsheets as he chuckled and pushed into her with his finger, his mouth never leaving the sensitive area where he flicked, teasing.

"Stop," she panted, and he stilled, raising his head to meet her gaze as she panted, so close to the edge that he had brought her to. "Not yet."

Every piece of her longed to finish, but she wanted him inside of her more. He stood as she rose to the edge of the bed, pulling at his waistband. She felt his breathing hitch as she unbuttoned his pants, pulling them down. She paused, taking all of him in with her eyes as he sprung free. Her own breath stopped for a moment as she grasped him, her hands running over him in long silky movements, as he found her hair pulling it into his fists.

Her mouth watered as he closed his eyes, her hands continuing to work, moving faster and faster as he groaned. The restraint he held lined his face; it was obvious as he rocked into her movements. She licked her lips as she found him with her mouth, and she chuckled as he gasped, plunging into her as she struggled not to be overwhelmed by his size. Her hands ran over his backside as he moved, lost in one another.

He dragged away from her, pulling her to her feet to stand in front of him, both of them naked now as his thumb circled her breasts again, his hardness against her belly as he took a deep breath, lowering his forehead to hers.

"I want to taste every inch of you, but I don't think I can wait any longer." He kissed her jaw, working his way down to her neck as she let her hands roam, again finding him in her grip.

"I can't either." She pulled him down with her on to the bed. He knelt over her, his hands sliding down her thighs as she pulled him closer, as he finally pushed into her with devastating slowness. She groaned, and he stilled, but she pushed her hips forward, and he smiled as he pushed the rest of the way in, as she stretched to accommodate him, thrown back as he moved inside of her, rough and relentless, what they both wanted, what had been building between them for so long finally released.

She forgot everything as his hands crushed her breasts, as pain moved into the threshold of pleasure as she was pushed toward her peak, so close to release, to falling over the edge of the earth. Her hands ran over his back, muscles taut as he rained kisses over her neck, her face. He pulled her up to meet him, so she sat in his lap as they moved together. His gaze locked on hers as he shuddered, finding release inside of her, and when his hand fell between her legs, with him still inside of her, and he pressed his thumb to her, she arched and found her own release, the pressure finally relenting as it flowed from her in waves.

They lay there, both quietly panting, his weight heavy against her. He propped himself up on his elbows and smiled at her, slipping out. She moaned softly in defiance, and he chuckled, lying beside her, a hand under her chin as he gently kissed her.

* * *

His eyes had long shut; his breathing turned to soft snores as she stared at him. The soft light of the fire and lamp danced on his ebony skin. Their legs still tangled, the dampness of the sheets, the wetness between her legs, seemed far away as she gazed at his face. She hadn't been with someone as attentive as him before. That he would delay his gratification to ensure her needs had been met was unlike anything she had experienced. Her past lovers, only two, both other servants in the order, had left her desires unanswered, had seen to their own needs before leaving her room, leaving her roiling with need, to let simmer or answer herself.

His touch had done something to her, and she had felt the shift between them when it did. She wondered if he felt it too, the decision they had made, in the throes of lust, neither of them caring or noticing how loud the bed had been, or the fact that the patrons downstairs had likely smirked and talked about the unlikely pair of outsiders fucking in their inn. As she closed her eyes, she wondered what Dorothea would see now if she looked to her future, as she had never been surer of her path ahead, of the person she would be with in the end, as she was in that moment.

22

Negotiations

"The wings won't join us for a reason. Perhaps Anika hasn't proven her intentions well enough," Mae announced. Anika and Jake had just finished debriefing Val and the others on what they had learned when they went north. Evidently, Mae had remained unimpressed.

"They also explicitly left despite the fact that you had been against it," she continued. Val held up a hand, silencing her.

They had discussed what to share with the group on their way back. They had agreed that there was no need to share the fact that Anika also had the power of water, but they shared the news about the possible futures of the rebellion, that Dorothea saw no way they could win.

Val looked at them both closely, as though aware that something had changed between them. She sighed, shaking her head and sitting behind the desk as the rest of their group — minus Hawk, who still had not reappeared — stared at her, waiting for her to respond.

"Hawk left for a reason," Mae started again, only to have Val hold her hand up, shooting a glare in her direction, this time finally silencing her. Anika looked at her, the long blonde braid as tightly wound as the scowl on her face. She didn't meet Anika's gaze. Mae had been cordial toward her, never seemed to have had an issue with her, and now it seemed that the large woman's mind had been changed.

"Hawk left us because she isn't ready. We can't fault her for that. We pressured her. That does not just lie on Jake and Anika..." She tapped her fingers on the desk. "Let's resume this later. The kids are putting on a skit, and they'll be devastated if none of us show, especially you two."

Flo and Roth nodded, leaving first, the others trailing behind them. Mae, still blatantly ignoring Anika's eye contact, left quickly, but Anika pushed ahead to reach her. A hand tentatively laid on her arm had the woman spinning, her height so much more evident as they stood face to face.

"What?" she spat.

"What did I do?" Anika asked, her voice near trembling. She wasn't sure why.

The large woman's mouth twisted, awkwardly glancing at the others who passed them by. "It's nothing that you did... it's who you are. You're a Naidisbo, Anika, the family who was such a threat to the order that they wiped them out entirely. I just started thinking after you and Jake left that maybe there's more to this then you're letting on. Why else would you have situation after situation that causes us to question you? Why would you sneak away if we're a team?"

Anika opened her mouth to defend herself, argue, remind her they'd been open about leaving or plead for some grain of understanding, but Mae continued her verbal assault. "We're supposed to be a team, so everyone has to be a team player, but you broke every ounce of trust you gained when you left. You proved you're a loner, and the worst part is that you dragged Jake down with you."

She shook her head as she turned away from her, barely glancing back as she finished. "And he was one of the good ones, until you."

Anika followed her toward the kitchens, her footsteps heavy from travel, guilt, and the weight of Mae's words on her conscience as she did. This trend, of being questioned, of being asked for her loyalty, was beginning to get old.

But part of her also understood why, of course, they felt this way. Naturally they would wonder what side she was on. She knew there would be a fall out from when they'd gone north but she'd expected it from Val, not the others.

She sat beside Jake, in the seat between him and Rae, who smiled at her, friendly as always, and yet Anika wondered if she too questioned what Anika's goals were. Jake's hand found her knee under the table, and he squeezed it reassuringly. The heat, the touch, a welcome reprieve to the anxiety clouding her mind.

She leaned in to thank him, but before she could, the children started to sing, Anika watched as they re-enacted a scene from the last rebellion. The young blonde girl who had spoken the most when she attended class was leading them, her skin and hair darkened to look like Val, or Val's ancestors, as she rallied her people. They each took turns showing what they had so far accomplished with their powers. A young girl, red hair long and curling down her back, happily extended her hands and flipped the apple in front of Flo into the air, squealing with excitement at her success as the young boy beside her frowned. With the swipe of his hand, he changed the direction of the apple, bringing it toward him shakily earning a slap from the girl as the show continued.

"They're improving quickly," Jake said to Hcrib on his other side, who nodded.

"It's too bad they're so young. We need more people with actual skill," he responded.

"But they are too young," Jake answered.

Hcrib's face hardened. He didn't need to broadcast his voice for Anika to hear him clearly. "At the end of this, it won't matter how old they are. If they are power yielders, they will need to fight."

"Is there something we don't know?" Jake asked, his head bobbing toward her, including her, she gratefully noted.

"I likely shouldn't say but Val received a message from Reynard and Grayson right before you two returned."

"How come she didn't say anything?" Anika asked.

"Probably so she could hear your news, and we're meeting again in the morning," he finished with a shrug of his shoulders.

Anika was about to ask another question, but a young girl jumped onto their table, demanding attention as she magically transformed her hair from its mouse-brown to bubble-gum pink, beaming at the applause.

* * *

The knock on her door came tentatively, and still was unexpected enough that she sat up in bed with a jolt. Jake opened the door and meekly poked his head in. Thor, seemingly without care, pushed past him and jumped into the bed in front of her, his long warm body stretched out comfortably.

"Can I join you?"

She nodded. "It's going to be a tight squeeze, though." Thor purred and stretched obstinately, but Jake simply shrugged as he climbed in behind her. They both shuffled around until they were comfortable, his hand draped over her waist as he settled behind her. As she struggled for words the comfort and warmth overcame her and she was asleep before so much as a goodnight.

When she woke, he was gone. Thor remained, sprawled on his back, paws in the air. She dressed quickly, the rising sun filling her room through the small window, and snuck out, leaving Thor snoring behind her.

He was in the kitchen with Edric, Brennan, Rae, and Kane, having breakfast when she walked in. She sat across from him, beside Brennan, and nodded in thanks as one of the young girls brought her a plate of steaming potatoes and sausage.

Two mouthfuls of the savoury dish were all she was entitled to enjoy before Val stepped into the room, her very presence demanding attention. She was already outfitted for the day, dagger strapped to her side, training leathers on, and apparently already broken in from the dirt on her knees.

"Meeting, now," she ordered, twirling on her heel and leaving as abruptly as she had arrived.

She took another bite, and with a longing glance at her food she fell into step beside Jake, whose hand lowered to her back briefly before flitting away. "You left before I woke," she whispered.

He nodded, looking briefly at the others. "I didn't think it was best to cause any more... disruption," he paused, looking for his words. "I just thought I should go before everyone was up."

She nodded.

237

* * *

"Before your safe arrival back to us last evening, Kane was greeted by a messenger while on sentry."

Anika watched as realization settled over the group, wincing as her friend's heartbeats escalated in their panic. And while normally she wouldn't wish one of Mae's growls on anyone, the sudden sound provided a brief distraction from the whooshing of racing blood that was overwhelming her senses.

"This means that Reynard and Grayson know where Santouri is located, or at the least, have a rough idea of our location. I don't know how they found us, but they have. Second, they've asked for a meeting with Anika and me."

"Why?" Anika blurted.

Mae rolled her eyes and Anika's brief appreciation for the woman vanished.

"To discuss the terms of this rebellion, to prevent all-out unrest, and to clarify your position moving forward. He claims that we can come to an easy agreement for peace."

"You can't actually be thinking of going, again?" asked Jake.

Val nodded, but it was Kane who spoke. "If he knows where Santouri is, then we risk being attacked if they say no."

Jake nodded; Kane wasn't wrong.

"There's no need for everyone to go and we need to buy time. We need defence on Santouri while we meet, in case this is a trap, an opportunity to attack us when we are weak. I spent the night thinking: Flo, Hcrib, Mae, and Edric will join Anika and me in Ferreya, leaving Kane, Rae, Jake, Brennan, and Roth here to defend the base."

"The children will need Flo," Roth interrupted.

"We will need her more," Val countered, although she didn't say why. She nodded to the group. "Pack your things. It's a good journey by foot, and Reynard's requested the meeting in two days' time."

* * *

It seemed like the moment she unpacked; she was packing again.

Thor gave her a lazy head rub as she picked up her newly packed bag and groaned, stretching her sore muscles as she turned to Jake, wishing she had time to say every thought racing through her head. Part of her wished she had the time and space to voice the fear of what she knew was coming, to provide him the reassurance he would so surely need; and yet, part of her was thankful for the rush.

"Be safe," Jake said from the doorway. Anika nodded, planting a light kiss on his lips, wishing she could do more, say more. She left her room, heading to the entry to meet the others. Mostly she wished they hadn't slept the night before. She flushed thinking about it. Turning to look back at him, he winked and strode forward, pulling her close. His kiss was rough and quick. He bit her lip as he pulled away and whispered, "I'll see you when you're back."

She pulled away and resisted the urge to look back again.

* * *

Hagio had resumed some sense of normalcy since their last visit. Despite Reynard's announcement the street vendors were out again, the space bustling with activity, and residents seemed to have moved on with their day to day lives.

They had been summoned to meet in an area that would be somewhat neutral. Reynard wasn't stupid enough to think that Anika and Val would walk into the church and expect to leave in one piece. Instead, and wisely, he had agreed to meet at a tavern.

"We could still be ambushed," Edric had commented, to which Val had agreed and laid their plan out before them. An hour before they were due to meet, and with their plan firmly in motion, Anika and Val sat in silence as the others embarked.

They had agreed to head to the tavern ten minutes before they were expected. Each minute they waited seemed to tick by slowly, the two of them avoiding the topic that hung heavy in the air between them, neither willing to relent and speak first. Finally, with a stern nod from Val, they left the apartment. Night had descended, and the streets were quiet as they walked to the tavern.

As they ducked in, Val motioned to the guard standing casually by the window. The tall man tipped his head and winked. Mae had shape shifted. Anika didn't want to know where the man's body was... or what he was wearing. Anika looked the man over slowly, earning a glare from Mae. It was the first time she'd fully seen her ability to shift. Mae's soldier form was dark, short, with a face that held a convincing two-day-old shadow. She stood slightly slumped, as though bored. Anika wondered if it were truly the man's form she had shifted into or acting that changed the posture. If Mae weren't as hostile toward her, she would have dared to ask.

Instead, she walked into the tavern behind Val, quickly scanning to see Flo sitting with Edric in a corner booth. The sight of Flo nursing a beer almost made her laugh, as uncharacteristic as it was. Flo nodded, and Anika nearly jumped when she heard her say, *"Good evening, love."*

She didn't think hearing someone else's voice in her head would ever be something she'd get used to. She heard Flo chuckling, felt her eyes glued to her as she answered her thought, *"I'd be concerned if you found this normal."*

Across the tavern, two soldiers stood at the end of a table, blocking the occupants from their sight, but they moved as Val approached, her head held high with confidence. Inside sat Reynard, a presumptuous red robe billowing around him as he stood, slightly bowing to each of them in turn. Across from him, and with far less grace and surety, Grayson stood and bowed. He stumbled slightly forward as his royal blue robe tangled precariously around his legs. The dim tavern lighting illuminated Grayson's face. She had been at such a great distance when she'd last seen him, that she was surprised to see he appeared even younger in close proximity. Just barely an adult, his nervousness radiated from him, and his heart raced as he quickly took his seat and hid his trembling hands beneath the table.

"Please sit, Anika," Reynard patted to the chair beside him, "Val."

Anika sat, taking a deep breath as Reynard leaned forward comfortably and ordered them each a beer. The soldier nodded and left without question.

"Stay in sight so I can talk to you," Flo said. Anika willed herself not to show any indication that the woman across the room was inserting thoughts into

her mind. She smiled, exuding false confidence as Reynard reached his hand over and patted hers softly.

"I have thought and thought of what may convince you to see reason, Anika. I'm sad to say it's come to this." He squeezed her hand.

"Come to what?" demanded Val.

"*Don't move your hand from his,*" said Flo.

"I had hoped you'd let Anika join us without need for bribery or games."

"Anika makes her own choices. I don't control her," Val spat the words.

Grayson watched them quietly, but Anika could feel his heart hammering in his chest. He was scared, of them, of Reynard; Anika didn't know.

"I've decided to show you that I can play fair, that I am more human than you give me credit for." His hand remained clasped on Anika's. She didn't miss the look Val gave it. "Let Anika join the order, and I'll release the children."

The soldier came back and sat two beers in front of them. "*Don't drink it yet. It isn't poisoned, but you should leave your hand in his for now. When he releases it, you can drink.*"

Val drank hers, a sign of trust in their meeting.

Reynard chuckled. Anika's hand felt colder and colder. "I have twelve children currently in the church, waiting, unfortunately, for their execution."

Anika tried to conceal the sharp intake of breath. Grayson's eyes appeared dark, giving no indication if this was true or if he was as appalled as they were. Reynard nodded, seemingly satisfied that he'd made his argument and finally removing his hand from Anika's he leaned back in his chair, a coy grin on his face. She picked up her beer and sipped, willing her hands to be steady.

"I've been collecting them for some time. My patrols have brought them back to me when they tested positive for being naturalists. I had planned to kill them, publicly, of course, as an example, but I'm willing to reconsider... should you let Anika join me."

"*He's bluffing,*" Flo hissed in her head.

Before Flo had a chance to finish, Reynard had started talking again. "Of course, should you say no, I'll continue with my public execution, but I will also march on your little camp, what is it you call that place? Santouri? I think it, and the people there could use an opportunity to amend their ways with the order."

Anika heard Flo curse, but she remained stoned faced as she turned to Val, an eyebrow raised. Anika could hear her heart hammering from across the table, but Val remained stoic and unimpressed as she said, "We'd have heard if you had children in the church, Reynard."

"Would you though, Val?" he smiled. Anika felt sick. "The rebellion is not as strong as you think. People don't have confidence in you. The order rules. Families brought their power-wielding children to me. I hardly had to search them out at all."

"*Lies,*" Flo exclaimed.

"What proof can you offer that if Anika joined you, you wouldn't still march on us and kill the children and us?"

"I hardly think Anika would allow such a thing. She knows that I wish her to be my partner, not my subject." He looked to her, his energy palpable between them.   •

"I hope it wouldn't come to this, but I'd have Grayson destroy your children in the same way I plan to destroy the children in the church." He nodded to Grayson, who slid his empty glass of water into the middle of the table. The droplet at the bottom began to shake, its edges blurring as it expanded. Suddenly, it was growing, the glass filling with water, a spinning vortex slowing only as he pulled back his shaking hand.

"I'd drown them." Reynard laughed. Grayson sat looking at his hands in silence.

Val growled. Flo remained silent in her head, leaving Anika alone with her disgust and awe of the water going from nothing to something in mere moments.

"Anika, my dear," Reynard placed his hand on hers again, "join me for a moment alone?"

"*I'll be here, listening. Val can use the time to talk to Grayson.*" Val indeed was looking at the young man. She gave no indication if Anika should join Reynard, so she nodded and stood, following him as he led her to a more private alcove. Flo's eyes watched as his hand drifted to her low back.

"Anika, I was angry when you left." He again reached for her hand, pulling hers on to his leg this time. She was very aware of the limited space between them, their stools uncomfortably close together, his robe touching her legs as they sat with their backs to the tavern.

"You must remember how well we worked together and what there is between us?" He pushed her hair behind her ear. She swallowed, relief flooding her as she felt sickened. "I wish I could make you see the potential as I see it. I heard you went north. I hear you know that you have both bloodlines?"

She chilled at his words. "How did you know I went north?"

"I have eyes and ears everywhere, Anika. So, you know you hold the power of water, as Grayson does?"

Flo was silent.

"I may have that bloodline, but I have never been able to use the power."

"You just haven't tapped into it yet." He leaned in, and she could feel his breath on her face, sickly from the beer. "Do you have any idea how powerful you could be? Together, the two of us would be a force to be reckoned with, the most capable rulers of all time! We could protect these people like no naturalist ever could. Anika, what's between us is more than what could ever be found with a naturalist."

His hand came up to cup her face. She resisted the urge to pull away, the memory of Jake's face swimming in her mind. She let him lay his hand there, waiting for her response. When she didn't move or speak, he leaned forward, planting a kiss on her forehead. "I know you feel it, Anika, the pull between us."

"*You have to say something*," Flo reminded her.

"No," Anika answered. She stood, pushing past him to meet Val, who was leaving Grayson. "You're wrong. You're wrong about all of it. We don't accept your offer."

"*Let's go*," Flo said. Anika watched her and Edric leave the tavern, and she turned to Val, who smiled, the first indication that she had made since they left Santouri that she hoped Anika would remain with them.

"Reynard, we do not accept your terms, and we do not believe your claims. This meeting is over." Val gave a low mocking bow as she turned and headed to the door, Anika on her heels. Reynard called to them; the other patrons were silent.

"This was your last chance, Anika. I will publicly execute those children, and I will find you, your friends, and those bastards you've hidden. I will kill them too, and then I will burn your world to the ground."

Anika turned and squeezed her hand into a fist, smiling as Reynard paled, his heart having skipped a few beats. The soldiers around him moved, raising their spears, and Val tugged her out the door.

23

Shifting Tides

"**A**re you planning on telling the others that you have the power of water too?" Flo asked over her tea the next morning. The two women sat in the apartment. The others, except for Hcrib, who remained scouting, slept soundly.

"Jake knows," she answered, hiding behind the steaming mug of peppermint.

"We could use that to our advantage, don't you think?" Flo didn't ask with any maliciousness, rather with curiosity.

"I've never so much as felt an inkling that the power was there. I can't even use it."

Flo only nodded as Val came out of the room, cursing and pushing her dark braids out of her face as she found the kettle. They had spent the last three days in the apartment. Edric, Mae, and Hcrib took turns scouting bars and shops for any information regarding the order or the children they claimed to have hidden in the church.

Val and Anika had to remain inside, too obvious, and most likely to be killed should they be seen in public. This resulted in a lot of time spent sitting, no time for training; while Anika had certainly wished to rest, resting alongside Val had not been exactly what she pictured. Flo's company she didn't mind; the woman exuded security and contentment, a welcome shift from how her and Val's energies seemed to collide.

"I fancy a sunbath." Flo stood stretching, and despite likely being totally aware of the tension between Anika and Val, left to the roof, leaving Anika scowling behind her. Val, for once, didn't seem to mind as she sat, putting her feet up and sipping her fresh tea.

"I've been thinking," she started. Anika tensed. "If we don't find out any information about the children, we will still have to act. Reynard declared war on us, children or no children..." She paused, sipping her tea. "We need to move first. We lose the element of surprise if we don't."

"Unless that's what he thinks we will do," Anika pointed out. "He knows we wouldn't leave children to suffer. If he's bluffing, which Flo said he was, then we risk jeopardizing ourselves. It might be exactly what he wants us to do."

Val nodded, her concentration heavy on her brow. "You know the church better than any of us. Was there a place where they held prisoners?"

She nodded. "Yes, sometimes they brought prisoners to me for healing, but I never knew where it was. I was just a healer there. I wasn't the Naidisbo." She scoffed at her own words.

"My father used to say that the best place to keep something hidden was a library. People associate libraries with learning and positivity. I think he just said that so that my sister and I would read all the books in his collection, though." She looked at Anika but wasn't really focused on her.

It was a rare insight into Val's life before the rebellion, and so, with a breath of bravery, Anika asked, "How did you come to join the rebellion?"

"You mean lead?" Val corrected.

Anika laughed, some relief rolling through her as the tension decreased between them a bit. "Yes, lead."

Val paused, as though considering if she would share her story. Finally, she nodded. "The Lezah, my family, were powerful. In fact, my parents would have known yours. By the time I was born, there were very few left. We were heavily hunted during the last two uprisings. Good warriors, all with the foresight to know where the next blow would land, and quick healing, we were a force to be reckoned with. My parents led the rebels before I did. My younger sister and I would stay at Santouri. They're all dead now."

246

"How?" whispered Anika.

"How does anyone die in a rebellion? My parents died in the last battle, both felled by fire wielders. Their foresight wasn't enough to protect them. I was old enough to lead by then, but my sister, she was much younger, and their deaths destroyed her."

"She died too?"

"Do you see her here or at Santouri?" Val snapped. Anika merely grimaced in response, but Val was shaking her head. "Sorry, that wasn't necessary. My sister, Lain, she killed herself a year after my parents died. She was consumed by her grief, and she hid it from us. I found her in her room when she missed our morning sparring session. She'd used nightshade and water hemlock."

Anika nodded. It was certainly a deadly combination, but Val continued. "I think she used plants as a way of punishing herself. The earth giveth us power and taketh it away," she quoted.

"I'm sorry." Anika could only offer the words, as empty as they sounded, as useless as they were.

Val shook her head in dismissal. "Lain made her decision. I miss her every day, but she also gave me a great gift in her death. She gave me something to fight for. I need to fight, to show the world that being a naturalist is nothing to be ashamed of, that having the power, this power," she lifted up the sleeve of her shirt, revealing an intricate scar, "is nothing to be ashamed of."

"What is it?"

"I don't carry wood like the others. When we were young, our parents tattooed these designs into our skin, using the sap of our tree."

Anika looked more closely. The tattoo, upon closer inspection, was a complexly designed fish, its lines crossing over one another, the glimmer of gold resin on her dark skin shining.

"I have a question, but I understand if you can't answer it."

Val nodded as she sat back in her chair again.

"You heal faster than most people, but that didn't save your sister?"

She shook her head. She either didn't know or wasn't willing to answer the question. Apparently, it also meant that their conversation was over, as Val picked up the book that she had been working on the last few days and went back to reading. Anika had looked, but the cover was plainly black, leaving no clue to what it was that she read. As a reader herself, she respected that when a person held a book in their hands, the intent was to read, not to discuss, so she stood and started the kettle again, about to have another cup of tea.

Two cups of tea later, and both Val and Anika looked up to see Mae slide in the door, turning expectantly as Edric and Hcrib followed closely behind her. Edric was slightly out of breath as he huffed, "We have news!"

"About the children?" asked Flo as she came down the ladder, her oiled skin glowing in the light.

"No," Mae said.

"Yes," finished Hcrib. "I found something out about them. "You thought he was bluffing because he was, about part of it. He has the kids, but he's holding them elsewhere, not at the church. I couldn't find anything out about a planned execution, though."

Flo was silent. Whether she was upset that she had been unable to discern Reynard's true agenda, or if she was devastated for the children, she didn't show it.

"Can I talk now?" asked Mae, earning a rude hand gesture from Hcrib. "There's fighting in the north and the south. Apparently, people are pushing back against the patrols. If they're told they have to join the order and refuse, they're executed. The children are being taken — see Hcrib, I could have told them that too," she added, "and apparently, the wings have made quite a bit of noise south of here."

"They slaughtered a village near Greyfork," Edric said, solemnly. "They resisted, and so they killed everyone. Apparently, in the south, they've managed to take quite a few of the wings out of commission, and they have more held hostage in Roland. It looks as though Reynard is holding them there for a special event he is planning. I heard that he's taken complete control of Balin and Roland and is keeping his soldiers there, to keep the people subdued."

"Your family?" asked Val.

"Safe, or no word of them being anything but," he finished.

"The wings, this could be the public execution we were warned about," said Mae.

"So, we're looking at the south being completely under Reynard's control. Any more word on the activities in the north?" Val asked.

Edric stood tall, looking proud. "They continue to fight and push back. There've been several attacks on soldiers in the smaller villages. People are gathering in Greyfork, prepared to fight. There are several young power wielders there, and my people won't let them be taken by the order."

Val looked a bit lost in herself as she sat thinking. Flo looked at each of them anxiously. "We can't go back to Santouri and leave children here."

"We don't know where they are. We have no way of getting them."

"They're children," she stressed.

"Yes, but we don't know which part he was bluffing about. He could have been bluffing about the executions."

"He wouldn't," she started, but Val cut her off.

"He could have been, and we can't very well do anything while we're here and the other half of us are in Santouri... the risk of Santouri being marched on is higher every day, especially if there is starting to be unrest in the north and the south. We need a plan; we need a way to reach out to these people, let them know the rebellion is still strong, is still willing to stand behind them."

"We need them to come to Santouri," Mae said.

"No, not yet. We need things to remain exactly the way we are. Santouri isn't where we can risk battling with Reynard." She ran a hand through her hair, unbraided and loose around her shoulders. "We head out as soon as the sun sets and push hard."

They nodded, Flo looking devastated by the idea.

* * *

Each journey seemed to be longer and harder than the last for Anika, but she didn't dare complain, not when people were dying in the north and the south. Dying because of her, she thought. If she had gone with Reynard in the beginning, would he still be holding hostages in cities, slaughtering villages?

"*Don't do that to yourself,*" Flo said in her head, earning a scowl from Anika. Flo ignored her and continued. "*You can't predict the future more than any of them, and you don't know what he would have done if you'd joined him. You certainly couldn't have prevented the wings from working against him. We don't know what would have happened.*"

Anika nodded, pushing ahead of her as they climbed a steadily growing hill. She worked to keep her thoughts blank, never forgetting that there was a mind manipulator in their midst: someone that could hear her thoughts, even change them if she wanted.

She stopped suddenly and turned, Flo nearly running into her. Flo stumbled, her pale skin reflective in the moonlight as Anika searched for a way to voice what she'd realized. "I don't understand. You can change people's thoughts. Why don't we just change Reynard's?"

"It isn't that simple. I have to keep my eyes on him at all times. I'd have to be with him constantly."

"But if you were around him, you could change his mind on something, at that moment at least, right?" she asked.

Flo nodded, indicating that would be possible. "So, if this public execution were to happen, you could be there and stop it."

"Well, yes, but it really isn't that simple. Any time you change someone's mind, the moment you leave, it regains its own control again."

"We're wasting time. Let's keep going," muttered Val. Anika nodded, turning and following, the burn in her legs an afterthought.

* * *

"Okay, Roth and Flo, you stay with the kids and the elderly. There should be at least three people on sentry at all times. You need to have your guard up as much as possible. If there is any sign at all of Reynard's men, you need to be ready to retreat to the second base. Over the next few days, outfit the second base with everything you'll need, and send some of the children and elderly's belongings, so they don't have to carry anything if you retreat. If all goes according to plan, you shouldn't need to be there. We should be back in time."

"Since it sounds like the south has been completely defeated, there is unlikely to be any fighting. We will have to sneak the best we can, but a bloodbath will only result in us losing lives, and I won't see that happen. Anika, Mae, Hcrib, and Rae will come south with me." Anika didn't miss the eye roll from Mae. "Edric, Kane, Jake, Brennan, you're our best fighters, and if there is a battle in the north, they will need you."

"Balin is my home. I go south," said Kane, Rae's hand resting on his knee in comfort and solidarity.

"No, Val's right, you're needed north. If they're really slaughtering entire villages, they'll need you. I'll go south and see if I can find any word of your family." Rae smiled sadly.

More time apart for Rae and Kane. Anika looked to Jake. He stood in the shadows of the room, arms crossed and looking down, his expression unreadable. Anika stood to the left of Val and looked to them all. She knew, at that moment, that she had made the right decision denying Reynard.

These people, stubborn, headstrong, and full of hope for a better world, were her friends, and she would do what she had to for them. They all filed out of the room, each caught in their own minds, thinking of the packing, the preparation, the goodbyes they would have to make before they left. Each looking forward to one good sleep before nights of sleeping on the ground snuck up on them again.

A hand grabbed her arm, its touch warm and familiar, and she turned to see Jake, his gaze heavy.

"Come with me?"

"I'm going south," she started, but he was shaking his head and pulling her in closer, not caring if the others heard or saw them.

"No, come with me tonight. Be with me tonight."

He embraced her, his mouth finding hers as she tilted her head back, his breath warm on her face, the smell of him sweet and inviting. All she could do was nod.

24

False Confidence

She lay beside him, her body damp with perspiration, her breath still a little uneven. He lay on his side, propped up on an elbow and gazed at her face, a hand running long lazy circles over her bare stomach.

"Do you think she makes us go separate places on purpose?" she asked, turning to him.

He nodded. "I do, but it doesn't matter. It doesn't change anything between us."

She pushed herself up on to her elbow, her blue eyes meeting his brown. "What is between us?" she asked.

"Something," he paused, looking for the words, "I don't know what you want, but I know I've never had anything like this before. I know that when we're apart, I wonder how you are, where you are, if you're okay, the entire time. I've never met someone who can pull me so far from the other things, things I should likely be focused on, because I want to be with her."

"Me too," she smiled as she leaned forward, kissing him lightly on the lips.

He smiled, his vulnerability obvious between them, so much so that she felt the need to fill the silence.

"When we met with Reynard, he tried to persuade me that I was supposed to be with him." She felt Jake begin to withdraw, so she reached a hand out, placing it over his heart. "And at that moment, I realized that Dorothea and

Val were completely wrong. There was no part of me that wanted anything to do with him. No part of me was drawn to him; no part of me was interested in his power, his vision, his evilness. I realized that even if I am both Naidisbo and water wielder, it doesn't matter. You've shown me that it doesn't matter. You've made me want to fight for naturalists, for us to be equals someday, to not hide in shame at what magic flows in our blood. You made me want to fight for us. For this."

His hand closed around hers, and he raised it to his lips, kissing each knuckle slowly as he moved up her arm. As he rose over her, he kneeled between her legs and rained kisses over her collar bones, each kiss as though he were savouring the very taste of her skin.

She sighed, and he stopped. "I said I'd taste every inch of you, and I meant it."

* * *

They eventually relented and slept; lust finally replaced with exhaustion. The window in Jake's room was bigger, and the sun woke Anika in the morning, heating her face. Jake slept on beside her as she lay there reflecting, aching pleasantly from the night, dreading what she knew the next days or weeks could possibly entail.

She snuggled into Jake, her nakedness convenient as she looped her leg over his hip, and smirked as she felt him grow hard as he slowly woke, his body responding faster than his mind as he pushed his hips toward her.

She cupped his cheek in her hands. "Good morning. I thought maybe we could..."

He didn't wait for her to finish as he shifted his hips, the length of him easily sliding into her, still wet from the night before. She moaned as he started to move, building his speed as his mouth found her throat. Whatever upper hand she'd thought she had shattered.

She pushed him back against the bed and moved on top of him, not letting him leave her for a moment as she readjusted herself to his size and started to ride him, his hands finding her backside as his mouth came up to find her nipple. He sucked, the hard and sudden climax rocking through her as they tumbled together over the edge.

She lay down on top of him, her legs still straddling his hips as he ran a hand through her hair. "Morning," he answered.

He scowled as she lifted herself from him. The sudden emptiness went beyond her pelvis. "I likely should have left earlier."

He shook his head. "No, I don't care. There's no point hiding it."

She stood, finding her underwear and cursing at the state of the room, and of them. She pulled her pants over her hips, his eyes watching her as she searched for her bra. She said, "I don't think we need to hide it either, but the others may feel differently."

"Who cares? They already know. That's why we never go on missions together, and Val hasn't even bothered to explain why. What else can she punish us with?"

"Do you think it's because she wants you?" The thought filled her with dread.

"Val!?" He sat up, the sheet forgotten as he kneeled naked in front of her.

"Yeah." She shrugged into her shirt and passed him his pants, which he begrudgingly accepted and began to dress.

"Val doesn't want me, at least not for sex. Maybe to co-lead the rebellion."

"So, she doesn't want you distracted."

"Maybe she doesn't want either of us distracted."

"She could use some distraction. Might help her relax a bit." Anika smirked.

Jake laughed as he opened the door for her. "I dare you to tell her that."

"Not if my life depended on it," she answered in laughter but was stopped as he pulled her in and kissed her lightly. She could smell herself on him still.

"Be safe." His hands ran over her arms as she stared up at him.

"Be safe," she echoed.

* * *

Roland was subdued, Anika thought, as they peered at the village. People who walked outdoors did so with their heads low, avoiding eye contact with one another and with the soldiers occupying the streets. The soldiers stood, swords at their sides, some with bows on their backs, confident and unyielding in their red uniforms.

Val tapped her on the arm and pointed to the small building east of them. Soldiers stood on the roof as well as its base. The two of them sat in the bush watching, the guards being replaced every thirty minutes. A wordless signal, and they were army crawling back to their camp, waiting for the others.

When everyone was gathered again, Val said, "I can't imagine they would bother keeping the wings anywhere else. That's the most guarded area. Seems like the perfect place to keep hostages."

The others nodded, looking at both Val and Anika. "What will we do?" asked Mae. She hadn't warmed up to Anika on their journey south, but she also hadn't said anything negative or offensive; a small win, Anika thought.

"We need more information," Anika said, surprised at her own sense of authority, but Val nodded, and so she continued. "We don't know who exactly is in there, what condition they are in, and if they are willing to fight with us. There are a lot more soldiers here than us."

"Our focus could be provided elsewhere," Rae said. Mae sent her a look of dissatisfaction.

"Hcrib, you get into that building. The sentry shifts every thirty minutes. Get a sense of how the people are doing, what they want. If we free them, they and their families will need to journey back to Santouri with us, provided we escape intact. Rae, gather information in the village, but be discreet. We don't need you to be noticed by a soldier. We will figure things out from there. There are still a few hours until the sun goes down; let's not waste them." Val nodded to each of them as she addressed them.

Hcrib and Rae took this to heart, leaving almost immediately. Val and Anika didn't bother to follow them, both trusting that they could carry out their respective missions with ease, but Mae watched them go, pacing and radiating impatience as she stretched.

"Mae, sit, relax, wait," ordered Val.

She grunted but obeyed and sat, eventually lying back and looking at the clouds, silent. Abruptly, she sat up. "Let me at least watch the sentry shifting. Maybe I can gain some information about who's coming and going."

Val sighed but nodded, knowing that it was likely futile to argue with the woman. Mae, finally satisfied, bounded to her feet and left, leaving both Anika and Val waiting. The minutes seemed to tick by slowly, the silence broken only by the chirping of birds or the sounds of nature settling in for the evening.

Twigs cracked, and branches broke as Mae thundered back into the clearing. Anika had jumped in preparation for an assault, but Val had held up a hand knowingly and said only Mae would run full-fledged through the scant brush to them and not expect to get stabbed.

Sure enough, the tall woman ran directly into the clearing and stopped, panting as though she'd run as fast as she possibly could. Anika could feel the excitement buzzing off her as she said, "They have a Lider and a Komandante!"

"Interesting," replied Val, looking in the direction of the village. "Why would they have such high-ranking officials here?"

The question had not been directed to either of them, and neither Mae nor Anika answered. Mae, finally having caught her breath, said, "This is the perfect opportunity, Val. A significant loss to the order, a statement that the rebels are alive and strong. We kill them both when we rescue the prisoners."

Val nodded. She didn't outright agree or disagree with Mae, who paced excitedly between them. Anika stood, waiting for Val to decide, to say anything that would provide some idea of where her thoughts lay. Anika wished at that moment she had Val's gift of foresight, even to just break the suspense.

Sun had long since set by the time Hcrib and Rae returned to their site. Rae filled them in on what she'd been able to find out. The Lider and Komandante had arrived with the soldiers over a week ago and rounded up the entire village. They had then announced that they would be taking the children and any able-bodied people with them to fight for the order. When the villagers had protested, many being unwilling to leave their homes or livelihoods, the soldiers had made it clear that there was no choice. That same evening, several of the villagers had tried to push back against them, attacking with whatever meagre weapons they had. When the soldiers fought back, they were surprised to find that more men and women had been arriving from the other villages and fought alongside them... unfortunately, it wasn't enough, and they'd been easily subdued.

"So, no word on the wings, then?" Anika asked.

Rae shook her head. "No, only villagers are held captive from what I've been able to hear."

"There's a good number of men and women there, at least twenty, but none are rebels or wings from what I can see. Just people, scared to lose their lives to the order. They're eager for freedom and getting angrier and angrier the longer they're held in that barn."

"Have they given them any food, water?" Val asked.

Hcrib shook his head. "Nothing for the last two days. They've hardly seen the soldiers except for a brief glimpse of a man who told them they'd all be answering to Alvar soon enough."

"Are they well enough to fight?"

Hcrib nodded. "They're tired, but they want their revenge."

"Fair enough," Mae huffed.

Their plan was simple. They would use the next day and evening to gather weaponry from the free villagers and empty houses. Hcrib would continue to sneak into the barn through his entrance between sentry shifts, but this time, he would take whatever weaponry he could, stockpiling the villagers. The next morning, their plan would be executed, with armed villagers to aid them and get their revenge.

Unfortunately, this plan meant that Anika was sitting around their camp, waiting for a full day and night. She volunteered for first sentry and prepared their supper, a sad assortment of fruits they'd picked along the way, hard bread and cheese, and what little greens they could combine to make a salad. Even so, she continued to lose her focus and concentration, thinking of the others and how they were faring. She wondered if the children were safe at Santouri, and always her mind wandered back to Jake, wondering how he was in the north — if they'd found battle, if they were safe, if he was hurt.

She was also curious about how Thor was doing by his side. Her affection for the cat had grown beyond what she could have expected.

As she lay down to sleep that night, she looked at the moon and wondered if Jake looked at the same one, and if so, what his day tomorrow would bring, and if it would be as risky and dangerous as hers.

* * *

Everyone was in their positions, each aware of their role, when they were to move. Anika stood at the edge of the village, summoning every bit of courage she had, slowing her racing heart. She would need to be confident and secure in her declaration. She would need to mask her fear.

She started walking down the road, the barn ahead by only a couple of hundred feet, though it felt like thousands. One foot in front of the other, she walked, steadily. The surroundings buzzed in her ears as she blocked out the whispering of the villagers who waited, watching and expecting something to happen.

She didn't see Val or Rae, but she knew that they were waiting, watching her walk up the path. She didn't know if the soldiers would recognize her. Just in case, she was ready to declare it for them. Only a hundred feet away now.

One of the soldiers pointed her out to his companion. The two of them stopped their slow circle of the barn as she approached. Fifty feet away, the older soldier stepped forward. She could feel him from there. His heart was slow and steady, healthy despite his older age. He raised a hand, and she stopped.

"What do you want?" he asked.

"Do you know who I am?" she scoffed indifferently; an eyebrow raised. She almost didn't recognize herself in the tone of her voice.

The man hesitated and Anika took the opportunity. She flipped her black hair over her shoulder and tilted her head to the side as she smiled. "I'm Anika Naidisbo. I'd like to speak with Reynard."

"The Naidisbo!" exclaimed the younger soldier. The older man glared at him quickly before turning back to her.

"Yes, yes, very exciting, isn't it, having the Naidisbo in your presence? I'd like to speak with Reynard, and I'm not fond of waiting."

"He's not here," the older man said. His hand dropped to the hilt of his sword.

She laughed, low and self-assured. "Do you think your blade can protect you against me, old man?" She finally took another step forward, breaking the invisible barrier between them. "If I wanted to, I could stop your heart in your chest with barely a thought."

The young soldier's eyes widened in fear as he looked to his companion, who glared at her. "Reynard isn't here."

"Bring me your highest officials then. I'm not interested in waiting."

The older soldier chuckled; the cue Anika had been waiting for. She lifted her hand and looked to the younger soldier. His heart was faster than the older man; he wasn't as confident, young and scared. She focused on the steady rhythm and slowly began to shut the hand that she held up in front of her, purely for theatrical effect, but it did the trick. The young man's eyes widened as his breathing began to slow, his heart racing, as he grabbed for the man's shoulder, gasping for air. He twirled back to Anika, who kept her face neutral, not letting the guilt show through as she watched his face full of rage.

"Stop!"

"Bring them to me." She opened up her palm, and the young man inhaled deeply, nodding as the older man looked to him for confirmation that he was okay.

"Matthew, go find the Lider and Komandante. Inform them of this... situation."

The young man nodded, but as he turned to leave, the tavern door across from the barn opened, and two men strode out, followed by a group of soldiers. Anika looked them over. The Lider wore a uniform of black, similar to that of the red uniformed soldiers. The Lider was younger than she had expected but had a hardness about him that made her unsurprised he became a Lider so young. He was harsh, and his very walk exuded arrogance and power.

She felt her own heart plummet, her mind suddenly fuzzy as she took in the Komandante, the very same one who had drunkenly cornered her so long ago, the night she had finally escaped. The same man that was the reason her entire life had turned upside down, and as she took him in, she didn't know what emotion she felt — fear, anger, disgust, all of them? He looked far less threatening today. His dark hair was long and greasy, and the silver smock hung limply around his thighs. She willed herself to give no inclination she knew or remembered the man.

But he remembered her, it seemed. His smile, as greasy as his hair, was plastered on his face as the two men stopped in front of the soldiers, taking her in. She was incredibly aware that she stood alone in front of them. She waited, reminding herself that she wasn't a servant in a dark hallway this time. She wouldn't show her fear.

"Did you think I'd forget? I'm the one who forced you to reveal your true nature," he drawled, his voice sending shivers up her spine.

"I'm glad I'm memorable. I can't say the same for you, though. We've met?" she taunted, forcing a smile on her own face.

"You've demanded to see us. What of it?" spat the Lider.

Fear coiled inside her, threatening to spill out to the fake exterior she wore. She willed herself to become this person that she pretended to be.

"I trust you've been in communication with Reynard, and if that's the case, then I trust you know he's declared war on me... well... the rebels. I'm sure you remember, Komandante, just what my abilities are."

She pushed both arms in front of her and closed her eyes. Their hearts began to beat wildly, in preparation, as she curled her power around them, slowing them both down long enough to bring them to their knees.

But then the Komandante looked up. Panting, he met her gaze and smiled, and she felt it. She felt the pushback on her power. The Komandante slowly stood to his feet as he pushed back against her abilities, his heart beating stronger. The sudden shift in her capability took her by surprise, and her focus on the Lider was gone. The same fear that had been coiling inside her began to overcome her as she reached for her sword.

Mae came into vision, her quarterstaff already raised as she ran to the barn, swinging it down to the lock and shattering it as she turned to the two soldiers, engaging them in battle as the doors flung open behind her and the angry villagers began to swarm out.

They were pathetically outfitted with what they had been able to find, but the knives, daggers, even one man with a shovel, were better than nothing. Anika focused. Her senses were too overwhelmed for her to use her power. She swung the sword upwards, and the Komandante pressed forward, his own sword drawn swiftly from his side, his eyes focused solely on her. She'd hurt his pride, it seemed.

More soldiers came out of the tavern. The Lider stopped to shout orders as Mae continued to take down male and female soldiers with her quarterstaff. A splatter of blood already covered her face as she threw a dagger to a young man by her side. Full of energy, he jumped on to a soldier's back, his dagger finding its place in the man's abdomen.

Rae had been waiting atop the tavern for this moment. As the soldiers struggled to get in formation, she leaped from the top. Her air slowed her as she hit the ground, and her sword swung in the middle of them. Soldiers dropped in shock as the air bender leaped into the air again, attacking them from above before they had a moment to comprehend what was happening.

Anika still hadn't seen Val, but she knew she was there, somewhere she would be fighting, rallying the villagers. Sure enough, she heard Val's cry, strong and confident, as she fought with the people: their leader, she would bring them justice. Ruthless but justice nonetheless.

Her sword met the Komandante's, the man's breath on her cheek as intimate as that night in the church. His sneer of disgust was prominent as he brought his sword down. She spun, avoiding it as she dodged to his undefended side, swinging only to be met by his sword again as he blocked her. They turned, locked in their own private duel as chaos reigned around them. She felt out with her power, looking for his heart, but again it seemed blocked, as though he held some shield against her abilities.

He lunged forward as she jumped back, falling down and scrambling to her feet again. He chuckled. "A poor fighter. I suppose I should thank the order for not training the servants well enough. Sad, isn't it? So useless when your power doesn't work."

"How?" she spat. She hated herself for asking, but she needed to know.

Sure enough, he didn't answer, his dark eyes glinting as he pressed her back toward the crowd fighting. Each time she turned, she saw death, villagers taking down soldiers together as a team, using the one advantage they had, their sheer number. The old man from before, panting and blood-soaked, turned toward her as two of the villagers attacked the Komandante from behind, the man laughing easily as he fought them both, distracted for a moment from Anika.

The old soldier spun his two daggers in his hand, but he was older and slower than she was. She deflected him only twice before her dagger sunk into his side, piercing his heart. He was dead as he hit the ground. She paused, her abilities still dulled. She didn't feel his life end. She twirled, looking to the Komandante, who stood over the two villagers, both dead on the ground before him, the young woman still clutching the bleeding wound on her stomach.

"First kill?" the Komandante nodded to the dead soldier at her feet, mocking, but before she had time to respond, he swung his two short swords in the air, his long sword gone or discarded — she didn't know or care — but she knew that she wouldn't be able to defeat him without her power and with only the blade in her hand.

She only briefly registered the high-pitched cry from afar as the arrow sunk through the Komandante's neck, blood spraying over Anika as he fell forward to his knees, blood gurgling as he tried but failed to form words.

And at that moment, whatever tether he held on her power was released. She found his heart and stopped it, a small mercy from whatever part of her good soul still existed, and he fell facedown to the earth.

25

Val

"**U**ncle!" she shouted across the development room at him, "this doesn't make any sense. You're scared to let me use my power, that's all!"

She sat down in the chair angrily, crossing her arms as her scowl deepened. Her uncle sighed and planted his feet on the desk, leaning back in the chair as she'd watched her father do so many times before. It still pained her to think about her father, about her mother. Her uncle ran a hand through his silvering hair, his black skin darker than her own as he collected his thoughts.

"Val, I don't know how many times we have to go over this. Your parents were explicit in their wishes. You're to use your gift for short term only, not long term."

"We could see what happens in the future. We could plan to win!" she argued, stomping a foot down for exaggerated effect.

"The future is never concrete. What you see today could change tomorrow. It's a power that consumes people, driving them crazy; they get lost in it. Your parents made me promise to keep you girls from relying on it."

"Maybe if they'd have looked further ahead, they wouldn't be dead." She said the words, knowing what effect they'd have on her uncle. It was the same effect that it had on her. The wondering, the anguish that didn't go away since there were no answers as to why they hadn't been able to use their foresight to prevent their deaths. She'd wonder forever how they both ended up dying in the battle. She continued. "Even if they couldn't use it to see the entire future, they should have been able to predict the next move of their enemies — they shouldn't be dead."

"I'm not saying you're wrong — I'm saying that we have to respect what they asked of me."

"You couldn't stop me." She raised an eyebrow in challenge of his authority.

"No, I couldn't." He nodded slowly. "But if you don't respect me, then I hope you'd at least respect your parents not to put me in that position."

She rolled her eyes, making no effort to conceal it as she stormed out and headed toward her sister's room. She didn't knock; she never did. Even if her sister protested every time, she barged in. This time was no different.

"Val, seriously, couldn't you knock?" Her sister lay in bed reading. One look at her and Val knew she hadn't bothered to get out of bed at all during the day. Her obsidian hair was wrapped into a messy bun at the top of her head, her eyes tired for someone who hadn't bothered to move out of her bed all day. She wore a tank top that she'd grown out of years ago and shorts that left little to the imagination. Val ignored all of this as she placed her hands on her hips and launched into a discussion.

"Sorsha, this is ridiculous. You can't spend your life hiding in this room." She pulled the chair out from her sister's desk and sat, leaning forward and pushing the book out of Sorsha's face. "Uncle won't let me use my power, and he wants to go engage them in battle. Why is he so unreasonable?"

She asked the question genuinely. Her sister was the calmer of the two of them, gifted but with no desire to use her power. She was a gentle soul who had earned a soft spot in her parents' and her uncle's hearts. Sorsha sighed and closed her book. Resigned, she sat it on the table and looked Val over.

"You need a shower," she stated bluntly. "You smell."

"I was training all day!" exclaimed Val.

"Mhm, anyway, you still smell."

Val smacked her arm in good nature as Sorsha sat up. She moved as slowly as an old woman, but Val was relieved that she had at least smiled — she hardly ever smiled since their parents died.

"There's no point in looking ahead, Val. We all end up in the same place." Sorsha shook her head, as though she were speaking to a child and not her older sister. She continued. "Alvar, Val, eventually, we all die. It's as simple as that. Wherever you look, whatever vein of the future you choose to see, eventually ends with your death. If you get to the same place no matter what, then why look at all?"

"Alvar, you're morbid." Val hated how she talked about death with such ease, as though she knew it personally.

"It's just the truth. Uncle is right. If he wants to engage the order in battle, then let him, but don't try to predict the future."

"Okay, but who determines how far is short term and how far is long term? He expects us to look at the short term, so we can fight more efficiently, but who's to say where that ends?"

Sorsha shook her head. Val could sense she was beginning to shut down, as though the simplest of discussions overwhelmed her. "You're looking for loopholes, Val."

Sorsha lay back down and reached for her book. Val took this as her cue to leave but not before she looked back at her sister in worry, just another one of the people she wanted to look into the future for.

* * *

She kicked the pebbles at her feet, cursing at them as they splashed into the brook in front of her. She kicked her legs forward and lay back, staring at the sky and thinking about her uncle and her sister.

"Idiots," she mumbled but immediately bit her tongue as she felt guilty. "They're wrong." She wasn't speaking to anyone. She knew if anyone happened to go for a midday walk, they'd find her muttering to herself, and they'd run to her uncle, claiming that Val had finally lost it completely.

She shut her mouth and thought things through. If she knew what would happen, then she could plan. She could look at all of the possibilities, no differently than when she was training with her uncle. She could freeze a moment of time when she looked at an enemy in battle and see every possible move he was considering. Then she could react to whichever he threw toward her. It had taken a long time not to become confused by so many possibilities, but she'd practised and worked at it with everyone she could convince to go into the ring with her, and she finally understood her power.

She more than understood it — she embraced it — and she wasn't scared of it. Her parents had been scared of it, Sorsha and her uncle were scared of it. But she knew it, knew that it was the very essence of her and a true gift from Alvar for her to help win this war.

She rolled forward and looked at the brook again. She knew that the future was constantly evolving and changing, but she had to use her power wisely; if she kept the results to herself, then she could possibly intervene to help win the war and prevent her uncle or any more people from dying unnecessarily. She nodded to herself as she made her decision. She would look, and damn them all.

Part of her thought about waiting for a special time, but it made no difference if she looked right now or alone in her room — no, she would look now while she still had the nerve to go against everything that her uncle and sister had asked of her.

She closed her eyes and looked — it didn't take much, just like a thread that needed to be pulled from a cloth to unravel it. She merely needed to tug, and she could see everything. So easy, and yet so much more overwhelming than the power she used when she trained — the information flooded her, so fast and furious that she couldn't slow it down, couldn't look at each possible sequence of events to see the consequences.

Worse than her inability to slow it down was the nausea that hit her like a fist, the knowledge overwhelming her brain as she stitched the possibilities closed again. She turned off the tap to her power as she gasped, her chest heaving as she sat back up, unaware she had even fallen down.

She struggled to remember the details of each possible chain of events, but there had been three that stood out clearly, and she knew she needed to act soon; otherwise, she would lose her uncle too.

* * *

She packed her bag immediately, as her uncle and his scouts were already a day ahead of her. She closed her bag and sat at her desk. She was nearly ready to go, but part of her hesitated. She wanted to look again, to make sure she was doing the right thing, but her uncle's warning echoed in her head. She resisted the temptation and instead pulled out paper and a pen.

Sorsha, I'm sorry – I know you'll be livid, but I looked, and I have to go after Uncle, or he dies. If I'm not back in two nights' time, then send help, please. I love you. Val.

She nodded, reading over the words again, short and to the point. She folded the letter in two and, on her way out, slipped it under Sorsha's door.

She'd never travelled alone before. She hadn't anticipated how lonely and cold she would be, but she pressed on, hopeful that she could make up time and catch them before the ambush she'd seen happened. She'd been walking for hours. She was exhausted when she finally stopped and let herself rest. Closing her eyes, she fell into a deep sleep before she'd even checked her surroundings.

It didn't matter. She woke, and everything was fine. No sign that any humans or creatures had been around her during the night. She picked up her bag and, swearing at her stiffness, set off again. She found them at the start of the first night. She had run into the clearing in her relief that they were all intact and nearly had her chest stabbed as a result, but nonetheless, she'd thrown her arms around her uncle and told him everything.

He had stood quietly for a long time, and she didn't know if he was angry or relieved. He never did tell her, but they packed their things and started the trip back to Santouri first thing the next morning.

"I'm not sorry, you know," she said to him as they walked the next afternoon.

"That doesn't help your case," he said to her side, but she caught the grin on his face and smiled as she skipped ahead, happier than she had been in a long time, finally feeling that she was doing something right for their cause.

They stopped on the second night to sleep. She had hesitated as she'd left instructions that she'd be back by now, but she disregarded the thought as she went to sleep, blissfully happy and confident in her powers.

They got back to Santouri early on the third morning. Val had started to wonder why they hadn't met anyone to rescue them like she'd instructed Sorsha. Still, she had assured herself that if she had used her powers so well that maybe Sorsha had finally gained the confidence and looked into the future as well and seen that they were in fact alright and didn't need help.

She unpacked her bag and ate lunch with the others. Sorsha hadn't come out of her room, so typical of her to stay there. Val thought she'd give her some space. Maybe Sorsha was mad that she'd used her power, but she could have at least come to say hello to them. Val went to her room, feeling restless and wanting to talk things out with Sorsha. She paced around the room before deciding that she'd just go and talk to her and face whatever it was that she was mad about. She stopped as her hand hovered on the door handle; she could look ahead and see if Sorsha was mad at her for using her power, or if she was just holed up because she was depressed still, or if she had even used her own power and was basking in delight.

Val sat on the edge of her bed and closed her eyes, looking for the thread, but it was nowhere to be found. She searched and searched, but still she could find nothing, just a void where a thread should have been waiting to see her future. Dread filled Val as she considered what it could mean. Had she tapped out her powers, or was there some reasons she couldn't see Sorsha's future?

Panic started to consume her that something was wrong as she ran from her room and down the hall, throwing open the door and coming face to face with her worst nightmare. She fell to her knees as she took in the sight of Sorsha's body sprawled on her bed, vomit dry and crusted on her pillow, the stench of urine strong enough that Val threw up on the floor.

"No no no no no no no," she moaned as she crawled through her vomit toward the bed, pulling herself to her knees as she grabbed at Sorsha's arms, shaking her violently. "Wake up! Wake up!"

She screamed it over and over until someone else came and moved her hands away from Sorsha, dragging her away. She only screamed harder as they pulled her away from the body.

When she closed her eyes, she saw Sorsha's empty eyes staring back at her. When she tried to take a deep breath, like everyone kept telling her to, she smelled death. She'd overheard her uncle talking to his men. They'd found Val's note in her room. They thought that she'd taken advantage of her uncle and sister being gone, or the fear of losing them both had driven her over the edge in her depression. Either way, no one had bothered to tell Val, but she knew the truth of the matter — she had killed her sister.

No, her power had killed her sister. And it gutted her.

* * *

She sat with her legs on the desk she often sat behind as she talked to their people. The memory came back to haunt her every time she used her power, no matter how far ahead she projected. Even in battle, she saw her sister's lifeless eyes staring back at her. She couldn't say that she'd completely learned her lesson, but she had taken time to refine her power when she dared to use it again, and she'd learned how to control the threads when she pulled so that the information didn't overwhelm her.

Still, making the conscious decision to take another look at the actual conclusion of the war was a decision that she couldn't make lightly. She'd done it once before in a sense. She'd looked specifically at the Naidisbo's fate, but that wasn't the fate of everything she stood for. No, this would be different. She tapped the pen against the paper in front of her, still utterly blank as she considered what she was about to do.

So similar to that day at the stream, she closed her eyes and braced herself as she pulled on the thread, opening the world of possibilities. Immediately, the information began to drown her, and so she paused, filtering away the possible endings until she only saw the possibilities in which the rebels finally won; not lost or co-existed but won.

Something was wrong, though. In each vein of possibility where she knew in her soul they would win, she couldn't see how it would happen — each event ended abruptly, in the midst of battle or otherwise and then went black.

She closed the thread of possibilities and picked up her pen.

Hawk. She hesitated. The last time she'd written a note from the force of her power, she'd lost that person. Hawk, though, was already in the wind, struggling — and the only person who would likely come back to Santouri before the next mission.

She wrote.

26

New Beginnings

Anika looked in the direction of the arrow. Recognition at the cry made her hopeful, but she hadn't dared to believe until she saw the untamed hair of Hawk as she ran down the hill toward them, another arrow already in the bow, ready to fly.

Hawk had killed to spare Anika's life. Smiling, renewed with energy, Anika turned as another soldier engaged her in battle, but her power was unleashed, surging with the death of the Komandante. She had merely played with the soldier and his swords for a heartbeat, two, three, before finding his mind with her power and shattering it to pieces. The man's eyes were empty as he hit the ground, and in a brief moment of shock at herself, her dagger pierced his heart, ending his life quickly and with surety. She felt unleashed, her power suddenly drawn out.

The sense of death filled her, but rather than letting it paralyze her, she relished it, letting it build her up, strengthen her as she pushed on, looking for her friends. Mae, Hcrib, and Rae each stood confident, helping villagers as the last of the soldiers fought against them.

Still, she did not see Val. She turned, momentarily reprieved from the battle as Hawk continued to run toward her, and then she spotted them. Moved away from the group, between the barn and another building, Val and the Lider were locked in battle, her sword meeting each of his strikes with confidence and a grace that only someone with the ability to predict her

271

future would be able to match. Hawk finally stopped beside her, breathing heavily from the run. Anika grabbed her without thinking, hugging the stiff girl, who didn't let the grip on her bow loosen for even a moment.

"Not the time for hugs!" she yelled.

Anika pointed to where Val continued to fight. She reached out with her power, but the Lider was too far. Hawk must have realized this as she raised her bow, waiting for the perfect moment to shoot him.

But as they turned in their dance, Val's eyes found them and she smiled as she spotted Hawk. Her foresight had not seen this, it seemed. That pause of vulnerability was all that the Lider needed as he lunged forward. At the same time, Hawk released the arrow.

The world seemed to quiet the moment the dagger penetrated Val's chest, her eyes dropping from Hawk to the blade as the arrow found the Lider's back, tearing through his heart. The pair fell together. The Lider's body went limp as it landed on Val. The blade pushed deeper as her hand fell to the side, unmoving.

Anika and Hawk were running as it unfolded, at the fallen pairs side before they registered the quieting of the battle behind them. Hawk pushed the man's body off Val, hands fumbling as she grabbed Val's face, arms, looking for signs of life. Anika stood over them, scanning her, looking for anything that she could pull on to save her.

But the body was quiet, already gone.

"Do something!" screamed Hawk turning to her.

Anika knelt, oblivious to the blood soaking into her legs as she reached for Hawk's hands, pulling them both into her own, but the woman refused to meet her gaze. Anika placed a hand under her chin, pulling her closer, though Hawk resisted. "I can't, Hawk. She's gone."

The words choked her, but she could do nothing for someone once they were dead. Hawk screamed, the sound shattering Anika's heart as she held back her sob watching as Hawk lay her head on Val's stomach, uncaring of the blood that soaked her face and hair. Anika reached up and pulled the dagger free from Val's chest, flinging it to the side as Hawk screamed again and again, "I'm sorry," ringing through the village.

A hand came to rest on Anika's shoulder. Rae stood beside her, tears streaming down her face as she took in Val's lifeless body. Wordlessly, she pointed behind them, Anika, shaking, stood and turned.

The villagers stood, silently and respectfully. Three soldiers kneeled in front of them, bound as Mae stood guard behind them, quarterstaff hanging limply by her side. Hcrib stood with the villagers, hand over his mouth in shock, unable or unwilling to come closer.

Their silence reverberated in the clearing as they took in the rebel leader. Their energy, once so full of life, now dull, weakened. Anika stood, leaving behind Hawk, Rae, Val's body, and between them, she looked to the people, forcing a sad smile to her face.

They waited for her to speak, and she felt it then, the shifting of their energy as they looked to her. Mae and Hcrib waited for her to say something, and she realized that she had to speak. Val would expect her to speak, to keep them going.

"Do you see what the order does?" The words were barely more than a whisper, but the people heard her. "They slaughter your people. They kill without thought or regret. These men," she gestured to the three kneeling prisoners, all looking at the ground, "these men are our enemy. Today is just a glimpse of what the order will do to us. They will stop at nothing to destroy our very lands we walk on, to take away our children, and for what?"

"Nothing!" cried a villager.

She nodded sadly. "Today marks a new beginning. Today is the day we send a message to the order that we will not take this lying down any longer. Today we show the Aita that we're going to fight for what is ours, for our rights!"

The crowd's energy grew; some of the men and woman nodded in agreement. Anika gestured to Val behind her.

"They kill us because they fear us, because they wish to control and stamp out what we're made of. No more!"

The villagers cheered.

"What now?" asked Hcrib. Anika looked at him and took a deep breath.

"We bury our dead, and then we prepare for war."

Mae pulled her dagger free and stepped behind one of the prisoners, her blade glinting at his neck as she pulled his head back, but Anika held up a hand, surprised to see Mae stop, waiting for her to speak.

"Leave him alive." It was the young soldier from before. Fear glowed in his eyes. "Let him take a message back to Reynard of what happened here today. Kill the others."

Mae smiled and, moving to the other soldier, pulled her blade across his neck, kicking the man forward into the dirt as she did the same to the next man beside him. Anika watched as their life bled into the ground, as she felt their bodies be released to whatever came next.

* * *

The villagers dug graves for their dead. Men and women were placed in the ground on the outside of their tiny homes, side by side as family members wept, placing small belongings with them. Hawk had remained with Val's body, unable to move as the others had knelt together and dug with their bare hands in the ground. No one picked up the shovel. Dirt streaked their already bloody bodies as they turned to Hawk, who shook her head.

Hcrib went to the girl and pulled her hands off Val's body gently, brotherly, as he whispered, "She'd want to be here, with the people she was trying to protect."

Hawk hiccupped but made no move to stop Mae or Anika as they lifted Val's body and placed it in the grave, both women holding back their sobs as they slowly covered her with the soil of the earth.

Rae stood over the head of her grave and blew a kiss toward Val, her tears falling on the fresh soil as she patted down the last of the earth. They watched as the green tendril of the Lezah tree began to push through. It was Val's last gift to the earth, the tree of her power sprouting, in hopes that there would be another power wielder to carry on the line someday.

Anika sniffed and turned to look at the villagers and the pile of dead soldiers beside them. There hadn't been many, but it was enough to cause damage to these people and the rebellion. She looked to Mae and said, "Let's burn them. Hopefully, Reynard will see the smoke before that boy gets to him. Let's send a message with his element."

As the smoke began to swirl in the air, the stench of burning flesh was strong and hot in their noses. Rae looked to Anika and asked, "What now?"

She nodded, thinking as she turned to the villagers. "When the order hears what happened here, they will seek revenge against your village. I cannot promise safety for your future, but I would ask that you join us as we journey back to our base. Join us as we fight the order. The elderly and the young will be kept safe. The journey is only a few days north if we press ahead now."

The seconds ticked by, but slowly the villagers began to nod, dispersing for their homes. As they returned, outfitted with their belongings for the journey, children rubbed their eyes from being woken from their beds. And Anika felt the first glimmer of hope that they would see a better future.

27

Jake

His blade met flesh with every turn, and it still wasn't enough. His breath rained ragged in his chest as he blocked a blade while cutting deeply in the thigh of another oncoming soldier. They were tired, and they were outnumbered, but they pressed on.

They had gotten to the village only an hour before the battle had started. They couldn't afford to wait. Soldiers had been plundering, taking anything they wanted from the villagers, tying the men and women who looked as though they were in good health up and placing them on wagons to transport them back to the order. They had asked no questions. Instead, Brennan and Edric had snuck in, cutting binds off of people as Jake and Kane acted as distraction. In the sudden flurry of battle, the prisoners had run to their homes, grabbing knives, swords, and whatever else they had, to join the four men in their fight.

It still wasn't enough. The order had sent a large group of soldiers north, and they were outnumbered at least two to one. Jake, with his ability to fight longer and more efficiently than the rest, gave them a distinct advantage with Thor by his side. But the enemy had been prepared and had journeyed with two foxes in their group.

Thor pounced forward, teeth sinking into the flank of a young female soldier, her scream shrill among the dull thuds of battle as she fell, struggling to pick up her blade to attack the cat. Still, he was already gone, leaving her victim to Kane's shoge sinking into her skull from where he stood, his other blade in a dangerous dance with a Lider.

Thor's habit in battle was to circle Jake and his opponents, taking the enemy down when Jake was unable, but the foxes now had Thor pinned as their target and advanced mercilessly. The two circled the large cat, flames spitting from their nostrils. Thor growled, tail in the air, stuck between the two of them.

One of the foxes lunged, teeth catching Thor's flank, burning as it bit into the cat's flesh, but Thor was fast and strong. He jumped for the fox's neck. Throwing his weight onto the creature, he pinned it on to its back, his hind legs gutting the fox's stomach as it shrieked. The other fox, shrieking in protest as its companion was shredded, made to leap on to Thor's back but instead was intercepted by Brennan's hammer. The animal's head twisted with a sickening crunch as Brennan laughed and spit on the sizzling animal in the snow before turning to continue the fight. Thor growled in thanks at the man.

Edric pulled a villager to her feet quickly. Turning and swinging his fists, they collided with a soldier's face, shattering bones. Edric, always one to enjoy a good fight, smiled as the soldier staggered toward him, blood running from his eyes as he landed another blow to his head. This time the soldier didn't get up.

Despite their effort, the soldiers outnumbered them, as villagers lay injured, dying, or dead in the snow. Kane and Brennan stood back-to-back as a group of soldiers circled them, weapons raised and swinging. Jake continued to fight, Thor with him again, Edric, the only solitary warrior.

Jake's head spun at the sound of Kane's bellow across from him, his eyes following where Kane swung, killing soldiers with a new intensity as the man screamed again and again. Finally, Jake's eyes found the reason for the man's newfound energy. Brennan lay, hammer still clutched in his hand, throat open, his blood staining the snow red.

Frozen and unable to think for a moment, he hardly registered the kill he made as he quickly calculated their chances of survival, let alone winning this battle, and he roared to the others, "Pull back!"

Kane remained oblivious in his rage, cutting down soldier after soldier as Jake began to back away from the battle, still shouting to the others. Thor and the villagers joined him. Finally, Edric, pulling Kane away from the soldiers, ran to him. The soldiers, exhausted and down in numbers, let them go.

"They won't give us long before they come after us," Edric panted.

Jake nodded and knelt in the snow, beckoning Thor to him as he pulled a paper and pen from his pocket, scribbling words out of sight from the others.

"Find her. Run."

Thor didn't need to be told twice. Jake watched as his best friend disappeared into the distance. Finally, he turned back to his friends, Brennan's body slung over the shoulders of Kane, who shook in rage and despair.

The villagers and his friends looked to him, waiting for his command as the blustery cold winds buffeted them. He shivered as he tried to find some kernel of courage, anything to keep going.

* * *

He looked up at the stars as everyone around him slept. He would never admit to the others how deep the ache was inside him for her, how it had nearly broken him when he'd tied that note to Thor and told him to go to her. How he'd pictured her face when Thor would greet her, how he knew she'd look up, and look for him. He knew that his words would gut her, and he'd felt guilty as soon as he'd sent Thor on his way, wished he'd written more, but his brain hadn't been working. He'd been rushed, panicked.

More than anything he wanted to hold her, he wanted to run his hands along her soft body, he wanted to cup her breasts as they lay together, he wanted to kiss her neck, breathing in the scent of lavender and rosemary that clung to her, like a drink he couldn't get enough of.

He had to stop thinking about her before it became even more unbearable, stop thinking about the little noises she made when he was inside of her, how she gasped his name when he brought her to climax. He stopped himself again and let his hand drift lower. He wanted so badly to find release, but he wouldn't, not when his friends were around him, not when they and he were mourning.

He stilled at the sound of someone rolling in their sleeping bag. He turned and watched as Kane sat up, hands running over his head as he cursed and threw the blankets up. Jake debated pretending he was asleep, but he would want someone to talk to him, so he sat up. Kane turned and gave him a nod as they walked away from the others, nodding to the sentry as they passed. When they were far enough away not to be overheard easily, Kane said, "I can't fucking understand it."

"He was a good fighter," Jake started, but Kane cut him off.

"No, I can't fucking understand this war." Kane shook his head and looked at him in the moonlight, Jake giving him the time and space to talk. "Sometimes I don't know if we even know what we are fighting for. Sometimes it feels like everything's become so jumbled and disjointed that we've lost sight of the purpose. Yes, we have the Naidisbo, but if she isn't a naturalist, if she really is a pure magic, then shouldn't we want to get rid of her too?"

Jake's heart stilled, defensiveness creeping into him, but Kane held up a hand at his reaction and continued. "I'm not saying that I actually think we should do that, but Brennan... Brennan was so literal, you know? I know that this is more than that, and I know that Anika isn't one of them, but Brennan told me that he didn't think it would work out because how could two people ever get along when one was pure, and one was a naturalist?"

"The Naidisbo have fought beside us for a long time though, man," Jake started, and paused. "And isn't this what we are fighting for, for the type of magic we have not to matter?"

"Doesn't it bother you sometimes, though? That she's *pure* and you're not?"

Jake paused to think about it. He could guess what Brennan had said. He'd been so honest — Jake forced himself not to go there, not to think of his friend in a negative light so soon after his passing. He shook his head; it wasn't something that needed thought. "No, I never feel like one of us is better than the other. I never feel like she will use her abilities against me. I know she stands with us."

"You questioned," Kane started, but this time Jake stopped him.

"I did, but I don't anymore. I can't explain it, but I don't have anything to doubt." He shrugged and looked at the sky. "I just know."

"I have the same thing with Rae." He sighed and kicked at a branch in front of them. "I can't believe he's gone; I can't believe any of them are gone."

"This is war brother. It's really here."

"This is war."

Acknowledgement

The Naidisbo wouldn't exist without my partner, and husband, Josh. In 2017 Josh and I had a conversation - about magic systems, about discrimination, about world building - and because of it, The Naidisbo was born. The Naidisbo would take time, a lot of time, to come to fruition because of the nature of life being what life is - chaos.

And life, since 2017, certainly has been chaos. Chaos as we navigated career changes, graduate school, and a global pandemic. And also the best type of chaos, welcoming our daughters Havin and Sage (who most certainly are responsible for the delays in the Naidisbo being released).

There are many others who need to be thanked, particularly those who collaborated on the Naidisbo, whether through their time, support or skills. The NWT Arts Council who provided funding and the push I needed to move forward with publication. Sigrid Macdonald from Book Magic, who provided her editorial skills and expertise, and most importantly her encouragement. To Ana Chabrand Design House for her magical capability in designing the exterior of my story, and bringing it to life. To Seth Tomlinson Cartography for bringing Torekan to existence (a significant upgrade from my crude pencil sketch).

When I think of how I ended up becoming a writer, I think of many different people. My parents, who let me spend ridiculous amounts of time reading. My sister, who writes with me, and believes in me. My Nanny and Grampy, who spent hour upon hour reading to us. And, my personal support team and friends. I can't possibly name them all, but they are the ones that cheer me on, keep me accountable, and let me complain about the situations I put myself in. You know who you are.

About the Author

Megan Wood can often be heard saying she is okay at many things, and not great at anything. Her most notable accomplishments are those that are rather 'normal'. She is happily married to her husband, Josh. She has two young daughters, Havin and Sage - who both fill her life with joy, and sleepless nights. She has a ridiculous number of hobbies - and has difficulty committing enough time to any of them to become great. Some of these include writing (obviously), reading, exercising, sewing, playing music, and more. Professionally Megan holds a Bachelor of Science in Nursing from the University of Prince Edward Island, and a Masters in Nursing from Memorial University. She was born and raised in Prince Edward Island, Canada and made Yellowknife, Northwest Territories her home. In her day to day Megan works in health - focusing on Mental Wellness and Addictions Recovery. The Naidisbo is her first published novel.

Manufactured by Amazon.ca
Bolton, ON

30814967R00176